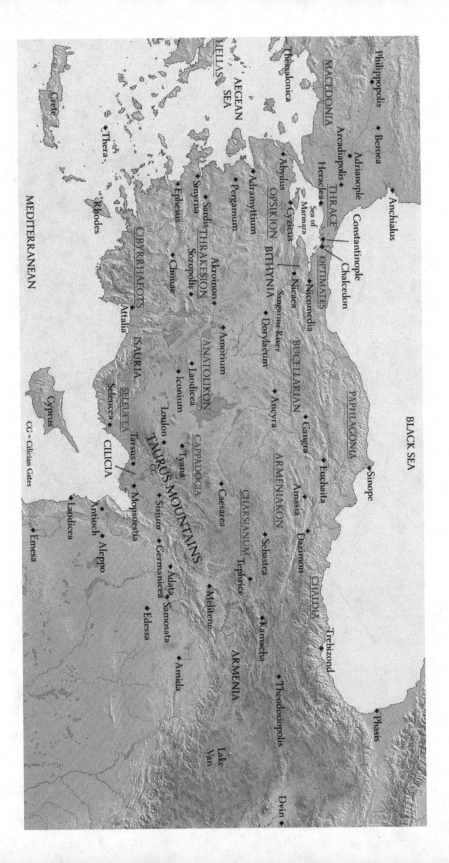

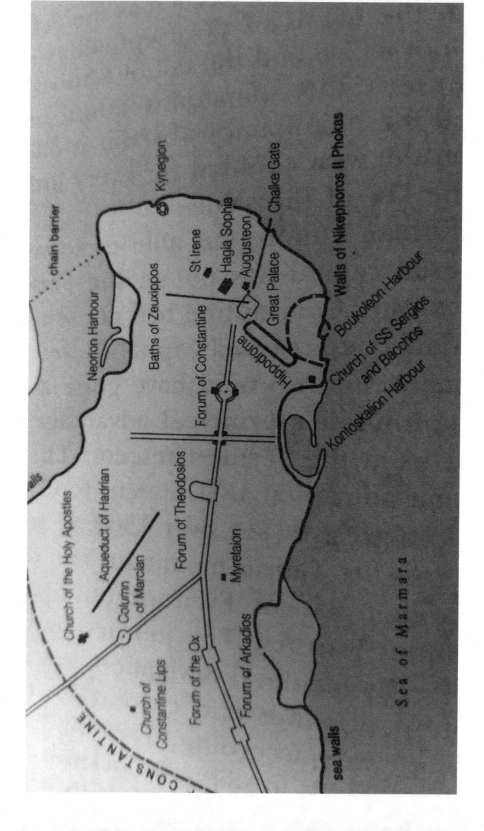

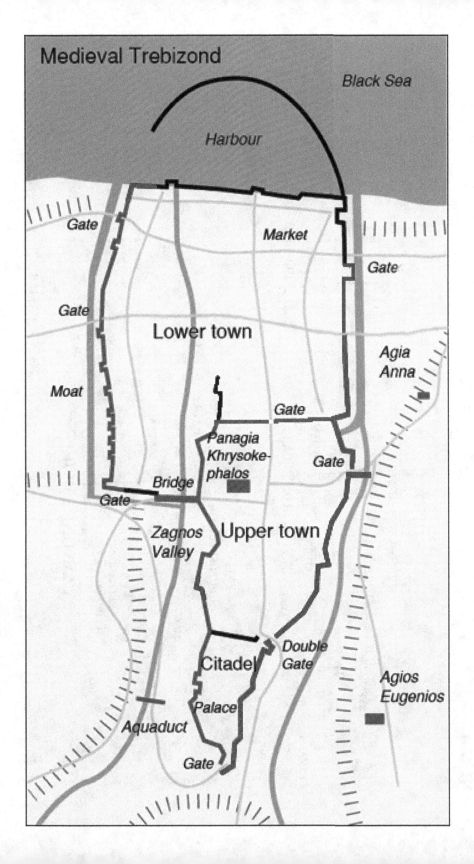

Medieval Trebizond

Black Sea

Harbour

Gate

Market

Gate

Gate

Lower town

Agia
Anna

Moat

Gate

Panagia
Khrysoke-
phalos

Gate

Bridge

Gate

Upper town

Zagnos
Valley

Citadel

Double
Gate

Agios
Eugenios

Aquaduct

Palace

Gate

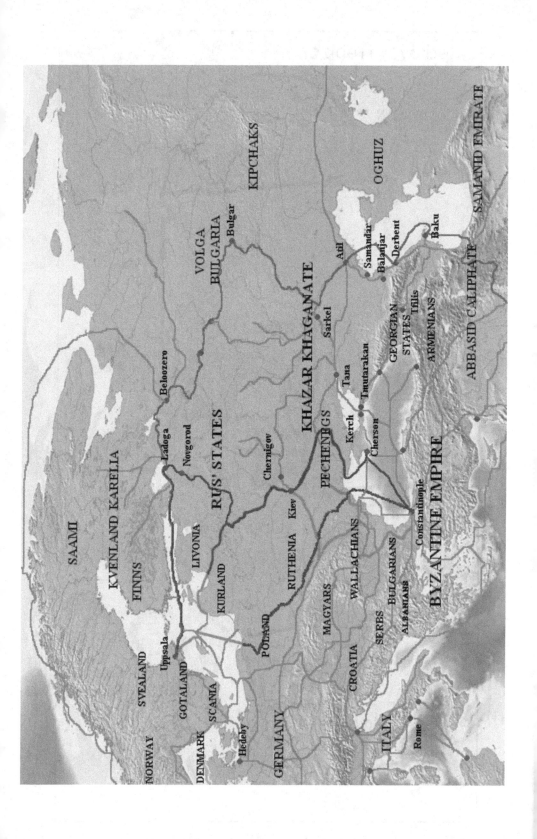

SIRENS' SONG

S. Catherine Jones

authorHOUSE

AuthorHouse™
1663 Liberty Drive
Bloomington, IN 47403
www.authorhouse.com
Phone: 833-262-8899

Published by AuthorHouse 09/05/2024

ISBN: 979-8-8230-3046-5 (sc)
ISBN: 979-8-8230-3047-2 (hc)
ISBN: 979-8-8230-3045-8 (e)

Library of Congress Control Number: 2024915131

Print information available on the last page.

Any people depicted in stock imagery provided by Getty Images are models, and such images are being used for illustrative purposes only. Certain stock imagery © Getty Images.

This book is printed on acid-free paper.

THE WILDERNESS

Chapter 1

The giant polar bear gripped the earth with its claws, tearing deep fissures in the rocks. Resisting its retreat north to the arctic, the bearlike glacier left jagged furrows that now, ten thousand years later, are filled with water. My father and his brother trudge along the edge of one of these channels, dragging a colossal tree they have just hewn between them. My cousins and I follow, gathering the twigs and branches it sheds for firewood.

The weight of sticks in the bundle on my back presses my small feet further into the snow, but I dare not fall behind, lest I lose my father in the late fall snowstorm. I can barely make out my uncle's sons fanned out beside me, until Lars veers into me, sending my armful of kindling scattering.

It does no good to cry, for they only ridicule the tears that will freeze my eyelashes together. I resign my collection for Larsen to scavenge and continue plodding after my father.

We reach our hamlet on the rim of the fjord, where we all heave the enormous log on top of the stack. When the waters thaw in the spring, the men will begin the dangerous task of floating them to the mill. For now, however, we seek our hut in the waning afternoon light.

In the sheltered woodshed under the low hanging eaves of our cabin, I doff my pack and untie the sodden wool wrapping from my legs. Leaving them to dry on the pile, I rush inside to my maman and sister. A pot of stew bubbles on the fire, and I stare hungrily at its dwindling contents.

Being the youngest of our extended family, I must wait last to fill my bowl. By the time Maman ladles shares for my father and uncle, then his sons and wife, all that is left is broth for Brigida and I. My stomach growls, picking up the scent and my sister offers me her bowl. Lars glares at us over the lip of his dish.

"My bride eats before you," he complains, "Brigida must be strong to carry my child."

"Here girls, have mine. I have lost my appetite." Maman's quiet defiance fails to shame Lars. Ever since Father promised to marry Brigida to his brother's eldest, meanest son, Lars has been behaving worse than ever. Maman tells Father the boy is trying to rush the bedding, but Brigida is not ready.

"I'm still hungry," Lars holds his bowl out for more, his hard stare fixed on me, that I need give my soup to him.

"We're all hungry Boy," my father grunts, tired of the fight, "and we all earn our food."

"Not Adila!" Lars shouts back, jumping up and pointing at me, "she never brings in any sticks for the fire, all she does is eat up all our food!"

"Liar! You knocked me down and I dropped all my...," he lunges at me and strikes me across the cheek. The soup sprays up into my face, disguising my tears.

"Enough!" Uncle roars, "I've had enough of your women and the trouble they cause. Take them and leave this place!"

"Maman, why is everything so hard for us? My infantile voice trembles with cold, fear and misery, as we nestle together on the wooden planks of our cart. On this frigid northern night, the feeble warmth emanating from my mother and sister's spare frames on either side of me, fails to chase away the bitterness.

"Because Odin wills it my child." My mother whispers back. Symbolic of her essence, the breath from her lips forms silvery puffs of condensation that appears magical as it rises into the moonlight. In quiet moments such as this, I almost believe the village tale that my maman was a Valkyre, a female Viking warrior angel, fallen from the mythical heavens when my father captured and enslaved her.

"Keep that lousy brat quiet." My father growls from the other side of my mother's protecting back. He would have had to trap her in order to keep a creature as compelling as Maman. Though her fabled beauty is faded with hardship, there remains an unearthly quality emanating from her robust person. I ease my lips right up against her ear, her flaxen hair tickling my cheeks.

"Why does he hate me so?" I sense the inside of her stiffen, then the familiar sound of her release. In this freezing, unforgiving tundra, my mother's voice lifted in song is a beautiful gift. It is only because of the sweetness of her melodies that I know there is paradise out there somewhere for me to live for.

I watch her lilting words waft across the star sparkled darkness above me, evoking an image of a spirited child, filled with hope and promise, and see myself dancing amidst the aurora borealis glowing in the night sky. Not even my father's begrudging grunt and subsequent snores can penetrate the mystical vision, as the heavenly mists seem to form a green pathway transporting me from under the threadbare blanket into a realm of paradise.

As I cross into a dreamlike state, the once bright moon fades into the frigid wilderness of this frozen desert from which we are escaping. The ethereal aura that lit my path, retreats deep inside of me, only to beheld in song, but no longer seen. Unable to perceive my mother's melodious words, life becomes tedious and full of suffering. I trudge along the frozen earth, toiling under my father's vengeful eye, but I learn that I can always find solace if I retreat into this core of light, certain that one day it will return to illuminate my destiny.

I awake abruptly to the harsh, steely morning and my father's cursing as he heaves himself over the side of the cart, followed closely by his deep sigh and sound of his stream hammering the permafrost. I cringe, anticipating his odious morning ritual.

"Adilsen," his gravelly summons cuts through the crisp air, I flinch involuntarily each time he barks my false masculine name. "Get out from under your mother's skirt, and come show me how you piss like a man."

"Adil" Maman pleads, "we're going to a new land, no one knows us there. Must we keep up this tale that Adila is a boy?" As my father turns his sneering countenance towards us, she rushes on, desperate to avoid his inevitable anger. "She just passed five years this autumn, there will be signs, people will find out..."

I yelp as my father lunges over the edge of the cart and grasps a handful of my thick, short curls. Maman's impotent whimper fails to save me from his grasp that drags me bodily across her and out of the cart, my back scraping over the rough planks. I don't even cry out, because the shame of having to show my father how I can pass water standing with my tunic lifted around my hips, is far more painful.

"If you were the boy you were supposed to be, we wouldn't have to go through all this trouble." He spits to me, then sprays his hateful venom upon my mother, "You're accursed, to give me two mewling females, so I've told you I'm taking this one for a son. She's built like a boy, fights like a boy, works like a boy, so she is a boy. I'll not hear another word about it!"

The familiar exchange cuts to the core every time, and I turn inside myself and listen for the silken strains of my maman's song to give me strength to get through this moment. As I call on this peaceful power for protection, a calmness comes over me so that my father's rough instructions to learn to shoot my stream forward, slides off the invisible shield around me, unable to take root in the vulnerable soil of my mind.

With the simple perception that only a child can possess, I reckon that my father is taking us south to more fertile lands. A few days ago, we loaded our cart with all that we call our own: one cooking pot, four horn cups, one woven blanket, a hunting knife, an axe, a hammer, and our most valuable item, grandfather's iron blade tree saw.

When his brother exiled us from the Finnish village of our birth, Father blasphemed Maman, berated Brigida and beat on me for not being a boy. When the storm abated, he hitched the ass to pull the cart, ordered us to help pull, and because we knew nothing else, Maman, my sister and I obeyed.

Used to constant industry and labor until we are too exhausted to think, it is easier to not have anything to do but walk. Which is when I learn to sing. Whenever Maman sings, it puts my father in a trance, so when she instructs me to try to repeat after her, he doesn't say anything. It takes us more than a full moon cycle to trek to the land of the Rus, and in that span I master all of the songs of the Norse that Maman knows. She teaches me to communicate the stories through the emotion I put in my voice, how to breath, warble and fluctuate my tone. Now, when my father rages, I can imagine this river of calm melody flowing just under the surface of my chapped skin.

The climate of this heavily wooded region is much kinder, the land fertile and the rivers alive with fish and fowl. My father's capricious mood swings wildly between fear of what the future holds, and eagerness over the abundance of the earth. We pass through several hamlets about the size of whence we came, but the people regard us with suspicion and have no work for us.

By the time I perfect all of the tales of Odin, Thor, Loki and Freya, and piss to my father's satisfaction, we find our new home. It is a village of some hundred souls carved out of the wilderness of Novgorod on the northern edge of the Principality of Kiev. Most everyone in the village are servants of the nearby abbey; which, I come to learn, is a religious place where men worship a God by the name of Jesus Christ. With the ease of youth, I readily accept this God when I see pleasant smiles on rosy faces of the villains bustling about their chores. The crop is so plentiful that the abbey takes on our family to sow crops immediately. The monks even provide a few rows to cultivate, the seed to plant, a single-room wattle and daub hut, and a garden for Maman to grow food for our family. We're already starting with more than we left!

Chapter 2

We settle into the daily rhythm of the busy village. Each morning, my father and I go into the fields to plow and plant. The soil is much more supple, and the communal plow cuts deep, straight furrows with only the ass pulling and my father guiding the blade. When the beast won't pull, I must coax it to go or take a turn in the harness myself, my father at the reins cursing and beating us both. The other boys helping their fathers, point and laugh at me pulling the plow. At first, hot tears would blur my vision, when they made donkey sounds at me. After a few stumbles and extra whips from my father, however, I've hardened my heart and sealed my ears to their japes.

My mother and sister explore the forest to dig for roots and find plants for stews and medicine. When I finish in the field for the day, I have no desire to mix with the other boys, so I help my mother cultivate the overgrown garden into vegetables for meals and herbs to treat ailments. In the solitude of our small homestead on the edge of the village, I chop at the weeds, water the plants, and sing to soothe my soul. One day my father finds me digging up leeks in the garden, and grabs me by the ear.

"From now on, you'll stay with me and keep company with the other men and boys in a pot of ale when we're done in the field for the day." My ear burns as he gives me a shake to emphasize his edict, "garden tending is women's work, my son needs to be with me and the other men!"

During these loathsome afternoons, I learn how to run fast or stand and fight. Like a pack of wolves, four or five of the boys make a game of separating me from the group of men. I usually try first to run, terrified of what they will do to me if they find out I'm not made like them underneath my short tunic and leggings. More times than not, the fear fuels me, and I dart like a hare through the forest and lose them in the foliage. Sometimes, after a long day when the ass won't pull and I'm tired from having to take over in the harness, they do catch me. Accustomed to my father's fists, theirs are mere bee stings in comparison, so I study their moves and mimic their punches.

Being smaller than most of them, I figure out how to duck under the melee so they end up hitting each other. Though I'm younger, I'm stronger from pulling the plow, and when I swing back and connect with a cheek or a gut I can knock them down.

Things go on like this day in and day out throughout the harvest, and I grow mean and surly. I relate to my father's permanent scowl and scornful demeanor, the thin thread of joy inside receding under the padded layers of my banded bosom. Only when I fall exhausted to sleep at night, massaged by the hand of Maman's crooning songs, do I dare acknowledge that secret place of peace deep within me.

As the winter season advances, and the days grow shorter, my temper eases with the reprieve from daily bullying. The harvest is in and the piling snow forces us to retreat indoors. Now its just back to avoiding my father's foul moods as he searches for an outlet for his aggression in our cramped hovel. For the first time in my memory, we have food aplenty to last us until the thaw, and the forest is teeming with boar, deer and fowl that we hunt and trap. We keep busy improving our circumstances, felling trees to add outbuildings to our lot, fashioning furniture out of the abundant wood in the forest, or stuffing new mattresses.

The abbey remains an awesome mystery to me, a foreign place, tugging at my curiosity as if I'm connected to its carillon by invisible cords. I marvel at its power to mark the time of day, just as the sun and moon determine the seasons. The deep tolls from the bells, the distant chanting, and the wafting fragrance, touch something in my core as strongly as my mother's heavenly voice. When the other villagers inform my father that, once the crops are in, all the menfolk are required to go to the abbey on Sundays, a thrill shivers down my back at the thought of going there.

My only experience with religion so far is Maman's belief in the Gods of the northman, Odin and Thor, and that they created everything and make everything happen. At the abbey, everyone gathers in a temple they call the Church, to worship the Christian God of the Romans. Whereas

Odin is hailed for being combative and cruel, like my father; the message I absorb about Christ is of a kind, loving creator. It is in this context that I find and fall in love with God.

I anticipate those peaceful hours on Sundays to get me through the rest of the weekdays. I quickly learn the songs, shocked when my father doesn't cuff me for singing them. The heady smell of frankincense, and the muted words of gratitude and glory from suffering, coax the shy hope from that hiding place in my heart. Each time I enter the stone walls of the church, its as though this all-powerful God is building walls of love and protection around me, filling me with purpose that there is something greater for me in this world, and that he will take me there.

Of particular interest to me is a breathtaking statue of Mary, the mother of Jesus. I drink in every detail of her serene face and wonder that this maternal woman is revered and respected among men. She is the first woman I have ever seen exalted and important. And there are other saints too, holy women, helpful women, loving women, teaching other women in this religion. Sometimes I can't stop the tears from streaming quietly down my cheeks, as the girl in me cries out to be known as the young woman I will inevitably become.

Chapter 3

Over the next year I grow tall from the heartier diet, and fit from the labor and fighting. Though I'm now able to outrun the other boys and fend them off most of the time, I have a new destination of escape, the abbey church. I sneak in and find a hiding spot and let the calm wash over me as I study the statue of Mary, or the stories depicted in the carvings of biblical scenes adorning the altar. Whether or not my father knows, he doesn't say anything as long as I get my work done. Maybe he's silently satisfied that I'm stretching up high like a white bark birch vying for sunlight. Conversely, my robust size makes me feel like a boy, and my only connection to my feminine self is the enduring softness I find in the presence of the beloved Mother of God.

Another season passes busily by in much the same fashion, marked by yet another growth spurt. I have seven summers, the early harvest marks my birth, and I have already surpassed Brigida in height, who has seen two more years than me. When my father takes a swing at me, which is a bit less these days, I'm usually able to dodge him or defect the blow. With this new confidence, I've taken to defending Maman and my sister from his physical violence, though I still can't protect them from his cutting words.

Lately though, his abusive tongue has lost some of its sting along with his fist, and he no longer curses Maman for not being what she used to be, or for not giving him a son. Perhaps our improved circumstances are mellowing him, for in our new homestead, we finally have enough. We have enough food to eat from the garden and the forest, enough work from the abbey fields, enough warmth from bear and deer pelts, enough wood to light fires. There are times, however, sitting quietly beside my father in the church on Sundays, when I think it might be something more that has sparked his mind to think before lashing out.

In these years of peace and growth, three things bother me. The boys still bully me, I have to deny myself as a young woman, and the disconnect from Maman. The daily separation of men and women is one cause, but the main reason for our distance is she clings to Odin and the old Norse gods. Every Sunday, I repeat the stories I've heard that morning to her and my sister, about the miracles of Jesus. One day I try to explain to her about Mary, and how these followers of Jesus Christ also honor his mother.

"My child," she looks at me sagely, "I've done my best to raise you in the old religion, to know the tales of our gods. The most important message from all of these creeds however, is to recognize that there is a powerful creator that makes everything happen. Some gods are warlike, jealous and vengeful, some are nurturing and awesome, but they determine everything in our lives."

"If Odin was so great, why did he make us suffer so before we came to Novgorod?" I challenge. "Since we came here, and started knowing God, look at how much better things are!"

"Are they really better Adila?" She counters, "Yes, we have food, clothing and shelter aplenty. Yet we still have to call you Adilsen, and you come home beaten and battered every fortnight!"

At that moment I gasp, seeing my father's menacing frame darken the doorway. As my mother turns to follow my gaze, he smashes his fist into her jaw. "I'll not have you speak to my son so ever again!"

"Leave her alone!" I stand up to him, "I started the conversation!" I immediately find myself on the rush-covered ground beside my mother, shaking the cobwebs from my ringing ears.

"Your name is Adilsen, boy!" He roars over us, "and from now on, we'll not speak of the old religion in this house!" Here he pauses, growing still, "not even in song."

I stare after his departing back, shocked that he denies us all the comfort of Maman's soothing voice. I reach out to help her up from the ground, but she swats away my hand, looking at me accusingly as if to say, "I told you so."

We enter the darkness of winter in silence, Maman's magical tongue stilled by my father's edict. We occupy ourselves building a loft for my sister and I to sleep, and for the first time we share our own bed, free from my father's rutting and grunting when he mounts his wife. Growing up needing each other for warmth, and seeing livestock procreate, has given us an education in sex and reproduction, so it is no surprise when my sister starts to bleed, thus making the separation necessary. Ironically, because of our new private space, as Maman and I grow apart, I discover a new friend in Brigida.

Whispering in our bed at night, I'm able to become a girl. I caution my sister to stay close to Maman, and which of the boys are mean and to avoid, and she shares with me what the other girls in the village are like. She listens to my adoration of Christ, and tells me what she learns from Maman about the spirit of this new land. Very quietly at first, I sing to her the songs I've learned in Church, then with more boldness when I realize that my father can hear but doesn't object.

Brigida blossoms with the spring bloom, the most vibrant of all the flowers in the fields. She has my father's smaller stature, but whereas he is wiry and bandy, she is petite and lithe. We both have startlingly light blue eyes and fair hair, as do our parents, but my hair is always cropped short while my sister is crowned with golden curls. I used to hear people say that before life hardened her, my mama possessed a beauty that was otherworldly. As I witness that same ethereal comeliness flourishing in Brigida, I can almost fathom my father's infatuation with the beautiful Valkyrie he imprisoned as his wife. Though its too late for me to rescue my mother from the dominance of men, I become fiercely protective of my lovely sister.

My father dictates that this year we will plant more rows of barley, he has his eye on bartering one of the other villains for the use of his ox next season, but he needs more crops to trade. I'm furious when he orders my mama and sister into the fields to drop seed, and the other boys and even some of the men stare at Brigida's bare calves, lustful intentions written on their agog faces. Fire flushes my face when I recall what they brag about doing to the pretty girls in the village, and I throw myself into the planting and pray to finish our rows quickly.

This all gives my tormentors fresh fodder to jeer at me, telling me what they think about my sister, and what they want to do to her. I caution Maman to keep her close, and even have the audacity to grumble to my father that she's not safe when he calls her out to the fields, directing his attention to the leers. I plead with my sister to stay with our maman, not go anywhere alone, and keep her eyes down whenever she goes outside with us. I scare her sufficiently, repeating how the boys say they're going to pass her around and use her. I'm so distracted looking out for my sister, that I forget to watch my own back.

It is a bright summer day, as I accompany Brigida to the abbey with our tithe of eggs, until I notice a group of boys behind us. I hasten her into the queue at the guardhouse, and elicit her promise to stay there with the monks until I come back for her. Returning to the gravel pathway, the boys are no where in sight, and I leave the road to check around overgrown corners in the abbey walls. In my concern to chase them away from my sister, I fall into their trap! Crouched, fists up and hackles raised and ready for a fight, I'm surrounded by half dozen of the most ill-intentioned boys in the village.

"Where's your pretty sister, Adilsen?" They laugh at my pathetic stand.

"He's comely like her, we could have fun with him first!" The blood rushes in my ears in terror of what they might discover. As they grow more serious about having sport with me, they start to jab step at me, and I pray for a cool head to confront them. I'm ready when they surge at me, and manage to dodge and punch for a few precious moments until my back meets the planks of the wall. They pummel me until I'm nearly senseless, I vaguely hear them shouting at each other not to knock me out before they can have me.

"Here's what I'm going to poke in your sister when I get the chance!" One of them sneers, and I feel his rod prodding my bruised face. Another holds my head and pries open my jaw. I feel my gorge rise as the stench of him fills my mouth.

Suddenly, all of the suppressed indignity and unrequented abuse I've suffered at my father's hands fills me with a cold rage. It fuels me with surprising strength and clarity, and with all of the anger in my being I bite down hard and spat him out. He howls loud enough to wake the dead, and while some of the boys run, a few of them try to quiet him, and one of them proceeds to beat me about the head.

At once, all becomes quiet, and I'm lifted up by a pair of robed arms and bore into the coolness of the abbey grounds.

"My sister," I moan, my lips fattening from bruises. I squint at the hooded figure as I'm laid down on a pallet, my eyes rapidly swelling shut too.

"She's safe," the resonate voice fills me with peace, and as I sink into oblivion, I hear him tell me, "and so are you now my child."

"Brigida," I mumble through bruised lips, everything is dark.

"She's safe," the same voice answers, I hear the monk lighting a candle. "Rest easy, she's back home with your parents." I slip back into the void, feeling nothing.

"My sister," I gasp, struggling against the pain in my body to raise myself from the pallet. Sunlight filters through the slits of my puffy eyelids.

"Brigida has been this whole time with your mama," the familiar calm voice floods me with assurance. "The boys who attacked you have been punished. You're both safe now, you can sleep."

I turn my face to the golden warmth and sink back into the pallet. Awareness leaves me again, and I succumb to deep restfulness.

I've lost track of the days as I drift in and out of consciousness, but eventually I wake up and stay awake. Exhausted in mind and body, I ease into my surroundings. It is daytime again, sunlight slices through a high window in the whitewashed wall. I lay on a pallet on the flagstone floor in a small cell with another cot across from me, and a table with a basin against another wall. There is a wooded cross hung on the other wall, and underneath, kneeling on a low stool, was the robed figure from my befogged memory, his tonsured head bent in prayer.

"My sister," I whisper, not wanting to disturb his meditation, but desperate to hear of her well-being. The brightness of his smile when he sees me lucid, dispels any fears I have of bothering him.

"As I have told you, child," his gentle voice is filled with kindness, "she has stayed at your home with your mama this whole week of your infirmary."

"I've been here for that long?" The air thickens once again at the thought of my father's fury that I'm not there to help him, "my father is going to kill me!"

13

"I think not," I look at him skeptically, he doesn't know my father. He continues placidly, "we've come to an agreement, your father and the order."

I listen intently as he explains how he's seen me not only attending mass, but running to the church for sanctuary and praying to the statue of Mary for solace. He's taken note of the stillness in my demeanor, and the light shining from my eyes when in the Lord's house.

"Especially," here he moves from his prayer bench to sit on the edge of his bed and face me, "many of us have heard your beautiful singing voice. You see, the Abbot has been commissioned by our superiors to assemble a boys choir, and we wish to add you to our growing group."

I drop my eyes and bow my head, so that he doesn't see my shame over my dishonesty, squelching the spark of hope that his request ignites. A glimpse of the glorious life I could have, filled with song, love and joy flashes through me, and I squeeze back tears of bitter disappointment, denying myself this illusion. I mumble something about this being a great honor, but my father will never approve.

"Oh, but he already has!" My head snaps up as I try to focus on his gentle brown eyes through the water now flowing freely down my cheeks. I dare to hope. "The abbey is to grant him lifetime use of our oxen to replace your labor. For giving his son to the church, God will grant him a new one."

"But my sister, Brigida," I lament, "if I'm to stay here with you, I can't protect her!"

"So you'll miss out on your destiny for your sister?" His query hangs ponderous in the small cell. Parallel lives stretch out in front of me; one, a continuation of my life as it is, and the other, a life in this idyllic haven. I look into his eyes, pleading even as I answer, "I can't leave her, she's my only friend, and I have to take care of her."

"Your father was right that you would not want to separate from her, he was very adamant that she had to stay with you." Here he opened his hands and shrugged, "It took some bargaining, but the abbot is going to allow your sister to live here with you, as long as she remains secluded from the flock."

I struggle to digest the magnitude of this boon, to have a female anywhere in the abbey walls is strictly forbidden. The monk continues,

"Your father wouldn't accept anything less. My child, I have seen you in my prayers, and the other monks are witness to your calling, so we were guided to make an exception to have you both live here. You won't be able to sleep in the dormitory with the other novices, but we can clear out a storage shed next to the kitchen for you and your sister."

My head is swimming, I feel as if I'm having a dream. With my sister here she would be safe, and my female identity would remain secret. A very shrewd maneuver by my father, which reminds me what the monk said about replacing me with another son.

"But I don't understand," I furrow my brow, desperately trying to process this turn of events, "who would become my father's son in my stead?"

The monk heaves a long suffering sigh, as if he's had to explain this many times. "As I've told you, I have seen you singing in my dreams, and God doesn't plant these seeds without giving us a plan to see their fruition. Like your father, you must believe in God's plan, and whatever it is that we, his children, need to do to carry out his will, we do! If its God's providence to take you into his house, he will replace you with a new baby for your father. I've instructed him to go to his wife and be kind to her, and he will have his new son before the year is out."

True to this prophecy, God makes everything come to pass. By the harvest celebrating my eleventh year, my sister and I move into a small storage room built up against the kitchen oven, where it is always warm. Each day I meet the other six novices in the choir for lessons, and before the next full moon, Maman is with child.

THE FOLD

Chapter 4

Several months pass swiftly, a blur of mass, prayer, learning and song. Brigida and I are ensconced in the daily life and routine of the religious order of the abbey, our old life fading into a romantic distortion of the harsh reality that it was. We even laugh and mock our father's antics, and fondly recall our mother's warmth and strength. The monk who rescued me, Brother Samuel, becomes my sage mentor and dear friend. In this gentle atmosphere, the jagged edges of hardship that shaped our character smooth over. I grow spiritually and in knowledge of the lord, and my sister matures in form and beauty.

Our abbey is home to roughly one hundred monks, not including myself and the other novices, and is like a village in itself. We adhere to the strict rule of the Order of Studiites, a religious group conceived by Saint John of Studious in Miklegard, and spread throughout the Eastern Roman Empire. Our chapter is one of the northernmost outposts.

The monks must all take a vow of silence, which allows them to talk only during chapter, matters of great importance, and to sing or chant. For the most part, they obey the rule, which is a great comfort to me in my dealings with them. There is little interaction, except in moments of instruction or private conversations with Brother Samuel. For Brigida, contact with others is prohibited, so she only ventures into the kitchen and yard when there are no monks or lay workers present. This arrangement suits us for now, and we're content to carry on with ourselves for companionship.

The only practice I detest, is the requirement of tonsure, where the monks must cut their hair short and shave it off entirely at the crown. Prior to entering the abbey, it was a means of silent protest that I would wear my hair as long as possible, tying it back, until Maman would trim it under threat of my father ripping it from my scalp. At night, I would take it out and feel the soft tresses start to curl around my finger like a golden coil, a secret feminine delight. Within the first week of our arrival, however, I drag my dispirited feet into our tiny room, and show Brigida my bald pate.

"Oh Adila, your lovely curls!" The pity in her voice appeases my bruised pride. "Why did you let them cut it all off?"

"I had to; all of the novices have to wear the hair like this." My bottom lip trembles with suppressed emotion, "It was all I had left to show I'm a girl."

I drop down on the pallet and burst into tears, self pity winning the battle. Brigida sits next to me and puts her arm around my shoulders. "You don't need outward vanities to prove you're a girl."

"You don't understand," I lash out unfairly, "you get to be who you are, you get to wear your hair out and walk like a girl. I can't even take a piss like a girl."

"To what end?" She snaps back, "I'm here in this cramped room day in and day out, what does it matter if I leave my hair out? There's no one to see it!"

"I'm sorry Brigida," her truth penetrates my sorrow. "Its ungrateful of me to be upset about my hair. We're here, safe, warm, well-fed, I should be happy to be so blessed. I must pray for a better attitude of sacrifice for my Lord."

"Do you wear your cowl pulled up over your head all of the time?" She asks after a thoughtful pause.

"Some of the novices take them off in the sanitarium or rectory when we eat, but I usually keep mine on. I try to keep as much of me hidden as possible."

"What if you just make sure to keep it covering your head, and I'll shear your hair as needed?"

I nod in appreciation, but I can't seem to shake the malaise of our having to always hide our identities. That night I start to bleed.

Throughout the frigid winter months, we are warm and happy. I pass sunlit hours in the scriptorium, learning to decipher and write letters, reading and reciting the bible, and singing and praying in the choir and at mass. Brother Samuel continues to teach us the word of the lord, and our small boys choir is generating some praise for drawing crowds from the surrounding countryside. Brigida and I erect a privacy screen outside of our room so that she can use the space outdoors as a laundry. Once a month, the monks toss over their habit and cowl for her to stir in her large vat of hot water and lye soap. When the ground thaws, we break the soil in our makeshift yard and plant herbs and plants for medicines, as we used to do with Maman.

"Tomorrow is Sunday, I will wash your hair." Darkness has just chased us to bed after a tiring day tending to our garden, in addition to my monastic chores. Bathing has become a sublime treat that we've developed to lift each other's spirits. We pull the vat inside and boil snow to fill the tub with hot water. Brigida makes a mild soap by diluting the lye in fat and adding rosemary and mint for a fresh, invigorating scent. We take turns scrubbing each other until our skin is pink and our hair is gild. The anticipation of a bath tomorrow immediately lifts my mood.

"Thank you, Brigida, you're becoming like Maman, always knowing what to say or do to soothe me." At her soul-deep sigh, I turn towards her, trying to perceive her expression in the dim light from the fire that seeps through the cracks in the stones from the shared kitchen chimney wall.

"I miss her so much," Brigida's wistful words evoke my own childish yearning for my maman's arms. "I was always with her, she taught me everything I know."

Brother Samuel is always trying to impress upon me and the other novices how we must follow the example of Jesus Christ and strive to serve others in everything we do. It is times like this, I see my selfishness, in that I don't consider my sister's circumstances and happiness. My days are filled with purposeful pursuits, and at night I draw comfort from my sister's care and nurturing ways. In my complacency, I forget that she has the same needs as I. As I conjure up the image of our Maman's steadfast gaze, her mystic music falls from my lips. I close my eyes and give myself to the profound pleasure of the honeyed melody pouring into the darkness.

I sing one of my favorites, the one that transports me into the night sky, and I see myself dancing among the stars. In my vision, my hair is long and swirls my head in downy white ringlets. The buds of my breast are unbound under a floating white tunic, my movements bold, willowy femininity. At some point as I fall asleep, the lyrics turn inward, and the spirit of the joyful child swells into rich dreams of following a celestial pathway to peace and eternal beauty. When we awake the next morning, Brigida hugs me and thanks me for my lovely singing. I realize that this is a way I can return love and comfort to her, and I vow to make a regular practice of reciting the ancient songs as well as religious hymns.

In these early months of her pregnancy, we visit Maman when we have the chance, promising to be with her for the birth of the child. A prosperous calm has settled in their lives, witnessed by the aura of health emanating from Maman burgeoning form. Her careworn brow seems a little less furrowed, her pale blue eyes now twinkle ever so slightly. Most telling, however, is the change in my father's demeanor. Where he was once rash and abusive, he has become quiet and thoughtful. With the tranquility that permeates our family home, and the freshness of spring in the surrounding countryside, we start to anticipate our outings to go home, especially for Brigida, who has to remain isolated on the abbey grounds.

After the birth of our prophesied brother, Samuel, however, these treasured times come to an abrupt end. A few of the older boys had continued to stalk and harass us, emboldened by short memories of the lash they received for punishment, and my new pious softness. While I was neglecting my physical strength, focusing on studying the bible, manuscripts, and music, they were still working in the fields and growing more muscular. We had been enjoying a prologued stay with Maman after her labor, when she asks Brigida and I to go into the forest for some roots. Lulled by the deep silence of the woods, I don't hear them come upon us, until I'm grabbed from behind.

They grip me by my forearms and force me to watch my screaming sister being tossed to the ground. I thrash against two pairs of restraining hands, as another of them holds her down and a fourth falls on top of her, crushing her feeble attempts to throw him off. In my frenzy of powerlessness, I vomit on myself when he violates her.

Something in me snaps, an animal roar escaping from deep within me. Rage clouds my awareness. Possessed by supernatural strength, I shake off my captors as if they were infants. I charge at the two boys abusing my sister, and knock the one off of her. I grab him by the arm and slam him into a nearby tree, where he crumples to a heap on the ground. A high pitched whining fills my ears as I turn on the rest of them, only to see them scurrying away, and my sister covering her bloodied legs. I have failed.

I had only managed to keep my beautiful sister protected for ten and three years. I drop to my knees beside her gathering her trembling form in my arms, my own body shaking with sobs of anger, guilt and failure.

After a while, my shock subsides enough to note the lifeless body of her attacker at the foot of the tree, but my muddled brain can't make sense of what I had done. Its Brigida who pulls herself together enough to quietly insist that we must leave. In my misery, I pick up her broken body and cradle her, stumbling and crying back towards our parents' home. She begs me to stop at a stream where she wades in to wash herself, then counsels me to rinse my face and cowl.

The cold water clears my head enough to comprehend that she said we must skirt the village and go straight back to the abbey. She cautions that father must never know, and I grasp her logic, we both know father will blame her. It will be more acceptable for me to get into a fight on my own, then have Brigida involved. She will be punished for bringing trouble on herself and kicked out of the abbey. I must pick up the yoke again and be strong, as always.

So hand in hand like scared children, we return to the abbey, where I deposit Brigida in our room and go to the chapel to pray. I'm on my knees in front of the statue of Mary when Brother Samuel comes for me.

Chapter 5

The monastic counsel rules that Brigida and I may remain at the abbey, if I repent and do penance. To purify myself of sin, I am to feel the physical ache of laboring in the abbey gardens, splitting and hauling wood for fires, and any other tasks that the monks call me to perform. I zealously complete my tiring chores with speed and vigor, praying that God overlook my wrong motives. When I hack at the soil in the garden, I'm chopping off male body parts. I attack the firewood as if I'm splitting open men's skulls. I punch at the sacks of wheat flour as I carry them, feeling the soft spots of a boy's belly. The exercise and exhaustion are precisely what I need to heal my guilt and rebuild my fitness.

Each night, I fall into our shared pallet too tired to speak, and I am up before dawn every morning for mass and prayer, until the day breaks and I have enough light to start my daily toil. I rest only to eat and sing, and answer the bells marking the canonical hours of service. Days, weeks, then months pass without respite from my rigorous routine, and I don't even notice how distant I grow from those around me. The other novices in the choir cease to engage me anymore, and I'm too weary to listen to Brigida complain about her clear, skin being pale and her radiant hair becoming dull.

The only event that distracts my narrow focus during these months is the arrival of an emissary from Miklagard, the capitol of the new Roman Empire almost a year's journey south along the Dneiper River. The leader of the small party, Bishop Stephen, is a diminutive, swarthy man, escorted by a pair northmen as enormous in stature as the Bishop is petite. The threesome dazzle our provincial imaginations, with their gold embroidered vestments and gleaming armor, and the monastery is abuzz with gossip over their sophistication. Though the hierarchy of the

Christian Church confuses me, I gather that this is an important visit, as the Abbot is in awe of the Bishop's person, and even Brother Samuel is taken by his intellect. It is the pair of Varangian guards, however, who attract my attention more than the pristine religious man, with their towering height and powerful builds. Each morning, as I draw water from the well, I espy them training with their heavy double sided axes and broadswords, envious of their proficiency with the weapons of war.

The intrigue over the foreigners has even permeated into Brigida's isolation, and she presses me for tales of the trio.

"I've heard they're from Byzantium," she queries one night, "an empire that stretches across the seven seas."

"Aye, Constantinople," I indulge, crumpling onto our pallet, "Brother Samuel calls their city Miklagard, which is home to more people than trees in the forest that surrounds us, and the Emperor of the Romans himself. The buildings are adorned in gold and marble statues, the grandest of which is the Hagia Sophia, the greatest church in the world."

"They say the women wear dresses of rich color and paint their faces," her eyes shine in admiration, "where no one toils over fields and yet there is still wealth beyond measure."

"Such stories you tell!" I yawn, slumber tugging my eyelids, "'tis a wonder how you hear all of this when you're here by yourself all day." Her response fades into oblivion.

Since the arrival of Bishop Stephen, Brother Samuel studies me intently, as if evaluating something, and I fear that he knows what really happened months ago in the woods. On the day marking my brother's one year since birth, my spirit is especially heavy as I drag myself into the monk's cell for our evening studies. The greek text swims in front of me, and the subtle theoretical differences of the iconoclastic dispute make my head ache. With a deep sigh, the kind monk sets down his tome and contemplates my mood.

"What troubles you, Child?" He takes a seat on his pallet to face me directly. "Your spirit is out of balance. When I used to look upon you in the chapel, your eyes shining in adoration of the Lord, I knew that you burned with the love of God."

"I still do Brother," I will have to repent the sin of omission as I reply only a half truth, "My penance has been a heavy burden, and I have

25

been very tired." I add on quickly, before he can think to lighten my punishment, "However, I joyfully accept God's judgment against me, and carry out his work with a light heart. It is also my baby brother's birthday today, and my sister hasn't seen our mama this past year."

"While your reasons are sound, I feel that there is something else you have not told me. Lately, I have watched you at your chores, at your prayers and studies as if you have been on a mission. What is it you are trying to accomplish my child?"

I avert my gaze to the floor, so he can't probe into my soul, "I have confessed to the Father Abbot of my sins, why do you remind me of this painful past?"

"I never brought up the incident. You did." my eyes snap back to his, realizing my slip, "I merely observed that your heart has not been as open to receive what the Lord is trying to teach you."

We stare at each other in defiant silence, he searching for the answer, me shielding the truth so precariously close to the surface. Reading my willfulness, he heaves another characteristic sigh and stands to answer the bell for evening prayer. The next day, he escorts my sister and I to visit our mama and baby Samuel.

Out in the refreshing spring air, I expect that Brigida is pleased to be going to see Maman, as she used to be. Instead, it's surprising to see her shoulders hunched and head down, not enjoying the beauty of the day. As we grow near to our parents cottage, her steps become slower and her feet sluggish. Always analyzing the thoughts of others, I assume that she's anxious to encounter them for the first time since she was attacked.

"Maman!" I cry as soon as we enter. In her sturdy embrace I fight to keep from sobbing, but her earthy smell draws out the little girl in me, and my tears wet up her broad shoulder.

"What's this child?" She gently draws away from me and scrutinizes my face. I close my eyes when she lays her work-hardened palm on my cheek, leaning into the healing strength of her spirit. I never thought I would miss her so much, and seeing her now brings a lump in my throat that I can't speak or swallow. She reads the emotion in my eyes and nods sagely, sparing me from explanation.

From the table behind Maman, my father stands up, holding baby

Samuel in the crook of his arm. For a moment, I can only marvel at the sight of my rough sire so tenderly holding his longed-for son.

"Father," I incline my head respectfully, reaching out for the baby, "he looks healthy!" I exclaim as I take his warm weight in my arms. I nearly cry again with the joy of snuggling my baby brother against my neck until he squeals in protest. I sniff him and smack his cheeks with kisses, the love for such a pure, innocent creature surging within me. In my rapture, I fail to notice the tense silence amongst the others.

Maman's patient gaze is affixed on Brigida, who stares back at her with an expression akin to horror. My father's brow is thunderously questioning, his head swiveling between the two. It is the ashen countenance of Brother Samuel who persuades me to ease the baby cautiously to his cradle and position myself in the fray.

"You heard me daughter," Maman chides steadily, "how long have you been with child?"

"What?!" My father and I both explode at the same time, but before I can process my thoughts, his quick temper spurs me into action. He lunges at her in fury, "Whore!"

Like lightening, I maneuver myself in between him and my sister, catching the blow that was to smash into her. It takes all of my self control to not strike him back and have my vengeance for a lifetime of abuse. My arm shakes with the exertion of holding his arm up in the air, his frenzied countenance turns on me.

"Murderer!" The spittle from his venomous tongue flies in my eyes, yet I still hold on, "a pair of snakes in my house!" He rips his fist away from my grip and points an accusing finger at Brigida and I, his words damning us, "a Whore and a Murderer!"

"I should kill you then!" I scream back, the rage boiling over, making everyone else in the room fade from view. Instinctively, I crouch into my fighting stance, ready to spring into deadly action. My father's form sharpens, as my senses hone in on him, his lip curls up in a menacing sneer as his muscles bunch in anticipation of my onslaught. Not even Brother Samuel's gasping cry, nor the baby's gurgling, can penetrate my thick red haze of intent.

"Adil," Maman's low, singsong voice breaks the spell. She crosses between us, her hand suggestively resting on her belly, and picks up baby

Samuel. Her calm gaze rests on her husband, as if compelling him to choose between his family and his fury. My full awareness is still affixed upon him, so I notice when his eyes shift to her hand on the mound of her stomach, and his visage softens. His posture eases, the anger visibly leaving his body. In this surreal moment, I believe that my mother indeed has some sort of power over him.

"They have to leave." He declares.

"In a moment." I've never heard my mama counter my father without fear of punishment. Then to my astonishment, she walks over and hands him the baby, which he readily welcomes into his arms.

Suddenly, my father morphs into merely a flawed human, not the raging ogre of my childhood nightmares. I feel the heavy beat of my heart, and my rapid breathing, and I realize that I have become that monster. The vile temper that I have always hated in my father, is in me! I fall to my knees in the rushes covering the floor, overcome with shame. Brother Samuel draws me over to the table and sits with me on the bench, praying fervently under his breath.

"When is the child due?" Maman's hushed query brings us all back to the dilemma at hand. My sluggish mind grapples with the time frame of that fateful day in the woods, our brother's birth, and the eight moons it takes for a baby to be ready to come out of its mother's stomach. My addled brain twists reality, and stretches her pregnancy over the past year to coincide with her rape, though logic suggests that I finished her attacker before he could finish in her.

"Its my fault!" My over loud voice is raw with emotion. I babble on, "that day...that day a while ago..."

"I know not when the child will be born." My sister's voice sounds cold, hollow as she interrupts me. Then she looks straight at Brother Samuel, "and I know not who the father is."

"What are you saying daughter?" He questions.

"You didn't know?" Her demeanor is almost scornful, "it was a condition of us staying at the abbey, that I was to be of service to them."

"Who," Brother Samuel whispers in horror, "who were you to...be of service?"

"Your brothers." Her quiet revelation shouts into the room, setting off a myriad array of responses. My rash father, as always is the first to curse and launch into a tirade of verbal abuse. Brother Samuel drops to his knees and reaches up to implore God to give him a sign. I'm numb from shock, and all I can comprehend is my mama nodding her head in sorrowful understanding.

Throughout the excruciating afternoon, Maman, my father and Brother Samuel hash out a new agreement for our future, and for once I have no interest in taking part. My befogged mind is consumed with guilt that I have again failed to protect my sister from the lecherous hands of men. I recall the endless hours I spent laboring around the abbey, at choir practice and studies, at prayer and services, and only seeing Brigida late at night when I would fall exhausted onto our pallet, to tired to listen to her recall her day and what she had been doing to occupy her isolated hours. I mull over all of the trinkets and comforts, tender morsels of food that found their way into our room, which I never questioned from where they came. I notice for the first time how she has filled out, more radiant than ever. I've been so wrapped up in myself, I have been blind of what was going on around me.

Trapped in thought, I don't remember much of the rest of the day and walking back to the abbey at dusk. I vaguely murmur a distracted congratulations to the stunning news that Maman is pregnant again, and absorb that we are to go back to the abbey to conceal Brigida's condition. Brother Samuel's even temperament is challenged, as he explains that Maman will take on both babies as twins. If my sister's child is a male, once he is old enough to take holy orders, he will become a novice under the tutelage of his fathers. A fitting end to the night, we pass into the silence within the monastery walls. I see our cozy room through a nightmarish haze, fighting the sickness arising in the back of my throat again.

In the tense stillness that thickens the small space, we prepare for sleep, laying down in our shared pallet next to each other as we have countless nights since we were born. Tonight, however, rather than snuggle close seeking one another's comfort, I squeeze up next to the rough stone wall, unable to bring myself to touch her. My swirling thoughts placed her under the rutting hips of countless falsely pious men. I imagine I smell the stink of their carnal use on her tainted body, and the visions of her as their whore erects an invisible wall between us.

As we lay stiff and awake for an agonizingly long time, her taciturn sobs wrack her form, and the core of my heart that will always love her, melts. I heave a sigh of resignation, and relax against her.

"You hate me," she cries, pity for her shattering my sordid fantasies.

"I could never hate you," I assure her, my own tears streaming down the sides of my face, "its my fault that I've failed you again."

"You shouldn't blame yourself, it is my lot as a women." Her words are heavy with worldly experience. "We are either tethered to a husband who beats us and controls our minds, or prostitute our bodies so that we can have our own beliefs and opinions."

"Not so Brigida!" I admonish, "we have a choice to not succumb to the evils of men. We don't have to depend upon them for our needs, we can choose to reject them and take care of ourselves."

"You mustn't scorn me Adila," she wheedles, "in your judgment of me you forget that you live as a boy. You've been taught how to fight and take care of yourself, and you've been given the choice to pursue your God."

"You don't think I would rather be myself?" I demand, self pity clouding my ability to consider her months of isolation, her need for love and humanly affection that I myself had denied her.

"Sister, please don't explode in a rage like father," the truth of her statement is a cold bucket of water, "you have no more choice to reveal yourself as a female then I have to survive without a man. At least the ones here are kind and gentle with me."

I drift into a troubled sleep, nightmares of the scores of monks, boys and their fathers taunting me to fight for my sister's honor intruding my respite. Throughout my visions, Brother Samuel stands to the side, chanting one word..."

"Powerless, powerless, powerless."

Over the next several months, my sister and I make peace as I come to accept her burgeoning stomach. Though I perform my penance with renewed diligence born of guilt, I'm mindful of Brigida's needs. I smuggle books from the abbey library to read to her, bring her wool so that she can spin and weave blankets and clothes for the baby, and fill the long winter evenings with songs I've learned.

On Sundays after mass, Brother Samuel accompanies us to visit Maman, though our father remains conspicuously absent during these afternoon hours. Around the time of the autumn harvest, Mama's baby comes due and Brigida, about a month from giving birth herself, and I go to stay with her during her labor. My father is visibly displeased with our presence, all but ignoring the both of us, but he had agreed to the arrangement that tumultuous day when we discovered my sister's pregnancy. As both of their fruit ripen, I grow from being amenable to their pact, to cautious excitement for this new life.

Just as the convenience of both babies coming due at almost the same time, it so happens that the Bishop Stephen prepares to return south at the spring thaw, and I, along with the other six novices, have been selected to join the emissary. Apparently, the Bishop has been on a tour of Christian monasteries in order to assess their orthodoxy. More pertinent to my situation however, he is recruiting boys for his great choir that is to fill the soaring domes of the Hagia Sophia with song. It is a supreme honor and momentous turn of events, and I am alive with anticipation of the adventure, especially upon hearing that my closest friend and sister are to come with us.

Brother Samuel is to lend his expertise to the Bishop to choose boys from monasteries along the way, and to teach and train us in preparation for our new lives in the glittering capitol city of Constantinople. Brigida will accompany me as my personal handmaiden, under dire consequences of mixing with the menfolk. She has conceded to leave her baby with Maman to rear, thus avoiding the scorn of the village and the scandal to the abbey.

My father's disposition improves when Maman bears another son, and Brother Samuel reminds him of God's fulfilled promise, that he shall have many sons in place of me, the one he gave to the church. Soon thereafter, Brigida endures an arduous labor to produce yet another baby boy. It is known throughout the village that Adil and his wife have been blessed with twin boys. Brigida is satisfied with the future of her son, as our father gazes upon his pack of boys with rare pleasure and pride.

When the first mild breezes from the south rustle tender buds on the forest trees, we take our leave of our family, tingling in nervous excitement. We cling to Maman, not knowing if we'll ever see her again, but she parts with those familiar words, "God wills it my child."

Father watches our emotional parting, drawing comfort from bouncing the pair of infant boys in the crooks of his arms. "I did my best with the two of you," he calls gruffly after us, "and now I'm going to do my best with my boys." He remains standing in front of his now-prosperous cottage with his sons around him, as our group sets out down the ancient pathway, beaten along the riverside by centuries of Viking traders.

THE FLOCK

Chapter 6

Brigida and I are useful on the trek south, drawing on our rural childhood knowledge of finding resources from the land. With Brother Samuel's support, Bishop Stephen's prayers, and the guardsmen's protection, we organize groups to forage for food, gather wood for fire and set camp at night. Brigida silences any questions over her presence with her hearty meals, and I volunteer for first watch, singing everyone to sleep, before curling up next to my sister for rest at night.

At first I am unimpressed with the dusky, petite man in charge of this expedition, with his flowing white garb, fastidious ways and dry personality. Within days however, I'm drawn to his generous degree of scholarship. The Bishop and the guards are the only ones mounted, and I become a fixture walking at his stirrup, badgering Brigida to keep up with the healthy pace. I eavesdrop on the conversations between him and Brother Samuel, who flanks Bishop Stephen's other side, my cowl carefully drawn over the glowing interest emanating from my mien. He explains that his official mission is to take inventory of the monasteries, but his real passion is to assemble a spectacular choir to sing praises to the Emperor Basil himself in the greatest of all cathedrals, the Hagia Sophia.

Within a fortnight we reach our next destination to the south, by which time I've become fluent in translating the Bishop's greek tales to Brigida. We travel close together, whispering of the vast Roman Empire that is to be our new home. I envision the people are small and swarthy, like the Bishop, hailing from all parts of the world beyond our knowledge. Just as our people are of the north countries, the Byzantine capitol is home to those from the south, east and west, all contributing their indigenous cultures to create a rich mosaic of humanity. My intellect is seduced by the fantasy of all things different: unique smells, colorful landscape, odd beasts, new warmth in the air, and strange shades and shapes of people. My mind blooms with the spring wilderness, fear dissipates like the ice on the river Dneiper, leaving in its stead cracks through which flows the refreshing purity of new life.

Farther south, the abbeys become more proximate and populated. The monastery of Minsk is the largest yet, its opulent comforts enticing the Bishop to spend a few extra nights, ostensibly to cajole the Abbot to part with more than the mere three novices they offer. The wealthy monastery depends heavily upon contributions made by their novices' families, which would cease if they were to join our mission. Since the religious house is situated within the city walls, Brigida has to lodge in a hut with a family outside of the Abbey grounds and I stay with her. Though they're kind people, he a lay worker for the abbey smithy, we have difficulty sleeping in the crowded single room dwelling, reminiscent of our early childhood living conditions.

It's a relief to reassemble our burgeoning troupe at the Dnieper, with the pleasant addition of a piper that the abbot conceded as a token to the Bishop's pressuring. Snaking our way down the riverbank, my senses dulled with lack of rest, I automatically fall in step with the Bishop's donkey, failing to note Brigida lagging behind. I'm deep under the spell of the Bishop Stephen's smooth-tongued stories, and the rhythm of the march, when one of the other novices from Novogod rushes up to me and pulls on my mantle. Instinctively I look for Brigida, and know that something's amiss. We race against the stream of black robed figures, who flutter like ravens as we push our way to the rear. The new novices are attempting to pull my squirming sister into the heavy forest alongside the dirt road.

The familiar crimson haze clouds my judgment, giving me supernatural strength and energy, and I gather my habit and charge at the thrashing group. With a roar I tear into the three boys, not caring that their soft bodies are crushed by my furious onslaught. Never having known any kind of physical exertion to defend themselves, they make feeble attempts to strike out at me until I send them flying to the ground. I pounce on top of one, intent upon pummeling him into the moss, when I'm plucked off and tossed on my backside. I launch myself at the offender, insanity blinding the reality of the massive Viking guard.

Only the element of surprise could have allowed me, with my twelve years, to connect a fist with the granite of his belly and elicit an "oof." After slapping away my fists a few more times as if they were pesky flies, he shoves me back to the ground, steps back and draws his longsword.

"Hold!" His commanding voice brooks no resistance.

"They attacked my sister!" Temper still feeds my bravado even as his steel winks at me, as if finding humor in my impotence.

"She is unharmed," he indicates my sister clutching the saddle of his warhorse, looking far more concerned about the height of the beast than the three inert novices.

"If you hurt her, I swear I'll kill you." I hiss, fear stoking the fire of rage when I visualize the ease at which the guard could violate her. I've heard the Varangians are the Emperor Basil's personal guardsmen, selected for their size, elite fighting skill and reputation for brutality. The bishop had told us of the treaty between the Eastern Roman Emperor Basil, and the Rus ruler of Kiev that started the Varangian guard. Prince Vladimir contracted to send to Constantinople thousands of these behemoths from the Viking clans of the north. So I assume that this platinum ogre is going to laugh at my oath, which adds to my anger.

Contrary to my limited thinking, he stabs his sword into the supple forest floor, and crouches down to stare intently into my burning countenance. Something in his calm, level stare reminds me of Maman, and I feel my face flame from a different kind of effort: not to cry.

"I'm not a beast," he switches from Greek to my native tongue, and bends his knee, placing a hand over his heart, "and I vow to protect you and your sister with my life."

"We don't want your foreign promises," I sulk, "God protects us."

"Perhaps God has sent me to help." He has my attention, "You see, I was taken from my village near Novgorod many years ago. I wasn't supposed to make this journey, the assignment was given to someone else, but with the intention of finding my family, I convinced the Emperor to let me go. Though I've failed to save my people, I've found you and I think that I am to protect you."

Skepticism warring with trust in him, an idea pushes through the clutter in my head, "If you want to help, then train me to fight. Teach me how to ride and use a weapon."

My outrageous request warms me and my heart beats with excitement. I'm holding my breath, watching him look from me to my sister and then skyward for divine inspiration.

"Aye," he stands and extends his palm to me. I clasp his hand and pull myself up.

"If you hurt my sister, I will kill you," I reiterate.

"Aye." We remain hand locked, our bargain sealed.

Our numbers swell like the River Dnieper with the summer rains. The southward current is our guide to the Euxine Sea on the fringes of Byzantium. We are a small village on the move, picking up more monks and novices as we go. To our consternation, a number of lay travelers have also latched on to our caravan, on their way to the promise of a better life in the grand city of Miklagard. Among them are merchants, farmers and tradesmen and their families.

In order to keep the monks separate, the Bishop and Brother Samuel organize us into tight formation and mandate study and choir practice. In these hours, I feel God's hand on me like never before, satisfying my craving for completeness. I'm able to dedicate my mind freely to the lessons, while our guarding angel, Nicolo, watches over Brigida. In the mountainous landscape as we advance on the sea, the humidity making our woolen habits cling to our sweaty bodies, I excel at Greek and delve joyfully into the intricacies of Christian theology and ancient philosophy.

For the first time since we left Maman's side, my sister is safe under Nicolo's vigilance to mingle with the other women who trail towards the back. When we make camp at dusk, she stays with the women to prepare food, while I train in martial arts and weaponry. At night, we curl up together, as when we were young and simple, and share our experiences of the day in girlish whispers of happiness. Ironically, I actually fear the delight that seeps through the cracks in the barrier of doubt I've erected around my heart.

Our stay at the monastery of Kiev, shatters this idealistic existence. It is a breathtaking setting, with the monks housed and worshipping in caves carved into the mountains. But it is by far the most debauched place that I have ever seen. Over the centuries, since the first Greek Christians lived in austere hiding in the dense forest and labyrinth of caves, their values have eroded like the granite of the hills in which they dwelt. The ostentatious riches of the city of Kiev, and the abundance of resources in the land, has attracted settlers accustomed to easy living, which seems to have seeped into its main religious house.

The abbey bells marking canon hours don't signal us to prayer, and the abbot and elders take their meals with the prince in his palace. There is little separation and seclusion between the government and religious houses, and the monastic administrators also serve the public. The bishop explains to us that in larger cities, it is important for the survival of the church to interact and take part in laic affairs.

All of this I sympathize with, and grasp the necessity of connecting with the outside world. That which I can't stomach, however is how their abbey has declined into an excuse for a brothel for boys. With Bishop Stephens and Brother Samuel quartered at the palace as guests of the prince, the only adult supervision left at night are the monks who hunt the boys in the dormitory for carnal purposes. I thank God that Brigida is lodged in the nunnery nearby.

As per my habit, I pull my cowl low over my shoulder length curls and fix my gaze on the ground at all times. This practice saves me from the fate of my colleagues on the first night of our stay. Well after nightfall, I awaken to shadowy figures snaking around the pallets on the floor, reaching out to lift a robe or blanket. They hone in on a few of the slumbering novices, plucking them from the floor, snatching them before awareness can wake them. The next morning, upon breaking the fast, my brother Dimitri from Novorod doesn't touch his food, his face blotchy and eyes red and puffy. For the rest of the day, he doesn't leave my side, to the point of trodding on the hem of my robe. I finally find a moment of privacy when I can address him.

"What ails you Brother Dimitri?" I whisper aside to him. A muffled sob escapes his bowed head. I feel the anger rise in my throat, anticipating the terrible cause of his anguish.

"They took me from the dormitory last night," he choked, "and they....they…"

"No need to go on Brother," the sickness that I'm starting to recognize preceding rage prompts me to interrupt him before the miasma takes over reason, "I have an idea of what they did." The heat rises from my neck into my face, my heart pounds with desire to avenge their abuse of my friend.

"Please help me Brother Adilsen," his plea stills my racing heart, giving me pause to listen. "We who know you, have seen how you protect your sister. There is rumor that you killed a boy in a fight."

"How can I help?" I'm careful not to elaborate on my past.

"Let me stay close to you, don't let them take me again…" His voice trails off, but I think I hear him say he wouldn't survive the shame. I tell him that I'm not sure what difference that would make, but agree to keep him close. That night, the six of us from Novgorod form a tight bunch and link arms as we sleep, so that when the eerie shades wind through the dormitory, they pass us by. In the morning we stay together and look for an opportunity to speak to Brother Samuel or the Bishop, I even try to get a message to my sister in the nunnery to no avail. The next night, we are not so fortunate.

Once again we lock limbs so that if one of us gets jostled, the others will awaken, and thus I fall into a troubled slumber. The darkness is so complete, that when I feel a disturbance from the brother next to me, it takes me several heartbeats to adjust my vision on my target. I focus in on the black habits that stand out against the whitewashed stone walls of the cave, as two monks attempt to subdue their prey between them. I throw an arm at one, catching him across the windpipe and spin on the other with a blow alongside his head. His yelp of surprise and pain draws other shadows from across the dormitory, and I have my hands full for several arduous moments. Though my lungs and muscles are burning, my thoughts remain cool, and I draw from Nicolo's training to deliver tactical blows designed to debilitate my opponents.

As quickly as the fight starts it is over, with five inert black forms strewn across the stone floor around me. I hear one of the novices striking a flint and I urgently stop him before he can light the torch. Instinct instructs me that we must remain anonymous if we are to survive.

Noiselessly, we carry them outside of the dormitory cave and leave them defrocked on the steps of the rectory. I have the idea that if we leave them in their skivvies, they won't be able to come back. Hours later, when we break our fast, the monks are gone from the steps, and there are gaps in the benches as we eat. All day there is an air of suspicious vigilance throughout the abbey, the novices receiving sharp looks from the elders. When we retire to the dormitory in the evening, I count four monks with lanterns posted along the walls. Unfortunately, the watch isn't for our security, but to catch the wicked boys who attacked the monks. Sensing trouble, I counsel my five brothers how we will need to distract and interfere with anyone attempting to make off with one of us.

Hours into the night, a ripple of tension passes through our close knit bunch, and I hold steady as a hem passes us. I'm about to release my pent up breath, when two pairs of white hands claw under my arms and try to extract me from the group. Just as I had instructed, my friends explode into action, scattering and sacrificing their bodies as missiles to trip and slow down the other monks who come running. The frenzy of activity infects the dozens of other novices, who join in the melee with zeal born of vengeance. The monks holding me, as well as the others standing guard, are swallowed up by the teeming mob bent on revenge.

Unnoticed, I slip out of the dormitory and race across the abbey grounds to the gate leading out to the city. I handily debilitate a surprised monk guarding the locked portal and take his key. Earlier that day, I had tried unsuccessfully to send a message Brother Samuel, so instead I had climbed the bell tower and located the barracks where Nicolo would be staying. My scouting serves me well, and I fly with surety to the soldiers' sleeping quarters and harry the sentry to bring Nicolo.

After taking a few moments to wake his comrade Cassius, and arm themselves, I breathlessly brief them as we hasten back to the abbey. I say a quick prayer for the monk at the gate, still shaking the fog from the knock on the head I gave him, and we sail straight through to the dormitory. As I feared, more monks have joined in the fray, and a mass of black cloaked fighting bodies has spilled out into the cloisters.

The shrieking war cry that erupts from the two Varangian guards arrests my stride, and I'm treated to the awesome spectacle of the hulking vikings charging the crowd. Swords drawn and glinting in the torchlight, white hair flowing against the night sky, my heart bursts in my chest in fearsome thrill. As their enormous legs swallow the courtyard, the tumultuous roar of the riot turns to shouts of warning and the robed figures scatter and flee into the darkness.

Night gives way to the pink freshness of dawn as we finish helping the injured hobble to their cells, patch the wounded, and clear away the wreckage of the fighting. The monks who had rushed into the fray, suffer the brunt of the beating at the hands of their vengeful underlings, who seem almost joyous when they receive word that they've been barred from the rectory to break their fast. There's an aura of confidence, power and righteousness permeating the dormitory, as they punctuate their whispered recounting of the event with jabs and kicks to their pallets.

The Bishop, Brother Samuel and Nicolo have many questions for me throughout the morning, so I join my brothers in fasting, while sequestered and interrogated. I explain everything to them, about the monks carrying away boys in the dormitory as we slept, how they violated Brother Dimitri, and how we finally had to band together to protect ourselves when we couldn't get word to any of them.

"The Abbot said that they're looking for one novice in particular who touched off the mutiny by abusing five monks the night before." The Bishop's intelligent gaze rests steadily on my face. "Do you know anything about this?"

"How could one small boy incapacitate five monks by himself?" Brother Samuel gives a nervous laugh, trying to cover for me because he knows my violent temper and history of fighting.

"Impossible," Nicolo chimes in conspiratorially, "I know of no soft novice to take down five grown men." I'm overwhelmed with guilt that he should be burdened with the secret of my training.

"I'm not asking either of you," the Bishop admonished, his keen attention never wavering from my demeanor, "I can't help keep our people safe if I don't have the truth."

Help, safety, truth, such basic needs, yet so illusive to me! As I ask God for guidance, a tranquil calm befalls my spirit and I return the Bishop's level stare.

"It was me, your excellency." Self incriminating words pour through me, holding my voice steady as I admit my capital sin to one of the most powerful figures in Christendom. "I was overcome with rage at what they did to Dimitri, and when they came for one of my other brothers, I defended him."

The Bishop ponders my words, and contemplates me for a few moments. He nods sagely, as if coming to a conclusion in his head, not at all looking disappointed by my revelation.

"You're excused Brother Adilsen," he inclines his head to the door that I should exit. "We will discuss a suitable punishment and course of action. You will return to the other novices in the dormitory and fast for the remainder of the day."

"Adilsen," Nicolo hies to catch up to me outside, "you will be safe among the flock, I'll stay and keep watch."

"I would rather you guard my sister."

"I've been checking on your sister daily, she suffers more from boredom than lack of supervision. The Nun's house appears to be administered with better principles than this hades." He lets out a beleaguered sigh as he surveys the compound of caves and buildings that comprise the abbey. Then, looking back at the edifice from which we just departed, "I fear you're in over your head."

"As you can see, I can handle myself in here." Fatigue dulls the effect of my brave words. The exhaustion from many nights without sleep deadens my limbs so they drag along the dusty courtyard.

"My concern isn't the physical battle, it is the power struggle that you've stirred up." He throws out an arm to encompass the rectory and the novice's dormitory in front of us, "On one side, you've got the Abbot and his brothers looking for revenge and a scapegoat for exposing their corruption to the Bishop." He turns and flings his other arm to indicate the chapter and library buildings behind us. "And on the other side, you have piqued the Bishop's interest in you for his personal agenda in this mission."

"Personal agenda?" The hard note in his voice conveys his displeasure. He stares over my head, weighing how much he should tell me.

"One of the reasons he agreed that I come with him, is because he knew of my desire to find my family. He thought that I would lead him to my people, so that he could bring them back with us." His grave pause draws my swirling thoughts to focus on his blazing blue eyes and long white hair, so similar to my own. "He means to build his own Varangian guard, his own elite army to protect him and rival the emperor's, so that the church won't be under the Emperor's thumb."

Though naive about the workings and politics of the church and the Roman empire of the East, I've gleaned enough from listening to the Bishop's conversations with Brother Samuel and other officials along the way to appreciate the significance of this. The Emperor Basil had fought to claim the throne from a series of military rulers and chamberlains, so any force amassed that wasn't commanded by him would be a serious threat to his leadership and life.

"Did you know of his motives when you requested to go?" His plea to the emperor to accompany Bishop Stephens would appear treasonous in light of this knowledge.

"The emperor suspected some underlying motive, but he didn't know exactly what, so he deployed me to look after his interests as well as his clergyman's protection." He takes my arm and guides me into the shade of the pillars outside the dormitory portal. "As we traveled farther and farther north, and the features of the villains grew lighter and larger like me, I noted his increasing interest as he scrutinized the menfolk like they were oxen."

A prickling sensation raises the hair on the back of my neck as I grasp where his story is going. My attention hones in on his viking features, seeing my maman's Valkyrie jawline and pronounced cheekbones staring back at me.

"We reached the southern border of Novgorod, and there, a village that was..." he trails off, his gaze distant, then continues in a hard voice, "he made us take captive three youths and two men. We got two days up the river before they overpowered Cassius and I, and they escaped."

"When we arrived at your abbey, he was still angry with us for letting them get away," his piercing eyes locked into mine, "then he saw you, and his plans escalated. Now he's also looking at these boys we are bringing back for the choir for the biggest, most robust ones. You're a living example of how he can have both a singer and a soldier, all in one!"

The import of his tale punches me in the chest, and the air explodes out of my lungs as if he had actually struck me. I had just given the Bishop proof that his scheme could work. My sleep deprived brain whirls sluggishly with images of singing in the great cathedral choir, and visions of fighting for the Bishop's army. I shake my head to clear the overwhelming fright of being trapped into a life not of my choosing.

"What can I do?" I can't run, can't go back, not with my sister.

"For now, get some sleep, let me stand watch over you and your young brothers. Nothing will happen until we get to Miklagard, so we remain vigilant in the meantime."

"Brother Adilsen," Brother Samuel buffets my shoulder, awakening me from a slumber so deep I had lost all sense of time. "We're all leaving, get up now."

"Brigida."

The kindly monk all but rolls his eyes in exasperation, "Nicolo went for your sister, they will meet us by the river. Wake the others and lead them past the barracks and continue along the road out of the city."

We file noiselessly into the night, moonlight illuminating the path out of the gate, through the city to the road following the river. There we rendezvous with the Bishop, his guards and Brigida, and a few other monks who the Bishop hand-picked to join us. Too tired and hungry to think, we sleepwalk through the forest along the river's edge, a silent endless snake slithering into the silvery dawn.

We walk on until golden beams of sunlight reveal a deep bend in the river to set up camp. As we regroup with our original brothers, and I reunite with Brigida, I'm surprised to see the change in our company. Gone are the lay men and women who had hitched themselves to our black robes in hopes of Godly protection. In their place are a dozen of the boys I recognize from the Kiev monastery. As when we started this journey, our numbers are mostly novices, chaperoned by a handful of monks, the piper, and the Bishop. Brigida is once again the sole known female, and the guards are the only secular travelers.

Ensconced in the embrace of the Dneiper, the Bishop relents to spend a day or two recuperating ere we press through the hostile territory of Bulgaria to the Euxine Sea. We fall back into old roles, Brigida preparing a quick meal, me organizing the boys to gather firewood and set up the

Bishop's tent. With food in my stomach and the fire warming me, for the first time in many nights I fall into an exhausted, unmolested sleep.

"Brother Adilsen," Brother Samuel cuffs my shoulder, awakening me from my coma. "You must rise, we need you." The tightness in his plea pulls me from the warm space beside my sister. The outlines of the encircling river and trees against the backdrop of gray sky, indicates that I must have slept half the day and through the night. Brother Samuel leads me around the heaps of snoring monks, scattered like rodent mounds across the leafy forest floor, to the Bishop's tent. Once inside, my eyes adjust to pick out four figures in the dim flicker from a single lantern. Nicolo bestows upon me an enigmatic glower, and shoves a chunk of bread and slice of ham at me. The Bishop pours a goblet of his heady Greek wine, thrusting it into my hand. The other Varangian Cassius, and another resourceful Brother Miro from Minsk, wait expectantly for me to eat.

"Fuel up, my son," the Bishop rather cheerfully insists as I sputter like a newborn on the divine bouquet of his vintage. "You're going to need your strength! The Abbot from Kiev has sent out a party to hunt you down and bring back the boys from the monastery."

"They have us sealed in our campsite with our backs up against the river. I surmise they'll let us know their demands at daybreak." The cold shiver of fear drips down my spine at Cassius's report.

"We think they will be satisfied if we turn you over to appease their damaged pride, but the Bishop has other ideas." Nicolo is quick to soothe my anxiety. "Their numbers are not so great, so if you mobilize the novices as you did before, we might fight them off and retreat before they can return with more men."

"What do you think, Brother Adilsen?" This is the first time the Bishop calls me by my father's name, "can you get the boys to fight like you did before?"

I chew slowly on the crust of bread as if they were my thoughts, turning it over this way and that before I swallow. "I think they would rather die fighting then go back."

"Then may God have mercy on us all," Brother Samuel's voice trembles as he prays over our mission. I wonder if he regrets taking me in with all of the trouble I've caused. I tamp down the twinge of apprehension, that I'm now further indebted to the Bishop for refusing to give me up to certain torture under the hands of the monks of Kiev.

The guards orchestrate a general plan, Brother Samuel and the few other monks are to use our fish nets, burlap sacks, branches, anything they can lay their hands on that will entangle and encumber the fighters. I am to lead the score of novices in a scatter attack, strictly to strike and run away, creating a distraction enough for the Emperor's two elite Varangians to dispatch them in small numbers at a time. Brigida is to hide, and the Bishop is to evoke the power of our Lord over us all.

"But where am I to hide?" Brigida queries when I tell her, surveying the sparse underbrush, the only vegetation that the thick canopy of pines and oaks will allow to survive. I alert her before the others to give her time to find cover. Gazing up at the web of branches and leaves, my sister giggles like a child.

"Are you mad?" I haven't heard her laugh in years.

"Perhaps," her eyes shine on me, "I have an idea."

The sun breaks over the river Dnieper with a roar from dozens of men from Kiev, as they charge our camp to reclaim their pride that we robbed along with the novices. Brother Samuel and his fellows trip, swipe at, net and evade, while Nicolo and Cassius answer our attackers with a rancorous onslaught of their own from the lofty backs of their warhorses. The novices from Novgorod dart about, surprising them with an occasional takedown, or ganging up on one for a swift pummeling. Within moments, the mounted vikings are swarmed, in spite of the pestering monks. I shout to my brothers to team up, pick them off and disarm them, and for the novices to take up the nets and sacks to throw them off guard.

The mercenaries pull Cassius from his horse, and I spring into action, grabbing a broadsword from a fallen villain. Without hesitation, I swing up into the vacated saddle and launch into the fray. Using my legs to grip the saddle as Nicolo taught me, I spin and hack my way to Cassius, protecting his back when I reach him, stabbing, punching and kicking anything I can.

There is a lull in the fighting as both sides assess the progress, and I see that the tight pack that had besieged us, has thinned slightly. At the top of my lungs, I cry for my sister to put her plan into action. The sky above us swirls with black winged creatures, swooping down upon the men from Kiev. The Rus scream in dread, dropping their weapons to cover themselves from the holy horror. The Bishop appears on his mount, cursing them, telling them they will not withstand the dark army of the Lord.

We let them flee, as we have no desire for more violence than necessary, and no means of keeping prisoners. The nightmarish vision of our counterattack will be enough to compel their retreat all the way back to Kiev and allow us time for our escape. I gaze around at the carnage, nauseated that I have been responsible for some of the slain. Amongst the bodies strewn across the leafy forest floor, I spot two inert robed forms and another few writhing in pain. Brigida is already tending to Nicolo and Cassius, who are both bleeding from several lacerations, and Brother Samuel is instructing the others to pick up three of the injured novices and lay them by the river to examine them.

Tears of guilt blur my vision as I approach the two lifeless black bodies. The larger is Brother Miro, the smaller my friend Dimitri. I fall to my knees beside my brothers, sobbing in grief, anguished to be responsible for their destruction.

"Death is a part of life my son," the Bishop's shadow drapes over me, his hand stilling my shaking shoulders. "It was God's will to take these two souls so that many more could survive."

"If you had sent me to Kiev, no one need die here today."

"Nonsense Brother Adilsen; twas I who gave the order to make our stand. For you to think that this is about you is to overstate your importance!" I lift my sorrowful gaze to him questioningly. "This fight is bigger than you, it is about the integrity of the church. We saved those boys from their odious fate in Kiev, and made the first step to dismantle their house as it exists. We gave them a spectacle of the might of our Lord that they'll not forget, and that my boy, is how Christianity takes root!"

"So you would have fought even if they had custody of me?"

"Absolutely," the fire in his usually placid eyes affirms his speech, "and you did a fine day's work here to seal God's victory. Now, let us take these two and lay them to rest with the honor of soldiers of Christ."

Dusk encroaches by the time we bury all of the dead, patch up the maimed and finally have something to eat. One of the other monks survives a stab wound in the side, and two of the novices had broken limbs from diving from the trees. We savor our repast amidst an air of mirth, as the boys describe the sensation of flying through the air, and the horror on the faces of the men as they jumped down on top of them. Brigida is hailed for her inspiration in the plot, and I growl at Nicolo to strike the admiration from his smile at her.

"Don't be so serious Adilsen," the big viking slaps my back, which is already aching from the exertion. "Were she a man, I would likewise appreciate the genius of envisioning the boys soaring from the skies. It was the terror of a supernatural opponent that caused them to turn tail and run!"

"You look too hard for someone sworn to protect her." I sulk, knowing that he's right but not willing to admit that she has thrived under his watch.

"Were you a man I would run you through for questioning my word." His voice lowers, his good humor gone. My heart actually skips a beat at the ferocity of his vow.

"What do you mean, 'were I a man?'" My life-long fear of being discovered as a young woman prodding me to bristle defensively.

"Were you a man, and not a puling little boy who knows nothing about twenty years of having only the integrity of my word to advance me in this world, I would take utmost offense." The heaviness of his brow lifts as he takes in the naive child that I am. "But like I said, you're not a man, so I forgive you. Take first watch tonight."

Grave tranquility mists the night air as I stand guard over our encampment. The crisp stillness of impending winter conjures memories of my family's move from the northern tundra, burrowing up underneath Maman for warmth in the open sky. Her honeyed voice pours from my mouth, old Norse verses weaving tales of battles won by warrior maidens, the Valkyrie, as heroines.

Brother Samuel approaches discreetly and sits cradled in the meaty roots of a nearby pine. He leans his head back against the tree trunk, eyes closed in reverence, his slight grin one of congenial contemplation. A pleasant tingle washes over me as I sing, and I realize how deeply I have grown to care about this man. He embodies everything my father is not: wise, educated, gentle, everything I strive to be. His very presence carries an aura of peace and good humor, a steadiness as old as the branches above where we sit.

"Your voice transports me to the heavens," he breathes when I finish the song, "'tis truly a gift from God."

"Brother Samuel," I address him after a moment of wrestling with my thoughts, "I fear I've brought much strife and conflict into your quiet existence. Do you miss the serenity of our abbey in Novgorod?"

"No child," he fixes me with his sage eyes, "God puts people in our path for his purpose. In you, he has blessed me with challenge and change, both which are so necessary for growth. My serenity lies in knowing that I'm following his guiding hand, and my peace comes from his holy spirit within."

"You change, and yet you remain unchanged." I conclude, gesturing to a giant oak, "Like this tree, you grow, but your properties inside stay the same."

"A function of living in God's will, contemplating his goodness every day." He considers the branches, deep in thought, "I've seen my share of bloodshed and heartache, my child. Hardship is God's way of teaching that which we cannot learn through complacency."

"Have you heard of a place called Ireland?" His query is so abrupt that I follow his gaze up to see if the answer to the riddle is written in the leafy ceiling.

"Aye, there was a masterfully illuminated volume about the island in the abbey library at Novgorod."

"Ah yes, I remember the tome. It was among the plunder that Viking raiders took from my home abbey Etar." He shakes his head as if to clear an unpleasant memory. "They slaughtered the entire population, sparing only the young and strong, like me, to man their ships." The distant flickering firelight glistens against the gathering moisture in his soft brown eyes.

"I was tied to the oars of their warships for five years, with only the love of God and the hope of securing those books that kept me alive. The chieftain took note of my devotion under the strain of abuse and deprivation, and I convinced him to accept our Lord Jesus Christ as his savior. After another five years of service in the fiords of the Norse, I was set free having converted the village population and established a monastery."

"Brother Samuel, I strive every day for your example of forgiveness and holiness." His tale humbles me.

"It was through serving God that my heart healed and I discovered my purpose in spreading his word." He continues, "I took all of the books that I could carry and made it my mission to pass along the gift of enlightenment that I learned from the Irish monks since the time I was a child. Eventually I settled in Novgorod, which is where God brought you to me."

"Thank you for sharing yourself with me," I'm at a loss to describe the deep gratitude that I feel for this saintly man, "you've taught me so much more than rhetoric and philosophy! I want to always do my best to be like you."

"Be wary of comparing yourself to others, child!" He counsels in his affable way, "Idolatry takes on many forms of worshipping things, people, even ourselves, above God. With that said, I do enjoy the task of mentoring you especially because of your willingness to learn."

"I'm afraid of what will happen to us when we reach Constantinople. The Emperor sounds so corrupt, the Bishop so worldly. I fear that we may lose connection with our Lord." I've been carrying the burden of my concerns since Minsk, it is a relief to be able to let it out.

"We each have our roles in this life, and we respect the purpose that God has for others, which will always be different from ours. I cannot speak of the Emperor, but the Bishop has a deep belief in Jesus, his faith is stronger than his self will." Samuel tutors me on the dangers of contradicting the Emperor in any way, as it is considered treason, and explains how the Bishop has very ambitious aims of autonomy for the church as an institution.

"As for your personal concerns," he continues pointedly, "this is a conversation we've had in many different forms. If you believe with all of your heart that God makes all things happen, then you will not fear, because everything will work out."

"Get some sleep, I'll take the watch over."

Chapter 7

The spectacle that greets us at first light, tests the limits of my ability to give my fears to God. My imagination protests under the mental effort to reason what I'm seeing, until an amazing shift overcomes me. Rather than forming opinions as is my custom, I curiously absorb the brilliant display in front of me without judgment. One particularly colorful figure commands my interest.

Her slanted eyes that stare back at me are narrow, inky slashes in an alabaster painted mask. The whiteness of the girl's face contrasts the blackness of her hair, which gleams in the morning sunlight like a raven's wing. Her red foreign garb is so vivid it hurts my eyes, as does the bright hues of the robes of the few women surrounding her. Though unlike anything I've ever seen, I recognize God's beauty in her lovely features. Impulsively, I smile at her and am rewarded to see the corners of her ruby lips raise slightly in return.

The Bishop and monks conference with the leaders of this astonishing band of foreigners throughout the morning, delaying our retreat from any new threats from Kiev. In an unusually strict tone, the Bishop orders us to prepare a feast for fifty people, and bewildered, we hasten to catch enough fish and foul. Brigida scours the forest for roots and nuts to add starch to the meal, so we are delighted when two of the women present her with a pot of white grains, called rice.

The clouds overhead are tinged with magenta highlights, the amber hue of the sinking sun casting brilliant rays of gold over the river as we serve our elders and visitors. We eat alongside these fascinating people, sitting cross legged on the earth, marveling at their use of sticks to convey the food from their bowl of rice to their mouth. The fare is simple, but well prepared and plentiful.

As soon as the novices are finished eating, Brother Samuel groups us together and we fill the torchlit camp with melodious praises to our Father. The girl with the painted face and her four attendants emerge from her tent with unusual stringed instruments that they pluck to create a rich, haunting music. The deep chords reach into my soul, touching that secret core that I've locked up so tightly inside, that only God and song can reach.

Their tiny, bejeweled fingers slide across the strings, and the resonating sound pulls reluctant tendrils of joy from the depths of my heart. Hypnotic waves rock me with their warbling notes, coaxing the breath passing through my throat to form a tune to accompany their instruments. After a spell, the song is finished, its lingering magnetism echoing through the night. I open my eyes to find my gaze drawn into the ebony, almond orbs that contemplate me so thoroughly.

"Why must you always draw attention to yourself?" Whispers Brigida, it is late as we curl up close to the fire to sleep.

"I swear to you sister, I'm not intending to, the music just comes over me," I try to explain my compulsion to sing.

"Well, your urge could lead you to peril," she admonishes, "like last night, you sang about a warrior maiden!"

"I was inspired by you!" I hiss, "and I was thinking of Maman. Besides, it was a Norse air, only you would understand."

"And Nicolo," she counters, "I saw him watching you. Please just try to curb your inspiration, lest it gets you killed."

"Brother Adilsen," Brother Samuel, shakes my shoulder, startling me awake, "you must come with me, you're being summoned."

A gentle blush tints the eastern sky beyond the river as I rub the sleep from my eyes and trudge behind my friend, my wits trailing farther still.

"I admit this is becoming a tiresome practice," grumbles the older monk, stalking out of our encampment.

"Now what does the Bishop want?" I yawn, summoning my sluggish brain to awareness.

"Tis not the Bishop who asks for you this time," he pauses to look back at me, "you have made quite an impression on our new friends. His excellency has been in meetings with the Chinese since early this morn, and they have requested that you indulge the princess with your presence."

"Who is the Princess?" I'm vacillating between excitement and trepidation. "What do they want?"

"The Princess is the painted girl to whom you sang last night. Beyond that, I know nothing, just be aware of God's will for you, and all will be well."

We arrive at a large, opulent tent, and Brother Samuel shoves me sternly in the back, pushing me through the parted opening into another world. No amount of reading or learning could prepare me for the sights, smells and feel of this silken cocoon. Before my eyes adjust to the torchlit interior, my nostrils inhale spicy incense, and I detect the whisper of soft fabric in the silence. The larger elements in front of me take shape, the bright floral vines decorating sturdy chairs and tables, the scarlet cushions strewn about the carpeted ground, so satiny that they gleam in the light's reflection. Embroidered curtains separate the tent into rooms.

I gape in wonder at the splendor of the items adorning the room, beaten gold plates and goblets, masterpieces of art woven into the rug under my crude sandals, and a delicate perfume permeating the air. Self conscious of my rough tunic and dirty footwear, I unstrap my patterns and untie the woolen bands used to keep my feet warm. My soles melt into the softness of the rug, and I close my eyes to better palpitate the luxury of touching something so fine.

A swish of silk and titter of hushed mirth snatch me out of my indulgence, cheeks afire in embarrassment at being exposed in my ignorance. Four women enter, heads bowed, and gesture for me to sit on a cushion, then retreat to hold the curtains open. The girl with the painted face glides through and takes a seat on an ornately carved chair, a veil covering everything but her slanted eyes. I'm captivated by her, trying to figure out if she's smiling or not, until I realize that I'm staring and beam at my own ridiculousness. To my astonishment, the black slashes of her eyes suddenly disappear into a mere slits, the girlish charm of her smirk widens my grin into a full toothy smile.

The glint of gold and gems from her rings draws my perusal to her small hands as they undo the fastenings of her veil. Her face, no longer painted white, possesses a fresh, natural comeliness. She seems young, within a few summers of my thirteen years, her pearly skin as flawless as the petals of the aidelveiss. Innocence emanates from her round countenance and black eyes, that I cannot help but feel drawn towards. I smile again to convey my friendship.

"Liang Na." She gracefully pats her chest. "Lang Nu." I bumble, not nearly as gracefully. "Liang Na." She repeats patiently.

"Liang Na." My tongue captures the foreign essence of her name. She dips her head a few times, pleased with my willingness, and reaches out to encourage me to do the same.

I freeze, my father's male version of my name stuck in my throat. For a brief moment, I stutter over the ugly syllables. I start to panic as Liang Na's pleasant visage falls in perplexity.

God help me.

"Adila." I savor the sweetness of my own name, palm to my heart. "Adila, is my name, Adila." The wave of peace that washes over me settles my pounding heart, reassuring me that I need not fear disclosing my name to this girl. The brightness returns to my new friend's demeanor, and she calls to her attendant's who bring forth their stringed instruments, and some filmy figures of people and animals on sticks. They arrange themselves around the chairs and pillows, and begin to play as Liang Na sings and the puppets brings words to life.

A tingling sensation engulfs me as the story unfolds, the lyrics translated by the papery girl and boy bobbing around the tent. Brother and sister play amongst the hills of pillows and the stream of a fountain set up in a corner of this curtained haven. The brother falls cripple and the sister takes care of him, provides for him, and eventually turns to fighting other boys to protect him. The girl then dons a man's tunic and joins the military to continue fighting for those unable to defend themselves. The similarity of the tale to my life is uncanny, trepidation grounding me into the plush cushion, unable to move as the twang of the last chord hangs in the spicy air.

Liang Na studies me closely, beckoning for the stick figure of the girl. She points to the girl, then to me, the corners of her mouth turning up into a reassuring expression. Tears of terror, relief and frustration at not knowing how to express that she must not tell anyone, stream down my cheeks.

I get up and take the girl and boy figures. I hold up the paper girl and shake my head, hiding her in the folds of my robe. I show them the boy, using the puppet to cover my face like a mask. A shadow of pity crosses her brow, and she inclines her head in understanding. She takes the girl figure from me and slips it inside her bodice next to her heart.

We spend the rest of the day thus, singing, using the stick figures and gestures to communicate. When we see each other again at supper, we each have our masks back in place, but our gentle gaze conveys our shared secrets.

It is late when we finish, and we have no time for entertainment this night, but Brigida, Nicolo, Brother Samuel and I gather to the side and share information. Our new friends are from a world far to the east called China. Liang Na is the daughter of the Emperor Tang, enroute to Constantinople to be given as a bride to the governor of the Emperor's eastern territories to secure their alliance. They want to join our company for the rest of the journey, as they lost their guides along the way, and in return they'll help defend us against any retaliation from Kiev.

While I pity her plight of being forced into marriage, I brighten at the prospect of being able to see her along the way. The next morning we break camp and make our way south, our group a bit more cumbersome, but a great deal more colorful.

Chapter 8

The Dneiper takes an eastward turn, its heavy currents detouring us along the bend as we seek a shallow location to ford. During these days I enjoy visiting with Liang Na each morning, fascinated by her toilet, as her attendants piece her together. I marvel at her youthful freshness buried beneath robes of position and ceremony. We develop a rapport of signs, symbols, song and stick figures, eventually picking up a few words of each other's language for simple conversation, punctuated by giggles at our stilted attempts.

The Chinese contingent brings up the rear of our troop, on alert for counterattack from Kiev, so we're well protected by their score of trained guardsmen. They report seeing a few outriders early on, but nothing more the further we travel. Nicolo and I chaff under the cheerful sluggishness of our caravan, and in the afternoons we scout the riverbed for shallows or, conversely, our next campsite. After about a week, we discover a slight narrowing in the span of the river where the water is chest deep, and the Bishop directs that we will make camp for the day and cross the water tomorrow.

Radiant sunlight touches us with rare beams of warmth the next morning, inspiring my sister and I to retreat for a few precious hours of female pursuits. We invite Liang Na and her ladies to join us by the river, where we picnic, bathe, sing and give ourselves entirely to the singular enjoyment of being girls.

I stubbornly ignore the whisperings of the other novices that I'm keeping forbidden company with women, and Nicolo's raised eyebrows when Brigida and I ask him to stand guard so that no one follows us. Perhaps I'm getting soft by spending so much time with Liang Na, but I crave to wash my hair, rinse my clothing and rid myself of my masculine facade for one sunny afternoon.

I drink deeply of the piney forest air, replenishing my soul with the music of nature. I lose myself in song, praising God for the beautiful day and the seed of joy sprouting within me. The water is cleansing, not only bodily, but it refreshes our moods as we play in the shallows.

Like a bolt of lightning out of no where on a clear day, a loud pop and cracking noise rends the picturesque riverside scene. A huge branch crashes into the deep waters, followed by such splashing and thrashing that I immediately sense peril and leap into action.

"Brigida," I bark out, "get Nicolo and take them back to camp at once!"

"Where are you going?" she cries as Liang Na and her ladies hasten to pull on garments.

"After the spy!" I shout back, already diving into the frigid depths in pursuit of the floundering figure ahead of me. The cold water does nothing to cool the heat consuming me as I pull myself in clumsy strokes across the expanse, to where the shadowy form is stumbling into the bushes at the far embankment. My lungs are protesting the swim as I reach the shore in time to locate my quarry, and dart through the underbrush.

The ever present fear of being found out summons my strength, and I sprint after him, unable to gain any ground. I must have lost my speed of the short chase in these past months, so I settle into to an even pace in effort to outrun the villain. As I fly through the woods, terror gives way to the wind whistling a peculiar euphoria in my ears. Losing all sense of time and distance, I draw supernatural stamina from this singing filling my head. It pulls me along as if some force has connected me on a rope.

After what seems like a moment, but in reality must be a significant distance, the forest floor starts to incline and I heed the jagged rocks from cutting my bare feet. The terrain becomes broken up with huge boulders and stoney formations, slippery with condensation. The climb sharply prods my heaving sides to protest that I've run for miles and I'm exhausted. Realizing I'm lost, panic provides a jolt of energy to close the gap on the spy. I'm close enough to see him look over his shoulder and stumble, which is all I need to launch myself at him and wrestle him to the ground.

He offers no resistance, merely lies face down in the leaves, and all concern for my own safety is immediately replaced by the nausea that I have killed another one of God's children. At the slight lift of his back as he takes in air, I roll him over, brushing the leaves from his face. My own breath explodes from me, as if I had been punched in the gut, with awe of what I behold.

He is the most beautiful being I have ever seen. Just as one pauses to admire the vibrant hues of a magnificent sunset, or the graceful flight of a proud eagle, I lean over him, arrested by his exotic features. I peer past the mask of his brown skin to admire the strong bones of his jaw and full mouth. Long, thick lashes, matching his black, tightly curled hair, rest upon his high cheeks. As I stare, his lashes flutter open to reveal molten orbs, glazed over in painful appeal. My gaze is sucked into the movement of his ochre lips, and the strained utterance of a plea.

Though I labor to understand his words, I hear the cry for help in his whisper, which snaps me out of my stupor. A cool breeze alerts me that this man is the only human being perhaps for miles, and he's hurt, and that we need each other in this moment, enemy or not. His rich coloring is already fading to grayish tones as I quickly assess his naked length for the cause of his anguish. It doesn't take me long to see bright red blood gushing from a deep gash in his side. Well experienced in having to patch up my own wounds, and educated in treating them from Maman and Brother Samuel, I tear the length of fabric from around my chest and use it to staunch the flow.

Gritting my teeth against the irritation of my tender breasts unbound for the first time in months, I press their binding against the man's side, training my focus on prayer rather than his sinewy ribs. Men's bodies are not unknown to me, as over the years they have been exposed to me unwittingly, under the belief that I was male, however this one is far more well-formed than those I have seen previously. His limbs are long and straight, not bent nor bowed from hard labor and poor diet, yet his muscles are fit and defined.

"God," I lift my prayer up to the patches of afternoon sunlight penetrating the high canopy, "don't let this beautiful being die because of my impetuosity."

"Nonsense my daughter," his response flutters in the leaves, "you didn't do this to him. He injured himself."

"But I chased him," I speak back to the wind. "If I hadn't pursued him, he wouldn't have lost so much life blood."

"You did what you thought was right," God's words filled my soul, "just as you must trust your instincts now to save him."

As I pray and keep pressure on his side, I study the foliage for something I can use to keep the flesh from rotting. The forest is thick with trees, some of which are birch, which will provide what I need. I check under the padding, and the bleeding has abated, the cut looks jagged but clean. I quickly peal off strips of bark, making sure to gather plenty of the antiseptic sap along with it, and gently stick them on the wound. The sting penetrates his daze, and he squirms and moans, then falls inert on his back. I'm fretting over how to secure the bark to his side without moving him, worrying about the whitish hue seeping over him and the coolness of his skin, when it suddenly dawns on me that I'm shivering in my damp shift.

Giggling inwardly at my bold solution, I throw my undergarment over a bush and press myself full length along his side. Positioned thus, I stretch my arm across his ribs and hold the bark in place, discovering that the swell of his chest makes a perfect resting place for my head. The contact of our naked bodies immediately sends waves of heat to warm us both, and I close my eyes to savor the erotic feel of his skin against mine.

The sensation of him consumes me. He smells of nature, the musk of leaves, the wood of the oaks and fresh water, conjuring comfort and an aspect of being home. His chestnut skin is liquid silk running over the granite muscles underneath. The rhythm of his shallow breathing and faint heartbeat under my ear lull me into dreams of his arresting features smiling at me.

I awaken with a start at a rasping sound, as he draws breath and his body quakes. I must have dozed off for a spell, but thankfully his heart sounds stronger and he is loudly sucking in the evening air. My shift is dry and I yank it over my head just as his thick lashes flicker open. His ebony focus settles on my open visage, studying my concerned expression. He utters something in a tongue I don't understand, and I shake my head, knitting my brow in frustration.

"I'm thirsty," his plea is almost lost in my relief that I recognize his greek words.

"You have a cut, but I'll take care of you." I vow in the same language, "I'm going for water, I'll return anon."

Sparked by the memory of slippery rocks, I retrace my path as far as I dare without losing my way, and encounter a narrow stream trickling between the boulders. I wash out my strip of binding, saturate the fabric, and race back to the man. He opens his eyes as I kneel beside him, and lets me squeeze water into his mouth. After a few more trips he holds up his hand, indicating that he's had enough. I take my turn to drink, then turn my attention to find a more protected place to rest. Espying a moss- covered dip between the roots of an oak, I pile up bushes and leaves alongside to fashion a nest. Dark eyes monitor my movements as I finish the task and return to squat beside him.

"I covered the wound with bark and sap to keep it clean. Now I have to tie this binding around you to hold it in place. Can you sit?" He nods, and I brace him from behind; he winces and reaches for his side. I brush his hand away before he displaces the set bark, and wrap the fabric snugly around him. He sucks his teeth at its coldness and starts shaking anew.

"Now, can you move over to the tree? I'll help you, we must go slowly so as not to open the flesh again." I half drag him the few paces and lay him down ere he slips back into unconsciousness. Pressing an ear on his chest, ensuring that he's still alive, I pray into the growing darkness for God to keep us through the night.

Removing my short shift again, I snuggle up next to him and use it to cover as much of us as possible. I pull the pile of bramble over us until we're completely buried. Not at all sure what the night will bring, I rest my head on his shoulder and sleep.

Distant rumbling resonates in the hazy fringes of my awareness, but I'm wrapped in a downy blanket of security and fail to detect any threat. I burrow deeper into the warmth, basking in its comfort that permeates every niche of my being. Its as if I'm being rocked by Maman, but the vision of her is dim, yet the peace is deep and abiding. The thunder grows more constant, but its jagged edges can't displace this aura of earthly belonging.

Like a boat tossed in a sudden storm, my slumber is shaken with a series of jolting snorts, my contentment capsized as I'm thrown about by a human force. Sensibility returns, a frigid gale; I'm being pitched from my cozy nest by the man whose snores I had fantasized were thunder.

Whilst he sputters leaves and thrashes about in the branches, I snatch on my shift and shield my shredded modesty behind a nearby trunk, until he exhausts himself and falls back onto his elbows to take in his surroundings.

"Don't do that," I call out to him when he scratches at the birch bark, now firmly glued to his side. He squints, trying to clear the fog from his sight, and I detach from the tree. He regards me obliquely as I near, his eyes searching mine as if to read my intent. I kneel down next him and point to the dressing.

"You mustn't take it off yet," he looks at the crusty bark bound in place, and back to me questioningly, "do you remember what happened? Tis a deep cut, so I covered it with birch sap and bark so it won't spoil."

"Thank you," his grave expression and the bass in his voice conveys a depth of gratitude belied by the two words. "I remember falling and something pierced my side, but someone was pursuing me so I ran. Then you were there…" His recount trails off as he squints at my face, his twin pools of molasses seeping into mine.

"…and you gave me water and kept me warm." Wonder is heavy in his accent.

"Aye," I dip my head in my customary way when I'm hiding from something. Not wanting to upset him, as he wobbles on his elbow, I refrain from enlightening him that it was I who had chased him. "For the moment, you must rest and regain your strength. I will find something to eat and bring water."

He drops back onto the green carpet, and once his breath is regular, I forage for something to sustain us. When he is hale enough to move, we will have to be fortified to find our way back to camp, so I thank God for the plentiful nuts for energy and fruit for drink. Sitting next to him on the sun speckled forest floor, we break our fast in silent companionship, instinctively aware of our need for each other to survive.

"How do you feel?" I take in his pale cheeks and the blue tinge of his lips. He leans his head back against the base of the tree wearily.

"Cold," my face ironically flushes with heat as he surveys me from under his long lashes.

"We have no way to light a fire." I point out rather dully.

"Yet you kept me warm through the night." Flames rip through my body, settling in my belly, making my legs tremble. I cease breathing and stare agog at the dark slits of his eyes. Not knowing how to react to these powerful sensations, I burst out in nervous tittering like the silly village girls I used to disdain.

"What is so amusing?" His voice is sharp, but the childish hurt in his widening eyes wheedles into my heart, tempering the fire and arousing my compassion for his vulnerability. I reach out and lay a reassuring hand on his clammy cheek.

"I'm unused to close male company," I blush, the paradox of living among men, but not knowing them striking me, "but I know we must share the heat from our bodies to keep each other. So perhaps it is best if we lay together until the sun climbs higher and warms the air.

The effort of squirming down into the natural bed created by the roots of the tree drains more of the color from his complexion. He falls asleep as soon as I curl up next to him, his arm wrapped around me as his even snores encircle my head.

The play of dappled sunlight across the smooth expanse of his breast captures my intrigue to explore his chiseled torso. Light as butterfly wings, my fingertips trace the lines of his rib bones to the tightly banded muscles of his abdomen. I lay my palm flat on the plateau of his breast, then probe the dip of his collarbone, enthralled by the silky texture of his skin. Some time during my contemplation of his narrow waist and hips, I cross into a misty dreamlike state, melting into his essence.

We awake thus to the midday sun's rays penetrating the forest canopy, coaxing our eyelids open. I can tell from the easy rise and fall of his chest that the rest has renewed a measure of his strength. My desire for information about him prods at my contentment, marshaling my wits for a way to broach the subject of him being a spy.

"Why are you naked?" I blurt out the most pressing question.

"I'm not naked," he mumbles, "I have my loincloth."

"Ok," I go along with the game, "why are you in these cold climes without proper covering?"

64

"Tis a long tale," he sighs. "Why do you want to know?"

"We're not going anywhere anytime soon, not until you're robust enough to walk. It was I who pursued you from the river, and I want to know why you were spying on us." With a grunt of discomfort he shifts so he can see my face. His molten gaze takes in my honey halo of short curls and bare shoulder draped across him, then back to peruse my features.

"Ah yes," he concludes his study, "the golden one. I would have remembered you at once but for my addled brain."

I bury my hot cheeks in his neck, but the spicy smell of him chases the heat from my cheeks down into my midsection.

"How old are you? Fourteen years?"

"Why do you ask?"

"You have an innocent boldness about you, passion seemingly beyond your years."

"Why were you spying on us?" I counter to deflect the extreme disquiet aroused by his nearness. He relaxes back, giving in to my interrogation.

"I wanted to see the Chinese Princess, Liang Na, without her knowledge. I removed my cumbersome garments so I could climb the tree undetected." My attention drawn to his brown skin, it dawns on me that he too, has travelled a far distance.

"Why were you trying to see her?"

"My company hails from the southern shores of the Euxine Sea, the princess is an important piece of an agreement between our peoples. We wanted to assess her before the pact is sealed, to ensure her fitness."

"She's a person...God's child," I raise up in defense of my new friend, "not just a pawn to be used by your people."

"Innocent and naive!" He scorns, "you must be from some mean village far from sophisticated government. This is the way of advanced civilization, to make promises thusly. She is not the only pawn." His arrogance has me not only seething, but also ashamed of my humble past.

"What do you know of the princess?" He demands to my rigid back that I present to him in childish temper.

"Princess Liang Na is a gentle young woman, tender to the harsh ways of the world." I envision our days of connecting with each other through song, sharing our cultures and learning our languages. "She's musical and intelligent, well-educated and sensitive to other's feelings."

"What has she told you of her future?" He presses.

"That she is to be married to a ruler from the southern reaches of the Byzantine Empire, to strengthen China's alliance with Constantinople, and allow traders from her country to pass through unmolested."

"Has she said anything about this ruler whom she is to marry?" Something in his petulant tone piques my attention, and I eye him coolly over my shoulder.

"She's scared. She's been told that he is a hideous, cruel giant who has many wives who he treats as chattel."

"Harumph," he protests, "people like me from the south have darker skin and tend to grow tall - much like yourself. Outsiders don't know our erudite history and advanced skill, they only fear our size and coloring, assuming that we're dangerous."

"Its the same with the Vikings, they're marked as ignorant and violent," my natural compulsion for enlightenment tickles my interest to hear him out, though I hug my knees to my chest, a shield against further insults. "The Emperor's Varangian guards have everyone across the empire quaking at the sight of their towering height and brawny muscles."

"We're not all like that," I call to mind my wise Maman and the fierce, yet refined Nicolo. "Tis unjust to put everyone together and deem us all alike."

"My point exactly. Now, if I could ask your small viking brain to figure out a way to help my monstrous frame to relieve myself, I would be much obliged!"

His humor eases my mood, and I help him stand and take a few unsteady steps to a bush. Leaving him some privacy, I set about restocking our pile of foliage in anticipation of spending another night. I wrest some edible tubers from among the tree roots and we add them to our feast of nuts, seeds and water.

"I can probably last another day or two on this diet," he squints into the sunlight after we share our meal. "The wound will keep for some time, but my head swims when I stand."

"You lost a lot of blood." Hunger is no stranger to me, but I realize that he needs meat to replenish.

"My forefathers developed a way to read the stars and navigate across the desserts and wastelands, so I have confidence that I can find my party. If I could just walk without fear of collapsing…". He limply tosses a shell in futility.

"I can keep us sustained using the forest's resources, but I think it best that we stay here until you are certain of your stability."

"Us?" He fixes me pointedly.

"Yes," I assure him, "I am responsible chasing you so far. I'll not leave you."

"What is your name, Golden One?"

"Adila," a thrill of joy ripples through my chest.

"Adila," his deep voice caresses my name and he extends his hand in formal greeting. "I am Majidi."

"Majidi," I repeat, our handclasp resembling the Chinese Yin and Yang that Liang Na showed me, black and white, flowing together.

We pass the afternoon conversing about our homes, families and travels, until the bite of chill in the late afternoon air reminds me that this is not a time of leisure. Never have I talked so much in one sitting, not even with Brigida. His intellect attracts me, but unlike Brother Samuel and Bishop Stephen, he asks questions of me and remarks introspectively on what I have to say. The heady combination holds me in thrall, and I'm reluctant to tend to the duties that are part of our reality at the moment.

As I scour the woods for anything edible, I espy a beaver splashing in the rivlet, and manage to maim it with a well tossed stone. Though we cannot eat the meat without a fire, the heart and blood may go a long way to restore Majidi's fluids, and I hasten to bring the necessary provisions back to him. He blanches pale when I tell him he must swallow the heart and eat the mash of blood and crushed roots that I prepare on a large piece of bark.

Amused at the sight of this sophisticated, comely man choking down the slimy fare, eyes bulging from effort not to vomit, I rush to bring him water and find something to disguise the taste. To my pleasure, I discover some late bunches of black current, knowing that God is watching over us for this provision. Majidi is still fighting his gorge when I return, and he stuffs the berries in his mouth, their sweetness easing the tension in his face. I'm moved by his trust in my knowledge as he ingests what I give him, especially when I don't think I could eat what he just forced down unless I was starving, and I've been countless times light headed from lack of nourishment.

Night descends with a cold heaviness, and we bed down to combat the chill with our combined warmth that escalates the instant we touch. He peers up at the flashing stars, explaining to me the ones he will read to map our route back to the Dneiper. He bemoans the heavy canopy that blocks the constellations, and I add that it clears a bit along the rivlet, suggesting that we might try to move that way on the morn.

Sometime near dawn, gauging by the gray tinge illuminating the treetops, my stomach jumps and I break out in clammy sweat. A few more gut twisting moments pass, ere I burst out of our nest in an eruption of leaves and branches. I manage to make it a few paces then drop to my knees retching the contents of my insides. My head is exploding, as I vomit until nothing more will come forth. The pain in my head is so acute, I moan in anguish, languishing on hands and knees on the ground over my mess.

"Adila?" Majidi calls, "can I help?"

"Nay," I can barely manage to moan. I roll over and rest on my back, gulping in the fresh air, letting it wash through me. A rustling in the leaves, and I feel his hand warm on my forehead. Visions of Maman's healing fingers ease the pounding in my temples, but it is his outline against the growing light sky, rubbing my head tenderly. Steadying under his ministration, I stagger to the rivlet to get some water to wash my mouth. Still feeling a buzzing pressure in my head, I go back and see that Majidi is laying back down between the tree roots, patting his chest for me to come to him.

Relief replacing embarrassment, I gladly sink into the meat of his shoulder and he strokes my hair.

"Did you eat a beaver heart too?" He jests, "should I anticipate getting sick?"

"'Twas some mushrooms I found," the throbbing subsides under his soothing touch, leaving me with a pleasant floating sensation that I recalled from years prior. "When I was younger I mistook the fungus for an edible mushroom and felt this way."

He caresses my cheek and neck, the arm supporting my head tightens as he grips my waist, pulling me close against him. The feeling of drifting through the clouds intensifies to a breathless plummeting when he presses his lips to my forehead. A mewling moan escapes me, expressing a need for something I can't identify. Instinctively, I shift my leg over his, then jump back when my thigh brushes the hardness under his loincloth, causing him to suck his teeth.

"I hurt you!" I cry, trying to pull away, "I'm so sorry."

"Nay!" He grasps my hip to keep me there and tips my head back so I'm gazing into the full force of his passionate expression. His eyes are coals of smoldering desire, sparking a lurking memory of lustful leers from the boys who attacked my sister and I. Panic overtakes the warm eagerness of a moment ago, and I squirm out of his embrace and scramble away. I stare at him in irrational terror, gasping for air to calm my spinning head.

"What is it Adila?" My name, spoken in gentle compassion. The whirling earth slows, then stops when I see his brow wrinkled like a walnut in perplexed concern. I take a few gulps, observing the leaves fluttering blithely against the pale blue sky, absorbing the refreshing breeze brushing through my hair, hearing the songs of the birds carrying about their business as if nothing extraordinary just happened. I contemplate the beauty of his confused aspect, and realize that he meant me no harm, the madness is confined to my head.

"I am afraid of being forced." The words tumble out in spite of my iron clad will, which governs all matters of my violent past.

"Forced?" His eyes widen, incredulous, "but twas you who…". He pauses as my gaze drops, mortified when he points out my boldness. "…and I'm incapacitated! I couldn't do anything if I wanted to!"

Tears gather to distort my vision into a watery portrait of colors all running together. Not knowing why I feel compelled to explain, the story bursts out of me in a torrent of shame, anger and fear. I tell him everything, my sister, the boys in the woods, how they attacked me, and even how I killed one. I talk and talk until the demons vacate my mind, and there's nothing left in its place but a peaceful void.

He is silent, reading the emotions as they play across my face. For a long time, we sit quietly, letting the ugliness of my past dissipate with the late morning mist.

"Tis a terrible ordeal, one I cannot begin to fathom." The sincerity in his voice touches me, "But I have never harmed a woman, and I would not hurt you."

"I just want to have the choice…with everything in my life."

It is well into the afternoon ere we break our fast and give each other privacy to tend to our needs. Our easy banter is strained and awkward from the morning's explosive events, but as the day proceeds we make our way slowly to the rivlet and follow its path downhill until we find a small clearing to pass the night. The trees are not as dense, so Majidi will have a view of the stars, and we find an area of heavy moss to cushion our respite.

"How do you feel after walking?" The going had been tedious, but his pallor no longer has the grayish hue of yesterday.

"Weary, but not as weak," he looks up from picking at the nuts I've scavenged, "once I get some meat I'm sure I'll recover."

"You must leave the bark," he has started picking at the edges since I removed the binding. "If you pull it off, you'll tear the scab forming underneath."

"Tis giving me a terrible itch," he whines.

"That's good," I chuckle at his childlike pouting, eliciting a scowl, "it indicates the wound is healing. The only way remove it is to soak it in warm water until it falls off."

"Harumph," he protests, assessing the waning sunlight. "I'll be able to tell our direction once night falls. How far do you think we have to go?"

"I chased you for quite some time," I calculate the distance in my head, mulling over the pace that we held and about how long we ran for. "I estimate we covered up to ten miles, and maybe a mile returning today."

"You ran that far after me?" Disbelief written in his eyes.

"Aye," I fire back, "the surprise is that you kept going!"

"You're a remarkable woman," he concludes. "You find food and shelter out of wilderness, you tend to my ailments, you can run for leagues, and you're keeping us alive out here."

"God provides, we merely have to look for his abundance." I shyly deflect his compliments, ignoring the tingling happiness they elicit. "Besides, I've had a lot of practice surviving the woods and being chased myself."

"You give a lot of credit to this God of yours," his earnest tone moderates any defensive reaction to his questioning my savior. "My ancestors brought Allah, the God of Mohammad, to the shores of the Euxine Sea in Byzantium. My people speak of Allah with the same reverence."

"He saved me," the tremor in my voice attests to the depth of my devotion, "my life was unbearable, and God gave me peace and hope."

"I think its admirable to have such a relationship with your creator." He opines, "Many become lost in studying the Koran that they lose sight of the reason why we worship, and have no real connection to Allah."

"Yes, I've been blessed with great teachers who constantly remind me that God makes all things happen, so I appeal to him frequently." As the sentiment leaves my lips I have a vision of Maman. "My Maman would always tell about the will of the Gods, so it was natural for me to accept this concept."

"Was she Pagan to have more than one God?"

"She venerates the Norse Gods, similar to the early Roman and Greek Gods." He is so absorbed in my tales of Odin, Thor and the others, that I keep going and entertain him with the rumor of my Maman being a Valkyre, and my father trapping her. I regale him with descriptions of my bandy-legged, bad tempered father matching up with the towering, lithe beauty of my mother. He throws back his head and roars with high humor, his mighty laugh echoing throughout the forest clearing, evoking the latent mirth from my belly. We roll like children on the mossy ground, holding our shaking sides, choking back tears of hilarity.

"Enough!" He surrenders, "your wit is going to open this wound you're making me laugh so hard."

"No one has ever told me I'm witty," I'm slightly sobered by the revelation.

"Well, I have a stitch in my side now from your comedy." His attention is back on the birch bark, "and I thank you for the pleasant distraction from this itching."

"Here, let me help," I kneel behind him and scratch his back and side around the dressing. He shivers and sighs in pleasure, goose flesh dimpling the flawless skin. He twists and squirms so that I can reach every area of his broad back, murmuring his contentment and gratitude. Despite the dropping temperature, I'm warmed with admiration of his lean muscles, narrow waist and long limbs.

I'm drifting into that drunken state again, where I feel overcome with a desire to mold myself to him, when I hear his teeth chattering and his shivers turn to tremors. I mentally shake myself and give him a friendly pat on the shoulder, telling him that we should bed down for the night. As I gather the foliage I had stocked nearby, he makes himself as comfortable as possible on his back and thumps his chest for me to come and lie down. Any lingering distress from the emotional day vanishes, as I seek my spot in the valley between the roll of his shoulder and the swell of his breast. We embrace tightly, our mutual need for the other's body both practical and passionate.

Through prayer and focus on the function of sharing our heat, I relax into the melodious timbre of his dissertation on the constellations.

Sometime in the night I become aware of the music of the forest, trickling water, breeze rustling leaves, crickets chirping, and the steady drum of Majidi's heart under my ear. These things fill my being, leaving no space for anything but a sense of belonging. I don't try to reason why I feel this ease, nor draw any conclusions. For once, I accept the intuition that this moment is otherworldly, and fall back asleep cradled in peace.

In the morning we make an effort to be about our business in friendly companionship. Majidi confirms that the rivlet is flowing in the general direction of his camp, so we follow the trickle, buoyed by its bubbling cheerfulness. Our mood is light, and I ask him about the land where he's from, entranced by his description of the tropical port on the shores of the Euxine Sea.

By late afternoon his conversation becomes labored, and I suggest we rest. Not even waiting until I discern a relatively comfortable spot, he drops to the ground and slumps over in exhaustion. Worry creeps upon me that he needs something more hearty to fortify him soon, or he won't have the strength to continue the trek. I'm staring into the ripple of water over the rocky stream bed, when I spot a black clamshell amongst the stones. Plucking it out of the ril, I see more of the small mollusks, and send up a prayer of thanks. By the time the sun is fading I have a pile stacked next to Majidi and I shake him gleefully showing him the clams.

His toothy grin rewards my efforts, and we pry open the sharp shells and swallow the slippery bodies while he explains his familiarity with shellfish from his marine diet. Chaldia, his homeland, occupies the south eastern shore of the Euxine Sea; her northern coast is our landmark to circumvent west to Constantinople. The Chaldians, he tells me, are mariners, sailing the seas for food and commerce, their ports renown centers of trade and culture.

"Is that why your people want to treat with the Chinese?" I reason, "To gain their business from the trade of silks and spices?"

"You're logic is correct," he drops another clam down his throat, "however it is the other way around. The border between Byzantium and Persia is rife with conflict between Christians and Muslims, they both prey upon commercial caravans traveling through the mountain passes along the silk road. Our military and ships are to provide protection and naval escort to the Chinese merchants in exchange for tribute to be confirmed by the Emperor Basil."

"Is that why your party is on your way to Constantinople?" I opt for the Greek version of Miklagard, wary of my provincial use of the norse name for the capitol of the new Holy Roman Empire.

"Aye, this was supposed to be a short sail up the Dneiper for a bit of scouting, but it has turned into an odyssey of its own!" He shakes his head in wonder at how it all went wrong and shivers as a gust of cold air rustles the bushes. "We must put into port before the winter sets in and the seas become too rough to navigate."

"I certainly understand your concern," I commiserate, hugging my knees to my chest, "the chill has set in early this evening."

I hustle to dispose of the clam shells, lest they attract any unwanted creatures, and scan the area for where we can rest for the night. I'm much heartened to see Majidi breaking leafy branches from the bushes and heaping pine needles underneath an overhanging bolder. Whether out of need for shelter, or returned vigor, I enthusiastically join him, approving of his choice. His movements appear less sluggish, as we build up a thick wall of foliage around the space under the slanted rock. He disappears for several moments and I hie to find privacy for my own ministrations.

Instead of laying on his back, he props his back up against the leaf lined rock, and gathers me close in front of him. I squirm deeper into his arms, and he clutches me happily, both of us pleased with our efforts to create a cozy nest. Suddenly he freezes, his breath exploding from him.

"Cease!" He grits through clenched teeth. I stop wriggling and turn to look at him in time to see his face contorted in a pained expression. He opens his eyes and the fire in the black orbs sears through me. Trusting his word that he would not hurt me, I reach up and smooth the tension from his handsome face. Wanting to give him something, I smile compassionately, desperately desiring I could give more.

"I've never beheld a man so beautiful as you," the truth tumbles out of its own volition. "Are Chaldians often so comely?"

"To the contrary," he perceives me with perplexity, "we've been rumored to be ugly beasts, as you've heard from the princess already."

"We both know that's not true," I relax my head onto the padding of his muscled arm, the intensity of the moment past. He describes how people of the southern climes are typically smaller in stature than he, his unusual height most likely because his ancestors hail from the African interior, not the desert. His portrayal conjures images of tanned faces, black or brown curly hair and earth toned eyes. I'm so entranced by the picture he creates, that I fail to note the tightening of his jaw and tension in his frame.

"Adila," I savor the sweetness of those three syllabi from his seductive lips, "I'm so cold. I don't want to frighten you, but can you stay close?"

"Of course, Majidi," I nestle timidly into the circle of his embrace. He wraps himself around me, nearly suffocating me in his effort to get warm. My instinct to comfort overcomes my shyness, and I let my body mold to his and stoke the innate fire in my northern blood, channelling the flames to him. The tremors shaking his frame abate, giving way to jerking spasms as his muscles jump before falling asleep.

Long after the gentle rhythm of his snores had lulled me to join him in slumber, his restlessness stirs me. I immediately perceive the plunge in the temperature, and the stiffness of his body, pitying his southern softness. I murmur an assurance that I will return shortly, and scrounge around in the dim moonlight until I collect a few armfuls of leaves to add insulation behind him. I cover the ground with another thick layer and lay on my back next to Majidi, pulling the brambles closer to bury us. This time, I bring his head to my shoulder and gather him to my breast, twining my legs in his to share whatever heat I could. I envision flames leaping from my core to him, rewarded as his weight sinks onto me.

"You smell like wood, rain and sunshine all at once." He sighs, burrowing his face in my neck.

"Mmmmm," I hum, still training my thoughts on passing my heat to his icy toes.

"Are you not cold?" He complains, breaking my concentration.

"Aye, but I'm accustomed to the frozen climes of the far north, even more frigid than this."

"How do you live in this? I'm frozen stiff!"

"One technique I've acquired is to visualize a fire inside of me, and as I focus on its heat, it is like adding fuel and the flames actually grow." We're silent for a while as he contemplates his inner conflagration, the sounds of the night serenading us in our cocoon.

"I heard you singing that day at the river." My mind turns back to the peaceful scene prior to his loud disruption when he crashed into the water. "Your voice was what drew me to find you, it was so alluring, like a magnet."

"My Maman had the gift that she passed along to me," I chuckle, "though I've never heard my singing described as alluring. She could cast a spell with her crooning, twas the only thing that calmed my father's raging."

"What was it you sang by the river?"

"A Christian hymn I was teaching Liang Na."

"Would you sing it for me?" Heartened that he would want me to repeat lyrics about Jesus, the pull of melody floods my being. I lose myself in the joy of my musical legacy flowing out of my soul. One song spills into the next, I lose track of time and space. I'm well into a childhood lullaby when I realize that his snores are accompanying my words.

Dawn's silvery aura paints the sky when the stiffness in my body prods me to waken. The warm heaviness of Majidi's inert form bears me into our bed of leaves, so that I feel every pebble and stem poking into my sore back. Though I have no sensation in my arm that supports his head, I train my mind to rejoice that we made it to see another day. In the moments when the moon is still visible against the backdrop of morning light, I attempt to read the stars to surmise our direction. I think I find the constellation which points to the east, and feel an uneasiness when I calculate that following the rivulet may guide us farther to the south of our encampments. As if sensing my disquiet, Majidi stirs and sighs against my neck, the stubble on his cheek abrading the delicate skin under my chin.

"I love the feel of you," he slurs, drunk with sleep.

Not knowing what to say, I'm silent, hoping that he is not yet lucid. Praying that he's aware. Confused by the stinging in my eyes, a bevy of emotions threatens to overwhelm my nativity. Few people have ever spoken kind words to me, and fewer still, compliments and expressions of love. I'm awed by the tenderness I feel for this man. Though he's a stranger, it is as if I've known him always, and his body against mine is as organic as the forest surrounding us.

Basking in this new experience of affection, I dare not move and spoil the moment. I watch the heavens take on an iron hue of the grave morning, savoring the warmth emanating from him, not wanting to face the reality of the damp cold day ahead.

"I wish that we could stay like this all day." He is definitely awake.

"Yes, but you're not the one being crushed!" I jest good-naturedly. He apologizes and shifts his weight to his side and scoops me up in front of him.

"There, now we can." He jokes back, "as long as you don't move."

We enjoy each other's comfort, conversing quietly about our concerns and what our course of the day should be. We decide that once we start to grow restless, we're going to break our fast and quickly be on our way. When we can no longer ignore the call of nature, we hasten about our private business and huddle together over our fare. Following the trickle of the stream, we set off at a jog, fortified by the meat from the clams. At this steady pace, we keep ourselves warm and make marked progress.

Of one accord to keep moving ahead of the impending winter winds, we slow down only to pick up food along the way as we encounter it, then resume loping along through the underbrush. I thank God for strengthening Majidi, so that he stays right behind me as I set a healthy tempo. Throughout the day we continue our momentum, stopping only for a quick break or snack, saving our breath for running rather than conversing.

As the evening chill descends, and we look for a place to bed down, I start to notice signs of human presence. Saplings have been chopped down, branches stripped of food, and bushes trampled. Soon we come upon a clearing that has been occupied within the past week, flattened undergrowth and cold fire pits left behind as evidence. Someone had cleverly constructed a temporary hut by bending young trees together and weaving branches in between, making the whole thing airtight by packing the gaps with moss. We welcome the convenience and retire into the dark shelter, pleased that the ground inside was piled with dry leaves and pine needles.

Exhausted from the taxing activity, I nestle into Majidi's welcoming arms and fall asleep immediately. Whether inspired by the relative coziness of our accommodations, or Majidi's granite torso molding to my back, my dreams are so erotic that they come to life in the opaque blackness of the dead of night. My heart pounds as I imagine his hands seeking out the crevices and curves of my body. His magic touch brings my skin alive, as he pushes up my shift and strokes my hip, moving upward along my ribs.

"You're so lean," his sensuous voice permeates my pleasurable fantasy. I arch my back to better enjoy his fingertips tracing my shoulder blades and back down to cup my buttock. The brush of his hand in the cleft between my legs awakens me with a jolt of lightning ripping through my belly. Before I can react to his exploring my thighs, he continues in soothing honeyed tones, "I won't hurt you. Your body is so unique, I just want to know it. Your skin is rough here on your hip, but soft on your belly."

The slight sting from the remark about my skin being rough is forgotten the instant he finds the swell of my sensitive breasts. I whimper in painful delight when he covers a mound in the warmth of his palm. He teases the hard tips until I'm about to shout, then leaves them throbbing as he works his way back down over my abdomen.

"You're built hard, like a man." He concludes, unaware of the path of carnal devastation left in wake of his examination. His statement however, has the effect of a plunge in the ice cold Dneiper, instantly stifling my passion with the reminder of my masculine form.

"Good," I spit, choosing anger over tears, "then I won't have to worry about you wanting me. You're much too pretty for my liking anyway."

"To the contrary," he pulls my backside into the firebrand of his rigid member, "your uniqueness adds to my desire for you. I made a promise to you; however, so I will wait for you to come to me."

An unearthly contentment descends upon me, and I lean back into his arms and feel his tender kisses on my neck and shoulder. Pushing away thoughts of the morning, I turn my face toward him to greet the fullness of his lips with mine. The pleasure of his mouth consumes my whole being, and we remain molded together for an eternity. We finally part for air, and he sighs deeply and settles back to sleep.

As purposeful as we rose the previous day, the dim cozy interior coaxes us to indulge in a slow start to this morning. Intuition tells me that this may be the last time we wake up locked together for survival, so I ponder the pale sun oozing into the hut in a pensive mood. If not for my mission to get Majidi safely to his camp soon, I could continue to exist in this make believe world with just him and I, exploring this passionate connection to its fullest.

"Stay with me Adila." He reads my thoughts. I sigh heavily, the vision of me walking with him through the golden streets of his tropical paradise swirling in my head. "Sail to Constantinople with me and come live with me in Trebizond."

"What of my sister?" I protest against the waves of magnetic energy binding me to the idea of waking in his arms every day. "And Brother

Samuel and the others. They need me, I have responsibilities that I can't just turn away from."

"You could if you wanted to be with me badly enough," the childish pouting in his statement prevents me from lashing back at him in anger.

"Would you give up everything and come with me if I asked you?" I counter gently, "besides, you're not even giving me promises about our future together."

"When we get to my camp, we will help you find your people." I chaff at his dictatorial tone. "Then you will see that they are safe and don't need you as I do."

A hush falls over my spirit. No one, not even Brigida, had ever said they needed me. The rush of someone verbalizing that they need me pulls at me with such force that I let my silence acquiesce to his edict.

We linger until nature's call chases us out into the cold to minister to our bodily functions and food. My jog east is not so jaunty as it was yesterday, leaving Majidi to take the lead, his easy lope aided by his misconception that these are not our last moments together.

We reach the Dneiper by midday and stop to rest and determine our direction. We press on to the south until Majidi gives a whoop when he espies an object flashing in a tree branch.

"My bangle!" His shout is swallowed by the rush of the river, "I took it off and hung it here with my other clothes on my way from our camp. We're close!"

He swings me up into a breathless hug and captures my lips in his. Unlike the desperate searching of our kisses last night, his mouth joyously conveys his excitement without need for words. I abandon myself to these final moments, sharing the celebration of our victory.

"Wait here, my love," he drops me clumsily on a tree stump, his boyish elation eliciting a smile from me in spite of my crumbling heart. "I'll be back anon!"

I numb myself to all thought and react. Not allowing myself a moment's hesitation, I bolt upriver in the opposite direction. I fight through currents of agony rushing against me, each step more arduous than the last. I stubbornly deny the metaphor that going against God's will is like fighting upstream.

The pain in my heart reaches up to squeeze my throat, constricting my breath until I feel I'm going to faint. Only the certainty that if Majidi tracks me down, he is going to convince me to abandon my will, keeps my feet following the river to the spot where, five days ago, I gave chase to this extraordinary being. The frigid water clears my head and washes my tears away as I plunge in, freezing the memory of the past days, as well as cleansing the surreal dream of Majidi from my mind.

Thankfully, my tunic is still where I had thrown it over a branch to dry, and I strip off my sodden shift in exchange for the dry woolen garment. Night is closing fast upon me when I reach the encampment, only to find it deserted. The fire pits are banked, tents gone, and not a soul in sight. Before the moonless darkness is complete, I'm able to scavenge some some morsels to eat and scraps of bedding to keep me through the night.

The biting winter winds penetrate the layers of fabric, deflate the tight ball I've curled into, and probe into the very core of me. I welcome the distraction from the ache in my chest, inviting my lifelong companion of suffering and misery to replace the tenderness of my feelings for Majidi. I cycle from sobbing over my breaking heart, to appealing to the freezing air to divert my thoughts, to dozing fitfully, haunted by imaginings that he is holding me.

With the dawn I set my mind to figuring out where everyone went and what I am going to do next. I assume that they thought I was lost or worse, and moved on with their itinerary, until I locate the spot where Brigida and I had slept next to a fire pit in the middle of the campsite. There, on the flattened ground, she had formed an arrow using white pebbles from the river. For once, I thank God for my parents for teaching us to be resourceful, for Brigida knew I would make my way back, and she was ready. Not only is the arrow pointing west, back towards the river, there's a fragment of fabric tucked underneath. I pull it out and unfold it.

"Going southwest toward Preslav on the Euxine Sea," someone had written in greek, "taking shortcut across hostile Pechneg territory."

My guess is a day or two ere I find the others, so I collect a few necessities and tie them into a light pack. I ford the Dneiper one last time, and set out at a jog keeping the pale morning sun over my left shoulder. Diverging from the river valley, the Bulgarian landscape grows more inhospitable, baring gnarled shoulders of rocky mountains above her heavily wooded mantle. Now I know why the Emperor Basil has been thwarted in his conquest of Byzantium's northernly neighbor, the territory alone is a formidable foe to any army. Though for one person, taking breaks only to eat, orient my direction, and rest for the night, the going is slightly quicker, and I catch up to my party late the following evening.

Everyone celebrates my return, telling me how my sister assured them it was safe to travel on and that I would find them. I leave them to their impressions that my tears are those of relief at being reunited. Only Brigida considers me in contemplative silence, and our roles are reversed as she holds me tight throughout night.

We continue to march at a grueling pace, aware of the exigency to beat the snowfall. There is little time to interact, which suits my sullen mood, the exercise exhausting my body, the twisted ravines characterizing my conflicted spirit. Over the next few weeks my footsteps take me alongside Liang Na's chair or Bishop Stephen's mule, where I find solace in gentle feminine companionship or intellectual stimulation. I'm not even upset that Brigida has taken to riding behind Nicolo, though it gives me a pang of envy seeing her curled up behind him to escape the wind.

With God's grace we pass through the perilous shortcut without incident. Rather than divert further into Bulgaria to recruit more boys for his choir, the Bishop deems it best that we get to Constantinople as soon as possible. Our Pechneg guide tells us that the coastal climes are milder than the interior mountains, which are by now covered in snow. By the time we reach the jagged cliffs of the Euxine, the emptiness within me has eased, and I appreciate the majestic waves crashing into the rocky shore.

Chapter 9

The route to Constantinople traverses the western shore of the Euxine Sea along well established paths that speeds our progress into Roman territory. To make up time from delays and stay ahead of the weather, we eschew the comfort of abbeys and monasteries further inland, and opt for the convenience of the road and towns along the way. Provisions are easy to come by, with the sea on one side and the forest on the other, though the Bulgarian villagers are wary of our large party.

I accompany our guide, running ahead and scouting where to set camp in the evenings, relishing the task to occupy the void in my heart. On a few occasions I glimpse the pointed sails of a Byzantine ship on the horizon, and I yearn to fly across the watery expanse and join Majidi on the sea. Like a mirage, she disappears, leaving the crash of waves against the rocky shore, and briny gusts to usher me back to the chore at hand.

It is after one of these excursions that I return to the caravan and find Brigida trailing behind, walking hand in hand with Nicolo. But for the irritation I feel for being seemingly the last one to know about their liaison, my reaction is uncharacteristically benign. My sister's horrified expression and protective posture, as she positions herself in front of him, speaks of her concern for her knight.

"I love him," she declares forcefully at my approach, her words a shield against my anticipated anger. "And he has spoken his love for me."

My silent perusal shifts back and forth between the two, processing their closeness, his enormous hand covering her slim shoulder. His towering form over her petite frame strikes me as similar to the incongruous match of Majidi and myself.

"Won't he crush you?" I admonish in good nature, they release their pent up breath simultaneously in relief.

"I wouldn't know," she grins back softly, tilting her head shyly. "He won't try!"

"Not until we're settled into my home in Miklegard and could talk to you," Nicolo chimes in gruffly. "I swore an oath, and I keep my promises."

The assurance of my sister's future safety in Nicolo's capable hands brings a palpable equanimity that I've never felt before. For the greater part of my fourteen years I've carried the burden of her physical protection, and now the fierce viking has lifted the responsibility from my young shoulders. His tenderness for my sister is touching to see, and I trust him as I have no other.

"I admit my shock that you didn't go into a rage over Nicolo and I." Brigida and I still share space next to the fire pit at night.

"I'm sorry that I've behaved like a tyrant in the past." The shame of my surly behavior heats my face in spite of the chill of nightfall. "I never want to turn into our father."

"There's something different about you since you went into the forest." Her cornflower gaze probes my face in the firelight. "You never did tell me what happened."

"You're becoming just like Maman," I muse wistfully, her coaxing eyes drawing out my secret, "able to see into one's soul."

The stars bedazzle the velvety heavens, bringing me back to the last time I contemplated the constellations with Majidi. The tale spills out of me, evoking tears anew as I conclude with how I deserted him. My raw emotions surprise me, I had thought I was forgetting him, but as usual I've been merely distracted with activity.

"So you love him then," Brigida determined.

"I don't know." I stare back at her, frightened by her conclusion of my powerful sentiments. Love always seems to be accompanied by pain.

"I know I love Nicolo, because I have this feeling like we're meant to be together." Her visage glows, mirroring mine when I reflect on Majidi.

"Like you belong," I add. She nods empathetically.

"What are you going to do about it?"

"There's nothing to do now." I concede, "its too late, he's gone."

"Its never too late."

83

THE PROMISED
LAND

Chapter 10

After almost a year of living on the move, we cross Thrace, the boundary between Bulgaria and Byzantium, and approach the outskirts of Constantinople. Though the civilization of the coastal suburban cities beckons us, Bishop Stephen presses on, alert for signs of social unrest. The war between Emperor Basil and the Bulgarian Tsar Samuel have left the land and people in upheaval.

We depart from the moderating maritime breeze of the coast and slice inward across the isthmus between the Euxine Sea and Propontis. The land is hilly and the climate damp, our heavy tunics clinging to our tired legs, sticky with perspiration. The trek becomes easier when we merge with the old Roman Via Egnatia, the timeless flagstones trod for centuries by armies, merchants, pilgrims, and St. Paul himself on route to Rome.

In spite of the overcast winter skies, which reflect my own lingering gloomy disposition, I'm enthralled by the sights along this ancient highway. I envision myself a disciple of Christ, passing through the territory on my way to witness Jesus' teachings. The countryside here is more settled, the woodlands less dense, and we encounter many travelers along the way. We finally pause in Melantias, a village within a day's walk of our final destination, to gather ourselves and prepare to enter the capital of the Eastern Roman Empire.

Melantias has long been a popular staging area for expeditions, so the villagers are accustomed to accommodating large crowds. We set up camp in the valley and rest for a week while the Bishop, Nicolo and a few of the other senior monks go on to arrange our admittance into the city. Thrace is crowded with other sojourners traveling to and from the city, yet the diminutive people are friendly and energetic, and the villagers hospitable, making our stay enjoyable.

Brother Samuel shepherds us close together, wary of his responsibility to our safety, and continues our worship, lessons and rehearsals. It is necessary for us to make an immediate impression on the Emperor Basil to justify the expense of the expedition; therefore, we are perfecting the score we will perform for his eminence as soon as we arrive. We put on a show for the villagers one night, eliciting exuberant applause from our rustic audience, bolstering our confidence in our preparation.

Interwoven in this rich tapestry of new and different tastes, smells, sights and sounds, is the ever-present thread of heartache. These are the last days I will spend with Liang Na and Brigida. Once we depart this staging location, I will go with the monks straight to the seclusion of the monastery, and I know not when I will see my sister again.

It is Brother Samuel who sympathetically guides me through my tumultuous emotions during this time. Only he and God know of the sadness I will experience to leave my sister, who I've never been without for more than a fortnight. My only consolation is that she will be content with Nicolo, whom I now believe was sent by God, as he pointed out when we first spoke. On more than a few occasions this week, my mentor finds me weeping on the hilltop overlooking our camp and offers his soothing company.

"I fear he will reject her once he finds out about her past." I cry out my concerns to his willing ear. "I haven't asked Brigida because she's been doing so well that I didn't want to bring it up and sour her mood."

"Nicolo knows." While I'm digesting my shock, Brother Samuel continues, gazing towards the Propontis Sea in the distance. "Confessions are strictly confidential, but I will tell you that your sister sought absolution from the Bishop, and part of her penance was to tell her man."

"And he still loves her?" My query is more of an awed observation of the strength of love to overcome such circumstances. Any disappointment I may have felt that my sister didn't tell me this, dissolves in the light of God's work, not only in bringing together two tortured souls, but in Brigida's compulsion to turn to Christ to confess her sins.

"Its part of why he loves her, because he's flawed too." He directs his attention to my perplexed expression, as I try to fathom why Nicolo could love her for her brokenness, and what could he possibly have marring his outward perfection. "He has a wife already."

"Which is why there has been no talk of marriage," I muse aloud, surprising myself with my lack of concern for the formality.

"Aye," he confirms, "he was taken from his family many years ago when he was captured and pressed into serving in the Varangian Guard. While on this mission, he went in search of his wife and sons, and found them alive and well in his home village."

"He told me that the Bishop was angry with him for losing some youths they had taken from a place in Novgorod." The hidden pieces of Nicolo's enigmatic past were falling into place.

"They were his sons." My mentor's voice strained with rare emotion. "He set them free to live with their bigamous mother and her unlawful husband, rather than subject them to the capricious power of the emperor."

"Brother, what have we gotten ourselves into?" Trepidation creeps into my speech, when I consider the lengths Nicolo went to in protecting his sons from coming with us. "Nicolo is in a position of honor with Emperor Basil."

"God's work child," he assures, "he has something planned for us, as he does for everyone. Tis up to us to listen."

The massive size of the city's fortifications is beyond what my provincial imaginings could have comprehended. We file through several curtains of thick walls, each one built up higher than the previous, then pass under the soaring arches of the Golden Gate and into Constantinople. Once inside, the ostentatious capital displays her splendor in the pale afternoon sunlight. The muted green of the gardens, white of the buildings, sapphire of the sea, and ochre of the earth, all soften the intimidating grandiosity of the structures.

My mind tumbles over the stone pavers as we walk along, gawking at the masterpieces of marble statues adorning the streets and ancient columns supporting marvels of man-made engineering. The monastery of St. John of Studius, our final destination, is a colossal russet-hued structure easily visible against the backdrop of the sea. Sooner than I'm ready, we're in the dusky shadows of its red brick walls, and Brigida and I step to the side to meet Nicolo.

My lifelong friend, my confidant, my source of pain and comfort, my sister and I embrace fervently, exchanging promises of love and encouragement. I'm thankful that our parting must be brief, as we have only a few moments before the monastery gates will close behind the last of the monks. I symbolically place Brigida into Nicolo's outstretched hand with a passionate word to keep her safe in all things. I'm touched when he drops down on one knee and renews his promise from the forest in Novgorod.

"I pledge my life to care for her always," he vows earnestly, rising to clasp my arm to seal the pact. "You know by now my word is my bond."

"I don't think I've done a very good job of telling you," I choke on the rusty syllables, "thank you, my friend."

"My pleasure," the irony of his broad smile actually elicits a reluctant grin from my tear stained facade. "I'll leave you with this bit of news I just found out; they want Brigida to stay with Liang Na and help serve her until she leaves. You will be able to see each other sooner than you think at the ceremony at the Hagia Sofia!"

My heart swelling with gratitude for the favor to my sister, I drift under the venerable arches of my new home. As it is late in the afternoon, we are all ushered directly through lofty arcades of the cloisters, to the Cathedral of St. John the Baptist, for the Divine Service of Esperinos. Melodious song rises to fill the soaring dome in praise, giving glory to God our creator. Renewed tears stream down my cheeks, overcome am I with the beauty of my surroundings, my circumstances and my lord's greatness.

After the short service we unceremoniously follow the resident monks past the lavatorium, where we wash our hands and face, and into the rectory to dine in reverent silence, but for the reader. The chosen text is a passage welcoming us to the abbey, which leads me to contemplate our humble reception to this establishment, along with the strict piety I'm observing, and even the tasty but modest fare we're served. By the end of the meal, I can only marvel at this oasis of simple devotion in the midst of the opulence of the city.

In the same unpretentious mode, we file into the chapter house for a quick synopsis of the regulations of the house and what to expect. At first I'm overawed by the international influence of the Abbot Nicolas, dazzled by his resume of running the oldest and largest abbey in the empire, until I realize that he has stopped talking and is looking directly at me.

"One of our rules here is to uncover our heads in the Lord's presence," panic squeezes my heart in its tightening grip as he addresses me, "is there a particular reason why you don't doff your cowl? There are many of us here with disfigurements, if it is a matter of extreme ugliness which injures your pride."

"God save me," My mind screams through the heat of embarrassment and fear that I will be required to remove my hood. I haven't cropped my hair this entire journey, and I worry that its length and feminine curls will testify to the truth of my sex.

"Forgive me Father Abbot, but tis humility why I retain my cowl." The words flow without thought, "I pledge a vow of anonymity to keep me humble. I have seen much evil from vanity over our outward appearances, so I prefer to remain physically unseen in honor of the holy spirit within me being the focus of attention."

"Unusual, but not unorthodox," the Abbot contemplates, and calls for a vote over whether or not I shall be allowed to stay covered. Praises sing through my relief with the string of "Ayes" from the section where the resident monks are seated, until one of the senior brothers who accompanied us from the north whispers something to the Abbot. Once again his somber perusal penetrates my woolen robes as if he sees what I'm trying so desperately to hide.

"Brother Augustus has informed me that God has blessed you with the voice of angels, that you are our most gifted chorister. This gift must be protected and nourished as a treasure of our abbey, and therefore you will have your own cell directly above the calefactory."

For a pregnant moment I struggle to close my gaping jaw, so much is my consternation over this boon of having a private cell. "As you wish Father Abbot."

"This leads me to my next subject," he continues as if my wild swing from panic to praise never occurred. "This monastery is famous for exalting the lord through our dedication and commitment to music and scribing text. Those among us who are anointed in these arts are to devote their six hours of manual labor each day to the choir and scriptorium, and may be exempt from attending nighttime services."

He goes on to explain their adherence to the rules of the monastery, including observing all seven divine services, labor requirements, silence and cleanliness. This last topic finally snaps me out of the lingering euphoria, and I listen intently to his instructions on using the baths adjacent to the kitchen on a rotating schedule. Perhaps due to my female nature, I've always been partial to bathing and sensitive to unwashed bodies. Even in the freezing northern climes I would brave the cold and threat of illness to heat a barrel of water or swim in the river. The idea of a bath that I don't have to prepare myself piques my interest, and I miss the Abbot's requirement of monthly hair shaving.

"Unless you have permission to go to the infirmary, clergy are forbidden from venturing beyond the kitchen and baths, lest we find ourselves in the public buildings of the abbey grounds." Following monastic rules of separation, our contact with secular workers conducting the business of the monastery, travelers staying in the inn, and guests of honor lodging in the apartments, is strictly limited. "This establishment has the honor of housing many religious luminaries and government dignitaries, one such party will be arriving on the morrow. His excellence the Emperor Basil is holding an official state greeting for his governor, the Strategos of Chaldia, and it is our great pleasure to glorify the ceremony with music from our new boys choir!"

An excited tittering ripples through the room until Father Abbot holds up a restraining hand, requesting silence. "I would remind you all that use of your gifts is to credit our Lord and our Monastery, not for personal profit. Especially so in a fortnight when we sing at the Strategos' betrothal in the Hagia Sophia."

By the bedtime service of Apodepnon, several of us are falling asleep from the soothing rhythm of the chanting and incense. I'm so exhausted that I feel my way into my cell without lighting a candle and fall onto the pallet, asleep by the time my head touches the blanket.

"Brother Adilsen!" Pounding on the thick panels of the door punctures my heavy slumber, and I stare up at the sloped alcove mustering my wits to recall where I am.

"Brother Adilsen, wake up!" Brother Samuel's muffled command snatches me out of the warm comfort of my pallet to open the portal, "Couldn't you hear me calling you?"

"I'm sorry," I remorsefully rub the sleep out of my eyes, taking in his ruffled aspect in the wan morning light from the window, "I can't hear a thing, the door is so thick."

"I'm forever your wet nurse, having to wake you!" The sting of his gruff words is softened by his sheepish grin, "I've overslept too, they put me in my own cell next to the school. We're not used to sleeping by ourselves, without the others in the dormitory to stir us."

"Is your cell like this?" I assess the spartan room, pleased with its mean comforts and having a window for the first time.

"Aye, a little bigger than back home," he surveyed the table and stool, and the curious pallet built into a triangle shaped cove into the wall. "We shouldn't tarry nor talk, we've already missed Prote Ora and breakfast. We can catch up with our brothers to tour the abbey if we hie this way."

He leads me through the corridor to the right, past the dormitory, then points to a portal and whispers to me that it is his new quarters. We descend the spiral staircase and catch up with the group in the chapel adjacent to the great basilica where we heard services yesterday. For the rest of the morning Brother Michael, our host, guides us around the abbey grounds, describing everything in an economy of words. It will take me weeks to find my way around the massive campus, but I make note of a few points of interest and how to get there.

The cloistered quadrangle is easy enough to locate, with the vast cathedral comprising the eastern side, and next to it the rectory, where the mouthwatering aroma of fresh baked bread elicits groans of protest from my empty stomach. On the other side of the square lawn is the chapter house and private rooms of the abbott and other administrators. Most of the activity of the monastery however, centers under the arcades beneath the dormitory, where there are carrels for studying in the morning sun, the lavatorium and calefactory. At this hour of the late morning, many of the residents are spending a few leisure moments taking air, meditating, praying or studying in the courtyard.

Standing in the center, Brother Michael indicates the second and third levels over the chapter house, which are suites for important abbey guests instead of staying in the common guest rooms beyond the cloister. Then he takes us up a spiral staircase and through the large scriptorium above the rectory which leads into the schoolroom and choir room, then back down into the kitchen. To the back of the kitchen we squeeze single file down a narrow corridor which grows warmer and more humid with each step, challenging my vow to keep my head covered.

We come to a halt and my eyes take a few moments to adjust to the flickering flames from the sconces mounted on the tiled walls, but when I recognize the fabled bath I forget my discomfort. White tiles gleam in the dim light, covering every facet of the room from floor to ceiling, to benches and the sides and bottom of the bath. The pool itself is not large, room enough for half a dozen people to stand. The real marvel is in the mechanics of the circulation and heating, which Brother Michael pauses to proudly explain the engineering.

The ancient architects of the monastery wisely connected the kitchen ovens to the furnace which heats water in a cistern. The hot water funnels down through a sealed aqueduct to pour continuously into the pool. There is a drain at the bottom of the pool that carries the used water out of the building where it is dispersed into canals to irrigate the gardens. The only negative aspect of this ingenious system, is that I must wait my turn until all of the senior monks have had a chance to bathe, which could take a week or two.

Back at ground level, we wind our way through the gardens and observe some of the lay buildings: the infirmary, stables, almshouse and guesthouse for the more common visitors. Entering the cathedral through its impressive front door, we take in Ekte Ora service and then head to the rectory for a midday meal. The light fare is to hold us through the next few hours of designated labor, for which I join Brother Samuel and the other choir members in the schoolroom to rehearse the hymn for the Emperor.

"We are ready," Brother Samuel declares confidently as last chord echoes in the room. "You have been practicing for months, and your work shows, for you sound like angels. God is most certainly smiling upon you, as will the Basilius tomorrow."

"When do we sing for him?" A fellow novice from Novgorod queries.

"During this same hour, thank you Brother Peter. You will proceed with the same daily itinerary as this morning, though I have to join the Abbot and Bishop Stephen in receiving the Emperor and the party of dignitaries who are to convene here. Our performance is to be for their pleasure after they banquet, so let us all be sure to eat well tomorrow. We don't want anyone weak from lack of nourishment!"

"I'm already faint with nerves," quips a brother from Kiev, "not only are we seeing the Emperor, but the Strategos of Chaldia!"

"Brothers, we must stay focused on our task, which is to glorify God through our voices that he has blessed us with." Samuel admonishes gently, "we're not to gossip and delve into worldly matters of rulers and generals."

Later that evening, stomach full from the tasty bread and fish served at dinner, I venture to Brother Samuel's cell as per my old practice from Novgorod. I interrupt his time of prayer and meditation, but yet he welcomes me warmly and invites me to sit at his desk.

"What do you think of this place Brother?" I open, feeling a need for his reassuring presence. "I'm trying to overcome its magnitude to find its heart."

"I know what you mean!" He laughs, "The size alone is intimidating, and one can become overwhelmed with veneration for the greatness of the Abbot."

"I nearly got lost walking straight down the corridor to get here," I joke and continue, "Abbot Nicolas seems very wise indeed."

"He is truly a great man, my child." My mentor nods somberly, "he manages the monastery along strict, but sensible rules, while maintaining contact with the outside world in a diplomatic capacity."

"You said we mustn't gossip, but are the dignitaries the Princess Liang Na and her party?" Seeing my friend and my sister so soon would be an unexpected boon, but he grins knowingly and shakes his head.

"The Princess, no," he goes on, "but the Emperor is receiving the military ruler of Chaldia as an official guest here at the abbey before sealing their agreement in a fortnight. You will see her and your sister in a few weeks at the Hagia Sophia."

"Are Byzantine politics always so confusing?" Lethargy is setting in from the good food, and my exhausted mind grinds to a halt before entering the complex web of government intrigue.

"It does seem so," he chuckles, "which is what makes this oasis such a wonder. The days are productive and ordered, the setting on the rocks overlooking the sea, the ease of administration of these hundreds of souls is amazing!"

"So you like it here?" I conclude from the approval shining from his aspect.

"I do indeed, my child," he determines, "tis a holy place."

Through the rest of the quiet evening, alone in my cell and into the morning, I carry my wise friend's opinion and see the monastery through God's eyes of favor. Brother Samuel is right again in his assessment, which is affirmed by the smooth mechanics of the great abbey's operation, much like the engineered flow of water through the baths. We break our fast and progress through services and the midday meal without the slightest notion of the revelries taking place on the other side of the cloisters for our distinguished guests.

In the choir room, we are giddy when presented with new robes for our audience with the emperor. The brown, tattered tunics that we had worn throughout our journey from the north would offend the royal guests to say the least. Garbed in gleaming white and black, I try not to twist and turn in feminine delight over the supple linen as we warm up our voices. When the time is upon us to file into the cathedral, my girlish pleasure yields to fluttering anticipation of seeing the Emperor Basil, and I adjust my new hood in the dimness of the chapel in hopes of getting a glimpse of him as he walks in, whilst maintaining my anonymity.

The resident monks have the honor of performing first and they rise to their feet, their chanting filling the cathedral to greet the emperor and his guests. There is a murmur and stirring amongst our youthful ranks as we shift and crane our necks in effort to get a better view of the spectacle promenading by an arm's length away. To our frustration, we glimpse only fleeting impressions of flashing jewels and vibrant robes in the gaps of the ranks of elder monks in front of us.

When we are finally instructed to stand, the emperor is seated in a throne facing Abbot Nicolas and the altar, with his governor seated to his right, and Bishop Stephen to his left. All we can see through the cloud of incense are the backs of their heads, the Emperor's encircled by his gem encrusted crown, the Chaldian ruler capped in a white head wrap with a gold circlet holding it in place. Brother Samuel garners our full attention, counting us into our hymn, and the knots in my stomach untangle as soon as I open my mouth.

The glory of the music we create brings tears to my eyes, blotting out everything but the beauty of song stretching into every corner. Sonorous melody twines around the sacred statues and soars up into the gilded domes. As the last chord intones off the granite pillars and warbles down to the travertine marble flagstones, there is a reverent pause while the magic of the hymn sinks into the pious souls of the emperor and his entourage.

"Beautiful," I strain to hear the compliment from the emperor.

"Beautiful!" He repeats, his forceful voice gaining wonder. He surges from his throne and addresses our group of humble novices. Like me, his ruddy cheeks are wet and the light shining in his visage is ethereal. He throws his arms wide and roars his approval.

"Beautiful!" His commanding cry sparks an eruption of shouts and applause, and I feel my heart near bursting as I take in the awestruck Abbot and glowing Bishop. Next to the Emperor, the foreigner unfolds from his seat and turns as well to give homage to our choir. The grace of this simple movement, the tall, slim frame as he squares his broad shoulders, the spicy hue of his hands as he claps, and the world grinds to a halt.

I'm frozen in place, unable to move, unable to breath, only aware of my heartbeat pounding in my chest. The eyes, heavily fringed in long, curling lashes, are molten with genuine appreciation. The proud jaw and sloping forehead are as smooth and bold as I remember. His smiling mouth takes me back to the soft insistence of his lips on mine, and I thankfully succumb to the darkness that creeps over my awareness.

Chapter 11

The lantern's gentle glow permeates my murky consciousness. The light expands to encompass the desk, the bed, until I recognize the surroundings of my cell.

"Thank God," I pray in my head, "twas a dream I had."

Anxiety over the upcoming performance must have given me a spectacular fantasy, leaving me with a spinning head, as if I drank strong ale. I prop up from lying on my pallet and shake my head at the vivid detail of Majidi's black eyes and sensuous lips. Taking a few deep breaths to clear my head, I look around my room, trying to piece together when I fell asleep. It must have been the unaccustomed heaviness of the stew I ate at midday that made me sleep so hard.

Suddenly the thought strikes me that it is dark outside, and I jump up, ignoring the swimming in my head. I must have slept through the performance! I stagger to the door, crying out in fright when a shadow materializes from the corner to catch me.

"You must not get up so quick!" The chimera admonishes.

"I've missed the performance!" I bat away the supporting arms while the dizziness encroaches.

"Oh my child," the words are curiously laced with humor, "you are truly addled!"

I pause in my struggling, perplexed. Amusement shines from the wrinkled visage that grins up at me, and I trustingly sit down at the small monk's bidding. Something in the aged, dusky features and wiry gray fringe of hair ringing a bald scalp puts me at ease, and I forget to pull on my hood.

"I'm known as Brother Constantius, but you may call me Constance. You don't remember falling?"

"Not really Brother Constantius, I must have fallen asleep after we ate." There is a comical air about the stout monk invading my personal space so that I can see white hairs sprouting randomly on the fleshy chin.

"Constance," my new friend corrects me, squinting into my face so that I sit back, realizing I'm exposed to perusal. "Forgive my intrusion child, I tend to all of the sick brethren, and I've left my spectacles in the infirmary."

"But Brother Constance," I redress, my sense of disquiet growing, "I'm not sick, I must have just eaten too much and I'm not used to the rich fare, so I fell asleep and failed to wake for the performance."

"Just Constance please." Arms akimbo, in a posture that my mother used to assume when she was about to lecture me, this whimsical being proceeds to explain that I did indeed perform exquisitely, but upon seeing the great Basiliscus I was overcome and fainted in the choir.

"So after the ceremony, they carried you back here and bid me to attend to you. I'm sorry that they left you on the floor for so long, but you must understand that we couldn't disrupt the diplomatic proceedings."

"God save me." It wasn't a dream. The enigmatic man I met in the forest had indeed reappeared before me, garbed in silks and adorned in precious metals.

"Yes, you've had a bit of a shock," through sheer effort, I concentrate on what Constance is saying, "but God has saved you! Now, why don't you tell me what's really going on?"

I'm dumbfounded by the direct question, dread holding my tongue hostage as I muster my wits to reply. My thoughts turn sharply from the riddle of Majidi being here, alongside the emperor, to how this intrepid monk could possibly have known of my association with the Stratagos of Chaldia.

"Brother Constance, I don't understand..." I mumble, stalling for time.

"Constance, my Daughter, just Constance."

"Excuse me?" Did Constance just call me daughter? Lord don't let me pass out again.

"Yes Daughter, what is your real name?" The open smile radiates understanding and sympathy, washing away all fear and confusion.

"Adila." I shiver at the joy of verbalizing my name. "How did you know?"

"You smell of blood." I gasp in shock, not realizing that others could smell my mensus. It is always a particular challenge to rinse out the rags thoroughly enough, especially so when I'm not able to have privacy for long stretches of time. "Don't be alarmed, Adila. I'm a medic, sensitive to the odor, where others detect nothing."

"I know how difficult it is to conceal your female nature, and I can help you. When you menstruate, come to me at the infirmary and I'll give you fresh bindings."

"You won't tell anyone?" Wondrous disbelief punctuates my query.

"Nay, to the contrary, I will protect you. Just like the others."

"Thank you," I release my pent up breath in relief, then the rest of the monk's promise penetrates my sluggish brain. "What did you say... the others?"

"There are a few more of us women here at the monastery." Constance happily takes a seat on my pallet, while I choke on the revelation that there are others like me.

"Us?" My mind lingers on the pronoun.

"Yes...Us. You are bright!" The proud motherly grin interrupts my whirling thoughts. "If it weren't for your angelic singing I would request your services in the hospital."

"Thank you," I smile back freely, the magnetic optimism is infectious. "Are you are a woman too?"

"Yes," she affirms, "and No. I'm sort of both, I like to call myself Hermaphrodite, man and woman together."

"You're a pagan?" My ease dampening at the prospect of the evil one at work in this sacred house.

"Oh dear no!" She laughs, "I've known nothing but the Christian Church all of my life, but I can see why the reference to the Greek God would confuse you. I have been accused of intellectualizing my faith, because I ask too many questions and pry into the mysteries of our religion, but my belief in one God is strong." She goes on to explain that Hermaphrodite refers to how she was born with both male and female genitalia. As she expounds upon her search to identify with one sex or the other, I empathize with her plight, pitying her painful childhood.

"What brings you to hide within the robes of the order Adila?" Her matter of fact personality holds no judgment against herself or me. It is the first time anyone has asked me thus, even I have never contemplated it myself, I've merely gone along with it.

"My father wanted a son, so he made me into a boy." My throat constricts around the memories called forth by my speech. The abuse and insults victimize me anew as I describe how he made me talk, walk and behave like a male. Then my spirit softens as I reminisce over when I first fell in love with God. Constance nods her head wisely as if she understands the solace I experience when I let myself trust in his grace. I summarize my tale by recounting how Brother Samuel took me in because of my gift of music, and brought me with him to sing in the great choir.

"What an amazing story!" She exclaims appreciatively, "you've been very blessed to have found God, and enjoyed the freedom of traveling the countryside to come into this haven."

"I know, but I get so afraid and frustrated always having to conceal who I really am." I'm so caught up in my sadness that I miss her message.

"Everyone has hardships my dear, that's how we learn and grow. You're no different in that respect. Our troubles are of a more unique nature, that's all." She spoke kindly, but I'm ashamed nonetheless by my complaining.

"What about you Constance?" I try to thwart my selfishness by taking interest in her, "how did you come to be here?"

Without a trace of self pity, she details how, due to her deformity, her Greek parents abandoned her on the steps of the Kassian Convent, here in Constantinople. The good nuns raised and educated her, until in her teenage years she started yearning for female flesh as her masculine traits grew stronger. There was a scandal with a novice, who's parents were prominent citizens, and they secreted her to the monastery where she has remained ever since.

"But don't worry daughter, I'm much too old and wise to take carnal interest in anything but my dinner meat!" She concludes, chortling at her own joke. I shake my head in admiration of her spirit.

"I'm humbled by your morale," that this extraordinary being could overcome such burdens and find happiness, puts my adversity in perspective.

"We don't get to chose our lot in life," she sobers, "but what we can do is ask God what his purpose is in our creation, and how we can serve him with the talents we're given. This curiosity of my body has blessed me with intimate knowledge of the anatomy of both sexes, which I have used to help both male and female."

"Thank you for sharing yourself with me Constance," I'm touched with supreme gratitude that I would discover female companionship in the most unlikely of places, "but how did you deal with the carnal urges?"

"I prayed a lot for God to help me do the right thing, which was not always what the church deems proper." She winks, her habitual smile returning, "and I turned my thoughts to helping others, which has been far more fulfilling."

"Now," she stood up bristling with efficiency, "I think you're feeling stronger, so I'll send up some dinner and you rest. Come see me in the morning and I'll give you those bindings."

Hours later, after finishing my food and Constance's lingering optimism has dimmed, I process the monumental events of the day. The Emperor Basil, the Stratagos Majidi, the Hermaphrodite Constance, such magnificent titles, yet real people dance circles around my head. The tears glistening on Basil's cheeks, a gaping gash in Majidi's ribs, male and female parts under Constance's robe, impress into my soul, that I'm not the only one who has human vulnerability. I pace the flagstones in my cell, digesting their reality, just like mine, disguised by robes. The only difference is, theirs are of silk and gold, and mine are of wool and linen.

In spite of the high ceiling and window, my cell seems stuffy, and the desire to air my thoughts urges me to poke my head out into the corridor. It is after Apodipnon Service, so all of the monks are abed for the night, a single lantern casting its wan flame into the inky hallway. Instead of going right, past the dormitory, I feel along the stone wall to the left, which gives way to an alcove just outside of my room. The lantern light refuses to extend around the corner, and I nearly trip onto the first cobbled step carved into the wall shared with my cell. Shuffling gingerly deeper into the niche, I identify the sloping ceiling above my pallet is this staircase.

My heart, already full from the emotional day, beats against my chest as I ascend into the gloom. After what must be two score steps, I relish the physical exertion, but I'm starting to wonder how far this will go on. As

I'm contemplating climbing my way to heaven, a wisp of fresh air tickles my cheek, cajoling me upward.

The whistle of wind and clapping of waves applaud my effort when I reach the end of the tunnel, rewarding me with a breathtaking view of the night sky and Propontis several stories below. I advance out of the arched doorway and onto brick ramparts that cap the perimeter of the monastery.

A briny breeze instantly clears my mind of its heavy thoughts, opening my awareness to ponder constellations glistening beyond the layer of clouds that shroud the city. The rhythm of the surf washes my soul of all afflictions, widening my heart to receive its aqueous harmony. Up here, separated from human complexities, the strength of God's presence is palpable, loosening my tightly wound insides with the soothing sounds of nature.

"Thank you God," I inhale deeply of his peace.

"You need this time alone with me," a gust whines through the crenelations, "seek me here in this quiet retreat."

"I need your guidance Lord," I petition, "I can't make sense of why Majidi is here. What does this mean?"

"I put people in your life for a purpose." His rumbling sea reminds me.

"But he is a great man," I argue, "and I am an ordinary child."

"I have put great love in your heart," God's breath caresses my cheek, "extraordinary love that stretches beyond the boundaries of our bodies and limitations of our minds."

"So that's why I love him still," I marvel, "in spite of how different we are, and how angry I should be to discover who he really is."

"He is who I revealed him to be when you first new him." Gentle wisps lift the curls from the back of my neck, refreshing my recollection of the vulnerable man I met in the forest. That man was strong yet tender, intelligent yet willing to learn, full of humor yet serious in his commitment. Does it really matter what other people have titled him? My tangled thoughts uncoiling, I take in the crescent luminance of the moon one last time then duck into the darkness of the staircase.

My slumber is light, allowing me to answer the peal of the bell for matins. The steady routine of the monastery is a soothing balm to the rash of fear that threatens to spread when I dwell on yesterday's turmoil. Brother Samuel and the others regard me with a mix of concern and disapproval for causing a stir during the ceremony, but as the day progresses everyone seems to forget and get on with their business.

The choir members are given the day to rest from our singing duties, permitting us to wander silently among the monks in the sunlit cloisters. There's a group of a dozen or so sitting around the large fountain in the center of the courtyard meditating, and I join them for a spell, but I'm unable to corral my drifting thoughts to focus on breathing. Savoring the splashing music of the water in the marble basin, I meander about the garden peeking into the shed to watch the monks experiment with pollinating different plants. Their labor of love shines in their faces as they handle the flowers as if they were their own infant children, and I admire the purposeful industry of the quietly bustling yard.

My roving footsteps take me to the row of scribes and illuminators sitting at their desks, taking advantage of the late morning sun to work on their craft. I surreptitiously glance over the manuscripts, appreciating the vivid colors illuminating the parchment and the skilled copying and translating filling the pages. One of the monks in particular captivates my interest, for his tonsured head is as brown as a hazelnut, the wreath of tight curls silky black as a raven's wing. Sensing my perusal, he peers at me over his shoulder, his coal eyes probing past the shroud of my hood, giving me the distinct impression that he can see through my disguise.

Before I make things uncomfortable, staring at the sharp bones of his ebony cheeks and jaw, a stout form interrupts my sightline. Constance's bespectacled countenance grins up at me as she nods and gestures for me to follow her, tacitly reminding me about my visit to the infirmary. She bestows a meaningful look upon the remarkable scribe, passing her spectacles to the monk, who perches the lenses on his wide nose and surveys me from the hem of my tunic to the tip of my cowl. He nods enigmatically and returns to his lettering.

Pondering their curious exchange, I follow Constance through the twists and turns of corridors and portals until we reach the bleached sterility of the infirmary.

Calling out a blessing here and encouragement there, the motherly monk leads me down the center walkway between rows of cots and into a room in the back that is stacked floor to ceiling with supplies.

"Everything is so orderly," here in Constance's domain the efficient management of the monastery is at its peak. She hands me a pile of spotless bandages and swatches of wool, then bustles me into a separate closet for some privacy.

"Just drop the soiled clothes in the wash basin and join me next door in my office." In her realm, her manner is even more cheerfully businesslike, and I follow her instructions to find her seated behind her desk scratching ink on a piece of parchment.

"Thank you," I express when she finishes her note, sands the ink and places the parchment in an unbound book. "I haven't felt so fresh in months!"

"I'll schedule you for a visit to the bath for next week when you're done with your courses." Heat infuses my face at her casual references to my unclean state, and I cast around for a diversion.

"Do you know the scribe who was looking at me?" My naivety elicits a chuckle from her portly belly.

"I know them all! Each and every one of them has been through my care at some point, and I remember them all because I record their ailments, and how they resolved in my medical book here." She shows me the page containing yesterday's date and her impressions of my condition:

"Brother Adilsen, age ten and four, fainted in ceremony celebrating the Emperor's guest the Strategos of Chaldia. Pallor and verbal diagnosis is low blood levels, compounded by overwhelming awe upon seeing Emperor Basil. Condition resolved with rest and food."

"As for the scribe," she shuffles the parchment back in place and closes the cover, "Dominic suffers from the same condition as Us."

"Brother Dominic is a woman?" I hiss, incredulous that the first two "Brethren" I encounter here are not even men. I envision the lofty cheekbones and prominent jaw framed by a full compliment of jet curls, picturing her clearly as a striking woman.

"How came she here?"

"Her's is an extraordinary tale," she settles back in her chair, eager to enlighten me. "She came from Africa, where the sun burns so fiercely that it laps up all of the water so no greenery can survive, or so she tells me. When she was very young, she evaded the slave traders by hiding amongst the robes at St. Anthony's Monastery in Egypt. There, she spent her early adulthood learning the art of translating ancient languages into Greek and scribing new codices out of the old."

"I have heard about this monastery, the Bishop Stephen told of how it housed thousands upon thousands of the most treasured tomes in Christendom." I recall, "but he said they've come under much persecution of late."

"Yes, which is why our friend escaped with a treasure of scrolls and manuscripts hidden under her tunic!" She rocked back, holding her heaving sides in mirth at my shocked reaction. Then she waved a hand, "her journey as a stowaway on a greek fishing vessel is a story for another time, but needless to say she boldly walked up to the doors of our venerable abbey and requested audience with Abbot Nicolas. As compensation for taking her in, she presented the monastery with her priceless parchments, along with the most astonishing piece of them all." Here, Constance paused and peered at me across her desk, all frivolity fleeing under the reverence of her next words. "She brought with her a fragment of papyrus containing the hand of the Apostle John, a most sacred text from his Gospel of the life of Jesus Christ."

The gravity of such an amazing artifact descended upon the room, dampening our levity under its solemn significance. With such a fortune in her possession, she could have bought her freedom anywhere. I praise God for bringing her here and preserving his word through her gift. Constance bobs her head as if in agreement with my prayer.

"She chose St. John of Studius because she heard of our renown piety, our dedication to translating christian texts, and our famed Father Abbot. With her mastery of several ancient languages, she told me that here she knew she would be appreciated, and be able to continue her craft, though she had to sacrifice her femininity to do so."

"Brother Constantius?" A call from the doorway interrupts the surreal culmination of her incredible account. Brother Samuel hesitates to enter until Constance gestures him forward.

"Come in, Come in Brother Samuel," her jovial demeanor returns, "I've been anticipating meeting you, especially after your heavenly performance yesterday!"

"I'm not sure of speech protocol in the infirmary," he relaxed, "but when I saw you leave the cloisters I wanted to catch you and inquire after Brother Adilsen."

"I could not give proper diagnosis without being able to touch or speak to my patients, so I praise the common sense of our good Abbot for loosening the rules within these walls."

"You gave us a bit of a fright yesterday, child," he addresses me in begrudging concern, then to Constance, "is everything well?"

"Aye, just overcome with awe I surmise." The efficient doctor pronounces, "but the youth must have meat each week to keep the blood thick."

"Hmmmm, is this a cure perhaps for a penchant for creating drama?" Samuel chides good-naturedly, "the child has a knack for garnering attention."

"That's right!" Constance's laugh fills the chamber, "twas you who Father Abbot singled out for covering your head in chapter!"

"Tis not my intent to attract notice," my dour tone was lost on them.

"Well, we must take measures to remedy that, so after your bath, when you're ready, come to me for tonsure." Her attempt to help fails to improve my mood, yet I incline my head submissively. "And you too Brother Samuel! I'll give you both a sliver of soap to wash your hair, then stop by and I'll trim you properly."

"What a good natured fellow the doctor is!" Samuel exclaims, walking back through the labyrinth of the monastery, "you seem to be making fast friends here, I saw you interacting with the scribe."

"Yes, that's who we were talking about when you came," I'm careful not to gossip, "I asked about Brother Dominic ere I offend such a singular person."

"Tis well that you did, the Father Abbot tells me Brother Dominic is our best scribe, tremendously gifted in translating ancient texts to Greek." The ponderous tolling of the bells guides our footsteps to the cathedral for afternoon service Enati Ora. We're the first ones to arrive, allowing us time for a last whispered exchange. "I am concerned about you being able to sing at the Hagia Sophia in a fortnight. If you become overawed again, your solo is just too vital..."

"I'll be ready Brother Samuel," I respond with conviction, ashamed at my weakness. I absorb the next hour of divine service thirsty for God's strength to fortify me in these self-induced strenuous situations.

After dinner, I'm back in my room lying on my pallet, bombarded with retrospection of the developments from these monumental few days. Staring up at the slanted ceiling, I contemplate the staircase on the other side, the urge to make the climb again prods me out of my room and into the ascending darkness. This time, I proceed with more surety, accessing the ramparts breathless from the exercise.

The fiery sun sinks beyond the Propontis, casting its resplendent rays over the sea as golden paint spilt over the water. Agog at the brilliant masterpiece, I gaze across the shimmering waves dotted with fisherman's boats paddling into harbor for the night. One moored vessel in particular arouses a memory of a similar single-sailed ship far out on the Euxine Sea as I loped along its coast, yearning for love lost.

"Majidi," was it God's voice again carrying his name on a waft of salty air? A shadowy form emerges on the pier jutting out from under the monastery walls into the sea. A tall, slender robed figure, raises a long limb to acknowledge the captain on board who called out his name again.

"Aye Tarik," I nearly fall over the parapet, my ears reaching to hear the bass of his voice resonate from below. The dreamlike occurrences of these past days sharpen into reality, the pining, the pain and the panic piercing through me like a thousand pikes. The echo of their conversation transfixes me, lulling me into a reverie, as if I'm hearing my maman's crooning. Long after Majidi retreats to the abbey, I'm still tingling with his lingering presence.

"In this house you will find answers," the whispered words draw me out of my rapture, I probe the growing dimness for the speaker. Then I catch sight of the crescent moon hanging beyond the shifting clouds, and I realize it is my heavenly father's voice, as I'm by myself on the ramparts.

"Why is everything so complicated and difficult?" It seems that every time I feel that I've arrived at a new place of rest, something invariably arises to keep me in chaos. Even in my logic; I had come to terms with my love for Majidi. My time in the forest with him, I had reconciled, is to be a warm memory, comforting me through the lonely, cold nights ahead. With his reappearance, however, those emotions that I had neatly sealed away in a jar, to be taken down and looked at when I wanted, now thrust me from cool comfort to heated passion. So, insides quaking with desire for his touch, I wonder why my existence can't be one of simplicity and serenity.

"Find rest in me," the mystical brightness of the moon winks in assurance, "knowing that I put hardship in your life to prepare you for greatness, but I will also give you what you need to endure."

"Like Samuel, Constance and Dominic," I muse, "I can learn from them and they will help guide me."

Pondering the people in my life, I feel a rush of gratitude for my sister, Nicolo, Brother Samuel, and those who have been there to walk beside me through this journey. Awareness bubbles from my soul that God placed Majidi in my path for some purpose, and to stay receptive to my instincts. Holding to that intuition, I seek my bed and sleep, dreams of his naked body next to me heating my slumber.

Chapter 12

Days pass, knowledge of Majidi's presence in the forbidden rooms beyond the kitchen weighing on my psyche. I heed Constance's advice and petition God to ease the torment of desire, which works until I'm alone in my cell at night, remembering his exquisite features and rocklike frame. These moments drive me to ascend the hidden staircase into the night sky, seeking the tranquility of nature's symphony.

Thor's Day has come around again, marking a full week since I embraced my sister and sequestered myself within the abbey. Chuckling at the irony of celebrating a norse deity here in the house of God, I harken to Maman's wisdom that most everyone believes in God, we just call him by different names. Forever steady, forever strong, from her I learned to love like a slow burning candle, gentle and constant. Though I miss her ethereal aspect, I sense her aura as I appreciate the regularity of the stars lining up in formation across the heavens. I envision Majidi's graceful hand pointing to the constellation in the north sky, and know that my maman is there, as always.

"It is as God wills Adila," I hear her singsong adage in the coo of a nesting pigeon, and I know it to be true now, as it was when I was a babe curled up at her side. I sit with my back resting on the parapet, imagining the clouds are her breath condensing in the frigid air as she warbles an ancient lullaby. Losing myself in the tale, my voice raises with hers into the twilight, our duet drifting up to the cosmos.

Our lilting words waft across the star sparkled darkness above me, evoking an image of a spirited child, filled with hope and promise, and I see myself dancing across the sky in pursuit of the moon. Not even the commotion of the week can penetrate the mystical vision, as the heavenly bodies seem to form a pathway transporting me from sitting upon the unforgiving stones, into a realm of joy.

As I cross into a dreamlike state, the once bright moon fades behind the nebulous curtain of this unfamiliar atmosphere behind which I'm hiding. The ethereal aura that lit my path, retreats deep inside of me, only to be heard in song, only to be seen by faith. No longer able to perceive my mother's melodious words, life becomes uncertain and full of mystery. I follow along through the monastery grounds, seeking to break through the facade of fear holding me hostage, but I know that I can always find solace if I retreat into this core of light, certain that one day it will return to illuminate my destiny.

A booted foot prods at my leg, summoning me to alertness. I squint, lifting my hand to shield against the brightness outlining the silhouette standing in front of me.

"I'm up Father!" I start at my sire's prodding, then rub some sense back into my eyes. With every movement, my muscles scream from the abuse of lying on the hard stones, bringing me to full attention that I must have fallen asleep on the ground. Affixing the hovering shade with cautious regard, I stiffly find my feet and adjust my hood so that the reticent figure doesn't have the advantage of seeing my face while I can't see his.

"No need," the husky tone stays my hand, and then my interest when the monk steps out of the line of the glaring sunrise so that I take in the sharp ebony features of the scribe Dominic.

"Brother Dominic, I..." I what? I know your secret?

"You may call me Dominic," she picks up a portable desk that she must have brought and loops the thick leather strap around her neck. "I come here many mornings when the sun is bright to work, though Father Abbot has granted me special permission."

"Yes...Dominic, ahem..." I stutter, unable to pull my wits together.

"Why are you here?" She continues arranging her ink blotter and quill.

"Well I, ah," why am I so intimidated by her forthright questions? "...needed some air and found the staircase. I must have fallen asleep, tis so serene."

"Not why are you up here on the ramparts, I find inspiration in the

111

fresh air too," she pulls out a sheet of parchment and secures it in place, then traps me with her probing gaze. "Why are you, a young woman, here at this monastery?"

All anxiety flees, deflating my mettle like a sail without a breeze, and I lean back against the parapet and summarize my saga. Unlike the tragedy I recounted to Constance, that same past becomes dotted with vivid examples of God's favor. It seems the more I tell my story, the less dismal it appears, and the more I look for the positive aspects of my upbringing. Her level attention never waivers, as I conclude with a statement of gratitude for her confidence.

"When I saw you with Constance in the cloisters, I knew you were one of us," her grave mien returns to her labor, "I assume she told you how I came here?"

"Yes, she did, you're remarkably brave!" I applaud.

"God grants us each the degree of courage we need to get through the day," she staunchly deflects my admiration, "we must strive for humility in all things."

The peal of bells calls our attention to the hour, and I leave my new friend to her labor and hie down to join the procession into the cathedral for Proti Ora. My body aches from sleeping on the hard surface, and though I'm tired and sore, my spirits are high with the reminder that God will get me through the day.

The next few days pass with regularity, routine and rehearsals in preparation of our appearance at the great cathedral. In Chapter, Abbot Nicolas stresses the importance of decorum and cleanliness in the Hagia Sophia. Our heads must be bowed and covered at all times, as the largest church in christendom will be crowded with citizens wanting to see the Emperor Basil. We are to secure time at the bath and launder our garments before we make the trek on Sunday morning. Mindful of my personal challenge to maintain my composure around Majidi, I seek God's voice every chance I have.

One such opportunity I take to sigh praises, is my first experience of going to the bath. The monks are very rigid in upholding the privacy of those using the bath, as in other establishments it is often a corrupt place. Therefore, as I luxuriate in the steamy water, I can give myself completely to my female senses, all but singing in my pleasure of the moment. The trickle of the spillover is like delicate crystals tumbling into the pool, the dancing flames in the wall sconces bouncing off gleaming white tiles.

I scrub my hair with a sliver of soap that Constantine slipped into my freshly laundered robe, and rub my skin until I'm pink as a newborn. I absorb the heat into my very bones until my skin puckers and the last grain of sand runs through the hourglass, marking the end of my bath.

By the time I don my short, under tunic, robe and cowl, my brow is glistening with perspiration. Not wanting to spoil my cleanliness with sweat, I bypass my cell and seek the refreshing breeze atop the monastery.

Filling my lungs with the mild evening air, I bask in contentment, my mood as light as my curling tresses drying freely in the wind.

"Please God," I pray, "help me to keep this feeling through the day tomorrow. Give me strength to face him again."

"If you stay focused on me," God's breath sifts through my honeyed locks, caressing the nape of my neck with tranquility, "you'll see him as the gift I have sent to you, not a source of worry."

"Your ways are indeed mysterious, Lord," I ponder, "this man is a non-believer, he is the ruler of a great nation, and he has multiple wives and concubines! Yet you've put this tenderness for him in my hard heart."

"You need him as he needs you." His whispered response wafts through my ears as I seek my pallet and drift into fitful slumber.

Subdued excitement permeates the rectory as we break our fast, remaining with us through Terce, intensifying as we form parallel lines in the cloisters and burst forth into the morning freshness. We file out of the monastery onto the Via Triumphalis that takes us through the city, ending at the Hagia Sophia. Like a gaggle of white pigeons with black hoods strutting along the pavers, we twitch and cluck, unable to suppress our enthusiasm.

In the dull wintery light of late morning, the city gleams in rich majesty. I envision great Roman generals over the centuries, parading in victory, carrying spoils of war from far reaches of the empire to the great palace. With several leagues of walking ahead of us, we can already see our destination, the pointed spires and round domes of the Hagia Sophia. We march along the main thoroughfare and under the crumbling ancient wall of Constantine, leaving behind the more humble structures of indigenous sandstone bricks. As we pass sprawling villas and grand, multi-storied city residences, the dichotomy unfolds before us: decaying forums from bygone dynasties, and newly- constructed, columned public buildings.

The urge to gawk becomes too much for those of us from the barren plateaus of northern tundra. Try as I might to fix my gaze on the hem of Brother Samuel in front of me, a few murmurs of awe slip out when I glimpse the grandeur of the vast city. The Via Triumphalis spills into the Mese, a huge rotunda encircled in a creamy marble colonnade. The plaza is a cistern of churning humanity, loud colors adding to the cheerful chatter of pedestrians on their way to the ceremony. Though they jostle one another, they maintain a respectful distance from our order, softly calling out for the monks to bless them or a loved one.

Laughter and singing tickle the musician inside of me, eliciting a smile within the confines of my cowl at the merry piety flowing through the crowd. My ears discern a pair of philosophers engaged good-natured intellectual banter, from a loving mother calling her child to stay close, and a deep bass striking up a ditty. Vendors hawk their wares, and guards bluster unnecessarily to maintain order.

Whether it is the mild, late morning sun, the buoyant citizens, or the pace of the walk, a warm contentment settles over me. Somewhere nearby, a child starts to sing an elementary hymn. Propriety melts under the spell of her sweet voice, and I join her song, losing awareness of all but the joy of melodious expression. The power of the psalm ripples outward, and soon the street is alive in chorus. One hymn after another, our praises pour into the square outside the Hagia Sophia. At which point awe strikes me dumb in the propinquity of the enormous cathedral.

The colossal structure is the single most impressive wonder I've ever beheld. Unmindful of the disapproving grunts of our elders to keep our heads down, I tilt mine back to take in the towering walls, capped in golden domes and spiked with conical spires. If not for the press of the crowd moving us toward the cathedral doors, I would be paralyzed in awe that human hands could manufacture such a spectacle.

My limbs continue their dysfunction as we advance through the archway, and I trip over the marble threshold and fall against Brother Samuel. A sharp elbow in the stomach brings me out of my stupor, reminding me of my purpose in this holy place. Inhaling potent incense, I drink in the divine atmosphere created by the sun's rays highlighting the altar, absorbing God's presence into my soul. Tears of veneration moisten my face, as they tend do whenever I perceive God's majesty.

"I am ready God." Calmness eclipses excitement, bowing my head in reverence. Not even the smooth hand that slips into mine as we advance towards the apse shakes my holy confidence. Glancing to the side at my sister's petite frame, I hazard a watery smile, her face more beautiful than I remember. Her fingers tighten around mine, fortifying my spirit, and I hold onto her as long as I can until we reach our choir box. With one last glimpse, she slides a roll of parchment up my sleeve and disappears into the masses. I pocket the note and take my place, training my attention on the proceedings.

At least an hour passes while we wait for the citizens to come to order, the foreign dignitaries to parade in, and the Emperor and royal party to regale the public with their deliberate promenade. Brother Samuel affixes me with a warning, and I nod back in assurance that I won't cause a scene.

Outside the cathedral, trumpets blare to announce the arrival of the betrothal party, a hushed murmur falls over the congregation. Anticipation tingles as the director's wand whips through the air, counting us into the hymn. Our triumphant voices burst forth in the sublime ecstasy of glorifying God's presence in this sacred monument. Melodious praise echoes throughout the domed apse, soaring over the heads of the multitudes, reverberating back to urge my soul to release the fullness of my gift.

By the time Majidi assumes his position at the altar, I'm so deeply enchanted by the magic of music, that I fail to mind him standing directly across from me. Brother Samuel shifts towards me, indicating my solo, and I train my gaze on the spectacular bejeweled cross suspended above the altar, alight with the aura of the almighty.

The aria flows from the depths of my being, reaching out to caress the symbol of our lord in profound adoration. Joyous emotion saturates each syllable, carrying supernatural love to rain over the throng.

When the Chinese Princess reaches the altar, the entire choir crescendos into a glorious finale, punctuated by deafening applause. Through the thunderous acclaim, my hooded regard alights on Majidi, and I hear the noise as if through a tunnel. His ebony stare is penetrating the protection of my cowl, searching to match my face with the familiarity of my voice.

The remainder of the ceremony is a blur of color, chanting and diplomatic pomp. I cling to the image of the cross lest I drown in the sea of fog that encroaches each time my gaze drifts to meet Majidi's probing eyes. I even attempt to divert my thoughts to prayer for him and my friend, but I cannot find Liang Na under the layers of ceremonial robes, veils and painted mask that she's wearing. Their binding kiss, sealing the bond between them, delivers a blow to my gut that nearly knocks me out. But as I raise my eyes to the brilliant cross in supplication, I notice the agony in Majidi's expression, which snaps me out of my own suffering.

Highlighted by the rays of sun shining through openings in the gilded dome, it is as if God is revealing to me Majidi's truth, twisting his beautiful features into an ugly grimace of self loathing, as he kisses the child who is to become another of his wives. In the wilderness, I had cried out my anguish to him over my inability to make my own choices, and he had listened with only words of understanding and concern. He spoke in cold terms of politics and customs, but never of his own inanimate role and impotence. Seeing him now, standing erect next to his bride who is not of his choosing, I begin to comprehend the purpose of the handsome Stratagos in my life. So powerful, yet powerless; ruler of a country, yet imprisoned by its traditions; his beautiful aspect a cover for a suffering heart.

It seems an eternity ere the Patriarch seals the betrothal and witnesses the signing of treaties. In the din of the recession, I am an oasis of tranquility, my enlightenment of why God put Majidi in my path casting new perspective on how self centered I have been. In this sacred church, I vow to fear less what each day brings, and anticipate the possibilities that lie ahead.

This joy of discovery is short lived. As tired and hungry as we are when we get back to the monastery, Abbot Nicolas leads us past the rectory and into the chapter house. I dutifully string in with the rest, assuming he wants to congratulate us on our performance. My curiosity piques, however, as he studies us for long moments before opening the meeting.

"Brothers, I commend you on a spectacular display of God's gifts. Our order is glorified by your work today." His comments are gravely humble, typical of his leadership.

"I am troubled, however, by the events that took place on route to the Hagia Sophia." He pauses, his stern perusal sweeping the room. "Our rules may seem stringent, but they have been the foundation of the Studite Order, and our strict adherence to them is a matter of survival. You were counseled on your decorum, and because there were those of us who were gawking around and twisting and turning heads, we will all forego our dinner this evening."

Around the ranks, tonsured pates droop between sagging shoulders. As one of the perpetrators, I'm distressed at having disappointed the abbot, and for bringing punishment on my brothers.

"Furthermore," he continues, "you are all well aware that we are forbidden to interact with the public, which includes singing along with them. Brother Samuel, I understand it was your novice who broke his vow of silence?"

"Father Abbot," my stomach jumps at my friend's weary tone, "I beg for mercy for Brother Adilsen, he has a penchant to be disruptive."

"God save me!" My oldest advocate has finally betrayed me. Surely they will throw me out of the abbey.

"I did not ask you to judge him Brother," Abbot Nicolas admonishes, "jealousy is unbecoming in a monk."

"Oh nay Father Abbot!" The error of his statement shoots me up from my seat before my reasoning can hold me steady. "Brother Samuel would never be jealous of anyone! He is the most kind and caring person I've ever known."

Silence hangs in the air as my impassioned plea fades, and the folly of my outburst sinks into my thick skull. My mentor and the abbot exchange a meaningful look, Brother Samuel holding up his hands, palms up in a conciliatory gesture. As I realize that I've just proven his case for him, a rumbling wheezing sound swells into the chamber. Chuckles shake the ranks of the elder monks, and snickers break out amongst the novices, Brother Samuel is grinning from ear to ear. The dignified, distinguished Abbot Nicolas tips back his head and laughs, the room full of humor.

"Ah! Tis so, tis so Brother Samuel," he hoots, "Brother Adilsen has made your point splendidly."

"Perhaps my wrongdoing lies in my doting protectiveness over the child, Father Abbot. He has not learned the consequences of his impetuous nature."

"Our lord is a faithful teacher, if we allow him. Sometimes it means that we are uncomfortable with how he uses our children to teach us as well." He considers his next statement carefully. "Our young ones are so innocent, unrefined and uncorrupted that God often shows his will more readily through their impulses than our most carefully crafted plans."

Nods of agreement abound, Samuel's patient smile returning as everyone comprehends the wisdom of our leader. He confers quietly with Brother Michael and Augustus, and I tacitly thank Jesus for softening their hearts to my fate.

"Tis not my wont to let infractions go unpunished," the sentence squeezes my stomach, "therefore, Brother Adilsen you will sequester in your cell for one week for breaking your vow of silence. Cook will leave bread and water at your door."

I bend at the waist in acceptance of the penance, breathing easily in assurance that I won't be banished entirely. Taking my seat, I witness Brother Samuel's shoulders sag in relief, and I regret the burdens I have piled on him. I contemplate how he shouldn't feel responsible for me, then I recall how fiercely I have protected Brigida.

Her letter in my pocket beckons me, and I look forward to the solitude to sort through a lot of things.

"As for communing with the citizens," he goes on, "I believe we touched as many souls in the street today as we did in the cathedral. This unifying joy brought forth through song is what I envisioned when I agreed to support the Bishop Stephen's idea of a great choir. Brother Samuel, I commission you to continue engaging the masses through these performances, knowing that this is God's work."

Dearest,

You will want to know that I am well. I accompany Liang Na everywhere, and as such, live in luxury that I never knew existed! I would describe the Great Palace and throne room to you, but my writing skill is limited to simple words, which won't do justice to their magnificence! Attending to the princess is easy, nothing like the work I'm used to, and not many people want to speak to her, so as her companion I mostly just converse with her to help us both learn Greek.

In spite of my splendid surroundings and fascinating company, I long for you and Nicolo. I see him every day, we take our meals in the dining hall with the Emperor's attendants, but we are both in our work capacities so we can only exchange a smile, touch or short word. I'm thankful for my growing friendship with Liang Na, but its not the same as having you to share these wondrous experiences, as we have all of our lives.

Once I get settled with Nicolo next week, we are going to effort his influence to visit you. Until then, God keep you, I know he will because he always does!

All My Love,
Brigida

In the waning light filtering in through my window, I let the parchment fall on my stomach as I recline to absorb the pleasure of Brigida's letter. Optimism over her station soothes my spirit, though the rest of me remains overheated. Usually I appreciate my warm room after the chill of the day, however today has been the hottest I can remember and the long walk in the afternoon sun has my body heat elevated.

I recall my sister's rounded face, glowing in health and contentment, elevating her beauty to new levels. Pondering the divine gleam in her cheeks, I finger my sweat dampened tresses, wondering if my softer life becomes me as well. Against my better judgment, I peel off my heavy tunic and unwrap the binding from my breasts. Clad only in my undergarment, I pour fresh water in the basin seeking to alleviate the stuffiness pressing in on me.

Poised over the wash bowl, I pause to examine the faint reflection of the young woman assessing me. Vaguely reminiscent of Maman's aspect, my features are regular and fair. Perhaps it is the giddiness from my stifling quarters, but I grin at the pleasant image, noting the tidy row of teeth, none chipped or rotten. Self-satisfied, I splash water over my head and neck, a momentary respite from the oppression.

Plucking the wet tunica from my torso, I glimpse the gentle curve of my belly and hips. Though my breasts are small, they are well shaped and suit my slim frame. My broad shoulders give the premature illusion of an hourglass figure, supported by long, straight legs. Is this what Majidi saw when he spoke of his desire for my uniqueness?

The furnace of my room, stoked by the flames of passion, becomes unbearable and I compulsively throw open my door without concern for my state of undress, nor my sequestering. Rashness born of desperation, I dart around the corner and up the stairs, my head spinning feverishly.

Dusk blankets the city as I burst through the arched portal, gulping the crisp evening air to cool my insides. Brisk gusts sweep me out onto the ramparts, invigorating my bare arms and legs with their salty scrub. The wind whips through my hair, massaging my nape and scalp with its fortifying fingers. The swirling gale pushes me farther and farther along the pathway, depositing me in the cloak of the archway to the forbidden section of the monastery. Suddenly, stillness descends, the chirp of the night creatures and swish of the sea soothing in the aftermath of the tumultuous breeze.

"You left me." The darkness from the portal beguiles me with the sound of Majidi's voice. Elation flutters up from my gut, gripping my heart in joyous anticipation so that I can hardly breath as he materializes in the flesh before me. My limbs quake hungrily as I consume his length, flowing in loose white tunic and trousers. His petulant eyes and pouting lips, compliment the ache in his tone. I search his exquisite features for any sign on humor, but the hurt in his molten orbs slows my racing pulse.

"I was coming back for you," he reiterates his need for me, and I'm lost. The world beyond us ceases to exist. "but you left."

"I am here now." A puff of air at my back pushes me into him. Of their own accord, as if pulled by strings from above, my arms reach up to caress his face and shoulders. The magnetic contact snaps the span of time and distance, and we melt into each other. I meet his demanding mouth, matching its insistence with all of the fire that has been smoldering in me since I left my heart with him in the forest. He crushes me against the granite of his chest, enflaming my passion with his own firebrand prodding my stomach. He presses me against the stones of the door archway, and I stiffen momentarily as the memory of being trapped by a wall flashes through my torrid brain.

He eases back, gauging my mood, stroking tousled hair from my face to read my expression. The strained tenderness reflected in his gaze elicits a gentle smile of agreement, and I let my body speak my desire for him. He lifts me up by my buttocks and I wrap my legs around his hips, allowing him to carry and caress me into the dark tunnel. By the time he shoulders aside the door to his chambers, I'm nearly crying out in desire.

Wordlessly, I draw his tunic over his head and untie the cord of his trousers, delighting in the graceful limbs and proud member, as he runs his hands over my own nakedness. He bears me into the coolness of the silken bed, covering me with his warmth. I'm shaking in anticipation of him as he touches me and kisses me deeply. His blunt heat pushes at me, and I rear up in impatience, a sharp pain piercing my loins. He holds himself motionless until the bite passes, leaving the sensation of his fullness in me. Wanting something more, I mewl and wriggle under him, wresting a throaty groan and slow thrusting movement from him.

Like the natural rhythm of the ocean, he takes me. I'm consumed by the physical, emotional and spiritual joining, and give myself entirely to our coupling. After an eternal moment of shattering sensation, he loudly proclaims his ecstasy and falls heavily upon me. I welcome his suffocating weight, holding his spent body until the last of the spasms jerk through his groin.

Serenading night sounds penetrate my intoxication, benevolently ushering me back to reality. Majidi props his head on his fist and takes in my flushed cheeks, wonder widening his regard. His gentle kiss is now a butterfly on my lips, my jaw, my temple, as I let my fingertips explore the back of his ear, the smoothness of his brow, the satin finish of his curls.

121

Though the urgency has passed, I feel him grow inside me again, and he pulls back and stares at me in amazement. He shakes his head and inhales deeply in effort to slide out and roll off the bed.

While he searches for something, I grimace at the spots of blood smeared on my thighs, relieved to not see any red on the purple sheen of the bedcovers. As if tacitly understanding that words could break the fragile mystique of the moment, Majidi returns with a damp rag and reaches between my legs to clean off the evidence of my torn maidenhead. He briskly scrubs himself as he goes around the room and bolts the doors and shutters the lanterns.

Lethargy causes my wits to lag behind his activity, so that I'm still trying to reconcile having this magnificent man bathe me like a babe, while he's already moved on to climbing back into bed. He gathers me in his arms and buries his head in my neck, sniffing my hair and sighing in profound satisfaction. To my amazement, his arms relax heavily around me, his breathing steadies, and he sleeps. I wrestle with my befuddled thoughts for a short while ere I follow close behind him into blissful respite.

His hands on my body rouses my ardor, gliding over my stomach and breasts, bringing my flesh to tingling peaks. In the gray coolness of the morning, his kisses across my shoulders rekindle the passion between us, and I arch against his hardness. I shift to my back to seek his face in the dimness, opening myself to him. This time, I let him go slowly, and I experience a different kind of pain, that of a pleasure so great it is akin to agony.

Our loving culminates as the rising sun casts her golden rays through the drapes, painting us in shades of amber. We lay side by side facing each other, absorbing the magic of the morning. Proti Hora service bells punctuate the tempo of waves rushing through the rocky shore below, and the gulls crying their melody above.

"How many years do you have?" He questions softly, so as not to break the hushed spell over us.

"I shall have fifteen summers come August," I assume his concern is for the possibility of quickening with child, "but I am not at a fertile point in my cycle, so I should not conceive right now.

"You're so young," he laments.

"I'm well past the age when most young women lose their virginity." I assuage his conscience, "my maman was two years my junior when she bore my sister."

"You're right, it's just that I never want to become the monster they say I am." He rises and pulls the drapes wide to expose the vista of the city, unknowingly presenting a far more appealing view of his long limbed form. He cracks the door and speaks to someone in the passage, then closes the portal and comes back shivering to recapture my warmth in his embrace.

"You do emit some beastly noise," my attempt at humor joins my previous rationale, both failing to shake his serious mood.

"I usually have an aversion to fornicating with girls under ten and five, that I'm so attracted to you is exceptional, and vexing at the same time." The genuine angst furrowing his brow, lures me from my own stewing over the content of our first conversation since our emotional reunion.

"You're not going to accuse me of casting a spell over you, as my father did." Now I'm only half jesting, ironically earning a wry grin.

"Nay, tis something that has bothered me ever since I have been pressured to marry brides and accept concubines who are mere children. As a rule, I have refused to consummate until they have reached ten and five."

"Why Majidi? You can't be that much older?" His unlined face and fit physique testify to a man with a score of years. "In the Northern countries, tis rare to live past two score years, so to wed before ten and five is quite common."

"Perhaps because I never knew my mother, who died from complications in delivering my brother and I when she was merely ten and two."

"You have a brother?"

"Aye," he confirms, "a younger brother by three hours, identical twins. And he shares my late father's penchant for bedding young girls."

"Ah, I see," my heart squeezes with pity for this boy without a mother, and brutes for father and brother. "But that isn't you! You refused to take me without giving me the choice, though you could have easily enough in the forest."

"Much good it did me!" He scoffs, "I couldn't put you from my mind!"

"I couldn't forget you either." I admit, emboldened by his confession.

"I tried everything…blaming you for turning on me, pitying myself for you deserting me, I even settled for a while on being angry with you."

"I'm sorry that I mislead you into thinking I would go with you Majidi," this man has a way of laying my soul bare like I wouldn't allow with anyone else, "twas a cowardly act, because I knew I couldn't resist you thrice."

"Then you feel it too? This inexplicable attraction?" The black pools of his eyes reflected my own wonder over this fierce and abiding gravitation to one another.

"I felt it immediately, as if it is the most natural thing." A discrete tap at the door interrupts the pensive atmosphere, and Majidi garbs himself in his trousers to receive a tray laden with fruits from his valet. The plump grapes and sweet dates remind me of my penance and disobedience. Nearly groaning under the effort to drag myself out of the voluptuous bed, I don my tunica, girding myself for our inevitable parting.

"Majidi I must go to my cell," I explain how I'm supposed to be in isolation, "if I don't take in my tray and leave a waste bucket they will think something's amiss."

"Promise me that you'll return," he grasps my hands and fixes me with the depth of his black orbs. "Regardless of what the future holds, give us this time."

"I swear it," I vow, confirming my oath with my greedy lips on his, elation that this isn't our last kiss whisking me to my room.

Affirmed by God's perfect timing, I finish my morning functions and put the bucket of waste outside of my door, just before I hear someone rattling a tray in the corridor. In a moment of levity, I chuckle at the complete reversal in my circumstances, from having to find my own food and be constantly on the move, to staying in my room and someone delivering bread to my door. Laden with guilt of violating my punishment, I hold onto a small seed of obedience that I will eat only bread and water, as per the Father Abbot's instructions.

Once I've broken my fast, I kneel at my pallet for a much needed conversation with God. After asking for forgiveness for my sins of disobedience and fornication, I ask for his guidance to show me what he would have me do with Majidi. My knees and back start to ache from my lengthy litany of reasons why I should not go back to his room. I list all of the sins, pitfalls and drawbacks I can think of, and sit on my bed to wait for God to agree with me.

Silence. The mid-morning sun fades behind a layer of thick, gray clouds, portending rain. The faint movements of daily activity echo in the courtyard under my window, as I listen. In the stillness of my cell, beads of sweat break out between my breasts, though I'm only wearing my tunica. Can it be that I can't hear him speak to me in my cell?

Raindrops pepper the earth, spraying mist through the oiled hide stretched across the window high up in the wall, and I wonder if this is my answer. Straining to detect his voice, I rise to fan myself as the perspiration rolls down my back and face. The rain acts as a barrier, shutting me in the oppressive furnace of my room. No longer able to concentrate, I toss my robe and cowl over my head, seeking the cool breeze from the top of the abbey. I race up the staircase, prodded by the resonant bells marking Triti Ora divine service.

"Go, Go, Go!" They toll, urging me on to the ramparts. The tumultuous wind coming off the stormy sea rips away my cowl, whipping hair in my face and plasters my robes against my back and legs. Blinded thus, rain drives me forward so forcefully that I run to keep from tumbling over.

After a few harried heartbeats, the gusts whisk me to the quiet darkness of the archway leading to the guest quarters. Still not heeding any divine message, I lament my mangled hair and sodden garb, wondering how I can face the man I just made love to, looking such a mess. With one final exclamation of exasperation, God sends a clap of lightning, causing me to start into the corridor.

"You don't have to understand my gifts to you." The thunder growls at my retreat, "but accept those that I lay before you."

Humor shines from Majidi's face when he opens the door to my sheepish, shivering form. He sweeps me into the chamber and sets me down with a resounding kiss that wipes away all apprehension. Taking me by the hand, he leads to a curtained alcove, keenly observing my gasp of pleasure when I see a large beaten copper tub. Candlelight dances on the steamy surface of the water, pungent incense scenting the air.

Unceremoniously, we doff our clothes and he steps into the water up to his thighs and offers me his hand. Delight flutters down my spine as I slip into the heat next to him. He produces a square of linen and lump of soap and beckons me to turn around. His hands slide over me, reaching into every crook and curve of my body, scrubbing and massaging the jasmine scented foam into my skin. He chortles mischievously each time he elicits an uncontrollable exclamation from my impassioned lips, then hands the cloth to me to return the favor.

Distracted by the satiny bunch of his shoulder muscles sheathed in bronze, my ministrations aren't nearly as cleansing as his. With measured strokes, I explore his chiseled form, with the care and curiosity of an artist paying homage to a beloved creation. My admiring fingers bring about a much different conclusion, which I discover when I dip the cloth under the water to bathe his lower limbs and brush against his hardness. He guides my legs around his hips and slides into me, showing me how to ride him astride. With each motion my muscles tighten around him until an unbearable tension squeezes my groin. He obliges my straining, faster and more forceful, sending water splashing across the floorboards. With a final surge, something bursts within, flooding my loins in pulsing release. I collapse against him, letting him take over the effort of his own finish.

Exhausted and sore, I drape over him until the ache in my hips becomes too uncomfortable and I ease off and lean back against the tub to face him. He shakes his head in amazement, twining his fingers in mine where they rest on the ledge.

"You are my first Adila." Confusion furrows my brow. "I have never responded to any woman the way I am with you. With you making love feels so natural, not a duty."

"I know what you mean," I'm touched by his eagerness to share himself with me, knowing that he's not trying to flatter me, nor blunt the truth of his conquests, "it just happens!"

"Aye, when you allow it!" He quips jovially, flicking water at me, then ducking under when I try to splash him back. He emerges, his black curls glistening with drops, and presents me with the soap in askance. Happily

I kneel to lather his short, thick mane, intrigued by the tight coils and sericeous texture.

"Haven't you had enough for now?" I laugh as he runs his admiring touch over my exposed torso, inspecting my bony curves.

"Never!" He replies vehemently before I push his head under to rinse out the suds. He spins me around and tilts my head back to wet my hair and massages the soap into my scalp. He comments on the length of my tresses, and compliments their honeyed hue. I sigh my gratitude of this simple task, remembering how my sister and I used to pamper each other.

"I miss my sister," sentiments spill from my heart whenever I'm with this man. "How is it with your brother?"

"Complicated," his reticence suggests a sensitive topic. He heaves himself out of the water and reaches over me for a towel. I notice the jagged line marring his ribs.

"The wound has healed nicely! T'will leave a scar though, I'm afraid."

"My physician was impressed by your resourcefulness in using the sap," he passes a fresh linen to me, "the bark came off easily upon soaking, and the skin had already started to knit. He said you even managed to line up the edges to minimize the disfigurement!"

He puts on a long tunic and searches for something for me to wear while I hang my wet tunica and robe. I make a comical figure, swimming in a similar chamise that he finds, though his warm amusement assuages my abused pride over my appearance.

"How did you come by this life?" He indicates to my monk's garb.

"Its complicated." I earn a wry look at my attempt at irony. "You first."

"Discussions over ruling Byzantine families are always filled with intrigue," he pulls me out onto the patio and bundles me close to him on a chaise. Usually not agreeable to being dragged about, I'm endeared by Majidi's manner of keeping me in tow. As the rain pours down, his story flows out.

"Ours is not a kindred relationship. I have wondered if, when my mother died giving birth to us, our nurses favored me, which fostered jealousy in my brother, Damian. His envy was fueled by my position of inheritance over my father's domain and my early successes as a military prodigy. When Emperor Basil recognized my skill in tactics and diplomacy, awarding me the governorship of Chaldia, I learned the full extent of my brother's covetous nature in a failed coup that he planned."

"So why not banish him?" My solution to everything is to get away from the problem.

"Firstly, if I keep him near, I can watch for signs of disturbance." I see why the emperor values Majidi's finesse. "But more importantly, I rely on his partnership. From the time we were children, we would play pranks on everyone and switch places, pretending that one was the other. We have become flawless in impersonating each other's antics, and because we look exactly the same, it is like having the ability to be in two places at once. When we were first born, our father branded Damian on his heel, and this mark is the only way we can be distinguished."

"That sounds like something my father would do," I grumble in empathy over having a cruel sire. I'm beginning to comprehend Majidi's yen for reliable human connection, why he was inordinately upset at my disappearance in the forest, and why he craves my touch. His childhood was one of cold business, whereas at least I had Maman and Brigida.

"My brother learned to appeal to my father's base nature for his attention, and joined in his orgies, developing a taste for young female flesh." His pretty mouth twists in a grimace of disgust. "So I took advantage of his depraved carnal appetites. I allowed him access to my harem."

He explains how in his culture, the seraglio is rigidly off limits to all but the wives and concubines who live there, and the castrated male attendants. To introduce another man into their female isolation is strictly forbidden. He expounds on the diplomatic reasoning behind his union with each of his wives, and the complex process of accepting gifts of concubines. to turn away either is akin to insulting the giver.

"I was only ten and three when forced into alliance with my father's vizier's daughter, who is ten years my senior. Then, for the next four years I was away on military campaigns with the Emperor Basil. As part of my assuming the Chaldean seat at ten and seven I had to take as a second wife the former governor's widow." The story he details makes me realize that there are many nebulous forms of enslavement. "Since that time I've been given a score of concubines in return for my favor over their families and territories. This is where my brother has helped me with the burden of managing the women."

He said he became overwhelmed at the prospect of keeping them all happy, which affected his ability to perform sexually, so he made a deal with the devil. Damian could have the concubines at his disposal, and Majidi would focus on siring a legitimate heir through his wives. His tale concludes with his latest wife, Liang Na and their return to his homeland in a few day's time. The rain whispers outside the balcony as I digest this sordid tale. In its pattering against the stone walls of the abbey, I hear the women of the seraglio weeping within the confines of their barriers of society and tradition.

"So that is why you understand not having freedom and choices," I opine. "You're just as trapped by your station and circumstances as anyone."

"This is why I abide Damian, he frees me up a little so that I can travel. When I'm on campaign is the only time I don't feel suffocated by familial duties. We just make sure to stay out of each other's way so the arrangement has worked over the years. There's been only one problem."

"Your new scar will identify you?"

"I hadn't even thought about that because I haven't slept with any of my concubines in a long time, only he visits the harem." The incredulity of his statement fills me with skepticism. I assume that all men take full advantage of the women at their disposal. "I've failed to produce an heir! My brother has sired several children, but my wives have not."

"Is this why you wanted to see Liang Na?" I recall his spying on her in the forest, "to see for yourself if she looked fertile?"

"Adila, I have never spoken this aloud to anyone," his heavy tone arrests my full attention, "but I think it is something wrong with me why they don't conceive. Tis why I'm not concerned about impregnating you, I'm unable."

"Perhaps you were not of age? Or they've passed their fertility?" My disbelief dissipates under compassion for his predicament and I yearn to soothe the panic underlying his velvety voice.

"Thus far I've passed the blame onto them being too old, which is why my vizier arranged for me to wed the Chinese princess," he pauses, listening to the muffled tones of Ekti Ora calling the brethren to noonday service, "and I'm away on military duties much of the time, so I haven't had the opportunity."

"You're right," I agree cynically, "'tis complicated! More so now that you have a young princess to beget an heir."

"At least I have some time before she turns ten and five, when the betrothal period ends and I must consummate the marriage."

In silence we contemplate the watercolored city beyond the marbled balcony. I nestle close to him, sharing whatever physical comfort I can provide, while I search for an answer to his dilemma. Its times like these when I talk to God about my own problems, and his wisdom washes over me that I don't have to know all of the answers to the great mystery of life.

"God will reveal all in time Majidi," I muse delicately. "I've had to tell myself thus many times to explain why I'm here in your arms right now."

I twist around and face him, engaging the intelligence I find in his dark regard.

"I don't understand this astounding attraction that draws me to you. I am a mere maid from mean beginnings, and you're so remarkable!"

"Outwardly we appear as different as the extreme climes from whence we come," he continues my sentiments, "yet you compliment me as no other being, I'm bare before you."

"This is precisely what I mean," I finish, "we can't always discern what everything means and where we're headed."

"Like letting your ship drift in a storm," he punctuates, "you don't know where she will land, but you have to know she will land somewhere."

A muffled tap on the chamber door interrupts our conversation, and Majidi disappears through the curtain and reemerges with a tray of food. My mouth waters at the sight of the plump fruit and fish, and I offer a prayer of sacrifice as I reach for a dry wafer. Majidi notices that I eschew the wine and meats, so I tell him of my penance and personal choice to honor at least the fasting, since flagrantly disobeying the isolation part of my punishment.

"Now that I've told you my deeply incriminating secrets," he prods, "its your turn to tell me why you're here as a monk."

"The afternoon grows late," I squint out over the balcony rail at the inky sky, seeking a starting point for my own somber tale. "Are you sure you want to start another heavy topic today?"

He folds his arms across his chest and fixes me with a condescending glare to communicate his willingness to listen. The shame of what I'm about to recount turns my stomach, but I remind myself that his revelation of impotency rivals that of my masculine rearing. I pick at a stray linen fiber on the otherwise flawless white sleeve of my borrowed chamois, marveling at my impoverished beginnings and how I came to sit with the ruler of Chaldia, sharing his company and wearing his clothes. With an incredulous laugh and a shake of my head, I meet his curious eyes and delve into my past from a fresh perspective of gratitude for where it has brought me.

"I was raised as a boy," I dive into the heart of it, "my father wanted a son, so he let it be known by everyone that I was male."

Other than an interested arched eyebrow, Majidi absorbs my disgrace unaffected, emboldening me to continue.

"For as long as I can recall, I did everything as a boy would do. I walked, talked, spit, ran, fought and even urinated like a boy."

"So that's why you were able to chase me down in the forest!" I'm stunned that he would take only that detail from my statement. My deepest shame has always been having to piss to my father's masculine approval. "But why would he go through such lengths to lie about your gender?"

"When I was younger, I thought he hated me because I was a girl," I choke on my childish pain, "but I've come to realize that he's just an angry, miserable person who didn't get his way. It wasn't my fault for being a daughter and not a son to keep up with his brother's many boys."

"Of course its not your fault! I'll never understand this obsession we have with male offspring," Majidi commiserates, "I would be overjoyed just to have a child."

"About four summers ago, I was attacked by a group of village bullies outside of the abbey in Novgorod. Brother Samuel found me and took me in. He made an agreement between his Abbot and my father to bring me into the fold so that I could sing for his choir, and my sister could stay with me."

"What a glorious use of your gift of song. I knew it was you immediately when I heard your voice in the Hagia Sophia, your talent is a blessing for sure."

"Since then I've hidden behind the robes of my order and given my voice to God. In return, I've gained fellowship, education, purpose, adventure, and most of all, peace."

"So the obscurity of the holy habit has been a blessing and a burden," he concludes, contemplating the watery landscape, "as are my state robes of Strategos of Chaldia."

"You say nothing about my masculine rearing." I observe wryly probing for a spark of disapproval.

"I already think you're extraordinary, your upbringing is part of what makes you so." He pulls me back up against him and wraps me tight in his long arms. Together we meditate on what we have learned of one another, the music of the rain and waves lulling us into trancelike silence. The toll for None breaks the spell, and Majidi squeezes his arms harder around me as if he could weld me into his chest.

"I love the feel of you close to me." That word again. He said the same to me in the forest, and, as before, I'm scared and exhilarated at the same time. "I know not what will come of this Adila, but stay with me tonight."

"Aye," I acquiesce before thinking, "I must return to my room so that they don't suspect I'm not there, but I will be back after Vespers."

"Sing for me Adila," silvery moonlight bathes our silken cocoon in her mystical aura. Nighttime has long since fallen, yet the cool wintery breeze fails to calm Majidi's unsettled pulse under my cheek, "your voice is so soothing."

I choose a gentle hymn that I had composed to the melody of Liang Na's wistful music, envisioning my vocal cords are the strings of her lady's instruments. My words of praise whine through the rain-washed air, transporting us back to the Russian woodlands.

"I've never heard anything like that," his fingers toy with my gilded curls, "what was it?"

"I created the lyrics to set to the music of Liang Na's melodies." I immediately regret my choice, as his hand drops from my hair. He stares reticently up at the brocade draperies covering the bed.

"I must see her tomorrow." His tone is laden with regret. "The

Emperor is having a banquet in our honor before we depart. I just got word while you were away."

"Is that why you're unable to sleep?" I rest my cheek on my fist to contemplate his mien, rather than the pain of sharing him with his betrothed slicing through my gut.

"Aye, my spirit is troubled." He faces back to me in the dimness, "I often think about when you sang to me in the forest when I need ease."

"When Maman used to sing to my father it would mollify him, almost put him in a trance."

"Can you recall any of her songs that made him sleep?"

"Aye, I know them all as I know how to breathe," I filter through her cache of ditties, selecting my favorite lullaby. "The tongue is old Norse, but the melody is soft."

Sitting up against the pillows, I gather his head to my lap and massage the tightness from his forehead and neck. The familiar lilting words waft across the star sparkled darkness outside of the bed curtains, evoking an image of a spirited child, filled with hope and promise, and I see myself dancing across the sky in pursuit of the moon. Not even Majidi's sleep spasms and subsequent snores can penetrate the mystical vision, as the heavenly bodies seem to form a pathway transporting me from under the satiny blanket into a realm of joy.

As I cross into a dreamlike state, the once bright moon fades behind the misty veil of this uncertain tenderness under which I'm hiding. The ethereal aura that lit my path, retreats deep inside of me, only to be heard in song, but not seen. No longer able to perceive my mother's melodious words, life becomes short and full of the present moment. I follow along through the sinews and valleys of Majidi's back, seeking to navigate the roiling sea of emotions I feel for him, but I learn that I can always find solace if I retreat into this core of light, knowing that one day it will return to illuminate my destiny.

The memory of waking up and making love to Majidi sustains me through the morning in my stifling cell. By the time the bells toll Ekti Ora, I can no longer pray away the heat or meditate on cooling my core, so I strip off my linen robe and cowl and sit against the outside wall to absorb some of the winter chill through the stones. The sweat drips down my face and great beads bubble up all over my flushed skin, but in the midst of misery, I thank God for this distraction from obsessing over Majidi being with his betrothed today.

This attitude bolsters my resolve to endure at least the day in penance, and I turn my thoughts to finding a way to be more comfortable. Rain continues to patter against the oiled hide stretched across the window set high up the wall, teasing me with its fresh scent. Upon inspection, I find notches in the stones under the window, and surmise that I may be able to leverage something into the holes to use as a ladder and reach the opening.

Surveying my room, my perusal rests on the small table, which I flip over and twist out the legs. The first gap in the stone wall is the height of my shoulder, and I shove one of the legs in until it is sturdy enough to bear my weight. Standing on the makeshift rung, I find another notch and repeat the process. The four table legs are just enough to reach the window and pull myself up into the deep sill. I wretch the skin aside and drink in the cold air and icy drops, nearly sobbing in relief.

I perch in the window watching the monks huddle under the cloisters until the bell for Enati Ora calls them to the late afternoon service. The melodic chants from the cathedral beckons my soul, and I sing along with my brethren, pining for the presence of God. My heart feels torn between the powerful, passionate desire for Majidi, and the steady, gentle need for Jesus. I'm not ready to have to chose.

The inky daylight is rapidly fading when there is a tap on my door and the sound of someone leaving a tray on the threshold. Stiff from hours of sitting in the cramped alcove, I gingerly swing down into the sweltering sauna and pull on my robes to open the door and bring in my daily ration of bread and water. I gulp the water thirstily, then reach for the roll when I notice a scrap of parchment resting on the tray.

"Do not to show yourself in the window."

Deflated, I drop into the chair, appetite gone. In spite of nightfall descending, the heat in my cell seems to have escalated. Through a feverish haze I make out the toll for Typica, knowing that the monks will be finding their beds for the night. In a fit of self pity, I hurl my hunk of bread at the door, where it wedges in the latch, compressing the iron lever down until I hear an audible click. The portal swings open under my stunned regard; I need no other invitation. Dropping my tray and waste bucket on my way out the door, I sprint up the staircase and burst onto the ramparts in joyous freedom.

The crisp breeze penetrates my sweat soaked robe to tickle a shiver from my puckered skin. Awash in relief, I voice my thanks to God for his mercy in escaping the hellish inferno of my cell. I rest my fevered brow on the waterlogged stones of the battlements and absorb its cool moisture.

"In listening for me, you are carrying out my plans for you." God's words bite through the heated layers of linen and skin to nip at my consciousness.

The drizzle has stopped, leaving the earth replenished, the air fresh and the night sky speckled in starlight. Tranquility seeps into my innermost being, as I take in the rush of the breeze, the chirping of the night creatures and the percussion of the waves lapping at the hull of the ship moored below. Placated in mind and body, I curl up in the crenellation, vigilant for more of God's instructions.

"Why have you brought me here Lord?" I ask that which is uppermost in my thoughts. "What purpose do you have for me? Why this yearning for a man who is of a different world? Give me something, a sign, a vision, anything to help me know I'm doing your will."

My queries dissipate into the darkness over the Propontis and are answered by the stillness of the sea. Moments pass anticipating a response, senses sharp for God's voice on the breeze. A quarter of an hour slips by, the ebb and flow of the waves washing along the rocky shoreline tug at my eyelids. From the deck of the ship, the reedy whine of a duduk pfeife weaves seamlessly into nature's symphony. The powerful stealth of music conquers my wits, and I sluggishly surrender my vigil to its blissful prison.

When the dream comes, and I become that spirit dancing among the stars, I smile in my sleep that she's still there. Arms gently pluck me from the heavens and pillow me against a beating heart.

"Adila," a whisper kisses my forehead, "why do you smile?"

"Maman," I breath back in childlike trust, "I had a most wonderful dream."

"Then stay there my love." Curiosity nags at the edges of sleep, trying to place the spicy scent, which is not of my maman. The rocking movement and rhythmic pulse put me back into the realm of fantasy, and I slumber on, comforted by the sensation of being cradled in adoration.

"Adila, are you awake?" I start out of deep sleep, confounded by my opulent surroundings. Pristine sunlight streams through rich blue and red brocade bed curtains, gleaming off satiny covers on which we lay fully clothed. My lethargic memory recalls falling asleep to the lullaby of a reedy instrument in the recess of a parapet.

"I am now," I raise my head from the pillow of Majidi's chest and grin tiredly, content to find myself nestled against him. It is as if no matter where I go, I somehow return to his arms. "How did I get here?"

"I found you asleep between the crenellations and carried you here." He chuckles, "You were dreaming and called me Maman!"

"Oh! I remember now!" I laugh at my childish antics, "I succumbed to the mesmerizing sound of a piper from your ship, and I dreamt that you were my mama carrying me to bed."

"Do you miss your mother?" He asks earnestly.

"I do sometimes," I harken to the times during our journey when I would miss her simple wisdom or the comfort of her nurturing. "But I feel her presence with me a lot, especially in song. What about you? Do you feel a void from not having known your mother?"

"Yes and no." I rest my chin on my fist to better read his explanation in his expression. "My nurse was always there to care and dote on me, but I often wonder what I could have learned from a mother had she been around. Even if just the knowledge that I'm like her and not my father."

I peer into his soulful eyes and notice the dark circles underneath and puffy eyelids. Such grave thoughts are at odds with the freshness of the morning, and I wonder if he's been alert for a while. Marshaling my sagacity, I share my own worries about being like my father.

"It troubles me that I have my father's vile temper, but I use that fear to channel it into something good." I tell him about the incident in the monastery at Kiev, and how I was able to use that violence to fight evil. "I've discovered that if I accept that part of who I am, I can ask God to use it for his purpose, which has helped manage my anger."

"So if I admit that I'm a child molester, I can use it to my advantage?"

"Good heavens Majidi!" I exclaim at his belligerent misunderstanding, "such a somber topic for the morning. Did you not sleep well?"

"Not a wink."

"No wonder your mood is bleak." I muse, "let us just agree that you don't seem to have a penchant for abusing young girls. Why didn't you sleep?"

"The weather has been unseasonably fair." He says cryptically. I wait for him to expound. "My captain informs me that we must take advantage of the fortunate winds."

"So you're sailing home soon?"

"We must leave the day after the morrow." His tone portends the end of our surreal time together. "I've been awake all night watching you, not wanting to lose you again."

"Can we not speak of it now?" Tears threaten to engulf the tranquility of the waking hours, and I stubbornly tamp them down. "I missed you yesterday, let's enjoy today."

He smiles indulgently and nods, tightening his hold around me. Burying his face in my hair, he inhales deeply as if memorizing my scent. His endearing antics remind me of the perspiration embedded in my robe and tunic. I recount my sweaty day to him, welcoming the change in subject and diversion of his attention from my smell.

"I could use a bath." I probe, remembering our previous experience. "And something to drink!"

"They've already stowed my bath basin on the ship, but I have another idea." He jumps out of bed to pour a cup of water, then cracks open the portal to murmur with the valet. "You may be thirsty, but I've been holding my water for hours! We have a few minutes to make use of the toualeta."

After almost a week of stooping over a bucket, I luxuriate on the marble seat in the small closet until I hear the servant tap at the apartment door. Finishing up with the sponge at hand to clean myself, I emerge as Majidi is shouldering the portal closed, bearing a tray laden with a bowl of steamy water and towels to a table beside the bed.

At his command, I gladly strip off my robe and tunic, feeling slightly exposed to be naked while he's fully clothed. I smile shyly at him and reach for the towel, but he intercepts my wrist and leads me back onto the bed. With a mischievous grin, he wets the linen and washes my hand meticulously and bestows kisses on each of my fingertips. Stretching my arm out, he strokes the cloth up and down my arm, his lips following his ministrations.

My other limbs are treated to the same ritual, then he pushes me onto my stomach and massages my back and buttocks. His mouth works on the sensitive skin over my shoulders and neck, and by the time he flips me back over to clean my face I hungrily meet his tongue with mine to taste the fulness of his kiss. His lips burn into my neck and across my chest. He wipes my breasts and torso, blowing cool air to tighten my nipples then devouring them, ruthlessly raking the hard nubs with his teeth.

By the time his stiff beard scores my abdomen, I'm desperately gasping for him to disrobe so that he can take me fully. I manage to drag his shirt off, but he captures my wrists again and holds them by my side. He shoulders aside my twisting legs and uses the cloth to rub the delicate folds between my thighs.

"Majidi!" I cry out as his mouth captures my venus mons.

"Yes Adila?" His rapt attention is absorbed in fueling the fire between my legs. "I want..." his probing makes me forget what I want, I grip the bedcovers. "What do you want?"

"I need..." a fissure of fire slices through my loins, I arch my back and squirm against the bedcovers.

"What do you need?"

"I need you inside of me!" I pant, clutching at his head and shoulders.

"Like this?" He slides a finger into my sheath, making me sob in agonizing pleasure.

"Enough!" The mounting pressure is unbearable, and I frantically yank at the chord holding up his trousers. "You must take me now!"

He frees his throbbing member, and in one thrust sinks himself deep inside, pressing hard against my swollen sex. Another stroke takes me to the precipice of tension and I squeeze his hardness, eliciting a throaty groan. One more plunge sends me tumbling over the top and my body jerks, the spasms prolonged as he impales me a few more times then stiffens with his own release.

He collapses heavily on me, the strain of our lovemaking draining from his frame, his labored breathing in my ear relaxing to a steady puff. I revel in the burden of his slack form, even as I work to fill my lungs, the muscles in my hips cramping. His member slides out of me, and still he remains inert, whistling snores extorting an amused giggle at his narcolepsy.

We sleep late into the morning, holding each other tight, our subconscious not wanting to let go. The bell for the sixth hour prayer service and midday meal triggers an answering grumble from my stomach, finally bringing us to awareness.

"Let me call up some bread to feed that dragon in you." Majidi quips, bobbing across the bed.

"My belly protests the unintentional fast of yesterday!"

"I'm not talking about your noisy stomach," he leers at me suggestively, "I'm thinking of that beast that was commanding me to make love to you!"

"Oh aye!" I titter bashfully, "What you did drove me mad with desire!"

"You inspire my lovemaking," he flops back on the bed with me, considering me admiringly. "I've never done that before, never been comfortable enough with anyone. Frankly, I've never cared much about pleasuring anyone other than myself."

"You're magnificent," the passion behind my curtness speaks more than flowery prose.

"How is this possible?" He articulates what I've so often wondered, "you and I are so different, yet I'm consumed by thoughts of you constantly!"

"I've had this conversation with God many times Majidi, because I feel the same way about you."

"That's precisely what I mean," he studies me, "your reverence of your God is so central to who you are. My faith is not like yours."

"But is not Islam a strict religion, like Christianity?" Since journeying to Constantinople, where awareness of one's spiritual identity is a source of individual pride and the subject of intense discussion, it dawns on me that I've not yet seen him on his knees in prayer. The rap at the door gives us pause in our discourse. I scurry behind the bed and snatch Majidi's discarded tunic over my head when he admits the valet with his tray. We break our fast on the balcony as the sun spills her splendid rays over the city harbor.

"Muslims are just like Catholics," he resumes between bites of fish and omelet, "there are some who are devout believers, some who use the Koran to justify their own beliefs, and some who go along with what others believe."

"And which category do you fall under?"

"I would say the latter," he intellectualizes, "but the lines of religion are so blurred from living in border country, that I question why we make such vital distinctions between our faiths. It may come across as blasphemous or apathetic, even heretical to speak thus."

"I've experienced life in the frontier, where paganism and Christianity vie for souls, so I understand how the name we give God can mean our survival." I commiserate, "however isn't Trebizond one of the strongholds of the orthodox church in the east?"

"Yes it was one of the original cities of the ancient greek empire, the first to convert when Constantine established the New Roman capitol here in Byzantium." I nibble on my hunk of bread, enthralled by his historical perspective, "so its native inhabitants are devout Christians. They abide me as a ruler because I allow them to practice their rites freely, as long as they tolerate my islamic traditions."

"Such as your practice of keeping several wives and concubines." I regret my criticism as soon as it leaves my lips. His handsome features fall, I have to take a drink of water to wash down my remorse.

"Aye," he nods, "the Harem is a necessary custom of my people. Strangely enough, the seraglio is one of the only observances that identifies me as a muslim.

The Armenian city where I grew up, Melitene, was constantly under attack because of where it lies on the mountainous border between the powers of the caliphate and the romans. It was always a matter of survival to capitulate and, if necessary, convert."

"I'm beginning to see how you've grown ambiguous to religion." I pity his lack of joy in knowing his creator. "I'm sorry for my criticism Majidi, these things are not always as they seem."

"I think one of the reasons I admire your belief, Adila," he regards me earnestly, "is that you've lived at large in the world, and yet you remain strong in your faith. In a place like this," he throws his arm in a sweeping gesture to encompass the view of the city, "you'll need to hold on to your love of God as you mix with people from so many nations."

Leaning back in my chair, rubbing my sated belly, I contemplate the rise and fall of buildings, parks and monuments that comprise the ocean of urban life. The patchwork of colors, red brick homes, creamy columned forums and groves of olive trees, teem with people as multi-hued and diverse as the landscape. I acknowledge Majidi's advice, recognizing my fascination with other cultures, and how that thirst could pull me from my relationship with God. Admitting to him how my search for knowledge will often clash with my trust in the Lord, I circle back to the start of our conversation, and reiterate that some things are best left to his mysterious ways.

"It still amazes me how in this short time that we've spent together I've already told you so much more than even my closest friends and advisors," he shakes his head in disbelief, "you know more about me and my private thoughts than anyone!"

"Who are those closest to you?" I note that he didn't mention his family.

"My best friend is Tarik, the Admiral of my fleet," he replies without hesitation, "we met in imperial service where we were in the division of Immortals together. When the Emperor Basil made me governor of Chaldia, I chose Tarik to go with me. He's the only other person whom I've told about my brother's utility, and he helps me watch over Damian."

"I may have espied him from the ramparts," I recall overhearing Majidi address him, what seems like many moons ago. "Who else do you seek when you want to talk?"

"Twas him you heard playing the duduk pfeife last night, he's an exquisite piper." Majidi provided, his face aglow with appreciation for his friend's cleverness. "There was another whom I admired very much, and would have followed him to the ends of the empire. General John Tzimisces."

"The previous Emperor?" The hair on the back of my neck prickles at the mention of the name I had heard whispered conspiratorially between the Bishop and Nicolo. Fear of the greatest conqueror in recent Byzantine military history had been fresh in the minds of the Bulgarian people, when we trekked through their territories on our way to Constantinople.

"Everything I know about war, leadership, administrating and governing, I gleaned from him." He confirmed, "he used to tell me that he saw himself in me, and took me into his inner circle to mentor me. When he was murdered, I grieved more than when my own father died.

I meandered through service in the meaningless battles between rival generals for control over the empire, until I met Basil."

"The current Basileous." My question was more a rhetorical statement to direct my spinning thoughts.

"Yes, but at the time he had not yet officially claimed his birthright, he was still in the shadows of his devious chamberlain who used him as a puppet." He explained, "I've always respected Basil for his dedication to serving his people. Though we don't have a warm personal relationship, we stay connected as colleagues, and I seek his political advice and support above all others. In turn, he appreciates my alliance and military endorsement."

"I've heard that the emperor is very spartan-like, refusing the carnal comforts of his station."

"Oh nay," Majidi chuckles, "he enjoys the luxury of his palace! You should see him perched on his golden throne, surrounded by gilded trees and mechanical birds that chirp on demand." He conjures the scene in the great palace Hall of Nineteen Couches, where platters of fruit are lowered from the ceiling and cisterns pump wine to flow from fountains, statues and columns. "You are correct, however, that he keeps everyone at arms length, especially women. It is rumored that the trauma of his mother's two marriages and love affair with Tzimisces left him scarred and cold to his own need for physical companionship."

"I can see how you would feel a bond with him over your issues with your mothers." One corner of his comely mouth turns down in grudging agreement. "But how do you reconcile over this practice of your multiple wives? He shuns marriage to one, yet he continues to grant his approval for your third betrothal!"

"Basil understands the benefit of recognizing the customs of those who he conquers, preferring to integrate his subjects slowly." I'm beginning to fathom Majidi's esteem of this solitary figurehead, "not only that, my tradition is a useful diplomatic tool to create allies along his borders and secure trade routes."

"Its all so intriguing!" I marvel at the web of politics that I've somehow enmeshed myself in, recalling Nicolo's warning about the Bishop's scheme to build his own personal viking guard. "But my brain could use a break, and I must put out my meal tray and bucket to keep up this facade for another day."

Evening clouds muffle the liveliness on board the saracen ship bobbing in the harbor below the ramparts, as I scuttle along the pathway toward the visitor's suite on the other side. Shades illuminated by lanterns dart to and fro, carrying supplies and wares below deck. I skid to a halt when I hear the pipe trill into a cheerful ditty, the jaunty tempo traveling from my ears to my feet. As if possessed by the tune, my unruly appendages tap and skip to the beat until I'm winded from the exertion.

"Don't stop," Majidi's graceful form materializes beside me, taking my hand and twirling me about. I feel the rhythm through his frame, my movements matching his, my footsteps following. His sinewy arm locks around my waist, guiding our motion to the clip of the cymbals and drum that weaves into Tarik's pipe. I stifle a merry giggle that I'm dancing with my infidel lover in my monk's robe and cowl.

Together we caper into the moonless night, thwarting the murky darkness descending on us. In hushed laughter, he instructs me to turn this way or that, the both of us doubling over in suppressed gales when we bump into each other or trip on the uneven cobblestones. As the music slows down, so does our mirth, and our swaying bodies join in a subdued ballad. When Majidi presses my back against the archway and sinks his lips into mine, there is no fright in my passionate response.

"Sing for me Majidi," I stroke the valley between his muscular chest, the sun peaking over the balcony as if hesitant to mark our last full day.

"I'm Strategos of Chaldia, I don't sing." He states unmindful of his scripted conceit.

"What's that supposed to mean?" I study his aloof mood.

"I have people to sing for me." He is distracted by illusions of his own greatness.

"That sounds very arrogant!" I gather the sheet around me and sit up to regard this rare show of vanity. He looks up at my indignant posture and drops his head back in a hearty guffaw.

"Men have been imprisoned or worse for criticizing their ruler as you just did!" He sobers slightly, "I could use more true counsel in Trebizond. My viziers and administrators always agree with everything I say. Tarik usually gives me an honest opinion, but he is away at sea more than I."

"My first impression of you was falling naked out of a tree." I tease, unimpressed. "Besides, you're not my ruler."

"Pity to the man who tries!" He throws up an arm to deflect the pillow I swing at his head. "What I really should have said though, is that song was not a part of my upbringing. My father was not a supporter of the arts, so other than my nurse crooning lullabies to me as a child, I never learned how to sing."

"Yet you dance!" I counter, "I was told that dance and instrumental music was forbidden by Mohammad."

"Tis a matter of some delicacy. Some muslims frown upon using instruments, but favor vocal melodies for moral purposes. I'm well versed in religious chants and hymns, as expected of my station, just not very good at it."

"How is it that you move so well in sync with Tarik's ditty?"

"Life in the roman legions hasn't been all drudgery." He reminisces, "we had a lot of idle time, so there was always camp songs and reels to keep our morale light. That tune to which we were spinning is a sailor's ditty, not at all permissible for a lady, nor a monk!"

"Would you teach me some proper steps?" The joy of music flowing through my feet again makes me forget all earthly circumstances. My pending religious vows, Majidi's high station, and our looming parting fade into the corners of my mind.

"Gladly! If you will help me to learn how to sing?"

"Agreed," I accept the fun challenge, "you know where my skill is, now let me hear your vocal range. Give me a sampling of what you sing in worship."

His keening lyrics saturate the room with the velvety quality of his natural base, which is not at all suitable to the nasal pitch of the hymn. I point out to him that he has a beautiful voice, but the sound must come from his throat. Soon, I have him repeating refrains from Tarik's ballad until he can carry the tune on his own. I join him in signing to the more sedate tempo, and he pulls me to the center of the room and guides my movements until we flow together through the motion.

We lose ourselves in the pleasure of instruction, hardly noting the bells tolling the passing hours, nor the occasional knocking at the portal to offer food or service. It is well into the afternoon when we can no longer ignore the call to duty and the grumbling in our bellies, and we break from our lessons to take refreshments. I muster the shards of my discipline and pull on my robe and cowl for the march back to my cell, the charade becoming onerous. Promising to come back within a few hours, I drag my now reluctant feet back along the pathway where just yesternight they had skipped so happily.

Keeping my oath to return after Enati Ora, Majidi answers my rap on his door holding a padded woolen tunic, trousers and ominous leather mask. Peering past his stooped shoulders garbed in crisp white linen, I notice the room is bare. Gone are the vibrant rugs that graced dull oaken floorboards and patterned tapestries that adorned gray stone walls. Empty pedestals mourn the loss of priceless statues and busts, the massive four poster bed bereft of its fluttering curtains and opulent covers.

"We set sail at first light in the morning, so we are all sleeping on board tonight," the sorrowful appeal in his eyes grips my heart, "the servants are coming back to stow the bed."

"What's this?" I point at the odd garments in his arms.

"Put this on and come with me on board?" His attempted command turns into a plea, "I'm not pressing you for answers, I just want more time with you. This is my old uniform from when I served as an Immortal, it will disguise you until we're in the privacy of my cabin."

The sudden emptiness of the apartments is like the desolate hole threatening to consume me from the inside out. Almost in a stupor I reach for the clothing, which he hands over and whisks me into the alcove where his tub once stood. We exchange a grim smile at my familiarity donning men's trousers, then he secures the mask and hood to complete the guise. With a firm hand on my back, he steers me briskly through the corridor and down the stairs to the pier.

The explosion of activity on board Majidi's ship further shocks my isolated sensibilities, and I gawk at the many shades of people the likes I have never seen. They all pause to salute their leader as we snake through the ropes, sails, barrels and other obstacles on deck. Comfortable in his leadership, Majidi greets his comrades pleasantly and murmurs for them not to interrupt their labors on his behalf. We duck under a low doorway and descend into his modest quarters, where we finally let out our collective breath.

"It isn't much," he refers to the austere accommodations as he unties the mask and helps me out the uniform, "but we've slept in meaner places than this!"

"'Tis luxurious compared to the forest floor," I continue the jest, not wanting to confront reason. As per his habit of steering me around, he takes me by the shoulders and guides me to sit next to him at the small table. Time slows down, yet my heart races ahead. There is a salty breeze from a nearby open window caressing my feverish forehead, bracing me to look into Majidi's expectant visage.

"Adila, we must talk about tomorrow," he gathers my trembling hands in his, "the idea of leaving you again sends me into panic. I won't try to explain the powerful feelings you awaken in me, I only know that I need you with me. When we parted before, there was an emptiness inside of me that hurt like nothing I have ever endured."

"'Twas the same for me Majidi," I began, but he held up his hand, interrupting me.

"I have to step out and find Tarik, so I want to give you a few minutes to think about what I'm telling you." He inhales deeply, "I want you to come with me, be with me always. You'll have your own apartments, your own servants…you'll never have to lift a finger again!"

"I've come to care for you deeply," I pause to consider my words, and he again jumps in before I can respond.

"And I you, which is why I want this to be your choice. I know how much your freedom means to you, so I'm giving you this time to decide."

He cradles my face in his palms and kisses me tenderly on the mouth. Then he scoops up a pile of scrolls from the table and ascends the stairs, closing the door on me and my tumultuous thoughts. What he doesn't seem to realize is how badly he missed in his assessment of my wants and needs if I were to go with him.

"God help me," I beseech the wind blowing in from the sea, "what would you have me do?"

As I have so many times, especially lately, I wait and listen for a reply. His briny breath from the window continues to soothe my brow and waft through my curls. His artful hand paints the late afternoon in shades of magenta and purple, glinting off the calm ripples in the bay that lap against the oaken planks of the ship. His gentle waves rock the vessel, all in hypnotic concert to dull my senses and deaden my eyelids.

Combatting the weariness, I get up and amble around the cabin, taking inventory of it tidy furnishings. Majidi's presence here on board his ship is more palpable than in the midst of the plush cushions and silken draperies of the guest apartments in the monastery. Though he seems to be comfortable in many different settings, it is here in this serviceable room where I imagine would be his choice of places to get away.

Trailing my fingers over a skillfully carved sea chest, I picture him asleep on his pallet nestled into the niche at the stern of the ship. Round portholes dot the walls, ensuring a fresh breeze and natural light throughout the space. I circle the room, marveling at the practical convenience of the water closet in the corner. As I pass a table holding wash basin next to the toualeta, I glance at the window above and startle right out of my skin.

"Maman!" I cry at the sight of my maman in the glass. She looks as astonished as I, her azure eyes wide, her squarely sculpted jaw agog.

"How is it that you're here too?" Confusion twists my wits as she speaks at the same time, then falls silent, her smooth brow furrowed. Sanity seeps back into my addled brain, and I peer closer at the flaxen halo of hair and rosy cheeks. No careworn wrinkles mar the pearly skin, no circles of fatigue dampen the light emanating from sky blue orbs. It is her, but it is not her.

Corralling my erratic notions, I inspect the glass more intently and discover that it is merely hanging on the wall, not an actual portal. Shaken, I stare back at the reflection in its smooth surface, watching realization dawn on those striking features that I'm gazing at myself clearly for the first time.

Majidi's tread on the stair fails to distract me from my image. His tanned visage appears next to mine in the mirror as I'm poking at my cheek, testing the reality that it is indeed my face in the frame.

"You have the most captivating face," he rests his head atop mine, contemplating our contrasting complexions.

"I've never seen myself before," I explain, still awestruck that I have the exact look of Maman. "Only vague reflections in a pool of water. I thought twas my mama outside the window!"

"Your mother must be very beautiful." The sincerity of his compliment draws my attention to his admiring gaze. I nod, remembering the tales of her famed beauty ensnaring my father. I had always thought that her fairness was passed to my pretty sister, leaving me wan and plain. But as I stare at our framed faces next to each other, there is a striking attractiveness in his earthy duskiness and my ethereal brightness.

"We do make a handsome pair!" He steals the remark before I can say it, then his infectious grin fades and he turns to face me directly. "Would you mind if I bring Tarik here to see you? I have spoken to him about you and he wants to meet you."

"Of course! I'm pleased to meet anyone so dear to you."

"I've brought this tunica for you to wear." He holds out a cobalt dress draped over his arm and pair of leather slippers.

"You would introduce me in a costume?" A stab of pain slices through my side that he would want to disguise me in one of his concubine's clothing.

"Nay my love!" He protests, "I want him to see you for what you truly are! Not as a monk, but a woman who has beguiled me with her artistry."

Still smarting with hurtful thoughts of donning another woman's garb, I eye the tunica suspiciously. The richness of the dyed textile coaxes my fingertips to explore its finely woven linen folds, finding the silken chamois underneath. Suddenly, the ache transforms into a desperate desire to be a young woman, if only for a few hours left in the day. I sigh in feminine rapture as I gather the gleaming fabric to my cheek and test its softness against my skin.

"I shall return with Tarik anon." I barely hear Majidi leave, as I hurry to cast off my masculine robe and tunic. I fill the basin with water and use a square of linen to scrub myself, noting in the mirror how the heightened coral hue in my complexion brings out the aquamarine of my eyes.

The watery touch of the chamois is like a cool cloud enveloping me from neck to thigh. I luxuriate in its nebulous barrier between my nakedness and the linen tunica. The garment cascades from its wide collar to hug my waist and drape to the wooden planks beneath my slippered feet. I check the arrangement in the mirror, admiring how the sheen of the fabric illuminates the glow in my face. A convenient comb brings my tangled curls to a shining mane crowning my head and shoulders.

Toiletry complete, I twirl and twist about, thrilling in the swirl of the skirt around my legs. Recalling the days when Brigida and I would parade around in the privacy of our closet, pretending that we were grand ladies, I strut across the cabin, reveling in the moment. I pause and marvel at the sun's golden beams bursting through the window, inhaling the breeze as it sifts through my halo of hair.

Turning away from the masterpiece outside, I smile to greet the Admiral as he dips his turbaned head under the low doorframe, followed closely by Majidi. The smaller man steps off the last riser and halts abruptly, his brown orbs open wide in awe.

"An Angel!" He cries out triumphantly and drops to his knees, bearded jaw agog as he stares at me standing in front of the window. Majidi maneuvers off the stairs around his friend, regarding his reaction in surprise.

"No Tarik, this is Adila," he holds out his arm in my direction, "she is..."

His introduction trails off, as he too gawks at me as if seeing me for the first time. Peering back and forth between the two of them in attempt to fathom what has them behaving so strangely, I catch a glimpse of myself in the mirror. The sun streaming in the portal behind me highlights the wispy curls billowing around my head, casting a glow across my face. The blue hue of the dress creates the impression that I'm floating in the sky, my gilded hair an aura of divinity.

"You do look like an angel," Majidi admits, prolonging the awkward moment. I step forward and reach both hands out to the dumbstruck Admiral.

"I am Adila," the thrill of my name dripping from my tongue sweetens my lips into a broad smile. "I heard you playing the pipe a few nights ago, twas beautiful!"

"Your voice even sounds sublime," he grips my hands and rises, continuing to study my face curiously, "there is something heavenly about your persona."

"We are all God's sacred creations my brother." My words strike a chord that seems to break the spell, and he closes his eyes and nods sagely.

"The Admiral," Majidi interjects, "is an orthodox believer in your God, Jesus Christ. It appears that he sees you exactly for who you truly are."

"I now know how my friend is so taken with you," he pumps my hands energetically, "your beauty is exceeded only by your lovely spirit. If there is anything I can do for you, please ask. It would be a pleasure to serve you."

"Thank you Tarik," I begin, touched by his devotion.

"She will tell me of her needs Admiral," Majidi separates our hands and moves to stand between us. The admiral regards him peculiarly and steps back with a bow, acquiescing to his rudeness.

"Of course, Your Eminence," the smaller man exaggerates, earning a piqued expression from his friend. He places his hand over his heart and inclines his head to me, "I must return to my duties."

"What was that about?" I query as soon as the door latches behind Tarik.

"I don't know!" The confusion in his voice, and worry gathering in his brow testify to his honesty. "When I saw the way he was looking at you and touching you, I couldn't tolerate it for even an instant! I've never been even mildly upset with Tarik before, but just now I felt such anger that he was holding your hands."

"I understand exactly Majidi," I stroke his face tenderly, sudden tears stinging my eyes, "that jealousy is the same for me, when I envision you with your other wives and women. Tis why I cannot go to Trebizond with you."

Wordlessly, he studies me intently as if trying to etch my image into his memory. He caresses my hair gently, brushing the tendrils from my forehead and neck, then drawing me into his chest, surrounds me with his essence. He crushes me to him as the sun disappears beyond the sea and darkness engulfs the cabin.

Chapter 13

Dawn exhales her wistful presence through the window above my head. Not wanting to break her peaceful allure, I quietly observe her transformation from somber hues, to joyous vibrancy that mocks my heartache. Her golden arms stretch down the pale stones of my cell wall, beckoning me to rise and greet her exuberance. Presenting my back to her cheer, I commiserate with the dull masonry of the interior of my bed niche.

Renewed sobs shudder through me, drenching my pillow, already soaked with sweat and tears from the past few lonely hours. Lamenting my loss, I play the memory of my last night with Majidi over again for the hundredth time since our parting in the pre-dawn darkness.

Scarcely speaking, we spent the night wrapped in embrace, relishing the touch of one another in desperation, seeing the end fast approaching. Sleep gave way to desire to absorb every moment together, we delighted in each other physically as our bodies joined; emotionally as our tears mingled; and spiritually in the merging of our heartbeats.

The passionate tenderness of his parting kiss quells the flood from my eyes, but inflames my body anew, causing great beads of perspiration to stream across my forehead. The inferno in my cell completes my hell, and I close my eyes and succumb to the misery within and without.

"Brother Adilsen," someone is shaking me, a candle flame flickers faintly in the back of my eyes. "Your isolation is over, you may join us for…"

The words trail off into the recesses of my awareness, murkiness smolders the light. Though I vaguely feel I'm being jostled about, I have no life in my limbs nor alertness in my thoughts. More voices are speaking, one raises sharply above the others, jarring my oblivion. Fingers poke and probe, failing to awaken me from my stupor.

I'm being hefted from my pallet, inwardly crying out at being carried precariously aloft through the black haze. Cold air penetrates my fiery core, gripping me in its frosty chill. I battle the convulsions that spasm through me, then mercifully surrender to the darkness once again.

Blurry figures float through my consciousness, silhouetted by a crisp whiteness surrounding us in sterility. The torrid heat is gone, replaced by a heaviness in my frame so great that I cannot move. I strain to open my mouth and ask for help, my eyes bulging out in effort.

"Adila, can you hear me?" Tears ooze down the sides of my face, I can't speak to reply. I slip back into the malaise that has claimed me for however long, I know not. Time either stands still, or flies by as I fade in and out of sensibility. At times I recognize the fuzzy images of Brother Samuel and Constance, but when they talk to me I can't understand what they are saying, nor can I respond.

"Adila, my daughter, "it is time to wake up." A crystalline voice arouses me from the depths of unearthly slumber. I open my eyes and behold a beautiful vision of Mary, the mother of God. The compassion in her gaze is unchanged after all of these years, since I first sought her holiness in the statue at the Abbey of Novgorod.

"Maman," I whisper in childlike innocence. Ignoring the lead in my arm, I reach out to touch her, but she morphs into a yellowish blue mist that seeps into my fingertips and travels through my arm to warm my core. Though it is dark outside, I'm filled with light and life.

"You still have a purpose to fulfill," this time I hear the resonant tone of my Lord Savior from within.

"God, what has happened to me?" My tongue is thick from disuse.

"You must wake up and pay attention, listen, be still, and the answers will come."

The new day breaks in blinding brightness to witness God's prophesy. I'm able to turn my head to take in the ward of Constance's hospital, and when the attendant comes through for morning rounds, I lift my hand and call for water.

"Constance, can you shave my head?" Two weeks have passed since they brought me from the fires of hell. I had been severely dehydrated, and the heat in my cell brought on a fever induced coma. Constance bemoaned that the workers in the kitchen might have killed me by stoking the furnace adjoining my cell, crediting a miracle that I survived my isolation.

"Shaving is not necessary," she instructs, her jolly demeanor subdued by my ordeal, "that is a northern practice. Here we just keep the hair trimmed and neat."

"I'm ready to join the community of brethren without having to cover my head." I picture my feminine reflection in the mirror, knowing that my curls will eventually give me away. "I feel like the hood separates me, and I desire to commit myself fully to the service of God."

"As you wish," she acquiesces in atypical seriousness. She sits me down in the barber chair and readies her shears with intentional slowness as if hoping I will reconsider. "Shall I speak to the Father Abbot about sponsoring you?"

"Thank you, but Brother Samuel has already agreed to be my sponsor." Seeing my honeyed locks blanket the floor tiles threatens my renewed resolve to dedicate myself to monasticism. "This must be how Samson felt when Delilah cut off his hair."

"Twill grow back soon enough," Constance encouraged, "but you must eat to regain your strength. You're so gaunt!"

"When can I rejoin the others in the rectory?"

"You can try this evening, though I recommend that you remain here for a few more nights so I can monitor your recovery as you adjust to a regular diet."

Her warning about transitioning back to normal foods, not just the broth and pap she had been giving me, proves to be prophetic. As soon as I eat a few bites of gruel at dinner my stomach lurches in protest. I spend the next two nights thrashing on Constance's cot in the ward, alternating between the vomit pail and the toualeta.

After almost a full moon cycle of liquid diet and sleeping in the hospital, I'm finally able to have bland solid food without it running through my gut like water. I'm still having bouts of sickness, but Constance determines that I can at least go back to my own cell. The Father Abbot even comes to visit me and apologize for the mishap with the kitchen furnace overheating into my quarters, and assures me that it won't happen again. My fear of being trapped in the heated room is further allayed by the frigid winds swirling through the monastery, encouraging everyone to linger indoors.

The toasty comfort of my room embraces me as if atoning it's former overbearing heat. I welcome the solitude of the winter nights in my own space to seek the inner peace that has been scattered in the winds carrying Majidi back east. The memory of his ship moored at the pier below the ramparts drives away any desire I may have to venture up the hidden staircase. Instead the divine companionship I discover in my quiet cell, stitches together the patches of my frayed heart, to wrap me in God's healing blanket.

Gently, I ease back into the steady routine of life in the abbey. In my weakened state, I surrender to Constance's supervision over my health and Brother Samuel's tutelage for my spirit. I'm touched by my brothers' support emotionally, and Abbot Nicolas' concern of my person. Once again, my faith rescues me from the precipice of despair, and I'm filled with gratitude for the power of the spiritual world in which I live.

As the weeks stretch into a month, my soul regains equilibrium, but the void of losing Majidi forever takes longer to fill. My heart won't reconcile its emptiness with my mind's decision to move forward from novice, into my anointing as a monk. The two seem to clash in my gut, keeping my bowels in tumult so that I have to sleep with a vomit bucket next to my pallet and carry a leather sack to catch my sudden attacks of nausea. What troubles me the most in all of this, is my loss of physical strength, which has always given me confidence to know that I can run, fight or muscle my way out of any situation.

It is this atrophy that drives me to make my way up the stairs to reunite with the more lively voice of God that spoke to me so clearly before. The moment I step onto the elevated pathway, I'm swept into an exuberant gust that whirls around me in joyous greeting. The wind twirls me out farther onto the rampart, sweeping away any dread over reliving my last encounter here with Majidi, and rejuvenating my laborious breathing. For the first time in many weeks, I tilt my head back and smile.

"My child, you are listening to my call again," the waves slap against the stones of the pier, just as God pats me down like a good-natured old friend.

"Lord, I'm grateful for your healing presence," his playful breeze flaps my robe, lifting my mood, "but I can't seem to make whole my heart this time."

"You carry him with you." The bracing words blow past my exposed ears.

"Aye, that's what vexes me," I speak aloud to my blustery companion. "I cannot let go of his memory, he stays with me like this turmoil in my stomach."

"Find my purpose for you." His blowing words abate, as if telling me to listen more attentively.

"I pray to know your will every day!" Impatience creeps in, "I'm in lessons with Brother Samuel for hours to complete my anointing. I shaved my head and give my life to you!"

"Heed my hand at work, and you shall know." His words are a muted brush encircling my bare pate. "Use the gifts that I have put in and around you."

Following his instruction, I take stock of my blessings, and recommit to applying them each day. Finding every opportunity for physical labor, I volunteer as a courier, running messages throughout the vast monastery. While my fitness slowly improves, I challenge Brother Samuel in my studies, pressing the boundaries of his knowledge so that we often have to consult the librarian for answers to complicated theology. It is only in my gift of song that I'm slightly thwarted, for in my absence a talented new novice had arrived to lead the choir with his sweet voice.

A stab of jealousy slices through my malaise when Ameer is awarded an aria for the Easter ceremony performance. I'm so accustomed to dominating, that the threat of competition is foreign, and I have to take a few deep breaths to cleanse my thoughts of this unbecoming reaction to another's success. My rusty vocal cords further remind me of their abuse and disuse over the past few months. Once I can see beyond my own ego, the beauty of his voice earns my appreciation and I succumb to the joy of hearing him sing.

Being of peasant Armenian background, the slight young boy is ill at ease outside of the choir room, and latches onto me like a duckling in tow. At first, I begrudgingly tolerate the misfit child, connecting with my own self pity over being an outcast. Then something familiar about his mien warms me to him trodding on my robe and trailing my every move, and I get used to him like my own shadow. Perhaps his tan visage and tight black coils on his head remind me of Majidi, and I thank God for the gift of his silent companionship to lift my spirits.

It is therefore, no surprise that he should be the one to knock on my door one morning and deliver a message that I have a visitor in the Bishop's parlor. Great beads of sweat burst out of every pore, my heart pounds. Majidi! Sanity flees my fevered brain and a different type of roiling takes over my belly. My shaking limbs refuse to coordinate in effort to find the way through the corridors, so I barely notice when Ameer takes my hand to steer me to the administrator's wing of the monastery.

We pass by the lavadorium where I pause in a moment of prudence to wash my hands and splash water on my face. The cold drives away the passionate visions of my long, dusky lover, and restores me to some semblance of decorum, ere I enter the elegant quarters where the Bishop stays when visiting the abbey. One bracing inhalation as Ameer raps on the portal steadies my pulse to greet my love.

"Brother Adilsen, my child!" Bishop Stephen's broad smile causes mine to falter. I cast around the richly appointed parlor, for another brown face, finding instead the ruddy features of my friend Nicolo. Fighting my way through a tumult of confusion, disappointment and delight over seeing the hulking viking still on guard, I kneel to the bishop and receive his blessing. In spite of his worldly lifestyle, his hand on my short curls steadies me so that when I rise again I can meet his joy with serenity.

"When they told me you would not be signing the solo at the Easter ceremony because you were ill, I had to come and check on you." His genuine concern moves me to express my gratitude and assure him that my health is improving each day. "Praise be to God for your complete recovery! You are my best recruit for this choir, I want to see you back to your robust condition soon, so whatever you need for your comfort you must tell me."

"Your consideration is overwhelming, Your Grace!" I bow to conceal my cynical grin over his ambitious motives for me, "but I'm quite comfortable here."

"Well, I know one person who will put some color into your cheeks!" I refuse to indulge my wild imaginings that the bishop would know of my connection with the Strategos of Chaldia, "right this way my son."

He ushers me through another small door leading to his private chamber and closes the portal quietly behind me. His spacious bedroom dwarfs a cloaked figure looking out of the window, dispelling any lingering absurdity that it might be Majidi. The slight person turns towards me and doffs the outer garment to reveal feminine skirts framed by the sunlight filtering through the mullioned glass. I gasp as I recognize my beloved sister, and we rush at each other, collapsing into a weeping embrace.

Moaning and sobbing unintelligibly, we surrender to our emotional reuniting, neither of us wanting to let go of the other. It is quite some time before our tears abate and we can interact sensibly, and we pull back enough to beam at one another.

"You've grown even more beautiful, Brigida," even the redness rimming her eyes makes them glow bluer, "you look happy."

"Aye, for the first time, I am Adila," the balm of my real name cheers me, "though I was worried when I heard that you were sick! What happened?"

We sit down hand-clasped on a plush bench at the foot of the bishop's great bed, and I backtrack from when I saw her at the Hagia Sophia. She sucks her teeth and shakes her head when I tell her of how I broke the rules, my isolation and the dangerous inescapable temperature in my cell.

"That was nearly four months ago," She laments, "and you're still so thin and wan!"

"Why thank you, dear sister," I tease, lightly prodding her thickening middle, "though t'would appear that you are in hearty health!"

"I'm with child," she places a protective hand over her stomach, gauging my reaction shyly. I whoop in joyous celebration, and we fall upon each other again, giggling as if we were back in our mean loft in Novgorod. "Nicolo is behaving like a peacock, strutting around like he's doing all of the work! Verily though Adila, he is wonderful. We live together now in his captain's quarters just outside of the palace, and everything is so grand..."

"Adila?" Try as I might to maintain a merry expression, the more she expounded on her life with Nicolo, the more I thought about my time with Majidi. "are you not content here?"

"No I am! I'm very comfortable. Its just that..." I choke on the suppressed tale, tears spilling anew over the aching loss, widening the void in my chest. Knowing that my secret is safe with her, I cry out my experience of seeing Majidi again. I can't bring myself to disclose our passionate lovemaking, lest I slip back into the deep depression that swallowed me into a coma.

She listens compassionately as I describe our lengthy talks, our shared grim childhoods, and our dancing on the parapet. I talk until I exhaust myself and the tears dry up, thankful to be able to unburden my clandestine affair to someone who understands. By the time I reach the part when Majidi leaves, I'm emotionally drained, but she reacts for me.

"You let him go again?!" She admonishes, "didn't you learn anything from last time?"

"There are so many reasons why I couldn't go with him Brigida." I itemize my responsibility to her and Brother Samuel, my vows to the order and the differences in culture and religious beliefs that all stand in the way of us being together.

"These sound like excuses to me."

"He has a harem," my voice grates harsh in my ears, "I can't give myself to him and have to share him with his other wives and concubines."

"Oh, I see," her resolve deflates. "That would be difficult. So you're just going to bury yourself here and forget about him?"

"I do like it here," I bristle at her tone, "I find peace in the routine and silence, I have friends in the brotherhood, and I get to study and sing all I want."

"I think, my dear sister, there's more to life than what you can find within these walls." She punctuates her kind words with a gentle pat on my knee, "and I'm close by for whatever you need."

"Oh yes! I do have something for you." I crack the door, knowing that Ameer will be near by. I whisper to him to run to my room and bring me the bundle from under my pallet. He returns some moments later and discreetly passes it to me. "Please take this with you, I'm afraid someone will find it in my cell and ask questions."

She unrolls the bundle and the soft blue tunica spills across the bench. She holds up the garment, exclaiming at its gleaming quality, testing the silk chamois between her thumb and forefinger. I explain that Majidi gave it to me, but I obviously can't ever wear it again, its more of a liability than a token to remember him by.

"I want you to have it," the blue sheen compliments her eyes, as it did mine.

"It could create trouble for you if someone were to find it in your cell." She folds it back up again with a nod, "I'll keep it for you."

We have time for one more hug, and I'm helping her shrug her cloak over her shoulders when a tap at the door precedes the bishop's muffled voice telling us they must depart. Emerging from the room, I elicit a last minute promise that she must let me know when the baby comes due. I congratulate Nicolo and bade him to send me word of Brigida's welfare.

"Your Eminence," I address Bishop Stephen, "I will do everything I can to gain my full strength for when I see you again. However, I do have one request."

"Tell me child," He adjusts the mitre to cover his head, I help him to tie it securely under his chin and pin on his outer robe. "My one last request ere I take my vows is to be at my sister's bedside when she goes into labor."

"Consider it done! Now get some fresh air and sunshine, the byzantine summer will enliven you!"

Chapter 14

The visit from Brigida does wonders for my mood and health. Though longing for the days with Majidi remains a gaping hole in my heart, the despondency and fits of melancholy from the previous month lessens, and my emotions settle into balance. Energy returns with my restored appetite, and the nausea in my stomach diminishes to a flutter of gas every now and then.

The climate turns milder, and I spend as much time as possible either in the sunny courtyard or on the ramparts. Bishop Stephen must have spoken to the Father Abbot, who has given me permission to take my lessons with Brother Samuel up on the parapet pathway, and I surmise that he relishes being outdoors as much as me. We often share the inspiring view of the sun reflecting off the indigo depths of the Propontis with Dominic, who we've discovered is an excellent resource, having translated many original Arabic texts.

Gradually, my indefatigable thirst for learning and music resurface, and I take renewed interest in my lessons and singing. Together with Brother Samuel and Ameer, we probe the boundaries of conventional musical scales and meter, incorporating the warbling style of islamic religious singing into our more monotone chants. The effect is hauntingly mystical, and we eagerly present our new score to Abbot Nicolas.

"As you are well aware, this establishment has long supported the arts." The Abbot leans back in his cathedra after hearing our trio. His reaction is hard to gauge, he listened to our entire score with his eyes closed, a stillness about his praying hands. "But this so-called hymn is extraordinary! I recognize the vocal fluctuations from our brothers in the eastern territories, and you've done a masterful job of integrating the melody to stretch the limits of conventional scales from the west."

"Thank You Father," we sag into a relieved bow, accepting his critique, "yet we give all glory to God."

"We have the Easter Ceremony performance for the Emperor Basil in a little over a month's time, so after that it would please us if you teach this new expression to the rest of the choir."

Its after Esperinos, and the monks have all retired to the dormitorium when I finally escape Ameer's ubiquity to savor the essence of the setting sun's hues. Orange gold rays stretch out from the disappearing bloody orb, highlighting the belly of blue clouds blanketing the Propontis. The temperate spring weather welcomes ships from abroad that bob in the benign bay like winged parchment cutouts, black against the multicolored backdrop of evening sky. Instinctively I scan the boats for Majidi's ship.

"Will I ever forget him?" I sigh in aching grief, "When will this wound in my heart heal?"

"Seek me first," God's balmy breath murmurs from across the sea, "where you find my peace and love, you will know."

"I'm listening for your word Lord, I'm looking for your hand at work, and I'm following your path for me, and while I'm grateful for your healing my body, my soul still craves him." Logically I should be whole again, and whenever my powers of intellect fail me, I struggle to understand. "I sense that there is some other purpose for me, but I can't figure it out! Is this what you would have me do? Is it?"

"Is it? Is it? Is it?" My plaintive wail bounces between the crenelations where a gust blows it against the abbey walls behind me until the echo fades to a whine.

"Is it?" I meditate, asking myself if all that I do is in search of God's purpose. Weary of thinking, I rest my head on the stone parapet and allow my mind to cease its work for the night. The emptiness in my brain cedes to my other senses, expanding to take in the loamy scent of the wet soil nurturing early buds sprouting vibrant green amidst the wintery grays and browns. The night creatures strike up a tentative serenade, providing a rhythm to which I hum a melody from a hymn that Majidi sang to me. An ethereal voice floats through the darkness to add words to nature's symphony, though I'm so steeped in the magic of the music that I hardly notice Ameer's appearance beside me. The song flows between us and drifts out across the waves, mimicking their pattern of crest and valley.

"God has blessed you with a wonderful gift, Ameer," I commend, forgetting, in the wonder of the moment, that he should be abed.

"And you too! We compliment one another." His heavily accented greek belies his foreign upbringing. "We must commit this to our memories so that Brother Samuel can compose it for the choir."

"Aye, and have two songs to teach them after the Easter ceremony."

"I hope you are not upset that I was given the solo." He is so downcast I nearly chuckle.

"Not at all, my friend," I respond kindly, "your singing is a joy to hear, I shall delight in listening to your aria."

"Good, because I'm very frightened of performing in front of so many," though physical contact is forbidden in the order, I reach out and place a reassuring hand on his arm, "especially the Emperor Basil."

"I was also," I commiserate, "but once we get inside the cathedral, there is an enormous cross suspended above the high altar. The sun illuminates it so that it appears to hover in an aura of heavenly power. If you fix your gaze on that cross, or any one of the sacred mosaics decorating the dome, God will give you the calm strength to raise your voice in praise above the multitudes."

"I shall take your advice," he vows, "for you are very wise and resourceful."

"God's grace has brought me through many trials," I deflect his adoration, my eyelids feeling the weight of the hour.

"I have heard many tales of your bravery and strength from the other novices and monks in the dormitorium." Surprise at his admission brings me back to wakefulness. I had assumed that my past was left behind on the road somewhere north of Thrace! "When I first arrived, you were in the hospital and there was a great deal of whispering over how you were too strong and full of spirit to get sick. Many of them didn't like me at all, they saw me as replacing you, and they missed your presence sorely."

"I had no idea." I murmur in bewilderment. "I hardly speak to anyone, but I am sorry that you have been unfairly received."

"There is a quality of confidence about you that creates belief in others." The moon's glow penetrates the lingering clouds enough to authenticate his truthful expression, despite my doubts that I could ever make such an impression on another. "We all see it in you."

"Why thank you Ameer," I'm amazed at how God continues to put such remarkable people around me, "for the kind words. I've also been told I have a knack for creating drama, so I caution you that I get into my fair share of trouble! With that said, let us find our beds ere the warden finds us!"

Chapter 15

Easter bursts upon us in an array of vibrant colors, smells and sounds. The week leading up to Jesus' resurrection started in the kitchen, with the cooks firing all ovens in order to have all of the baking done in time to celebrate on Sunday. As midweek approaches, we hold daily hymn services for the laity to receive their blessings and communion, during which our boys choir joins the somber bass of the monastic chorus to fill St. Paul's Cathedral with solemn music. Finally, on Good Friday, the women of the city shrouded in black, decorate the Epitaph of Christ with vivid blooms and mournfully tour their wooden caskets throughout the churches.

Father Nicolas allows us to watch the procession from the solar windows in the chapter house, so that we can understand the traditions of the people. The day of our Lord's crucifixion has always been a sedate event for me, but the lugubrious observance of the people of the eastern roman empire is a stirring spectacle. Drops of tears roll down the father abbot's face as he bears the Crucifix around the monastery. The brethren trail behind in similar fashion, some weeping, some praying, some silent.

Through all of the pious cortege of the day, I struggle to maintain a state of meditation on Jesus' suffering. The heat from the ovens has again evicted me from my cell, so I have been sleeping in the busy hospital ward again, even helping the overworked staff during the nighttime hours. Rest has been sporadic with the monks' fasting and vigil for lent, ensuring a steady succession of dehydrated and malnourished brethren at all hours.

A buzzing in my ears nags me after our supper of bread and water, but I pay it no mind once we file into the cathedral for our last singing mass of the day. Once I open my mouth and the sound streams through me, all distractions give way to the power of the music. When we finish, the senior monks deliver the sermon and enact the passion of christ, moving me to tears. After the lengthy service, we commence our candlelight vigil, and I'm thankful that my surge of emotion carries me through the evening hours of praying, kneeling, standing, repeating.

The droning hum crescendoes with each cycle of praying, kneeling, standing, until it drowns my senses in its pestering ubiquity. Through the din in my head, I realize that everyone is standing, and I rush to my feet. The bodies around me spin into one mass of white robes, and the dome above spirals down to encircle me in its whirling mosaic. I don't even feel myself drop to the flagstones beneath.

"How is Brother Adilsen?" The affable glow from Brother Samuel's lantern embodies his gentle nature, penetrating my consciousness.

"Should be fine, tis not like last time." Constance's pragmatic response stirs my wits, filling my body with palpable reassurance that I'm not in a coma. "I feel partly responsible for this, the child has been up during the nights helping me. That in addition to the fasting must have been too much."

"Thank God for that," I'm about to fully open my eyes, but pause at his next words, "but I fear that he may not be suited for this life. It seems as though monumental occasions overwhelm the boy, and rigorous discipline only weakens him. As his sponsor, I'm praying for guidance whether or not to anoint him."

"Much has been required of this one Brother Samuel," I remain still and let Constance speak for me. "We must not forget that when God blesses one with gifts such as this one has, they often come with heavy burdens to bear."

"Thank you for the reminder, brother," the relief in his tone is apparent, "he is the closest I have to family, and I care about him deeply."

"You have invested a lot in the child."

"I have brought him up as if he was mine own; as a parent desires for their children to be happy, so do I want the best for Adilsen. Tis why I pray and question if this is his true path, or if God has a greater purpose for one so richly blessed."

"Your devotion is unmistakable, Brother Samuel," I blink in effort to bring Constance's shadowy bulk into focus, "and you can trust that God will reveal all of the right answers according to his perfect timing."

"Oh he's awakening!" The lantern's incandescence falls on Brother Samuel's concerned countenance. "Brother Adilsen, can you hear me?"

"Brother Samuel," I croak, "you are forever having to wake me up!"

"Aye, my friend," he grins at my jest, "because you are constantly sleeping, and need a nursemaid to stir you!"

"I am sorry to be such a thorn in your side," I sober slightly, sitting up slightly to take a cup of water from Constance.

"Nonsense child," he grows serious as well, "your light has brightened my life in ways you cannot comprehend. We just have to make sure that you're properly rested and nourished, Brother Constance tells me that you haven't been sleeping nor eating."

"You dropped in a faint a bit ago during the vigil," piped in Constance with her practical diagnosis. "dehydrated, just like all these other poor souls whom you've been helping at night."

"Praise God that's all it was," refreshed from the water, I sit up and try to stand, but the dizziness returns.

"I'm going to move you to my pallet so that you can sleep uninterrupted while I tend to the ward." She drops a restraining hand on my shoulder, "Brother Samuel, I'll watch over your protege if you want to return to the others to resume your vigil."

"Yes I will, thank you," he hesitates, "it sounds very selfish, but do you think he'll be okay for the ceremony on Sunday?"

"With some rest and sustenance I have no doubt."

Satisfied with the report, Brother Samuel left with a wink of encouragement, taking his benevolent glimmer with his lantern. Constance gives me more water and some bread with a bit of salted fish, and bids me to lay down while she readies the bed in her room off the main hospital floor. Much fortified, I move into the crowded cubicle, drawing comfort from the clean scent of herbs, medicines and parchment.

My eyelids grow heavy again as I scan the rows of tomes and scrolls that line the walls up to the ceiling. Nearly hidden among the tapestry of books, I espy a small round window paned in vibrant stained glass. The image is of Mary holding the broken body of her beloved son Jesus. The rendition of her expression captures her agony so effectively that my throat convulses with emotion, and tears stream down my temples.

Gaze fixed on her countenance bowed in pain and sorrow of

witnessing her son tortured and crucified, I find a meditative state so deep that I drift in and out of sleep, not knowing where conscious thought ends and vision begins.

Saturday dawns in anticipation of the resurrection celebration. Restored in body and spirit, I switch roles with Constance, and while she sleeps, I administer to the infirmed. Meals and services throughout the day are simple and perfunctory, robes and cowls are laundered, and Father Nicolas mandates baths for everyone.

Aware of my terror of overheating, Constantine asks Brother Aaquil, a suitable name for the monk in charge of the mechanics of the waterworks, to instruct me how to control the flow of the hot and cold water in order to adjust the temperature. His enthusiastic demonstration, pulling levers and hopping around the gears in the tiny closet off the bath, evokes an indulgent grin in spite of my trepidation. I convey my thanks and take a deep breath, closing the door on the steamy bath.

The contrast of having my head and shoulders bathed in the cool water from the spillover, and standing in the warmth of the pool is the most pleasurable experience I've had since my affair with Majidi. Stress washes from me, and I delight in my first real bath in months, scrubbing my skin until it gleams a healthy pink. Rinsing in the waterfall, I lament my soft belly and rounded hips, chiding myself for running to fat in my complacency. Regret is short lived, however, as I massage the soap through the stubble of hair, cleansing away layers of grime with a sigh of delight. Thoroughly refreshed, I don my clean tunica and robe and join the brethren in the chapter house to discuss our itinerary for tomorrow's celebration.

"We expect everyone to adhere to the rules of our order," begins Father Nicolas, "heads covered, maintain proper decorum, and fall in rank and file. We have decided however, to relax the restrictions on interacting with the people. We have seen the benefits of connecting with outsiders through our fellowship and joy. Therefore, if you are moved to administer prayers, or share religious song, you may, as long as there is no physical contact with anyone. Brother Leontius, please go through the song list for us."

The head choirmaster stands and reads the program with all of the performances, starting with the Hagia Sophia secular choir, then our senior Studiites, through our boys chorus, and finishing with a grand finale Hallelujah of the combined groups. The choral numbers will take an hour or so, during which we will be required to stand.

"Tomorrow will be a joyful celebration, but also an arduous ceremony. We will break our fast in the morning with our Easter feast, and I encourage you to eat plenty to ensure your strength throughout the long day ahead." He directs his pointed gaze at me, eliciting a rueful frown, until he winks in good humor. "The Hagia Sophia will be crowded inside and out, and once we're in place, the patriarch's flock and Emperor Basil with his court will proceed to their places by the altar of the cathedral."

My mind wanders to the letter I wrote to my sister in hopes of seeing her again, telling her of my improving heartiness and the lump of emptiness in my chest that is taking longer to heal. Distracted by thoughts of Brigida's well-being, I half listen to the Father Abbot counsel us on the lengthy sermon, consecration and communion, warning us that it will be nearly Espirinos ere we return for dinner.

"So let us disperse from here to the rectory with my blessings for a nourishing dinner and fortifying night's sleep!" Preoccupied with our individual concerns, expectations, and festive musings over tomorrow's activities, we all mechanically drift with the tide of routine through the rest of the evening.

"Constance, I don't want to displace you from your pallet again tonight," I hide my yawn in the back of my hand, wanting to bed down for the night. "You heard what Father Abbot said, that we need to be well rested for tomorrow's ceremony."

"No need to worry about me Adila," she bustles around her room, collecting the items she will need to tend to her patients throughout the night, "I've been excused from the excursion so that I can stay here and attend to the needs of the sick."

"What a sacrifice!" I exclaim, shocked at her selflessness that she would miss the glory of celebrating Christ's resurrection amidst the grandeur of the Hagia Sophia. "You really must stay behind?"

"I'm not that saintly," she chuckles, "'tis my choice not to attend. When you've been to as many of these things as I have, you find that quiet reflection can also be a pleasing way to glorify Jesus. But you can return the favor by telling me all about it when you get back."

"I feel God's presence in the majesty of the cathedral," I recall the beams of light illuminating the massive cross above the high altar. "The way our voices saturate the entire space, from the glittering dome to the gleaming marble flagstones, is a testament to his delight in our praise."

"Ah my child," she tilts her head to the side and regards me wondrously, "you truly do have the spirit of Christ burning in you! How you shine when you speak of singing to God's glory."

"I see a similar delight in you when you are nursing the sick," her compliment gives me solace that she can still find God in me.

"Exactly!" She pats my cheek and returns to her task, "now be a good girl and get some sleep, and remember to stuff your pocket with the grapes and roll I brought for you so that you can have a bite during the service when no one is watching!"

The trek along the Mese seems distinctly lengthier, the hills steeper and the weather warmer then when we trod the cobblestone thoroughfare almost half year past. Gleeful sun laughs jauntily at the renewed earth, casting its unfiltered delight in rays of orange, gold and magenta over the bleached buildings and tender foliage. Our pace is slow, so my breath is strong as I join in jubilant song with the joyful masses that throng the broadway. The enthusiastic crowd sweeps us along until the mountainous Hagia Sophia swallows all through her colossal opening.

The coolness of the mosaic flooring welcomes all grateful visitors to the refreshing interior of the cathedral, ushering us up the nave to the choir. Keeping my head as low as possible, I peer from under my cowl at the multitude of faces for my sister. It is a bit of a challenge to hold onto an image of Brigida's cobalt eyes and alabaster complexion, with the grandeur of the soaring domes and massive construction competing to capture my attention. We assume our position in the apse, and I stifle a twinge of angst that I couldn't locate Brigida, a daisy in a forest of chestnuts.

In the partial privacy of the apse, I'm not the only monk to discreetly gawk at the wonders of the greatest church in Christendom. I marvel at the sheer height of the walls stretching to the heavens, making insects of the congregation. Boldly admiring the decorated domes, I notice the cross and banner of our order sway precariously.

Ameer has been honored with bearing the standard, and I slide into a gap next to him just in time to catch his sagging frame against me.

Instinctively I know that the boy is in a faint, and I silently bless Constance for supplying a tiny vesicle of urine and vinegar to break open in case I get lightheaded. I pop the pea sized sac and hold the pungent liquid under his nose to revive him immediately. His watery eyes thank me, as I slip a bunch of grapes in his hand and point to the massive cross above the altar to remind him to stay focused on God. I return the staff bearing the Studiite icons to him, as trumpets announce the arrival of the Emperor.

The fanfare of the imperial retinue commands the hundreds of eyeballs in attendance, making me forget all else to take in the dazzling porphyry and gold costumes signifying the family born in purple. Absorbed by the extravaganza, I nearly miss the light blue regard of the giant Varangian beckoning me until I meet his eyes. A wink and a reassuring smile from Nicolo puts my mind at ease that all is well with my sister, allowing me to concentrate on our forthcoming performance.

Anthony, the Patriarch of Constantinople, is the last to take his bench next to Bishop Stephens, completing a glittering array of worldly wealth. I imagine God beaming through the arched windows that crown the lofty dome, looking down upon his children, pleased with the rich tapestry he has created. Tightly woven together in his vast house of worship are all shades of humanity and artistry. Our beauty is his masterpiece.

Punctuating my musings, the cathedral choir erupts into a base chant that rumbles through the very stones under our feet. Their deep voices reverberate in my soul, grounding me in veneration of my lord. They continue with a celebratory hymn, and our monk's choir follows with a psalm that transports me to ecstasy in its beauty, so that I'm startled out of my trance by Brother Samuel indicating our turn to sing. In the sanctified hush between numbers, he directs Ameer to begin his solo, counting him down to begin. Instead of the saintly aria we're used to, I hear a faint gargling croak and feel him clutch my arm. Distressed by his crushing inability to overcome his anxiety, I rub the remainder of Constance's compound under his nose, heartened by his jolt to attention. I nod at Brother Samuel to restart his count, praying for God to strengthen the youngster.

To my chagrin, a mere whisper escapes the petite form at my side. Intuitively, my voice reaches out to bolster his, the lyrics of his solo taking flight from my lips to ascend the mighty walls and spiral through the cavernous basilica. I squeeze his elbow until I elicit a heartier timbre, then allow my singing to fade into his. He finishes his refrain with his own tongue, then the other novices join in for the remainder of the hymn. For the rest of the musical performances, he leans weakly against me, my arm under his for support.

The afternoon wears on, my feet and legs heavy like tree trunks from standing through the tedious service. I watch the sun shift from one side of the church to the other, amazed to discover paintings in the dome that I hadn't seen before because of direction of the light. I share my portion of bread with Ameer, my attention drifting from my churning stomach to the patriarch standing behind the ornate altar. Once the service concludes, I try to shuffle close enough to the emperor's recession hoping to shove Brigida's letter at Nicolo, but can't get close enough without being obvious.

Father Abbot eventually leads our brethren out into the square teeming with masses of people who weren't able to fit into the cathedral. Though the temperature has cooled, the mob percolates feverishly, zealously shouting biblical references. As we cleave the undulating crowd, my senses sharpen to perceive angry undertones piercing the air around us. On high alert, I mutter to Ameer ahead of me to step lively and keep up to the older monks ahead of us. No sooner do I issue the warning, then someone brandishing a club breaks upon us screaming something about killing the bearer of icons.

My violent past serves me well, and I jump in front of Ameer to intercept a blow that would have crushed the boy. Covering him bodily, I absorb the bludgeoning about my back, feeling no pain as the erstwhile red haze clouds reason with anger. In between beatings, I strike out and catch the offender's wrist, feeling bones crunch in my viselike grip. I'm about to pummel his exposed ribs, when a hulking figure jerks the club from the villain and pushes me back with a shake of his helmeted head.

Nicolo's calculating assistance rescues me from the fog of rage ere

171

I do something I will live to regret. He easily restrains the zealot, and encourages me to hurry to catch up so no one else gets hurt. I start to follow his advice, when he adds that this is why he wouldn't allow my sister to attend, and that she's doing well. Remembering my letter to her, I shove it inside his breastplate, pick up the fallen cross and bustle Ameer forward.

By the time we reach the monastery I'm in such agony that I can barely walk upright to the hospital. My whole body is in spasm, the pain radiating from my bruised back to wrench my gut. Constance takes one look at me and immediately pulls me back into her room and lays me down on the pallet. She calls out to her aide for some linens and buckets of cold sea water, then strips off my cowl, coaxes my cassock down my shoulders and cuts away my bindings, exposing my throbbing back.

Soaking the towels in the icy water, she gently covers my back, bidding me to lie prone and let the chill take away the sting.

"My stomach hurts so," I gasp, gripped in a cramp that twists my loins. "I'm trying to stay still but the pain…"

"Ah my poor dear," she shakes her head in exaggerated pity. "I'm afraid you may lose this one."

"What do you mean?" I pant between waves of torment ripping through me, each one harder than the last. "I've taken worse beatings than this and survived!"

"Your baby," my befuddled brain snaps to attention, "I don't think we can save the babe growing inside of you. Not to worry, Adila, the pain will pass soon and there will be others."

"Baby?" The word tumbles around my head, refuting my attempts to coral its meaning. I peer dumbly at my distended belly and groan in disbelief, "He told me he couldn't conceive!"

"Good God," Constance reacts to my startled expression, "you didn't know? You're still very slim, but you must be what, five months along?"

"How did you know?" I slur incoherently, laboring to follow the conversation.

"You forget that I'm a physician," she pours a syrup into a spoon and holds it to my lips, "just a drop t'will dull the pain. Besides, you haven't come to pick up any menstrual bindings in many moons. But there would have been other signs too, nausea, tender breasts…."

She continues to list the symptoms of my pregnancy that I had attributed to illness. The elixir slides warmly down my throat and eases into my stomach, allowing for a temporary pause to digest the stunning reality of my predicament. My addled thoughts won't behave long enough to sort out the spinning tale of Majidi's inability to conceive. Did he trick me? Was it all a sham? Another spasm rips through my innards, etching the agonizing doubt into the backs of my eyeballs until burning tears spring forth and I groan in anguished rage.

Shrugging off Constance's restraining hands, I lunge to my feet, growling in perverse pleasure, welcoming the shards of lightning stabbing my loins. Anything to dull the brand of betrayal searing my brain. My stomach lurches and hardens in effort to evict the tiny life, while my soul screams to hold on to this kernel of love. Keening sobs seep through the bars of my gritted teeth and my body releases its burden in a slippery crimson gush. Unable to look at the bloody remains puddling at my feet, I search for a diversion and find not one, but two dark pools glazed over with moisture, reflecting my own trauma of treachery.

Brother Samuel's tacit shock invades the cell like a wide-eyed gargoyle, yet his form remains frozen in the doorway. His regard encompasses my tunic gaping from my breasts, the gore between my legs, and Constance wrapping what is left of the fetus into a bundle, reciting prayers to speed my child's passage to heaven. Truth registers coldly on his visage, and he turns his back and departs with a finality that shoves me back onto the pallet. In the span of a few seconds, I've lost my love, my baby and my best friend.

The stoppered vial of opium syrup beckons from where Constance placed it on the shelf before she left with the soiled bindings. If such a small amount could provide temporary relief from physical discomfort, I ponder what a larger dose could achieve.

A prickling desire to dull the reality of my misfortunes nudges me forward again, prodding my hand to reach out. Suddenly, a piercing ray of blue light blinds me and I fall back, searching for the bearer of the irradiate sword.

Once again, Mary rescues me from tumbling over the precipice of pain into the abyss of self pity. The same benevolent soul who drew me into the embrace of the church as a child, now caresses me with the compassionate gaze of a mother who lost her son. The setting sun illuminates her cerulean eyes and cobalt robes, creating the blue blaze that intercepted my selfish intention, reminding me of all that she had to endure.

"You are not the only one to suffer loss, Adila." The glass drops of her tears speak to me.

"Holy Mary," I beseech to the glowing window, "I try to listen for God's will, and follow his path for me, but I find only loss and misery."

"God teaches us in hard times," the dust mites carry her silent message along the beam to settle upon me, "but he always brings us through. Just as he restored my son to me, so there will be others for you."

"How can there be other children if I am to take vows?"

"That is an inquiry for tomorrow, child," Constance's logical voice gives me a start. "For now, let me help you don this fresh tunica on and get you patched up."

"Thank you," I grasp her forearm, arresting her attention, "I don't deserve any of this."

"Nonsense," the smiling creases in the corner of her eyes are magnified behind her spectacles, "everyone errs from time to time, but I still see the spirit of Jesus in your aspect."

"I've made a terrible mistake, will you hear my confession?"

"I think the less I know the better," she catches my chin as it drops in disappointment, lifting my gaze, "but know this Adila, there's no sin that won't be forgiven. There is one more suited than me to hear your confession soon enough."

Inky silence paints the contents of the room, penetrates the crannies between the shelves, and hangs, nebulous in the air. A single candle burns steadily on Constances's desk, casting a feeble glow into the opaque space. At times I detect Mary's luminous visage, outlined faintly by the moon outside the portal, though I may be dreaming.

Sleep teases me in short stretches until the bruises on my back wake me to relive the trauma of yesterday. As if a bystander to the drama of my life, I drift through the recent events, some times alert, other times in fantasy. My sore body reminds me of the very real pain of premature childbirth, then I fall into the realm of slumber and envision my baby lying in the straw of a manger. I haven't had anything to eat or drink since the morning before the Easter service, and my tongue feels thick and fuzzy.

The candle flickers, a draft in the airless cell, my senses sharpen to its source. A slight shade flits around the perimeter of the cell, I clutch my tunica to the pulse pounding in my throat. Not sure if I'm dreaming or not, I stifle a cry when the shadow approaches my bedside and reaches for me. A familiar musk reassures me that I'm indeed awake.

"Ameer," I sag back onto my stomach with a sigh of relief. "You gave me a fright!"

"I had to come and tell you myself," he kneels down at the side of my pallet, "thank you for your help with the performance yesterday."

"I'm pleased to hear that you don't think I overstepped."

"I don't think anyone even noticed that you sang for me," he paused. "More importantly, you saved my life. You took the beating that was meant for me. I don't know how I can ever thank you."

His childlike gratitude sparked a realization that grows to warm my entire being. I gave the life inside of me to save his.

"Can you sing to me? Something new that I haven't heard?" I request, "the balm of your voice is all I need in return."

The wistful thread of words he weaves together masterfully into a melody is as elegant as a spiders web, ensnaring my attention in its silky net. For some reason beyond my ken, the fibrous tune transports me back in time to a crisp night sitting atop the parapets, surrounded by the music of the wind whistling off the propontis.

The dream, when it comes, fills me with unprecedented joy in the knowledge that the hopeful sprite still dances within me. Through all of my misdeeds and trials, I feel the pull of purpose yet, something out there in the heavens that drives me onward.

This time, however, I am no longer a boyish child spinning energetically along the starlit path. My image is of a young woman, pregnant with graceful power, sashaying towards an unknown destination.

Chapter 16

"Forgive me Father, for I have sinned. It has been six months since my last confession." I kneel at the feet of Abbot Nicolas, humbling myself before his authority. "I have deliberately lied before God to everyone about my gender, masquerading as a boy when I am in truth female. Then I disobeyed your orders to remain isolated in my cell, and defied the rules of the monastery to avoid the guest quarters."

It is a difficult task in itself to pray to God alone and admit my shortcomings, but the humility of confessing my mortal sins to another human being is more challenging than any physical feat. Though my body has had a few weeks to heal from the beating and miscarriage, I'm weak and trembling as I summon the strength to finish.

"God help me," I inhale deeply, the smoke of incense in my nostrils clears my head. Stillness permeates my limbs, commanding them to cease shaking so that I can continue. "Among my numerous venial sins, my last mortal sins are of fornication and adultery, for I have fallen in love with an infidel."

"You may rise my child, and receive the salvation of Jesus Christ for your sins." The abbot delivers prayers of forgiveness and absolution with the gentle stoicism of one who has seen and heard much of carnal sin. "What is your true name, and that of your fellow sinner?"

"My name is Adila," with the first public proclamation of my name, it is as if scales of deceit and dishonesty fall from me and I'm light as a cloud. "And his name was Majidi."

After a heavy pause, during which I stand, head bowed, before Father Abbott, he shuffles across the room where I hear the jingle of crystal. I suffer a moment of panic that he may not finish my penance, until the swish of his robes reappears before me.

"By the power vested in me, I baptize thee, Adila, as a daughter of Christ," sobs of ecstasy wrack my frame he anoints my forehead with holy water, "in the name of the Father, the Son and the Holy Spirit. Amen."

"Adila, beloved child of God," his words lift my chin and square my shoulders, "your sins are forgiven, and you are born anew into the church as your true self."

"Thank you, your excellency!" I'm floating without the burden of sin to weigh me down.

"Now return to Brother Constance's cell and pray for the remainder of the day. Your confession is as extraordinary as your person, and I must seek guidance as to your penance." My feet find the floorboards again, "I will send for you on the morrow."

The two hulking Varangians who show up the next morning to escort me to the Abbot's chambers, put my reborn faith to test. That fragile resolve is further shaken when they usher me into the presence of Abbot Nicolas, and see Constance and Brother Samuel already there, and Bishop Stephens occupying the abbot's ornate chair. They all scrutinize me in my plain laic tunica as if seeing me for the first time.

"Your Eminence, Brothers," the father abbot recognizes the group, "it is my pleasure to introduce our daughter in Christ, Adila."

His kindness turns my lips up in a timid smile, which evaporates under the cool regard from Brother Samuel. Constance winks conspiratorially, while Bishop Stephens inclines his mitered head in businesslike greeting. The abbot indicates I'm to take up a place beside them and continues.

"Those of us in this room are the only ones who know the truth of this matter of sex, and I want to keep it that way. I will bear the burden of one last deception and let it be known that Brother Adilsen has perished from his injuries." The gravity of my dishonesty weighs in his ponderous tone. "We have determined that Brothers Samuel and Constantinius had no knowledge of Adila's gender, and are therefore not responsible in any way for harboring a female in our midst. You both may return to your duties but communicate to no one what you have seen or heard."

The finality of his statement tolls like a death sentence, punctuated by the thunderclap of the portal behind the two dear souls, to whom Adilsen is now dead. Were it not for Constance slipping a piece of parchment into my hand as she brushed against me on her way out, I would have crumpled to the floor, as lifeless as I am proclaimed to be. Instead, the hand of God props me up to receive my penance.

"From the first day of your arrival here at the monastery," the abbot speaks earnestly, "I perceived a strong spirit in you, a quality that your silly cowl could not hide. In that short amount of time since, you have stirred our hearts, aroused our intellect, and enchanted our senses. I have prayed all night for another way to harness your gifts for our order, but God will not allow me to defy the trust of the brethren and knowingly house a woman in secret."

Each word drops like clumps of dirt from a shovel, burying Adilsen in monk's robes. This is the moment I had feared every day that I've lived this facade, and though I'm deeply saddened with loss, I am prepared to accept the inevitable. Levity of truth replaces the burden of carrying on this charade, helping me to accept banishment from the monastery. The grief of leaving my friends, my mentors, my studies and my music, is altogether another feat for grace to uphold me tomorrow.

"I would not be doing justice to God to throw you out of the order and into the streets on your own, that is not penance, but punishment." He reads my thoughts,

"Nor do I believe his end for you is to wither away the days living under your sister's roof, your gifts are too grand to not be put to use. To this end, I have consulted Bishop Stephens and together we have prayed for inspiration as to how to nurture God's purpose in you."

"We have contemplated sponsoring you as a noviate at the Kassian Convent, our sister order," when I recall Constance's tale of her beginnings in the nunnery, a warm seed of kinship tickles my psyche. "They are dedicated to the arts as we are, though they study in seclusion, unseen and glorified to the outside world."

"Not the right place for the woman who has finally captured the cold heart of the Strategos of Chaldia." Bishop Stephens douses the spark of enthusiasm with his harsh interjection. It strikes me that the only times I've seen the bishop with his ceremonial headdress have been in his official diplomatic capacity. "We deem it useful to the church to cultivate this connection."

"You're making too much of a temporary affair, Your Grace," rising alarm emboldening me to contradict the bishop, "he does not love me!"

"The matter of your penance is not up for negotiation," he bristles, "though I will indulge your incorrect opinion with my own insight on the Strategos' feelings for you. While on his visit here, he declined all but the mandatory engagements that he would customarily have attended. Throughout the events that he did appear at, he was distracted and anxious to leave as soon as possible. Our inquiries revealed that he had a female companion, whom he was very taken with, which is highly out of character for our militant friend. He is renown for his frigid views on women, so twas a rather humorous rumor that one had finally warmed his heart."

"We are therefore in the process of negotiating with the Strategos to release you into his care." The abbot's cavernous parlor dims with his pronouncement. "You will remain under Nicolo's watch until it is time for you to travel to Trebizond." The air in the room stifles my wits. "Your task will be to abide with him there, and convert him to Christianity."

"No Your Grace!" His sentence knocks me to my knees in supplication, "you are wrong about him! Even if he did care for me, if you make me a pawn he will hate me for it. To him I will be just another obligation, another responsibility to cast aside!"

The masonic press of the walls grips me in a vice of panic as the room crowds in, and the Bishop shoves himself out of his throne and towers over my prostrate form. I dare not raise my face to his outrage, for surely no other being besides the Basilius has ever challenged him thusly. I partly expect the hand of God himself to strike me dead.

"Who are you to question my authority?" For such a small man his voice reverberates mightily through the shrinking space. "You should be bowing down in thanks that we don't send you to the dungeons or worse for impersonating a monk!"

"You are right, your Eminence," Father Abbott punctures the tension with his sharp wisdom, "this impetuosity is exactly why the child is not suited for a life of quiet contemplation, but it is also what makes her valuable. She provokes others to think about their ways and customs."

"Yes, but Adila," he resumes his seat and I hazard a glance at his hardened countenance, "you must adjust your temper to reflect your gender. You have lived as a boy, and as such have been allowed certain privileges that people won't tolerate in a female. Your mental acuity will be frowned upon, your physical capabilities will be a detriment and certainly your verbal outbursts could be deadly."

"How will I fight without my weapons?" My mind cries out to the hollow span that's left between the squeezing walls.

"God will go with you my child," the almighty voice of God speaks calmly through the Abbott, girding me in his divine armor for yet another war, "he will fight this battle for you."

Chapter 17

Hot breath stirs the hairs of my nape, arousing me from the trenches of slumber. A luxurious sigh teases the corners of my lips up into a content smile at the thought of my insatiable lover. When I don't respond, he nudges my shoulder aggressively, tossing me forward in the bed.

"Majidi!" I drowsily roll back, "haven't you had enough?" I jest, the memory of our lovemaking still fresh from what seems like moments ago. His silken face caresses mine, until his prickly whiskers finally tickle me awake; but the great sable eyes that greet me are not set in the handsome visage of my love.

"Belasarius!" Nicolo's warhorse snorts in retort, then returns to snuffle me affectionately to full wakefulness. In the mental void between torpor and awareness, I savor the simplicity of my surroundings. Nestled in a stack of hay in the corner of Belasarius' stall, hugged by a large woolen blanket, I'm warm and comfortable while my eyes adjust to the morning's light peeking over the half door separating the animals from the first level of Nicolo's apartment. Within the silence of the stable, the rhythm of the giant horse's breathing fills the space with soothing natural melody; while without, the staccato of busy pedestrians provides background vocals. Seeping past my cellmate's pungent aroma, the smell of food cooking draws me from the last vestiges of sleep. I prop myself up on my elbow and contemplate the majestic creature lipping the crop of straw on my head.

"You're not quite as handsome as my last bedmate," I scratch the swirling hairs between his eyes, my bawdy wit shocking the Christian in me, "but I would rather ride you than he!"

Recalling yesterday's trek to the multi-leveled apartment, built into the apron wall that encompasses the sprawling palace grounds, I can only laugh at the absurdity of the sudden turn of events. The joy of reunion was overshadowed by my shocking predicament, and Nicolo's embarrassment over not having suitable accommodations for a houseguest. The Bishop hadn't even forewarned them, but sent his orders on a scroll with the guards who escorted me into his custody.

"What say you Belasarius, shall we escape to the forests beyond Thrace and lose ourselves in the twisting ravines where no one will find us?" My old friend from the journey down the Dneiper banks, shakes his mane and puffs his lips.

"You are right, we couldn't do that to Nicolo," I concede to his wisdom, the limpid empathy in his gaze evoking further contemplation. The irony of going from a monastery full of chaste men, to a harem occupied by concubines festers like a tumor, threatening to consume the years of Brother Samuel's teachings to accept God's path.

"How will I survive in a house of polygamy and sexual slavery?" I pose to the understanding creature.

"The same way you survived in an abbey of monks." He stretches out his neck so that I can reach to stroke behind his ears, his basic nature and response so profound. God will show me what to do, and this time I won't have to wear a disguise.

"You certainly are a smart horse," he rubs his head against my arm, and I wonder at the lord creating such an endearing beast. "What shall I do when Majidi doesn't like me anymore because they're forcing me on him?"

"I like you," he nickers softly, "even after all this time, I remember how you would pet me, take care of me, sing to me. You give of yourself, and others love you for it."

Sill musing this sentiment, the nearby peal of a bell announcing Proti Ora summons my habitual response to make my way to the day's first service. By rote, my feet mechanically march toward the sound to the Hagia Sophia, and deposit me in front of the massive altar cross, a beacon for the third time. I sate my soul on the symbol of Christ's presence, nourishing my confidence that he will be with me no matter where I go. My courage is short lived, however, as an ornate miter spikes into my view, Bishop Stephens affixes me with an incredulous look.

"You must adjust your behavior to reflect that of your true self, Adila," his imperious demeanor is not as sharp sitting in Nicolo's kitchen, as it was in the great cathedral an hour ago. The wise and holy Bishop Stephens who led us from the forests of Novgorod, now talks to us as he did then, competent, kind and patient. He stretches his hand in bidding to my hugely pregnant sister, "Brigida, can I charge you to instruct your sister on how to employ her womanly wiles and instincts to guide her through this journey?"

"Yes your Grace," she promises, "'tis the least I can do now that you've fulfilled my wish to have her by my side for my labor."

"While your piety is admirable," the bishop turns back to address me, "I'm sure you didn't intend to trouble Nicolo by absconding to the cathedral. If you swear to me on his life that you will remain here and accountable to him, I won't have to put a guard to follow you around."

"I swear by the Holy Mother Virgin Mary, on the life of my brother Nicolo, that I will not stray from here without leave from him or you." I vow, heavy with the regret of bringing upheaval into their quiet home. "I am sorry for causing problems, I wasn't thinking!"

"Nay Adila," his rough voice is tender with my real name, "'tis I who owes you an apology for not being able to accommodate you. My sister deserves better than to sleep in the stable!"

"Nonsense Brother!" I rush to assuage his embarrassment, "I would much rather have Belasarius at my back than most people."

"Which brings me to my next request," Bishop Stephens interjects, "Nicolo, you are well versed in court intrigue, will you teach her how to navigate the treacherous wilderness of palace life?"

"That's easy enough," the cynicism in his tone belies sarcasm, "don't trust anyone."

"That's a start!" We all stand when the bishop rises and places his mitre back on his head. "I have to get ready for the next service, but Adila, next time you must wear something suitable to your station and stand in the balcony with the other women."

Summer swells pregnant with heat and rain clouds bursting at any moment, like my sister's belly. Humidity seeps into my bones, thawing all remaining permafrost from my past, then sweats back out of my skin to be whisked away by the cooling sea breeze. Paradoxically, the sultry climate seduces my norse blood to bask in this sultry warmth.

Only at night do I toss and turn in my straw bed, jealous of my bedmate's swishing tail and twitching hide. The bite of mosquitoes ails me more than the afternoon fever that lingers past Esperinos. Not even the netting that Niccolo strings up can compete with the lure of Belasarius' feral aroma, that attracts the heartiest sort of flies to pester my slumber.

Accustomed to keeping strict hours, I arise each morning with Nicolo at Proti Ora, attend service and spend the early hours learning the ways of the Byzantine court. We start with etiquette and decorum, how to courtesy, how to address the layers of nobility, how to eat, drink, stand, sit, basically relearning even the simplest daily function. My dear brother, however, instructs me how to do everything inconspicuously, so that I can move about unnoticed. Hiding has been my way of life, so I pick up on the importance of this skill to survive the slippery intrigues of bureaucratic life.

Together we tour the palace grounds, where he points out staples of Roman domestic living that I might find in Trebizond, and how I am to comport myself in each setting. Though the Senate building intrigues me, Nicolo cautions that I must stay away from the men and their business, but then shows me how to sneak in through the side door and hide behind the tapestries to listen. The ostentatious throne room consumes a whole morning session to watch the theatre on display: the Emperor descending in his chair from the ceiling, amidst the cacophony of mechanical birds chirping and golden lions roaring.

We finish our lessons in the catacombs below the hippodrome, where I attain the darker skills I will need to defend myself. Though Bishop Stephens defrocked me of my monk's robes and male status, God equips me with a new set of armor; how to use poison and stealth to defend myself. Cloistered in his cell under the stadium colonnades, the court apothecary shows me medicines and herbs that he dispenses to cure and how they are misused contrary to God's will. I study the qualities, smell, taste, of plants meant to do everything from prevent conception, to increase ardor, even death.

Deeper in the bowels of the arena's underworld, Nicolo introduces me to the royal armory and its morbid array. He has me strip off my outer tunica and straps on leather armor over my short chamois. Rather than select the familiar viking axe or broadsword, he arms us with slim, short rapiers and proceeds to train me for close combat. He shows me the vulnerable points in the armor to stab through, and the exposed skin to slice at. He even challenges me to use every part of the knife to stun, throw, maim or kill. I master defensive parries, footwork and how to use my hands as a weapon. For the first few days, my memory balks at the closed heat of the armory fires, but eventually the exhilaration of physical exertion and intellectual stimulation takes over and I develop and appreciation for these sweaty sessions.

Especially when he leads me out of the murky recesses of the hippodrome, and leaves me with Brigida at the spacious Bathhouse of Zeuxippos. From there my sister picks up my domestic education, cultivating my feminine core. We soothe our sore bodies in the cold and tepid pools. While we relax in the bathhouse, or stroll the palace grounds, she shares her insights on how to employ our woman's wiles to influence others. I would never have guessed the power of female intuition and guile, without Brigida's tutelage. She in turn, had observed how maman could put an idea in our father's head, and make him believe that he came up with the thought himself. She passes along nuances from her time at court, like how to act demure and subservient without compromising her dignity.

"Try to saunter with your hips forward when you walk Adila, like thus." she thrusts forward her mountainous torso, gasping at a cramp pinching her back. We fall onto one another, in a fit of giggles at the ludicrousness of social custom.

"So we must cover our hair as to not overtax the male sexual self control, and we train our gaze to the ground in submission, but I fail to understand the purpose of straining our backs to walk in such a fashion."

"I'm no expert," we continue our stroll through the palace market, "but prominent hips suggest fertility."

"Well that should garner you plenty of attention!" I laugh at the ridiculousness of what we go through to please our male counterparts. To punctuate my jest, we pass a trio of leering guards who hiss and whistle at her. "See! You've already stirred their feeble imaginations!"

"Oh they're not for me, their admiration is for you!" I dare a glimpse over my shoulder to catch six dark beads fixed on my backside. "Sister, tis important that you recognize your attractiveness and anticipate the attention you will draw. You already have a sense of the danger in being caught unawares, but you must also be keen on the subtlety of seduction. A compliment is a powerful tonic that lures us to do things we wouldn't normally do."

Her indirect admonition of her own transgressions sobers us, as we weave our way through the plaza teeming with merchant's stalls and citizens haggling over wares. We find our destination, the candlemaker's kiosk, where we purchase candles and oils of citronella. The apothecary recommended the lemon extract to repel the mosquitoes, so we have been anxious to buy the vials. On our return, the eave that the guards had been loitering under was vacant, prompting me to look around and see them following us. Instinctively I push our packages at Brigida and shove her in front of me.

The first oaf makes the mistake of gripping my shoulder, triggering Nicolo's trained reflex. Like an arrow loosed from a taut bowstring, I shoot out my arm and chop him in the windpipe. Gloating at my perfect execution - no one, not even the guard sees what I did - I nearly tumble over my sister who has dropped the bundles. By then the next guard is upon us, colliding with her backside as she stoops over abruptly. Before I can react, she steps back, her sharp heel trodding hard on his toes. In one swift motion, she gracefully retrieves her wares from the ground and stands upright, catching the dolt under the chin so that he chomps on his tongue. His howling brings his third comrade to his rescue.

"Oh dear me!" Fusses Brigida, "I dropped my packages and didn't know he was so close behind."

"Not to worry Madam, he'll be fine," brushing aside her contrived concern he kneels in the dirt to retrieve her wares. Over his helmet, my sister winks at me to punctuate her point. I begrudgingly grin in understanding that not everything requires force and fight, but finesse and a little bit of farce. Suddenly her eyes bulge and she looks down and gasps. She sweeps aside her skirt to reveal a puddle at her feet.

"Its time," with the calm courage that takes ahold of the bravest of warriors as they walk into battle, Brigida reaches for my arm, "send this good man to Nicolo and take me home."

"Do you know Nicolo, the Varangian Captain?" I bark more sharply than my laboring sister, "seek him out and tell him his lady is about to give birth!"

In a touching tribute, Nicolo and Brigida name their baby Adilsen. He is christened by the bishop in a private ceremony; and at the same time, I receive his blessing over my travel to Trebizond. Whatever seeds of wisdom I have managed to absorb will have to suffice, as I am to leave my family in a fortnight and take on perhaps the greatest challenge of my life.

Though Bishop Stephens won't disclose the agreement he reached with Majidi to send me there, Niccolo shares with me what he hears from the barracks and palace halls.

"There has been excitement among the troops because the Strategos has finally agreed to lead an expedition of elite immortals into the heart of the southern Armenian mountains to invade a large monastic city." The kitchen fire burns low, softly crackling as it eavesdrops on our quiet conversation around the table. Its glowing embers throw conspiring shadows across the three of us ere we retire for the night.

"Several years back the roman city was taken over by muslims, the bishop imprisoned in the cathedral, and the army quartered in the monastery. The city had been a christian stronghold for centuries, and Bishop Stephens has lamented its loss of revenue and resources." Nicolo explains, "due to his proximity in Chaldia, the Strategos was petitioned numerous times to help him recover the city, but Majidi declined every request."

"Why did he refuse to help the bishop?" Brigida questions, "the ladies at court say his passion lies only in military matters, and he agrees to any expedition that allows him to roam about."

"The official excuse he gives is that he is preoccupied with business for the Basilius," sarcasm tinges his tone, "but I've heard the emperor opine that, while his governor does not strictly observe islamic tenets, he does hold onto the customs of his people. He prefers not to upset his populace by coming into direct conflict over religious matters between muslims and christians. But now he has suddenly changed his mind, and delves directly into the heart of ecclesiastic politics."

"So you think his willingness to go now has to do with me?" I envision myself carved of ivory, with the conical helmet and armor of a pawn piece.

"Aye, my guess is that Bishop Stephens is using you to sweeten the pot." He affirms, "if the Strategos will retake the cathedral, overthrow the infidel and reinstate the bishop, he will send you to Trebizond."

"He must certainly love you Adila," romantic idealism shines in my sister's lovely visage, alighting on the olympic profile of her viking rescuer. Her desire for me to share in her happiness softens my rebuke.

"Tis not love Brigida," my wistful words convey pessimism, "nor is it about religion or allegiance. This is statesmanship, ownership; and I am now officially a token in the Strategos of Chaldia's game of chess. Tis all he knows."

"Then you must beat him at his own game." Her abrupt simplification cuts through the morbid thoughts crowding my head. Our eyes meet across the oaken planks, and for a moment I feel as though Maman is staring back at me in her slightly disturbing way when she was particularly prescient. "Do you remember what I told you when you feared you had lost Majidi in the forest?"

"You told me that it is never too late for love."

"Yes, Adila," her voice is filled with conviction as she gazes upon Nicolo and Adilsen asleep in his cradle, "and love can always win if you believe in its power."

Chapter 18

Clinging to the back of the giant warhorse, a raft bobbing along an undulating sea of endless gravel, we drift down the road hugging the southern shore of the Euxine. Belasarius is my only friend, a temporary gift from Nicolo, but even he will only take me as far as the Chaldian border, where we will rendezvous with the Strategos' people. So I bury my tear stained face in his mane and let him carry me along the current of change to my unknown fate.

The guards sent to escort me ride in tight formation, giving the appearance of a mountain on the move. My hair, bleached white in the stark summer sun, streams down my shoulders, which are clad in the blue tunica that Majidi gave me many moons ago. From my lofty perch, I am the snow covered peak and the swarthy guards, on their diminutive Arabic horses, the slopes. When the pale ribbon of road disappears into the night sky, they erect a small tent for me and bring a plate of salted fish and bread.

Over the next week, I learn yet another treasured skill from my compact entourage, their Armenian language and muslim practices. Five times a day we stop and dismount for them to kneel in prayer to the East. Their humility and discipline impresses my monkish upbringing with a deep and abiding respect for their religion. Although they call God Allah, just as my maman used other names for hers, their belief in the power of something that makes all things happen is the same. While I connect with the loving nature of Jesus, I understand their attraction to the austere guidance of Muhammad.

All too soon we reach a narrow pass between the mountains and sea, marking the beginning of Chaldia. Greeted by a mixed band of guards, eunuchs, immortals and administrators, I bid farewell to the faithful Belasarius who shakes off my clinging arms encircling his neck, and nudges me toward their waiting vessel. With a grunt and puff of his nostrils, he nods at me in assurance that everything will work out.

The boat taking us the rest of the way to Trebizond is slim but sturdy, easily accommodating the few dozen of us; crew, guards and myself. One of my new companions, a stately looking man with pointed features and turbaned head, ushers me directly into the captain's quarters at the back of the boat and cautions me to remain there for the duration of the trip. The squeeze of captivity grips my chest, but instead of feeling the press of the cabin walls, I find the windows and study the landscape as it slides by.

The mountains are puce silhouettes against a magenta canvas of the evening sky, when a soft rap on the portal finally draws my attention from its travels along the distant Chaldian shore. The muted glow from a lantern enters, illuminating a broad grin set in a familiar dusky visage.

"Admiral!" Joy at the sight of Majidi's friend leaps up, and I throw my arms around his shoulders and kiss his cheek heartily. An imposing figure of a guard trailing the captain, presses me back with what sounds like a feral growl behind the impassive mask of an immortal.

"I thought you could use some fresh air and company to dine," he invites with a sweep of his hand and a sheepish bow that hides his pleasure from my exuberant reception.

"But the man with the turban bade me to stay in here." With all of the difficulties I've caused for friends and family, I'm sensitive to stirring up trouble for Tarik.

"I command this ship for Majidi and God," how refreshing to hear the lord's name from another's lips, "Damian's vizier has no authority on board, so you need not heed his command over my wishes."

"Then I gladly accept!" His defiance stiffens my resolve, and I step out onto the wind swept deck and whisper a thanks to the star speckled heavens for sending a friend. Over the tasty fare of fish and bread, he counsels me on the hierarchy of the noble household. From his truculent tone, I gather that he is not fond of the vizier and eunuchs who accompany us, and he goes so far as to warn me about the head eunuch especially.

"The others in the harem may be jealous, and their eunuchs are their agents who carry out their ill intentions." He advises, "as a newcomer, don't even trust the eunuch and servants assigned to you."

"What about Liang Na?" In spite of her marriage to Majidi, she is the only hope I have for companionship. "Will I be able to see her?"

"The princess is in the highest and most fortified tower of the seraglio complex," he shakes his head, "it will be difficult to get past her guards to see her. You are strong and intelligent, and you have God on your side, so I know you will figure it all out. If you ever have need of me, however, one of my ships will always be at anchor in the small harbor under the citadel. You will see when we get there tomorrow."

THE GARDEN

Trebizond tumbles down verdant valleys and spills into the bay waters of the Euxine. We glide past merchant ships, fishing boats and sailing vessels of all shapes and sizes, flying flags of many empires to attest to the multicultural metropolis. Though colors of many nations bob happily in the bay, the buildings of the city, by contrast, are like white knuckles, pale from the strain of clinging to the precarious slopes. Crowning the highest peak, the walled Citadel bathes in the golden glow of the morning sun, a gilded tiara that rests heavily on the heads of its inhabitants.

Formerly built as a church dedicated to the patron Saint Eugenious, to commemorate where he cast down the statue of Mithras to end paganism in this greek outpost, the Citadel is now the seat of Chaldian government. In order to reach my new domicile, we toil up the paved streets, winding like a serpent through gleaming stuccoed residences and marbled edifices and statues. The mountainside is so steep that the route zigzags deep into the valley among flowering oleanders and azaleas, towering spruce fir and corpses of oak and beech. The strenuous climb has me breathing heavily and sweating right through my kirtle and tunic. I'm so embarrassed by my disheveled state, I don't even mind that Majidi wasn't at the docks to greet me.

The mounted Vizier and eunuchs round the far corner of the walled compound and are swallowed into the yawning portico's jagged teeth. Bringing up the rear on foot, I sharpen to my surroundings, as the guards behind me prod me to keep pace through the mercifully flat citadel grounds. Without so much as a pause, nod or backward glance, the vizier leads us through a disorienting maze of tower staircases, corridors through the keep, and ramparts connecting another gatehouse. One last set of guarded doors delineating the men's world from the women's domain, and we end our journey abruptly in the middle of an airy receiving room.

Finally able to catch my breath, I survey the luxurious suite of apartments opening out to a balcony overlooking the seraglio. A eunuch garbed in a flamboyantly tailored dress, whom I speculate is the head eunuch, speaks in rapid Armenian to another bald, tanned servant, assigning him to oversee my household. Two female attendants await in the background, and the immortal guard seals off the doorway from whence we came, trapping me in this opulent prison with his eerie masked stare.

"Adila!" The hollow ring of my name brings a fresh sweat to my nape, but no butterflies in my belly. "My new favorite, how good to see you again!"

He approaches, arms outstretched to receive me; but he is not Majidi. The opaque glaze coating his eyes is impenetrable to my search for the soul of my love. Outwardly he is the same tall, lithe beauty that impassioned me to break my sacred vows, but on the inside, this man is not the real Strategos of Chaldia. Repulsed by the thought of touching this innate being, I drop to my knees.

"Sire," I supplicate at his feet, "I am not worthy of your presence after the long journey. I have the dust of the road, the smell of horse, and the curse of blood upon me! Please forgive my uncleanliness, and grant me reprieve to tidy myself."

Damian retreats a step at my dramatic performance, while a muffled laugh emanates from the direction of the guards. With a sniff of pained impatience, he motions me to stand, and forces a cordial mien.

"Of course! I am eager to see you again after making such a fuss to bring you here, so you will pardon my impetuous greeting." His gross conceit stuns my wits so that I dumbly succumb to his perusal. "Surely you've grown since I saw you last, you're as lanky and sturdy as a colt! At least your face still holds the freshness of your tender age."

Bowing slightly as his insult punches me in the gut, I hide my repugnance behind feigned submission. Adequately acknowledged, he spins in a swirl of silk and brocade and departs, snapping orders to the servants to have me scrubbed and scented. Like fish trailing the shark, his vizier, the Archieunuch and personal servants swim after his menacing form.

"Mistress Adila," the lone remaining eunuch drifts to my side, his curtsy as graceful and flowing as his vivid orange gown. "I'll take you down to the bathhouse now, as you'll be wanting a bath."

From the gleam of the sun reflecting off his shaven pate, to his manicured toes peaking from under his gauzy linen chemise, I see the eunuch as if for the first time. A pall of regret clouds my heart with a moment's sadness, for the toll of the unnatural effects of castration on a mature man. Outwardly he is well formed and comely, but his complexion is that of a boy and his stature is that of a woman. Kohl lined eyes belittle me, even as he inclines his head in subservience.

"No, I don't want to go to the bathhouse now." I'm too exhausted to temper my tongue. A sigh from behind me draws my awareness to the immortal guarding the portal and the serving girls standing in the passage leading to another room. Though hidden in the shadows, I imagine one of the girls' shoulders shake ever so slightly in suppressed laughter. A gust of briny air calls my attention back to the balcony overlooking the walled seraglio and beyond, the city and harbor. Inhaling the sweet sea breeze, I know that God is with me, speaking through me. "What is your name?"

"I am Nerses, and I am at your service." The sugary tone of his accented greek thinly disguises his resentment in having to take orders from a lowly female. His snobbish mien tickles my memory of being bullied as a child, but I resist the urge to prepare for battle, recalling what my sister taught me about using my female wits instead of my fists.

"Thank you Nerses, but I am much too tired to take another step today. It has been a long journey and I need to rest."

"Of course Mistress," he acquiesces, gesturing to the serving girls, "there is also a hip bath in the water closet so you can wash in private. I will have the servants bring water and refreshments."

Though I want to clap my hands in agreement, I merely nod my dignified consent and dismiss him to carry out his duties. He crooks a finger to the servants to do his bidding and clears out the room with a sweep of his outstretched arms. Releasing the well of breath imprisoned within me, I relax into the stillness of being alone for the first time in weeks.

Despite my heavy limbs, the tiled frescoes on the walls around the room beguile my fancy, inviting exploration of the pleasant apartment.

Leaving the arched balcony, I wander across the colorful rug, past the marble-sashed main portal and trail my fingers along the wooden furniture padded with brocade tapestry. A small round table and chairs next to the balcony and a few comfortable divans along the perimeter, compliment the purity of the creamy alabaster stones - the foundation of the Trebizond architecture.

A distant rush of water beckons me to cross the threshold into the bedroom, where it is slightly cooler in the shadow of the afternoon sun. Intentionally ignoring the opulent bed shrouded in curtains, I pursue the sound to another balcony on the other side of the domed room. Stepping out onto the platform, I gasp and clutch the marbled portico to catch my balance. The sheer plummet into the valley below is both terrifying and breathtaking to behold. The fortress curtain wall merges into the heavily forested mountainside, watered by a river flowing a league below. I shudder at the perilous beauty, retreating back into the sanctuary swathed in silken cushions and plush rugs.

The two young girls return, each shouldering yokes with buckets of steaming water. I follow them through another door into a spacious bath closet. They pour the water into a waist high cylindrical basin, and light several sconces to supplement the dim light from the windows, then scurry in and out until the tub is full. As they toil, I admire how the marble flagstones and tiled mosaics continue from the other rooms, though here the smooth slabs are unadorned with rugs or curtains. A smaller bowl and urn for washing hands and face sits atop its pedestal, partially obscuring the toualeta built into a niche in the masonry.

An ornately carved cedar chest crouches against the opposite wall, and a tall framed pane of glass lounges next to it. Before curiosity snares me into lifting the lid of the trunk, or peeking at my image in the mirror, the girls have the bath ready and close the door. The three of us stand awkwardly looking at one another.

"Mistress," the taller one with an angry scar puckering her cheek, takes a half step forward, addressing me in childish Armenian, "may we help you disrobe and bathe?"

"I can do it myself," I reply in my limited knowledge of the language, thankful for her rudimentary speech. They both bow in graceful confusion and stand to the side as I discard the filthy blue tunica and once white chamois. The scented liquid engulfs me to my shoulders when I sit cross legged in the tub and lean back against the rim. Cramped but content, I melt into the polished stone and let the warmth seep into my joints.

Engrossed in pleasure for several moments, I forget about the two silent figures still awaiting my whim. I point to a sponge and bar of soap, which the smaller child passes to me, eyes downcast. Vigorously sloshing about, I unceremoniously scour the grime from my skin, my spirits rising as my tanned complexion gleams happily in the soft light. Twist and turn as I might, however, I can't find a way to get to my back and hair. I glance in askance at the girls.

One look is all it takes. The girls are well trained and attuned to meet every need, and they heft a bucket and pour the water over my head. Scrubbing soap into my scalp and massaging my back, they transform the bath into a whole other experience altogether. For the better part of an hour, I'm rubbed, buffed, oiled and brushed until I finally step from the basin cleaner than a newborn babe.

The chamois they bring floats over my head and settles around me like a cloud, which they cover with an orange tunica of linen so supple it flashes like liquid fire. Guileless admiration beams from two pairs of hazel pools, as the girls urge me to the mirror to view the fruits of their ministrations. I brace myself for the shock of seeing Maman in the glass again, but the elegant, vibrant image that I encounter is far too sophisticated to be my mama.

Maturity and experience have rounded the sharp angles of my face and frame. The ease of surrender softens the frown that was previously etched between my brows, enhancing the allure of innate contentment. Whether due to the fecund changes of pregnancy, or the improved diet of privilege, my hips and bottom show a promising slight curve of the woman I will become. Only the marine eyes that stare back at me are those of Maman's, replete with tired smudges underneath, reminding me of my travel fatigue.

Saying a tacit prayer for God to keep me while I rest, I crawl fully clothed into the draped haven and burrow amongst silken cushions of the vast bed. As my vision narrows with slumber, I glimpse the inscrutable mask of the immortal guarding my repose.

Chapter 19

The bell tolling for Proti Ora peels back the layers of sleep, until I awaken in dismay that I'm late for morning service. I scramble through the tangle of luxurious covers, I must have fallen asleep in Majidi's room in the guest quarters of the abbey. Adding to my groggy confusion, is a vivid nightmare that I was expelled from the Studiite monastery for miscarrying a baby, lived openly as a female, and forced into the bondage of the Stratego's harem. The dream was so detailed, were it not for the outrageousness of it all, I would think it actually happened.

The gong ceases by the time I tumble out of the plush nest and plunge through the netting hanging from the bedposts. I take a few stumbling steps in the semi- darkness and stop short when I come upon two young serving girls holding trays of fruits and fish. The scar on the cheek of the taller maid jars my reluctant cognizance into obedience. I slump back down on the bed, beseeching God to still my spinning thoughts.

As if in response, a keening voice punctuates my plea. Its haunting song calls me to a window overlooking the harem, where I locate the sound emanating from a minaret beyond the walls of the seraglio.

"Allahu akbar, Allahu akbar," God is greatest, I translate the Armenian chant, "Allahu akbar, Allahu akbar."

"Thank you Lord," I whisper back reverently, "for reminding me of your greatness."

Shivering slightly as the stout sea breeze penetrates the light fabric of my new clothes, I pull back from the sill and cast about the room for something to stave off the chill. The diminutive serving girl materializes before me holding up a velvety robe, which I slip into with a grateful smile.

"Will you break your fast now, Mistress?" The other girl leads us to the sitting room and places the trays on the table, then opens the doors to the balcony. My stomach groans in affirmation, but before I break fast I must break water.

"I will be there shortly," I hie to the water closet and relieve myself in the touleta, using a nearby sponge on a stick contraption to clean up. My heart sinks momentarily when I inspect the sponge for blood and find none; my mensus is finished. Hunger winning over worry, I wash my hands and wipe my face, anticipating eating for the first time since yesterday morning.

Quickly blessing the food, I reach for some dates, but both girls put up their hands in outcry and stop me from touching anything. The more talkative one speaks rapidly so I can't comprehend, until she makes a dramatic charade of eating then choking.

"We must taste your food first," she slows her speech, "poison."

This reminder of invisible danger sobers my appetite, and I sit quietly and watch the girls nibble from each dish. They smile and nod that they are still alive, and for me to proceed with my meal. With significantly less enthusiasm, I pick at the fruits, bread and boiled eggs under the steady observance of four hazel and green orbs.

Studying the girls for the first time, resemblance to someone I can't quite identify pesters me to probe. Both are slim and petite, with skin like nutmeg and comely features. Thick chestnut and brunette hair is loose under linen veils that match the modest cut of their dress. Growing up in a community where everyone looks the alike, I'm aware of my innate prejudice to lump others with different qualities together, seeing them only as one and the same. As a child of unusual upbringing, however, I have always viewed everyone as a unique and beloved individual, peering past outward discrepancies.

It is their eyes that attract familiarity, large and thickly lashed, the older girl's slightly more green, the younger's like golden honey. The light of innocence shines from them both, and I know with confidence that they will be my allies in this shrouded battle.

"What are your names?" A startled pause answers my unexpected query. An imperceptible glance at one another, then a decisive shrug.

"My name is Mariam," the older one curtseys, "and this is Lusine."

"Why doesn't Lusine tell me herself?" I note that Mariam is the only one to speak.

"Beg your pardon, Mistress, but she does not have the power of speech. She has a still tongue." The younger's somber gaze confirms her defect.

"How many years do you have?"

"With God's grace I will have eleven years this winter, and Lusine has nine."

"You are Christian?" I lean forward in joyful interest at having company in Christ.

"My father, the Admiral, raised me to follow the teachings of Jesus Christ. My sister's sire left her to the muslim traditions of our Armenian grandmother, though my mission is to make her a disciple." The doting smile she bestows upon her half sister tells me of her love for her savior and younger sibling.

"Is your father Tarik, the Strategos' captain?" At her nod I send God a silent thanks for this angel, "He is a pious man, what does your mother think about him bringing you up a Christian?"

"Our mother died when I was very young," regret for my callous questioning wells up in my eyes, but she continues as if she's recounted the tale many times, "but our grandmother took us in and cared for us as if we are her own. She was the Master's nurse, so she had much experience in rearing children, and prepared us well to serve in his household. She even knew how to maim me, and silence Lusine's tongue without causing pain."

"Excuse me?" Did I understand her correctly? The shock of what I think she said eclipses my sorrow, "your grandmother did that to your cheek?"

"She had to do it!" Jumping to her grandmother's defense at my horrified exclamation. "It was the only way we could work in the harem without suffering abuse. She knew how to use herbs and medicine to make the mark without hurting me."

A sharp rap on the portal rescues me from the disturbing conversation. I'm almost relieved when Nerses floats through the entrance, his disquieting presence pressing the girls back into the fringes of notice. He scans the receiving room as if I'm not sitting there at the table in front of the balcony, then a tiny perplexed furrow mars his smooth brow. Unable to suppress the grin as recognition snaps his eyes back to me, I rise proudly under his appreciative perusal.

"Mariam and Lusine have done wonders to refresh me, Nerses," the bath, rest and food have my mettle high, "will you be so kind as to guide me on a tour of the premises?"

"It will be my pleasure mistress," he acquiesces, sweeping out to the balcony for a bird's eye view.

"The main walkway runs down the middle of the harem," he points at the paved pathway between buildings, "and past the main fountain in the central plaza."

"I can hear the sound of the water from here." Its aqueous babble seems to be everywhere in this place.

"What you perceive now is coming from the aqueducts directly behind your apartments, which flow downhill to supply the rest of the citadel and city." As he explains, I notice the narrow arched channels like arteries throughout the body of the complex. "To the left side are concubine apartments, then the bathhouse. To the right, are more residences and the pool and gardens."

"What is that tower past the gardens?" I indicate the daunting fortification rising above the far end of the gardens.

"That is the old keep, which now houses one of the Stratego's three wives." My attention sharpens, "the others are in the far west corners of the curtain wall, which are not visible from here."

"Which quarters are for the Princess Liang Na?" I lean over the balustrade, straining to glimpse the structures to the left.

"That is none of your affair," he sniffs. "You will have no contact with them, so you need only know not to venture along the perimeter of the harem. Concubines are to stay in their place in the center of the enclosure."

Smug in his restored authority, he leads me out of my apartments, through a corridor and down a wide sweeping staircase connecting to the central walkway. As we pass in between the multistoried apartments rising on either side, the prickle of eyes upon me scratches away my earlier bravado. Hushed voices fall silent and curtains are drawn when we pass by shadowed doorways and windows. A babe cries from an overhead suite, and a child giggles from the depths of rooms to the right.

The tiered rows of ivory dwellings open into a plaza with a grandiose fountain splashing playfully into its shallow fish pond. The sun climbing over the garden immerses the rotunda and surrounding structures in its brilliant glow. Dignified cypress and friendly olive trees encourage future exploration of the shady park extending for acres up to the forbidden tower in the far corner of the encompassing wall.

"Though the plaza is empty now, as things are generally quiet in the mornings," Nerses explains, veering to the left around the fountain towards a domed building blushing rosy in the early light, "this is the heart of the harem, where most of the women and their children gather to pass the time. And here we have the bathhouse, another favorite place, as the master has spared no expense for your comfort."

He points out the various amenities and features of the cavernous space, evoking my reluctant agreement of its spectacular attributes. Three separate pools are divided by wafting white curtains hanging from the painted frescoes on the vaulted ceiling. Murals of goddesses blowing cool, balmy and sultry breath, adorn each section's walls, indicating the water temperature as cold, tepid and hot. Waterfalls spill into each basin and circulate fresh liquid, reminiscent of the monastery bath I loved so much.

Cases of bottles containing soaps and oils hold the seductive promise of scent like the eucalyptus incense burning from pots dotted throughout the room. Polished granite benches scattered throughout are evidence of the need for ample seating during busy hours. So far however, the only other souls we've encountered have been a few scurrying serving girls and a pair of bathhouse attendants. At least I'm assured of being able to find privacy early in the day.

"There you are Nerses," a chiding voice interrupts him describing the responsibilities of women assigned to the bathhouse, "my servants tell me that you have not yet prepared my food for them to bring to me."

"I beg your pardon Mistress Zoe," his impudent tone contrary to his words, "I did not think you would be about at this hour. I'll see to it immediately."

Without so much as a glance in my direction, he glides away to do her bidding, leaving me alone with the flawless woman. Her heavily kohl-lined eyes scour me from head to toe, one corner of her red stained lips curling up in a derisive smile.

"Well, if it isn't the Master's new favorite." The syrupy syllables ooze from her tongue and congeal on the cool marble flagstones under her small pampered feet. "It appears he has replaced one beastly lover with another monstrosity!"

Snickers from the attendants goad her to make fun of my robust stature, an old taunt from my childhood that nonetheless still stings. Pausing in prayer, ere I let her insults sink into my soul, I search her ebony glare for signs of vulnerability that would cause her to disparage someone whom she doesn't even know. Her mouth moves, but the scornful slight that I'm not as ugly as his previous preference, bounces off impotently.

"I dare you to say that to Keket," a voluptuous figure, with a young boy nestled in the curve of her hip, joins the fray. "She would eat you alive!"

Her bustling energy crowds into the room and circles around behind me. Self assured in her motherhood, she views me with a glimmer of convivial challenge in her pleasant visage.

"You're up early Hayfa," the daintier woman spits, "and with the boy too. Come to mark your territory?"

"A word of advice, love," I sense duality in Hayfa's care of my being, "don't take potions to keep you from having children. Twill make you grow bitter, like Zoe here."

"It is much too early for all of that ladies!" the spacious interior is starting to fill with yet another addition to the group, their servants flitting in and out. A breathtaking young woman approaches and takes me by the arm, steering me outside. "I am Indira, and I'm pleased that you are here."

"I bet you are Indira," Zoe hisses as she trails out of the shaded building and into the heat of midday, "so you can try to seduce her to your perverted preferences."

"Hush your vile tongue! Jealousy is unbecoming of your station as the emperor's daughter," my petite patron admonishes, "besides, you know our master is virile enough to keep us all content. If not, however, you can find comfort with me!"

"Aye, she's mannish enough to attract your fancy." A sultry figure lounging on the wide rim of the fountain adds to the outrageous conversation. Indira releases me and whirls on the lithe beauty with a flurry of incomprehensible verbal banter.

The once placid courtyard bursts with feminine chatter, colorful dresses and graceful figures. The womanly scene warms me like the benevolent sun, reminding me of the days spent traveling through Russia with my sister and Liang Na. I peer curiously up at the aloof tower, then back at the walkway beginning to bustle, and slip away unnoticed into the garden.

Neat rows of herbs and vegetables give way to brambles of berry bushes and grape vines. A tidy grove of citrus, olive and nut bearing trees thicken into a forest of fragrant cypress and cedar that extends downhill as far as the eye can see. I wander about the underbrush, feeling nostalgic for Majidi and the time we spent lost in the wilderness. As if reading my thoughts, a hare sprints out from under a bush in front of me.

"I could survive in here forever, the land is so bountiful." I lament out loud.

"That is not why I brought you here," the grumble of thunder carries God's message, punctuated by a gust of cold wind portending rain. Resigning to his will, I navigate my way back to my suite as the rainclouds release their fury. Sodden and shivering in my thin dress, I'm ill prepared to combat Nerses' stormy expression confronting me in my receiving room. He chastises me for my disappearance, lecturing me on my deportment as he shutters the windows and sets about lighting sconces.

"I have other concubines and responsibilities under my care," he complains, "and I cannot be nurse to a wayward charge. These tempests arise quickly from across the sea, and you must be nearby to secure your apartment against the damage that the water will do to its contents."

"I will exercise caution henceforth," I grit through teeth clenched against the chill. "I wasn't aware that the weather changes so suddenly."

"Autumn is our rainy season, so nearly every afternoon we experience these downpours." Seeing my quaking limbs, he takes pity and directs Mariam and Lusine to stoke the fire. "You've missed dinner, but I'll have a plate sent shortly."

He departs abruptly, fuming from my lack of compliance. In awkward silence, the subdued girls helped me out of my wet clothes and wrap me in the plush robe. Mariam sets a hassock by the fireplace for me to sit, and brings a comb to tame my errant curls, while Lusine hunkers down on the carpet and rubs the circulation back into my feet. As the rain patters against the stones outside, the crackle of the fire, the gentle tug of the comb, and the warm friction of soft hands, conspire to snare me in a trap of contentment.

In a trance, I perceive Maman's sweet song comforting me with its airy tune. Her hazy countenance transforms into a shadowy visage playing pipes, which fades into the night sky as awareness dissolves.

Her lilting words waft in the wood scented darkness around me, evoking a vision of a determined young woman, filled with poise and purpose, and I see myself floating along a starlit river in pursuit of the moon. Not even the preposterous contents of the day can penetrate the mystical apparition, as the twinkling stream seems to form a pathway transporting me from swaying precariously on the stool, into a realm of musical joy.

As I cross into a dreamlike state, the bright moon forms a fiery ball that spreads from its grate in the wall to flood my consciousness. The ethereal aura that once lit only my path, now intensifies to drown out the melodic voice, arousing me back to reality. I perceive her gentle warning to stay alert, now is not the time for fantasy. She tells me I must wake up, and share the light that I can no longer keep inside.

"You must not sleep now," Mariam's plea echoes my maman's advice, and I open my eyes to cheerful sunlight pouring in from the balcony and windows, where Lusine finishes pulling back the drapes.

"My how quickly the weather changes in these climes!" I yawn and rub the remnants of Maman's specter from my face. Without warning, the door bangs agape and belches forth the malevolent presence of the Archieunuch. Startled, I jump up, swaying dizzily from springing upright too fast. He takes in my bowed posture and washed aspect with stately derision.

"Where is Nerses." He demands, his arrogance hailing the hairs on the nape of my neck to stand at attention.

"I do not know," I straighten to my full height, sizing his long frame against mine. He is a full head taller than me, but very thin, so I judge that I could easily best him in a physical confrontation. Then I remember my sister, and Nicolo's painstaking teachings that this will not be a battle of might, but of mental acuity. Thus I wait on his explanation for his intrusion, which doesn't take long, ere we hear the slap of sandals running in the corridor. Nerses scuttles breathlessly into the crucible of the head eunuch's ire, who unleashes a tirade of rapid Armenian.

In any language, the flourishing gestures and angry tone transmit their displeasure in my attendance. The taller man shakes his beringed, tapered finger in my direction, saying something about my whereabouts, to which my beleaguered servant points out toward the seraglio and counts off a number of names. They continue to argue back and forth, while I study them in amusement.

"Silence!" The Archieunuch barks, then addresses me as if I am dung on his shoe, "is the curse of blood still upon you?"

"Yes!" I seethe in retort, because indeed the hematic haze of old throbs through my head, blocking out reason. "And I would caution you to announce yourself before you intrude into my quarters."

"I take my orders from the Vizier, not a common whore like you!" Mounting righteous rage deflects the injurious intent of his abuse. Trembling with the craving to bury my fist in his gut, I drop my heated gaze from his malicious orbs, ere their gloating goads me to sinful action.

"You are to inform me as soon as her courses are finished." The slam of the portal behind him discourages retort or resistance to his orders.

"You should not have provoked Zinvor," Nerses forebodes, "the Archieunuch oversees the entire seraglio, and answers only to the Strategos and his vizier."

"To what end?" I question, "will my food arrive late? Will my bathwater not be hot?"

"Tis folly to trivialize his influence, he has the power to make life happy or wretched in this place."

"For you perhaps," I perceive Nerses' fear of anything that will disrupt the glassy plane of routine in the harem, "but as for me, God alone gives me joy and peace."

"You better pray that your God will protect you from his vengeance for disrespecting him."

"Disrespect him?" I laugh at the irony, "it is acceptable for you to quarrel with him, yet when I confront his slander, I'm the one who is disrespectful?"

"You are a woman, a concubine," he regurgitates the labels that male customs have twisted to mean subservience, "and you will do well to remember that."

"Yes I am a woman," the essence of feminine force stiffens my resolve, "but I will never be a slave."

After yesterday's tumultuous introduction to life in the seraglio, I embrace the freshness of a new day. Having slept well in the knowledge that I have purchased reprieve at the expense of Damian and Zinvor's offended pride, I wake prior to the gong of the Proti Ora, and step cautiously onto the miniature platform outside of my bedroom. The morning mist in the valley below is so thick, that it obscures the forest and river in its depths, creating the illusion that I'm in a castle built in the clouds. The rush of water grounds me in nature, as the sonorous chant of monks drifts across the gulf.

Locating the source of the music of morning service coming from a monastery high above the opposite side of the chasm, I kneel at the balustrade and join them in song and prayer. Thus fortified to meet the day, I emerge from my sanctuary to greet my young companions, as they arrive with baskets of strips of cloth and tufted wool.

"For your mensus, Mistress," Mariam meets my quizzical expression, with a trained guileless grin. I follow them into the bathroom to perform my morning functions and poke around among the bindings I am to use to absorb the blood that has ceased to flow. Among the padding, I find a tiny dark red bladder and bless my coconspirators for providing false evidence of my continued bleeding.

The delicate serenity endures through breakfast, and invites me to descend to the vacant plaza. I drink in the fountain's cheerful babble and soak up the sun's amiable radiance, having the cosseted courtyard to myself. When the shadows grow shorter, signs of life from the women's quarters spur me to retreat into the coolness of the garden park.

With more intent than yesterday, I use glimpses of the ivory-stoned keep rising above the leafy canopy as my compass. The trees continue all the way to the citadel wall, which I trace all the way back to where it intersects with the residential buildings. Dismayed that I didn't find a way to access the tower, I check my direction to backtrack into the foliage and notice the ominous sky.

Sighing at the prospect of having to cross through the plaza while the other women are about, I search the hewn masonry for a way to climb up in hopes that the wall has a passageway similar to the parapets at the monastery. The stones are too even for a foothold, but I make note of wet stains high along the structure and surmise that it could be one of the aqueducts branching behind the apartments and supported by the curtain wall. Without a means of getting up there, however, I square my shoulders and train my ears to pick up the crystal siren of the fountain to guide me back.

Rhythmic clapping impels me towards the center of the grounds until I discern the melody of instruments. Like an apprehensive toddler, clinging to a mother's leg, I crouch behind cedar trunk and watch the scene taking place in the plaza. A gregarious cacophony flutters around the fountain, a kaleidoscope of vibrant butterflies flitting about in scores. Netted by the strands of their merry tune, I hum along to the chorus, deftly picking up the lyrics. Entranced, I cavort through the garden to the periphery of the party.

"Come!" An enchantress takes me by the hand and draws me onto the paved surface, "Let me show you."

She whirls me around, then guides me into steps and another spin. Giggling playfully, she moves my hips in a seductive sway, then twirls me by my arm above my head. Delight overtakes reservation, and I sing and dance along with the others as if we were sisters of kinship, not lordship. The divertimento ends in squeals of exaggerated distress as the heavens shower driving rain to scatter everyone to the shelter of their apartments. Once again, I return to my suite soaked, but in better spirits.

The next few days are a repeat of morning prayer, exploration and diversion. I find the remaining wives' households on the western curtain wall, and am convinced that Liang Na resides in the tower. Though I have yet to discover how to access any of the wives apartments, I plan to search the interior corridor behind my quarters.

In the meantime, I probe the outskirts of harem society, tentatively getting to know its colorful inhabitants. As in every community I have lived, I encounter good, bad and all types of individuals in between. The novelty of this company, is how the women are brought in sexual servitude to the same man, but bound by sisterhood to one another. Contemplating the diverse personalities I've met, in the solitude of my receiving room, I converse with Mariam to improve my knowledge of the language and people.

"What is the significance of the dot on the forehead of some of the women?" I savor the delicate white fish on my dinner tray, using a hunk of bread to sop up the olive oil and lemon sauce.

"The Bindi is a sign of good fortune," it is easy to forget that she only has ten years, her intelligence and maturity surpass her age, "there is one especially beautiful concubine, Shamila, whom I serve, and she told me that among the Hindi…"

"Liar!" Accusation reverberates against the marble, preceding the seething Zinvor. Dread churns the food in my stomach when I espy the strips of fabric he brandishes. He casts the fraudulent blood stained bindings at me and snatches my upper arm in his tentacles. Apprehension switches to outrage when he yanks me up and tears at my chamois to expose my nakedness. The brawl that follows flashes by in an instant, but in my mind drags out the moment so it seems much longer.

Intending to free myself to repair my modesty, I swat his hand away and shove him a step back. He backhands me across the face so hard that I hear the clunk of his gold signet connect with my cheekbone, shattering my self control. A hard chop to the throat disables his attack, and I go on the offensive, pummeling him into a cowering heap, melting into the plush rug.

The sight of Mariam's scarred face marks the return of my humanly faculties, so that Nerses and the girls can drag the addled archieunuch away. Collapsing back in the chair, I immediately lament beating Zinvor, not because I fear the repercussions, but because I failed Brother Samuel, Brigida and God. Disconsolate, tears of contrition sting the blood oozing from the deep cut on my cheek. Far from condemning, a pair of awestruck spheres peer at me from around the arched frame of the portal.

"Lusine," she ducks into the corridor, "I won't harm you child, please come back."

She inches uncertainly through the open door, her visible apprehension knifing straight to my core of painful memories. With a heavy heart, I heave from the chair and lead her into the bath room to inspect the slash in the glass. Perceptively, she lights all of the sconces, tapers and torches to shed as much light as possible. The cut is all the way to the bone, and must be cleaned and stitched or it will fester.

"Do you knew how to sew?" A small confident nod confirms her well rounded upbringing, "I will need you to find a needle and thread to stitch this closed."

She stares doubtfully until I implore her to hurry, then sprints out to do my bidding. Pressing a cloth to the wound, I pull a dark green tunica from the chest, and a bottle of wine from my dinner tray. Lusine trots back in with the sewing supplies, and I soak them in the wine and take a drink to dull my anxiety. I sit on the flagstone floor with my back against the trunk and angle my head in a position of easy access to my cheek.

"Please Lusine," I reassure her as I give her the sanitized needle, "just pour wine over the cut and sew the edges together."

The brave girl nods solemnly and sets her lips in determination. With a sharp intake of breath at the sting of liquid cleaning the wound, I train my mind on all of the occasions that God brought me through physical pain. Mentally counting and praying, I purposefully ignore the pierce and tug on my skin, surprised at how swiftly the ordeal is over. The adept stitches are neat and close together so the scarring will be minimal.

A heady moment of gratitude takes over me, and I sweep Lusine up in a hug and plant a juicy kiss on her forehead. She beams with pride when I set her down and request her assistance in donning a clean chamois and tunica. Calling quietly from the antechamber, Mariam rushes in, wringing her hands in distress.

"Zinvor has yet to recover his wits," she relates, "but Nerses seeks audience with the vizier to explain what happened. They will punish you with the strap Mistress!"

"Tis not the thrashing that scares me," I set about the apartment, gathering items I will need to vacate, "but the humiliation that is certain to follow when the Strategos hears that I deceived him."

"What will you do?" she dubiously watches me rip a panel of drapes from the bedstead. I pause and take in these two loyal servants, suddenly aware of the precarious position I've placed them in.

"I won't tell you," I affectionately lay a hand aside her face, marking its innocent beauty for when I will need to draw upon a fond memory, "lest they question you. Now both of you go see to Zinvor, may God protect you!"

Nightfall abets my flight down the steps and through the harem. Skirting the plaza, my heart pounds with victorious exertion, as I flee past the garden and reach the shelter of the wooded park. Running on until the darkness of the thick corpse halts my escape, my feet actually lighten with the distance. Wan moonlight highlights a cedar to serve as my hideout, and I swing myself up, climbing its sturdy branches towards the heavens. Obscured amongst the pattern of waxy leaves, I string up the pilfered curtain and make my bed in the secure embrace of the tree's arms. Snug in my brocade cocoon, I sleep better than in my silken bed, safe from the reach of retribution.

Chapter 20

Tendrils of the bell tolling Orthros service filter through the forest of the citadel and wrap me in the solace of routine. Harmonized chanting sweeps across the valley, intersecting with the beseeching call to prayer which emanates from the minaret on the opposite side of the walled compound. From my central position, the christian and muslim services intertwine, forming one song so melodic that my trained ear cannot separate the strains. Enraptured by the perfect unity of sound, I hum along with the fusion of Islamic and Greek words of praise to God, committing the musical creation to memory.

Invigorated by the unexpected pleasure of receiving mass to start my day, I emerge from my nest and peruse the landscape below. Dawn exposes the bird's eye vantage of the entire seraglio, aiding my study of its layout. As I had surmised, there is a walkway on top of the wall that originates from somewhere behind the harem apartments and disappears into the tower. An aqueduct clings along the lip of the parapet and intersects with a bridge channel that stretches across the valley, carrying water from the caucasus mountain caps way off in the distance.

Midday approaches and I still can't spot a way to get to the top of the the wall, which rises at least three stories on all sides. Taking a break from my study, I watch the minuscule bodies start to move about the courtyard like insects emerging from their colony, unaware of events beyond their cloistered existence. They suddenly scatter when a disciplined rank of army ants marches through, a compass pointer indicating my direction. It must be the guards setting out on the hunt. Calculating how long it will take them to penetrate this far, I descend to relieve myself, and happen upon some meaty saffron mushrooms. I bundle and tie the fungus in my skirt, chuckling over my reluctance to stain the gauzy fabric, and hie back to my perch.

In the span that it takes the search party to near, I eat my fill of the mushrooms and some food I had brought from the remains of my dinner tray. The glint of sun on steel signals the guards' position far below, my only indicator of their otherwise stealthy progress. If I can't see them, I rest assured that they don't see me either, so I lay my head back against the tree and monitor the burgeoning gray clouds building over the sea.

Ominous rumbling stirs the waves into white frothy peaks, dispatching the brewing storm to batter the rigid shoreline. As the grumbling escalates to raging roars of thunder, the guards abandon their mission and race back to the citadel. Heavy drops announce that it is my turn to seek shelter, and I twist my hammock around me, creating a water tight pod with the curtain. In spite of the boisterous bedlam thrashing my aerie, the silk cords and dense brocade thwart the wind and rain and stave off its attack.

Under the cover of the waning storm, I venture out into the sodden woodland to scout a way to breach the wall. The entire stony expanse is expertly planed and slick with damp moss, forbidding any attempts to scale its lofty height. Dusk drives me back to my nest to contemplate the sun setting over the Anatolian mountains, and how to access the imposing fortress.

"I don't even know for certain that Liang Na is in there," I speak to the wind rushing through the treetops. The breeze replies with the familiar whine of music that I recognize from traveling with the Chinese women through Russia. The tune wafts from the tower, confirming my friend's imprisonment within.

"If there is no way to climb up, how can I get into the keep?" The tassel from the drapery chord flaps in a gust of wind, tickling my neck to bring my attention from afar. "A rope ladder?"

"Go up and across," the croak of branches answers, shaking their rangy lengths to demonstrate their soundness.

"That may work!" I squint into the night, envisioning a tree close enough to the wall that I could crawl out on a branch and throw a tether across to catch the rampart. Darkness obstructs further planning, so I slide into my curtained cradle and listen to the haunting strains drifting from the princess' apartments mingle with the bedtime calls to prayer in muslim and christian fashion.

The next morning is a repeat of the previous, only my surveillance is directed at the trees scratching at the wall, instead of the structure itself. By the time the guards emerge, then are chased back inside by the afternoon showers again, I've selected a gigantic cypress with sprawling branches to serve my purpose. A brisk jaunt through the sodden forest puts me under its rambling canopy, and I clamber up its wide spread branches until I'm within a stone's throw of the parapet walkway. From here I can toss a rope ladder and catch the lip of the aqueduct to anchor it within.

Encouraged by the prospect of reuniting with my friend on the morrow, I munch on a cold dinner and enjoy the solitude of the late afternoon back in my cedar perch. A curious falcon swoops down on a nearby branch, hopping closer to scavenge my errant crumbs. I squirm under its haughty scowl, then set out the remaining food for the hawk to pick apart. Finishing the last crust of the two-day old roll, the large bird cocks its head, taking in my reserved admiration of its white and brown plumage.

"I'm not much for birds," I confess my apprehension, eyeing the sharp beak and clawing talons, fashioned for ripping flesh, "but you are a very pretty specimen."

Graciously accepting my compliment, the falcon scratches the side of its head and ruffles its feathers, as if showing off its attributes. I marvel at the splendor of God's creatures, that he would mold something so pleasing to behold. Gradually my unease dissipates, while my downy companion prunes its snowy breast.

A lilting melody drifts from the tower, stirring the memory of a ballad Maman used to sing when she would catch sight of an eagle climbing in flight. The tune soars from my lips, thrilling at the freedom of the open skies, plummeting with the majestic kill. As if the falcon comprehends, it spreads its enormous wings and jumps along the branch towards me. I shrink back against the tree trunk, my voice faltering when it lands on my leg. Its talons grip through my skirt as it walks steadily along my leg. Not knowing what else to do, I mumble through the song and extend my arm to receive the fierce raptor, as I've seen falconers do. A hunch that someone has trained this one gives me slight ease, and I relax into the spell of music.

The last chorus fades into the dusk, and the hawk teeters precariously in a trance-like state. Ever so gently, I pull my arm in to cradle its weightless form against me to prevent it from toppling over. Other than for prey, I have never handled fowl, but this one's trusting vulnerability underlying its formidable appearance, sparks my nurturing instincts. Gingerly, I stroke the soft feathers on its head, watching its eyes blink sleepily.

The setting sun bathes the mountains steel blue and highlights the buildings of the city ghostly white. A deep calm descends as the moon spills its sparkling reflection upon the rippling sea. Hearth fires glow warmly from windows, dotting the sloped landscape, blurring together under my drooping eyelids.

In my dream this time, I envision the lights from the city merging into the moonlit path, creating a watery slide that I glide along until it flings me up into the dark sky. An enormous silvery falcon scoops me from free fall, and we soar among the stars, overtaken with breathless liberation. Transported in joyous fantasy, not even the chill of the night breeze can deflate my euphoric flight. Only when I feel my balance list sideways, does awareness set in to snatch me in time from tipping off the branch and into the darkness of the forest below.

With one final caress, I place the sleeping bird in the crook of the cedar that I had just vacated and slither into my cocoon. My bold plans for the morrow seem trivial compared to my gratitude for this creature that God sent to arouse my loving nature, that I tend to bury when challenged. Prayers of praise fill the last vestiges of mindfulness, as I commend myself to my lord's shelter for the night.

A twinge of loneliness gives me pause in the morning to see the empty space where I had left the falcon. But for a few dun feathers, I would think that I had imagined the whole episode. That, in addition to the grumbling in my stomach over having shared my food, confirms that I did indeed encounter a new companion, and that I must now find something to eat before pursuing my old friend.

Having decided to wait until after the rains wash away the threat of the guards, I spend the morning scrounging for berries, nuts and mushrooms to fuel my adventure. With one eye keeping watch for signs of human approach, my other eye longingly scans the mounting clouds for the falcon, envisioning it bringing prey for me to cook. The lack of protein these past few days has me feeling slightly listless, eroding my confidence in my fitness to survive off the land as I thought I could. Giving myself a mental shake, as I have no bird to hunt for me and no means of making a fire, I take my hoard back to the cedar just ahead of the stealthy search party.

Providence foils my plans, for the first time since my arrival in Trebizond it does not rain. The bay of hounds sniffing through the seraglio and outskirts of the garden signals the end of my holiday, Damian is done playing hide and seek. Thankfully dusk halts the dogs' progress into the forest, but I know now that I must be over that wall at first light. I hazard a foray into the brush to relieve myself and gather a handful of dates and hazelnuts to sustain me for another night.

I barely sleep for fear of being found out. When I do doze off, I startle myself awake with nightmares of dogs tearing at my skirts and falcons snatching my hair. Finally giving up on rest, I study the network of branches marked by moonlight, and decide to bundle up my bed, and attempt to cover some ground to the tower. It occurs to me that if I descend, however, I will leave a scent trail for the hounds to track. So instead, I tie my curtains and chords onto my back, and prowl along the trees' outstretched arms, a lynx progressing through the elevated network of foliage.

The blush of dawn outlines the tower and wall directly in front of me, when I finally pause to rest in the cradle of the cypress I had selected as the closest point to the aqueduct. Exhausted from a dearth of sleep, food and focus, I inhale the crisp freshness of the forest. The tang of citrus and pungent eucalyptus clears my head, while rose gold rays fill me with hope in the success of my mission. Sunlight bursts over the caucus mountains, flooding the stones of the imposing structure, seeping through cracks and revealing gaps in the masonry that were previously unnoticed. As if God points exactly where to cast my rope, a blinding beam funnels through a perfect "V" in the aqueduct.

A howling ruckus echoes throughout the park, and I surmise that the hounds have located the cedar that was my temporary home. The noise quickens my pulse, spurring me into action again. I unravel the chords and tie a jagged piece of shale to one end, then crawl out as far as the branch will support my weight. Calling on the strength of my Valkyrie ancestors, I draw my arm back and hurl the stone at the notch in the aqueduct lip. My aim is low, and the rock ricochets loudly off the bricks. I recoil the rope, take a deep breath to steady my nerves, and heave again. This time, the anchor catches inside the aqueduct a few meters from the notch, so I flop the rope until it wedges into the space, giving it a last tug to ensure it won't budge.

The forest behind me is alive with activity, leaving me no time to celebrate my acumen. I scuttle to the very tip of the cypress branch, and say a prayer that the chord will hold. Gathering the rope, I let go of the tree and hold on tight as I swing into the wall and bounce off twice. The apparatus does its job, and I pull myself up using loops I had resourcefully tied at each length of the chord. Wanting to shout in triumph, I reach the rim of the aqueduct and heft myself into the icy water in the trough. I scramble headfirst into the low part of the wall crenellation, anxious not to test the integrity of the narrow channel.

Burly hands grab me under my arms, dragging me through the gap, snatching my moment of victory. Twist and kick as I might, my waning vigor is no match for the expert arm lock that I can't escape. Tears of defeat build in my eyes, I'm so close to the tower that I can see the pale faces of Liang Na's ladies peeking out of a window. As the princess's sentry forces me back along the parapet away from my goal, sobs wrack me into submission, blurring the path ahead so I know not which way I'm taken.

After a surprisingly short walk, I'm back in the receiving room of my apartment, awaiting Nerses. Not even the cheerful atmosphere of the sun filtering through the curtains can lift me out of despondency, and I float in and out of slumber propped in the corner of one of the low divans. Fatigue, hunger and depression ooze into my core, contaminating my spirit of hope so that I feel like giving up.

When Nerses arrives with a whole squadron of eunuch guards, he's so repulsed that he can't even look at me as he gives orders for me to be taken to the bathhouse. In contrast to my first day in the harem, I succumb to his decree without argument, although a bath is hardly worthy punishment for my perceived crimes. They escort me down the spine of the seraglio, stomping triumphantly as if taking a criminal to prison. A spark of defiance lifts my head and straightens my shoulders, my pride not allowing the other women see me beaten.

The parade halts at the bathhouse and the guards shove me inside and slam the door closed. Their shadows darken the windows, as they take up post at each opening lest I flee again. Two bathhouse attendants move around the room, drawing shades to ensure my privacy, and setting out toiletry items to tend to my hygiene. They pluck off my filthy garments and dip with me into the warm pool. Under the spillover, they scrub my hair and scour my body. They repeat the process in the hot bath, massaging moisturizers into my hair and oils on my skin. From there, they plunge me into the cold water which, after the initial icy shock, stirs my blood and invigorates my mood.

Just as I grow accustomed to the cold temperature, a sharp bang explodes throughout the marble chamber. A hand wrenches my head by my hair and hauls me out of the basin and throws me against a table. Damian pins me bent over, my hips digging into the planks, and fumbles with his hands at my backside.

"I have been far too lenient with you, whore," he hisses. "Since you have violated my kindness, I'm going to abuse your cunt!"

My pulse pounds blood through my head, until the sound of it gushing in my ears blocks out all else. Panicking in total immobility, I strain to stand, but his body is leaned over mine, denying me any kind of leverage. My sister's face penetrates the thick red fog that rapidly obscures my sight, but it is not the visage of her as a victim that I see. She winks at me, and throws her head back to bloody the nose of an attacker behind her.

"Use your wits," she instructs, "not your fists."

In a surge of hot fury, I tuck my head and slam it into his as he whispers vile threats into my ear. He roars in injured bewilderment, and stumbles back a pace to give me the ground I need to gain my balance. Covering the side of his face with one hand, he snatches at me with the other. Slippery as an eel from bath oil, I slither from his grasp and dash to the door. On the way out I snag a bath robe and shrug it over my nudity, ere I burst out into the busy courtyard. My modesty becomes my undoing, the fabric gives traction for the eunuchs to seize my arms and detain me at the behest of their livid master.

He strolls menacingly towards me, probing a small cut over his brow. Apprehension suspends all movement in the plaza, the weight of the women's stares burdening me with the charge to bear whatever is to come with fortitude. Old habits die hard, and I tighten my gut as Damian steps in front of me and smashes his fist into my stomach.

"So you like it rough?" His other fist catches my chin in an uppercut, but I'm ready with my jaw clenched so as not to bite my tongue. "I can play nasty too!"

"I'll never give myself to you!" I grit through my teeth. He grips my throat then punches my face and ribs. Doubled over, I hide a grin because I can already feel an ugly bruise swelling over my eye. His outraged pride will batter me beyond his desire to have me.

"Oh?" He jabs at the side of my head, taunting me, "Never is such a strong word. Because I guarantee that you'll be begging for me to take you!"

"I have no desire for you, and won't be forced into sex with you!" I cry out and brace myself for the onslaught. I laugh as he strikes my face, tasting blood in my mouth, knowing that my skin will heal but his ego will not. He beats on me until exertion overtakes him so that he braces his hands on his knees.

"Get her out of my sight!" He yells at a visibly unnerved Nerses, then spits at me, "You disgust me."

The welts distorting my face disguise a painfully broad smile as the guards lug me past a stunned audience. Gawks of horror transform to confused wonder, as I fix the women with my one good eye, conveying victory in my gaze. I have purchased, at an agonizing physical price, my freedom from sexual slavery for the near future.

Out from under the cloud of Damian's malignant presence, I actually delight in the modest sophistication of my suite. Though imprisoned in my chambers by the eunuch guarding the corridor outside my portal, the sense of freedom within the rooms borders euphoria. Afternoon sunlight streams through my patio door, unmitigated by the usual rain to cool the air. Seeking reprieve from the heat, I splash cold water from the bathroom basin on my face and dab the dried blood from my mouth. I hold the cool cloth to my eye, now completely bruised over, and inspect the damage in the glass. Thankfully the stitches that Lucine sewed in my cheek to close the cut from Zindor's ring, held up under Damien's fists.

The reflection in the mirror is otherwise unrecognizable, as bruised and misshapen as it is. I'm sure this is what I used to look like when I was young and took beatings from my father and the boys in the village, because the throbbing soreness feels the same. At least on this occasion, my frightening image will serve to protect me from Damian's odious attention. Seeking relief from the heat in my face, I wander to the shady bedroom, lured to the balcony by the drone of monks at midday Enati Ora.

Faint cries from the more distant muezzin filter into the monastery prayers, which I bolster with my own voice to add melody to the monotone chant. Long after the muslim call fades away, I continue to practice weaving the Armenian words into a hymn. As usual whenever consumed by song, I become heedless of my surroundings, so when a piercing screech peals through the valley, I duck and throw my arm up to defend my tender visage.

In an awesome display of swooping feathers the falcon lands gracefully on my wrist. Flapping its wings to balance itself, while I figure out that I must hold my arm steady, it settles to fluffing its alabaster plumage and cocks its head to regard my startled mien.

"You found me again!" I maintain a singsong tone, remembering how it seemed to soothe the temperamental bird. "But I have nothing to feed you."

"Aaawwkk!" Its talons clamped on my bare wrist tighten testily. Mentally sifting through my catalogue of tunes, for once I can't make a selection to sing under the pressure of its stern displeasure.

"What shall I call you, my pretty friend?" I make up my own ditty about naming the bird, "how about Eugenious? For you are an angel, like Saint Eugenious, sent by God to serve Christians in Trebizond."

Eugenious preens its creamy feathers, content with the moniker, and perches quietly as I recall a local psalm about the saint. I bear the becalmed falcon on a tour of my apartment, ending at the portico overlooking the seraglio. As abrupt as was the bird's reentry into my world, Eugenious' departure is just as precipitous. He jumps suddenly from my arm, catches the breeze and dives down the middle of the harem apartments.

Feminine shrieks arising from the courtyard, attest to the raptor's whereabouts. A watery crash and more screams, then a vivid fluttering as the women flee from the frightening fowl. Like an avenging angel, Eugenious arises over the buildings, spreading its enormous wings to carry the weight of its prey. Proudly tossing a live fish onto the marble tiles of my patio, the falcon alights onto the balustrade, awaiting its portion with an impatient scowl.

Laughing so hard in spite of my aching ribs, I entertain Eugenious with a humorous ditty as I search for something to cut and clean the flopping carp. The best I can do is use the edge of the small ash shovel to chop off the head and tail and toss it to my benefactor. I kindle a fire in the hearth, and crack open the portal to ask the guard for utensils. Snores fill the corridor, not even faltering when I emerge from my suite and snicker at his incompetence. I easily pluck his knife from his belt and close my door softly behind me, not wanting any more adventure this evening.

Expertly, I descale and filet the fish, laying it on the grate over the banked fire. Without seasoning, the meat tastes fresh and gamey, but I'm so thankful to eat protein that I finish it all. Warm and sated, I slouch back in the chair and rub my stomach, repeating "Allahu akbar, Allahu akbar," along with the muezzin calling muslims to sunset prayer. Lethargy presses me into the plush cushions, battling with reason telling me to go to bed. I doze off without knowing, and when I awaken sometime in the night, the fire has died and my friend has flown away.

Muffled in the soupy mist of morning clouds loitering in the valley, the ring of the abbey bell summons me to the balcony. Kneeling at the balustrade, I contemplate the awe-inspiring vista of the monastery steeple piercing the clouds, no longer afraid of the plunge under the platform. With no self induced exploits pressing me into the day, I linger in the stillness of the hour until after the sun burns away the fog.

As I push away from the rail and turn to go inside, I notice a slender aqueduct clinging to the wall over the portico. Daring to lean over the balcony, I follow its course toward the sea, where it disappears around the curve of the citadel tower. It would be a small undertaking, as compared to the enterprise of yesterday, to swing up into the channel and explore its path. As my calculating mind assesses whether or not I am physically up to the task, God soars in to answer with a shrill "No."

"Good Morn, Eugenious," I intone affably, unhesitating this time in offering my arm as its perch. "You're looking very fine and satisfied. I trust you had a good night's rest?"

"Who are you talking to Mistress?" I spin at the sound of a female voice to find Mariam tidying my bedcovers. The falcon clucks jealously and launches its feathery bulk into the void, where it circles then glides away. "What a beautiful bird!"

"We met in the forest a few days ago." I explain, "I'm terribly sorry for the trouble I have brought on you and Lucine."

"No need to worry," she assuages, "no harm has come to us, but they are very upset with you. I have orders to bring you only bread and water to eat."

"Tis a feast for me!" The smell of fresh dough makes me forget the aqueduct, though I save a hunk to return favor the next time I see my friend. Stuffing myself with the warm bread, I catch up with Mariam on the doings of the harem. Lucine taps on the door and enters, carrying a bucket of steaming water and linens.

"You should be a doctor, Lucine," I submit to her nursing the cuts and bruises on my face, "look at how well your stitches held!"

"Thank...you," she forms the words with deliberate effort. Wide eyed, I stare at her proud grin, looking to Mariam in confusion.

"She has been practicing," her older sister boasts, then adds seriously, "no one else knows. Her learned speech is our secret, but she wanted to tell you."

"I am humbled by your confidence," hot tears of emotion building, I envelope the slight girl in a tender hug and kiss Miriam on the top of her head. "I promise I will never tell anyone!"

The girls help me change into a clean chamois and tunica, then depart with the soiled linens and empty tray. As they open and close the door carefully, I glimpse the guard outside leaning motionless against the wall. From what I can tell in that brief moment, the stout form and disheveled uniform are the same as I recall from last night. Hazarding to crack open the portal, I stick my head out and get no reaction. Heart in my throat, I step fully into the hallway without so much as a break in the steady breathing from under his low helmet.

My brain berates my rebellious feet for carrying me silently into the dim corridor. Logic churns my stomach in painful reminder of my injuries and malnutrition, trying to turn me away from the darkness of the unfamiliar territory and back to the rest of the citadel before it is too late. The impulse to explore is too strong, however, and hurtles me away from my suite, the guard, and the harem.

The unlit hallway ends in a circular tower with a staircase spiraling from below and continuing to the floor above. My head, still fuming at my errant limbs, refuses to make a decision whether to go up or down. A shaded figure ascends, blocking the archway to the stairwell, taking away both options altogether. Daylight filtering through lancets in the tower bathes the ebony beauty, illuminating her arresting features.

Obsidian gems set in alabaster glower sullenly through fringed lashes so long that they garnish her overlarge, penetrating eyes to make them alluring. The bountiful pout of her mouth adds to her sulky mien, though further study reveals open cuts marring her youthful cheek and brow, as perhaps the source of her discontent. Her powerful build looms over me, earning my admiration with rippling stomach muscles exposed under her short cropped chemise. The physical impact of her essence strikes me dumb, leaving me to stare agape at the only female to ever eclipse my robust size.

"Ah, the Stratego's new favorite," her lovely lip curls up on one side in contempt, as she measures my frame.

"I have no wish to trouble you, my friend," I soothe, peeking over my shoulder to ensure the guard is too far away to hear, "please allow me to pass."

"You are no friend of mine." Her rich voice fits her forceful persona. "There is no where to go, but to my apartments below, to which you have banished me."

"You must be Keket," I continue in a hushed tone, praying to avoid confrontation. I recall the name from my first encounter with the other women, and Zoe's reference to replacing one beast for a monster. This specimen of feminine magnificence hardly matches their derogatory description. "Perhaps you can help me to find the Princess Liang Na, I think she resides in the tower up these stairs."

I take a step to circumvent her, but she shifts to the side to stay in front of me. When I go the other direction, she mirrors my move and bodily blocks my path again. After a few more dancing paces, I change tactic and jab one way to get her off balance, then spring the other way around. As agile as I am, she crouches and cuts me off with an upward lunge, catching me under the arms and nearly lifting me off the flagstones. I recover and swing my arms underneath hers and grip the swell of her biceps so that our arms are locked as we scuffle for position.

Grappling like a pair of wrestlers of ancient times, we strain against each other, twisting and pitching in attempt to topple the other. Her strength is palpable in the bulge of muscles I can feel gliding under onyx skin, and the leverage it takes to hold my ground against the might of her haunches trying to drive me backwards. Fighting savvy tells me to ration my energy, and let her tire herself like a wave beating against a rock. In my weakened state however, my typical stamina betrays me, my flanks laboring painfully to breathe.

At the very moment I can no longer maintain the stance, she breaks her grasp, and we both stagger back. Hands on knees, heaving from our efforts, we glare at each other in frustration over being so evenly matched. Not even footsteps climbing the stairs interrupt our challenging regard.

"What's taking you so long my dear, I only sent you to get cold water from the aqueduct..." her query hangs in the tense air. I hazard a glance past my opponent, who straightens to a hunch, rubbing her neck as she turns slightly so that I recognize my rescuer from the insults in the seraglio on my first day. "Ah, I see you have met Adila!"

She clucks her tongue and continues on up the spiral staircase, muttering in her foreign language, though still conveying her disapproval.

In the brooding silence, we hear a faint splashing, then the sound of her slippers descending. She reappears in the archway, and shakes her head, piqued at our juvenile antics, until she notices Keket favoring her neck.

"You see this?" She tenderly peels back Keket's hand to reveal swollen welts the size of fingerprints on her throat. With tears melting her hazel eyes to liquid honey, she laments, "this is what happens when you upset the master."

"Hush Indira," husky with emotion, the taller woman brushes away her concerns and warns me, "he does this when he is not angry too, it is part of his game."

Lovingly, the diminutive Indira wraps an arm around Keket's waist and steers her back down to her rooms. As they sink lower into the stairwell, I dare to creep to the landing under the archway, touched by how the intimidating Africana drapes her arm around the narrow shoulders of her companion, leaning on her for support.

Tamed by my own infirmaries, I retreat into the darkness of the corridor, seeking the comfort of my suite. Noiselessly, I approach my portal and freeze at the clink of metal, warning me that the guard is awake. I retrace my steps to the spiraling staircase, where the late morning sun slices through narrow slits in the round tower. The cheerful rays are much more agreeable than the ominous passageway, so I proceed up through the staggered beams sparkling with dust mites.

The risers end in a sparsely furnished loft to the right of a low window framing the gorge. The precipitous vantage is similar to my eastern view of the valley, though here, the direct line of sight to the narrow road below, indicates its function as a lookout. A nearby gurgle of water whets my inquisitiveness, so I stretch out over the sill to discover the source of the sound.

The same aqueduct that I discovered above my balcony, spans the valley farther inland and clings to the citadel the entire length of the curtain wall, hugging the tower underneath this window. The channel is so close, I can easily reach out and test the icy water up to my elbow. This explains the splashing that I heard earlier when Indira came this way, she wanted the frigid water to compress Keket's swelling bruises.

Craning my neck seaward, I pursue the aqueduct's course as far as I can, but the tower juts out too far to see much beyond the corridor to my left. Gasping excitedly, I recognize the covered passageway opens into the rampart path. This is the route to Liang Na's apartments that I had been seeking! I rush through the arched portico onto the parapet path, and run smack into the plate covered chest of a sentinel.

"I'll go back!" I promise, pleading clemency to the armored soldier, "Just please, do not alert Nerses! I don't want to cause more trouble."

"How did you get by the eunuch guarding your chambers?" He growls, his proper greek unmistakable after weeks of the Armenian dialect of the harem.

"He was asleep at his post," I whine, reasoning with the only male to speak to me directly since my captivity. "I don't want anyone to get hurt because of my rash curiosity."

"That is the last thing Majidi would want." The ring of the true Stratego's name, and the sentry's professional demeanor, alert me that he has served as a soldier. With a firm gauntlet on my back, he marches me back to my portal and confronts the guard. "You lazy oaf, you fell asleep and let her out! I should tell the Strategos of your ineptitude, but if you vow to do your job better I won't have to bother him with your trivial mistake."

"No need to tell anyone!" The eunuch grovels, the sentinel is obviously higher ranking, his offensive verbal attack ensuring compliance, "I will bar the portal and be more vigilant, I swear."

"Very good then," he concludes, then shoves me firmly into my quarters and closes the portal. The grind of the metal bar sliding into its groove finalizes my confinement, though not without optimism for the morrow. For now, I am grateful for the solace of my suite to recuperate from my injuries and rest from further toil.

While attending Ekti Ora service from my private gallery, Mariam and Lusine arrive with my midday ration of bread and water, to hear me chanting the closing hymn. Their delight in my singing reminds me of how Brigida and I would revel in the sweetness of Maman's voice, and how she passed along her gift to me. In homage to her, I encourage the girls to hum along with me, as my maman instructed. Especially motivated to hear the melodic sounds emanating from Lusine's throat, I continue the lessons in Armenian as the muezzin calls the Islamic faithful to afternoon prayer.

"Do you know how to braid hair?" Having worn out our voices, we relax in mutual companionship, Mariam brushing my hair as Lusine tidies the bedroom. At her nod I describe Keket's head of small, tight plaits streaming to her waist. I am still getting used to my hair being long and loose, and the thought of the serviceable fashion appeals to me, "Would you be able to style my hair like hers?"

"Oh no Mistress, that would be disrespectful!" She explains how the concubine was the daughter of an African chieftain of the lower Nile, and the braids are a symbol of her noble status. "Not that you aren't important, but your hair is lovely curling free and unadorned, so you have no need to copy hers."

"I understand," my unsophisticated upbringing embarrasses me, so I redirect the conversation, "if Keket is royalty, how did she end up here?"

"From what I have heard, the Strategos took fancy to her and abducted her many years ago."

"Is that how the others come to the seraglio?" The thought of Majidi loving Keket births a dull ache in my heart. I prod the soreness with visions of them together in the bed the next room over.

"Nay, the concubines are mostly given as tribute, or for favor." My throat grows thick as the discomfort in my chest spreads up to cloud my judgment. He must love her, as he claimed to be enamored of me. Depression encroaches when I visualize her long legs visible under her shortened skirt, her ebony skin glistening with the sheen of perspiration when we clashed. "Besides, you don't want small braids like that. I saw Indira's servant this morning, and she told me that the master ripped one out last night."

Her appalling revelation rattles me out of the mire. I think of all the times that my father yanked me by my hair and how much it hurt, but he never actually tore out a chunk from my scalp. Then I recall the welts on Keket's throat, and my pity turns from myself, to the the tortured woman I met earlier. No one deserves to be treated like that, not even my worst enemy.

Sensing my reticence, the girls excuse themselves to return with my evening portion of bread. Preferring solitude, I let them leave the tray on the table in the receiving room, and tell them I won't need them for the rest of the night. The lord has other plans however, and sends Eugenious with another fish, for which I can reward him promptly with the crust of bread. My weary voice can't even muster a hum, so I listen to the evening services without joining in. Bored without my nightly entertainment, the falcon dips over the balustrade and disappears into the murky vale.

Eugenius' departure sucks any remaining levity in its wake, abandoning me to my sluggish mood. I drag my leaden limbs into the bath room to prepare for bed, managing only to pass water, wash my face and hands, and pull off my tunica before I collapse in amongst the downy covers. Burrowing into the billowy nest, I happily cede the day to the void of slumber.

Chapter 21

In my dream this time, the sparkling pathway arises from a nebulous mist canvassing the earth below. I fearlessly step from my solid platform to tiptoe along the crystalline course that flows around confining walls, guiding me to freedom. Muffled gongs punctuate my precarious dance, urging me to awaken to the present new day. I must have walked onto the balcony in my sleep, because I'm standing in my night clothes on the toe curling marble, fog from the yonder void floating around my ankles.

I inhale the sharp air to clear the vestiges of vision from my head, and the soak in the sonorous singing from the monastery to soothe my spirit. Though not quite as daring as in my dream, I proceed to hold tightly onto the porous door molding while balancing on the rail to test the reach up to the aqueduct. Freezing water greets my probing fingertips with shards of ice shooting down my arms, forcing me to retreat back into the portico to quell my shaking limbs.

Energized with curiosity, I rummage through the chest of garments in the bathing room until I find a woolen tunica, pair of heavy pantaloons and oiled leather boots. Mariam and Lusine arrive with my ration of bread and water and to assist my toilet. At Mariam's raised dubious eyebrow when they see my unusual garb, I usher them out of the apartment so they won't have to lie on my behalf. By the time I finish my simple fare and look after my personal ministrations, the fog has receded to carpet the valley below.

Before I balk at following my dream, I take a fortifying breath and jump up to grasp the slick edge of the aqueduct. Pulling myself into the shallow basin is more challenging than I anticipate with the heavy clothes, slippery masonry and glacial water. However, the channel is mercifully wide enough so I can slosh through and carefully hold its outer rim to facilitate my progress around the curve of the tower. The water resistant boots keep my feet dry, but the rushing current pushes me into a skid down the track. Clutching frightfully between the curtain wall and the aqueduct rim, I skate precariously to where it straightens along the rampart and prepare to vault down onto the parapet.

Out of nowhere I espy the guard patrolling the pathway, and I panic and plunge into the glacial water to avoid being caught again. After a moment of air sucking cold, I peek over the side to see his back recede into the portico. Limbs sluggish with chill, I command them to heave my sodden weight over the low channel wall and drop clumsily onto the stone walkway. I scramble into the shadow of a crenelation to gather myself for the sprint across the long side of the harem wall to the tower in which I will find my friend.

The mad dash seemed to go on forever, and my reward at the end was another guard to evade, and spiral staircase to climb. Exhaustion tempers my bravado with reality, as I continue to ascend, I lose my bearings and collapse on a platform. As if I landed in an aviary, bright colored movement flutters around me like several silken wings. Small white hands coax me from the stair, and urge me through a portal and into the welcoming embrace of Liang Na.

"We have been expecting you," the princess's broken greek belies her lack of practicing the local language, "ever since my ladies saw you try to scale the wall. We have been casting lots as to how long it would take you to break through!" Gales of giddy laughter enliven the vivid chamber even more with the joy of our reacquaintance. After Liang Na's attendants rushed me inside, where the prying eyes of the guards and servants couldn't spy, they peeled off my freezing clothes and wrapped me in a soft robe by the fire. Sitting amongst friends, I am myself. The opulent suite, silken trappings and restricted life matters naught for the moment, and I relax into the lull of gentile conversation.

"Tis a pleasure to provide your entertainment!" I banter, taking in the surrounding rooms. "Are you comfortable here?"

"Yes, they have provided for our every need, and the apartments are magnificent!" She gestures with a delicate sweep of her arm, "let us show you around."

"The furnishings are beautiful, but I can hear the waves of the sea and would love to look around."

"We'll start on the top floor then, the view is stunning!" Another climb opens into a large marbled patio, partially covered but mostly exposed to the panorama of city, mountains and sea. It is like a courtyard in the sky, replete with padded lounges, granite tables and a raised pool occupying the entire far side of the tower wall.

"When the weather is mild we spend much of our time up here," Liang Na explains, "Its so peaceful, with the sounds of the wind and the waves. On hot days we even swim in the pool, but the water is very cold!" As she continues to show me around, I can see that there's another aqueduct bridging the valley that supplies fresh water directly from the snow capped mountains into the pool.

The rest of the tour through the princess' chamber is a blur, as I am tiring from my escapades and contemplating the journey back. With a heavy sign, I tell my friend that I must go, and promise to come again tomorrow. Understanding my reluctance, her ladies help me don my still damp clothes, and stuff my pockets with fruits and cured meats.

Silently spiraling down to the parapet level, I hesitate before emerging from the shadows of the tower, scouting any sentineling obstacles. As always, God comes to my aide as the crying voice of the muezzin wafting from the minaret. The mid- afternoon call to prayer sweetens the air, answered by the subtle movement of the faithful kneeling, dotted throughout the harem, including the guards stationed at the ramparts.

"Allahu Akbar! Allahu Akbar! Allahu Akbar!" The sonorous words carry me forward, fully exposed onto the parapet. "God is Great! God is Great! God is Great!" My heart beats with the tempo of praise whispered from my lips as I drift soundlessly along the high wall pathway. Filled with holy strength and confidence, I hoist myself effortlessly up into the watery passage, wading against the upward current and bending towards my chambers. The last turn tests my fear of heights, for the afternoon sun has dried up the nebulous web that had hid the abyss below on my previous trip.

Here, the gong from the monastery drones out the muezzin, marking Nones prayer service for us Christian counterparts. The resonant tone gives me a boost of supernatural energy that I need to reach the haven of my apartments. I disembark from the conduit and collapse on the balcony floor, resting my head back against the balustrade. Closing my eyes, I absorb the low chanting to steady my pulse and slow my breathing. The hypnotic music caresses my fatigued frame into lethargy, though my mind warns that I must get up and change my attire.

"Auuukkkk!" The deafening screech echos in my ears, and a dramatic plumage of snowy feathers swoops down on the rail and flaps its wings regally.

"Good Evening Eugenious!" Happily relieved to have the jolt to attention, I thank my fierce friend for waking me. Having learnt his desire for attention, I compliment him on his magnificence, "You're looking very grand today!"

He hops to the floor, nearly as tall as my slouched form, and I treat him with some of the meats from my pocket. Saying a blessing to Liang Na and her ladies for the food, I share a meal with the falcon next to me and tell him of my exploits. The chill from wet clothes sets in, prompting me to unstrap the boots and doff the oiled outer garments. Eugenious calls farewell and stretches his wings to catch the evening breeze and soar away to his nightly pursuits.

The new day follows a similar pattern as the previous, though I time my visit to Liang Na better, exploiting the calls to prayer as cover to traverse between our tower apartments. The fatigue of yesterday weighs heavily in my thews, and the princess' nurse attendant suggests a plunge in the cold pool followed by a hot bath. The treatment invigorates me, and we lay in our undergarments on the patio furniture and absorb the sun's benevolent rays.

"These walls have many ears," Liang Na and I converse quietly as her ladies play strings and bowls under the eaves. "I heard that the Strategos took a fancy to you during his stay at your monastery."

"I am sorry my friend," guilt over my relationship with Majidi causing her injury floods my tone with tremor, "I did not know who he was at the time, nor that he was in any way attached to you."

"Ease your conscience Adila," she reaches out to touches my hand,

"I am aware of your innocence, and that you would never betray our friendship. More than anything, I'm elated to have you here, we are sisters now!" Crestfallen at her reference to sisterhood, my gaze sinks at the thought of our kinship made through our bond to Majidi. Mistaking my jealousy for pining for my own sister, she gasps at her error, "Forgive my insensitivity! You must miss Brigida terribly."

"I do yearn to see her," my response is sincere, "but I know that she and Nicolo are very happy, and they have a son!"

"What wonderful news!," she claps her hands as I detail the robust baby boy, Adilsen, and we commiserate vicariously in their joy of parenthood. "I do wish to have a child, but the master refuses to visit me."

"You are so young and petite," I chose not to disclose that I know of Majidi's vow not to take a bride under ten and five years. Not to mention the Strategos is away on some clandestine mission, his brother assuming his harem responsibilities. His wives and concubines are unaware of the murky delegation of who serves what carnal purpose. "I fear for your health, were you to become pregnant."

"It is my duty to my family, my country and my husband, to provide an heir and strengthen our alliance." She recites the mantra that women have been programmed to accept our whole lives.

"But what about you," I challenge, "and your happiness?"

"I see that your outward transformation to womanhood has not changed your masculine perspective," she jests, "I remember having this discussion with you many a night on the road to Constantinople."

"Ah yes, I do recall," those discussions helped open my eyes to my unrealistic view of myself living as a man, "and we always came to the save conclusion that the only true joy comes from our own holy spirit within."

"Besides, I am very content here," she smiles gently at her ladies and gazes out over the seascape, "even more so now that you are here!"

Her low threshold of a pleasurable existence puzzles me, I don't know whether to admire its simplicity, or pity her ignorance to the euphoria of real freedom. The confusion suddenly wearies me, and I beg their pardon that I must leave ere I grow too comfortable and fall asleep in their amenable company.

On the way back I again let the singsong muezzin and monks aide my progress, but instead of pushing me along, the haunting rhythms lull me into a clumsy trance. I slosh about in the aqueduct until I slip and fall face down in the trench. Fortunately none of the guards notice, and the chill from the water refreshes my sluggish brain.

This time, when I crumble onto the solid safety of my balcony platform, the vestiges of Nones service transport me into dreamless slumber.

Blinding light floods my aching head. I throw my arm across my eyes to ward off the piercing sun, only to cry out at the acute soreness upon moving. My tongue is thick with thirst, and I effort a glimpse at the tray of bread and water left at my bedside. With herculean effort, I drag my stiff bulk to sit and drink. The liquidly sweetness is manna from heaven, and I drain one ewer and reach for the second. After guzzling the extra pitcher of water, it dawns on me that there are two rations on the tray.

"That's strange," I reason with the ewer, "why is there double bread and water? Have I been asleep this whole time? Did I dream that I found my way to Liang Na?"

In search of answers, I forget my aches and pains and wander to the bathing room. There are no signs of the heavy clothes I thought I had worn, though I nearly jump at my reflection in the mirror next to the trunk. My eyes blaze bright blue from my pinkened face, and I surmise that the midmorning sun has me overheated. All the better opportunity to test the chilly conduit to look for the princess. I find a suitable thick linen tunic and leggings, and a rather flimsy pair of leather slippers.

Automatically, I boost up into the channel and slither around the tower to drop onto the parapet. Assured by the returning certainty that I hadn't dreamt this, I gather my might for the sprint up to Liang Na's apartments. Buoyed at the prospect of seeing her again, I race up the stairs and tap on the portal. Her attendants open the door and flit about to pat me dry and sit me by the fire next to my friend.

"We thought you weren't able to come today," she confirms, "but you made it! And burnt from sitting out on the terrace yesterday!" She beckons to her nurse attendant, who brings a pot of salve to rub on my face and neck. No wonder my skin looked so red in the mirror, I am not used to being in the sun for so long anymore. Recalling when I was young and got tender burns while working in the fields with my father, I remember how Maman would put the gel from an aloe plant to soothe the hot skin and make it turn tan. "The sun's rays are strong up there, I forgot how it will color the complexion if you are not used to it."

I tell her how I fell asleep yesterday and woke up disoriented, not knowing whether I dreamt our visits or if they actually occurred. As we continue to chatter affably, the heat from the fireplace creeps over me until a high pitched whine consumes our conversation. Recognizing the sense of panic that comes over me when I get too hot, I stagger to an open balcony and let the briny air blow away the old fear of heated enclosed spaces. Once my head clears, I explain to the distressed huddle of ladies hovering around me, the traumatic memory of almost dying in my monk's cell.

Still lightheaded, it occurs to me that I haven't had anything to eat today, and beg a morsel from my hostesses. They hurry to set a table for me between the open doors, laying out fruits, bread and smoked fish. As delicious as the fare looks, I have no appetite, and can only choke down a piece of bread and several cups of water. In spite of the breeze, food and drink, I can't shake the buzzing in my head nor the heat in my body. Deeming it best to tackle the return trip to my apartment before it worsens, I say farewell and fight my way through the burgeoning haze clouding my vision.

Welcoming the icy contents of the aqueduct to lower my body temperature, I slosh away, not caring that by the time I reach my apartment I'm trembling with chill. Sodden and shaking uncontrollably, I stumble into my bed room greeted by the startled countenance of Lusine. She takes in my dripping clothes and shivering form and grips my hand to haul me into the bathing chamber. Sage beyond her years, my young protector strips me bare, dries me and garbs me in a light chemise. Clucking in disapproval, she tucks me in my bedcovers and puts a cloth soaked in rose attar on my forehead, then departs with a halted promise to return anon.

"Mistress, where have you been?" Mariam's strained whisper penetrates my doze.

"She is sick," Lusine's unfamiliar tongue puts to words the problem that had eluded me. She props me up and holds a spoon to my lips and commands me to drink.

"Nerses is on his way to check on you!" Mariam hisses, then springs away at his knock on the portal. Through my discomfort, I grin smugly that he doesn't burst in anymore. The girls show him in and melt into the periphery as the eunuch and his entourage darken my bedroom with their portentous presence.

"The master wants to know if you are fit to receive him yet." He disdains to request my self assessment.

"I'm ill," I croak, swallowing shards of glass instead of spittle.

"You do look terrible," he sniffs almost triumphantly, "that flushed countenance and dark circles are symptoms of ague. I will inform the Strategos that you are not worthy of his visit."

In a swirl of vivid robes, he whirls about and departs, slamming the portal with the finality of a judge sentencing me to another week of incarceration. Never have I been so pleased to be insulted and jailed in the span of a moment. I close my swollen eyelids and succumb to Mariam's concerned displeasure and Lusine's gentle hand stroking my face and neck with the cool cloth.

Fever grips me in a stifling stronghold, and for the next day I battle with the bedcovers for relief from the oppressive heat; then in turn, for warmth against the chill that rattles my bones. Scared of the hot air trapped in the bed by the newly replaced drapes, I try to sit at the table on the front balcony to catch the late autumn wind and rain sweeping over the seraglio.

"Mistress, please stay in bed!" Mariam begs after I push away the broth she smuggled to me. The thought of drinking something warm renews my anxiety of overheating.

"I have a phobia of getting too hot," I explain so I don't upset her further. "Not yet a year past I was serving penance in my room, that was adjacent to the kitchen furnace, and it heated the cell up so hot that I got very sick and thought I was going to die!"

"Well, you'll surely die from this ague, exposed to the rain like this," she admonishes, "if you will try to let go of your struggles from the past and focus on getting better, maybe it will help conquer your fear of dying.

Lusine will remain with you to keep your head cool with rosewater if you can manage to stay under the cover. Once you break the fever you will feel much better."

So I turn my thoughts from the past, and give myself over to prayer and Lusine's cool towel. The remainder of the day and night, I thrash under the sweltering grasp of pyrexia. By the afternoon, one would think that the downpour outside was in my room, because my bedcovers were drenched with sweat. The fever has broken, leaving me weak and listless, but at ease. Contented to simply be, I allow myself to rest in the tender care of my two young angels, Mariam and Lusine.

Chapter 22

"We are to blame for you getting sick!" Liang Na cries a few days later when I am well enough to tackle the journey to her tower. "I should have known the moment you showed up here wet and cold!"

"The fault is all mine princess," I assure, trying to avert distress. "I so enjoy it here with you." We are up on the veranda again, listening to the water spill into the pool, mimicking the crash of the waves in the turbulent sea. I close my eyes and hum to the plucking melody her ladies play.

"I wish you could stay here all the time," she picks at her silken chemise, "but I hear that the master is anxious to have you."

"Huh!" I snort, "He only pursues me because he knows he will never posses me."

"And yet he discards me as if I do not exist." Her fallen countenance stirs the compassion in my heart.

"Tis not true Liang Na, he values you so much that he does not want to put you at risk from his carnal attentions until he is assured that you are fit for bearing children."

Even as I speak the words, it sounds ridiculous to me that we are only valued for our ability to carry an heir.

"You say that, Adila, and it just confirms that I am an unworthy bride!"

"There is more to being a wife than producing sons," I counter, growing tired of this recurring trend in our conversations. "You have so much more to offer your husband, and it begins with your kind and loving spirit."

"What is he like?" Her innocent query unleashes a dizzying rush of conflicting thoughts. Which master do I tell her about?

"He is very intelligent," I opt for the real Strategos, for I owe it to her to create an image of her real husband who she will know one day soon, "and noble, with good intentions."

"That is not what my ladies have told me," they exchange a dark knowing look, "they have heard that he is cold and even sometimes cruel."

"T'would seem he is different with the concubines," I scramble for an excuse for Damian's infamous reputation, "but he speaks of his wives with great respect, as he has of you my dear."

"He does not even acknowledge my existence!" She pouts. The pleasant music has stopped and thunderclouds burgeon on the horizon.

"I best not tarry," I point to the harbinger of weather gathering over the churning waters, thanking God for the timely incentive to conclude our afternoon discussion. Bidding them good day, I traverse the aqueduct uneventfully to retire quietly to my quarters.

After another hard night's sleep, I wake much refreshed in body, as the peal of the monastery bell washes my spirit. The jolly sun tempers the crisp chill in the air, portending an agreeable morning for a visit to the princess. Emboldened by my subterfuge, and ebullient by my determination to share the spirit of love strong in me this day, I hurry to eat and dress. With renewed vigor I hoist myself up into the channel and glide along its course around the tower to where it crosses over the ramparts. Well practiced by now, I hop down onto the parapet stones. In my haste to get there, however, I have mistimed the muezzin's call to prayer as my cue to dash into the cover of the next tower.

"Halt!" The sharp command propels me up the pathway in hopes of outrunning the bulk of the armored sentinel. Heartened as I stretch my lead, I swallow a whoop of victory when another guard emerges from the far archway. "Seize her!"

His hulking frame crowds the parapet, but I easily dart under his encumbered arms, spinning him clumsily into a crenellation before he recovers his balance to give chase. Hesitating at the spiral stairway ascending to Liang Na's apartments, I dare not bring this trouble to her abode, so I continue my escape through the tower's opposite archway and onto the rampart separating the lower citadel from the city. From this great height, the wind whips up my hair and tugs at my clothes, eliciting an uncanny laugh from the child inside of me, as if playing a game of tag.

Another guard charges from the distant keep, which I presume houses another one of the Strategos' four wives. He too is heavily armed with plate and mail, strong but plodding like the others encroaching at my back. Drawing from my childhood experiences, I coordinate our clash so that we all meet at once equidistant along the wall. Darting around one, scampering past another, I create such a melee amongst the three of them, that I'm able to speed on to the next corner tower. I flee down the descending staircase to ground level, where it spits me out into a palazzo behind the harem bathhouse. From there, I follow the slash of water to find my way to the central plaza.

The temperate midday air has encouraged most of the women to flock to the pool, all of whom turn and stare agog at my sudden ruffled presence. Behind bejeweled hands and chiffon veils, kohl lined eyes squint into smiles. Giggles bubble forth like the fountain in our midst, laughter rippling through the throng. They point up to the rampart wall and snicker at the guards still trying to untangle themselves and figure out where I went. Our shared mirth humbles me to a halt, and I pause to enjoy a moment of levity not directed at me for once.

Prominent amongst the tans and peachy faces, Keket's sable cheeks gleam taut from her approving grin. Next to her, Indira shakes her head in nervous amusement, her reserved humor reminding me of the consequences of ruffling the fragile ego of their master. Basking in the warm smiles bestowed on, not at me, I parade by to slip up to my apartments unnoticed by the eunuchs. Catching a wink from Hayfa, and a begrudging nod from Zoe, I finally notice the ominous specter darkening the promenade.

Malicious brown orbs prey on the lively scene, eyes sucking every detail to exploit at a later date. His pointed chin nodding slightly in nefarious satisfaction, Zinvor alights his gaze on me and grins. All of the shouting and thrashing in the world would not have frightened me as much as seeing his bared teeth in a twisted farce of a smile. He claps his hands in sarcastic amusement, overpowering any remaining frivolity. In the hush of the courtyard I hear the clink of his heavy rings knocking together, and my hand involuntarily jerks to the raised scar on my face.

"'Tis good to see you fit and mended, whore," his dichotomous words churn in my stomach like poison. He gestures to my harried eunuch scurrying to a halt behind him, "Nerses, will you be be so kind as to take the Strategos' favorite back to her quarters?"

Without waiting for a response, the Archieunuch strides purposefully up the thoroughfare and disintegrates into the upper citadel. Nerses chides me the whole way past the harem apartments, warning that Zinvor's vengeance takes many forms.

"We learn not to upset things around here, and all will be well." The nods and mutters from the women attest to their unwillingness to challenge this structure, "But you seem unable to grasp this concept, so it may be time you learn another way."

Rather than barring the door and trusting the guards, Nerses takes up residence in the chair before the hearth and directs orders from there. He sends Mariam and Lusine to fetch the bathhouse attendants and fill the basin in my room. Then he sends for the kitchen hands with instructions for the chef. The continuous stream of eunuchs and servants flowing in and out of my chambers is more disconcerting than if they had just locked me inside by myself.

The masculine press of eunuchs in my receiving room forces me to take refuge with the women in my bathing chamber. Their presence alone is enough to ensure my compliance in laying low in the tub while they scrub and rinse away a week's worth of grime. It is when they apply a noxious lotion to my legs and underarms to remove all bodily hair, that I comprehend what my punishment will be. The ritualistic cleansing is to prepare me to receive the master.

Perfumed in cloying musk, stuffed with rich food, and dressed in sheer silks I sit cross legged in the middle of my bed and await my fate. Like a warrior on the eve of battle, I anticipate my foe, refusing to wait on his pleasure. Girding myself in prayer to calm my spirit, and meditation to still my heart, I place my physical being in God's hands.

Night descends, and Nerses lights sconces in the antechamber, murmuring directives to his underlings while I sit in darkness. Into the inky blackness of twilight I detect every movement; the rattle of a tray for the eunuchs' supper, the pop of a cork from a wine bottle, the shuffle of sandaled feet as messengers carry out orders. The monastery bell tolls the eighth hour vigil, which I have not attended for many months, so I gladly join the haunting chants emanating from across the vale.

A loud yawn from the other room indicates Nerses' nonchalance, which plucks at the tension in my nerves, keeping me on guard. As the sky outside my window blushes in silvery predawn aura, my mind starts to succumb to the strain of unanswered questions.

"Why didn't Damian come?" Fear whispers.

"It matters naught, you are here unharmed," reason answers.

"What is he planning?" Anxiety prods.

"God will protect you," awareness reminds me of all of the occasions my savior has gotten me through.

"Mistress, please come and break your fast," Mariam's tentative entreaty interrupts my private conversation.

"I am not hungry," my petulant response draws her lower lip into a trembling pout.

"You must eat," tears swim in her molasses eyes, "you will need fuel for strength."

"Can you bring the tray in here?" I concede, "I don't want to eat with him out there." The sweet savory aroma of honeyed meats and fruit makes my stomach lurch, but the thought of dining with Nerses brings forth nausea. I choke down a few bites, chasing the dry morsels with wine.

"Eat," Lusine holds a chunk of bread to my lips, I close my eyes against the tide of queasiness.

"I cannot," I push the laden platter across the bed, shaking my head, "I feel like I'm going to get sick!"

They accompany me into the bathing room and splash cold water on my face. Much revived, I sit docilely while Mariam styles my curls. Lusine sets out an array of cosmetics and moves to make up my face.

"No paint," my firm denial stays her hand, "I'll not wear the mask of a whore."

"Please do not fight him Mistress," the older girl puts an arm around her sister, quelling her quivering shoulders, "tis best to just give him what he wants."

"You too Mariam? Lusine?" The wine gurgling in my empty stomach, points an unwarranted finger at these two innocent allies, "doesn't anyone here understand that by constantly giving in to him, you have turned him into a monster?"

"Tis time to go Mistress," Nerses nasal command held a finality that brooked no resistance. Saving my mettle for bigger quarry, I square my shoulders and march determinedly to do battle. He leads me down the main avenue between the closely packed apartments of the women's quarters to where Zinvor stands surveying the crowded courtyard. I hazard a glimpse into his sardonic visage to read his mood, and quell at the smug gratification in the upward curve of his thin lips.

"Well done, Nerses," his sharp gaze penetrates my gauzy chamois, "you are dismissed for the remainder of the day."

I mark his departure in the soft slap of his sandals on the pavers, alert to the air of anticipation thickening the humid morning. Training my warriors instincts on my surroundings, I note that the hour is early for such full attendance, usually the women do not gather until well into the afternoon. The trudge of boots announces the imminent arrival of guards to add to the restive scene.

"Ah! I see everyone is turned out in anticipation of some diversion!" Damien's voice booms overloud in the strained peace. I eye him sullenly as he slithers past, having a sinking certainty that today's entertainment will involve me. His convoy of eunuchs fan out and take up positions encompassing the group, thwarting any attempts to escape on foot. As the pretender snakes through the throng, fondling one, groping another, I whet my wits for a different kind of fight.

"I hear that it amuses you to ridicule my guards," he addresses the rhetorical statement to no one in particular. "So t'will give me great pleasure to mock your desire for my sexual favors!"

His snarl is accompanied by a startled scream from Keket as he unexpectedly yanks her by those flowing braids I had so admired. He drags her to the stair next to me, twisting her head painfully with one hand, while undoing his robe with another. Exposing his engorged member, he thrusts her down in front of him.

"Keket! Show her how an obedient concubine is to serve her master." His command carries a fissure of fear across the gathering. Separating herself from the huddle, Indira steps forward, palms up in supplication.

"Allow me to demonstrate my particular oral skills on you my lord," her stunning bravery stirs my conscience. He rudely shoves the slight beauty away so that she tumbles over Keket and they both sprawl at his feet. He throws his head back in a throaty guffaw, mimicked around the courtyard by his small army of eunuchs. Their rough laughter gives way to a musical titter, and the sea of ashen faces parts to allow Zoe to emerge. She approaches Damian, hips swaying in exaggeration of her skill, and reaches out to stroke him. Bile bubbles from my gut, and I avert my gaze, searching for mental footing in this slimy situation.

"Sire, you know I please you the most," she purrs.

"No!" He slaps her arm away, "Although it is very enthralling indeed to be so coveted, I am curious to see how much She lusts for me!"

I stare aghast at his finger pointing directly at me, his erection signaling his game. This is his retribution, he wants me to beg. With a slow wag of my set chin, I maneuver to my knees in front of him and close my eyes against the vile task I must perform to save the others from worse fate. He grabs my nape and shoves himself into my mouth, my eyes bulging in panic as I recall a similar invasion from my youth. He jams his penis all the way to the back of my gullet, forcing my throat to gag and stomach to heave involuntarily. With a glorious retch, I spew vomit all over his torso and legs. Staggering to my feet, I spray the nearby Zinvor, who is so taken aback that he deserts his master and flees. Bile dripping from my face, I leer victoriously at the women, then compose a look of contrition to Damian.

"My most sincere apologies," I exert my best lie, "if you will allow me to take you to the pool I will wash you."

"You will have to do more than that!" He snaps, shaking the flecks of my breakfast from his robe. I bow and lead him to the bathhouse, resolute in what I must do next. Mechanically, I disrobe him, a cruel copy of a body I once loved. I trail his wake into the warmth of the pool, where I wash him with manufactured care.

"Enough," he grunts, pulling me out of the water and laying down on a nearby bench. "How much do you want this in you?"

Seductively peeling off the wet silk so that his attention is on my gleaming skin rather than my steely expression, I linger on foreplay in hopes of speeding up the act. He clutches at me and mutters in a frenzy, and I know it is time to mount him and put an end to this hideous drama.

Mercifully, he is so over-aroused, that he grunts a few times and growls in climax.

Having made his point and delivered his punishment, we return to my chambers where he takes me again. Exhausted, hungry and beaten, I cede the battle to his gloating conceit and curl up into a ball in the middle of my bed.

"Wagging tongues are still lauding your name, Adila," Liang Na and I laze in the mild sun-drenched terrace high above the citadel. "One would think you are a myth!"

Her reference to being a fantastical creature makes me think of my maman, and I feel closer to her now, than when she held me as a child. Having suffered abuse at the hands of men, I now pity her submission and understand her plight to persevere. It has been a tumultuous couple of weeks since Damian had his way with me, so I cherish the tranquility of these moments with the princess and her ladies.

"Is there word of my visits here?" If the eunuchs ever found out, the repercussions would be terrible. Exercising utmost caution in evading the sentinels, I had belligerently traversed the aqueduct the very next day to prove myself bested, but not defeated.

"Nay, only of your exploits in foiling the Strategos," we carefully avoid discussion of my subsequent confrontations with Damian. Assuming that he had broken me, he attempted to violate me a few days later, only to find my fists less agreeable. Keket and Indira both took the brunt of his rage thereafter, for I saw their colorful bruises when Nerses took me to the bath house for a ritual cleansing. Recognizing the pattern of preparation, I spent two sleepless nights before the eunuchs drugged me and their master raped me. "The women all seem to admire your independent spirit."

"Yet they continue to appease him," I envision Zoe demeaning herself to him. "If they could just set aside their petty competitions and join together, they could change everything! There are so many of us..."

"Dangerous thoughts like these should not be put to words," Liang

Na interrupts, "We will pretend as though we do not comprehend your greek."

"What tune is this they are playing?" I change the subject to hide my disappointment in her response. The princess' attendants strum a familiar chorus, "I recognize it from one we used to sing on the road."

We unify our voices in song, content to let the melody mend the brokenness within and between us. Other than my sister, Liang Na is the only other female friend I have known for this long, and I am reluctant to test our relationship with ill will towards one another. Just as I attempt to show the others that we must beware of complacency in the form of appeasing our captors, I know that the time will come when our bond will be similarly strained; but not today.

Chapter 23

Autumnal squalls abate to mild wintery mists that hang damp in the air throughout the shortened days. The laden atmosphere depresses the desire to be out of doors, and I assume that the other inhabitants of the seraglio sit by their hearths to stave off the chill as do I more now. Whether attributed to the dull climate of late, or the poor sleep since my confrontations with Damian, my energy to do anything wanes, and lethargy saps my usual robust strength.

"Tis over a month now since you arrived, Mistress," Mariam comments as she helps me into a warm robe in the bath chamber. Her innocent remark suspends me in dread, our eyes meet in the mirror, reflecting alarm back to one another. I dare not speak life to what could be growing inside of my stomach. She is correct about the timing, it has been a full moon cycle since I came here on the heels of menstruating. Dazed, I brush past her and drop to my knees at my balcony rail.

"Lord tell me this is not true," I implore fervently, "I pray it is not your will for me to carry his child!"

Anxiously, I gaze out over the valley shrouded in nebulous film. Listening intently for God's faithful response, I grow impatient at the silence and give in to the whirl of thought spinning in my head. Counting the weeks, replaying the horrors, noting my fatigue and tender breasts, I emit a keening cry that echoes eerily across the canyon.

The haunting screech that replies is not the voice of God, but the utterance of the fierce fowl spiraling from the heavens. As always, Eugeneous' majestic descent takes my breath away, only this occasion I have no compliments for his beauty. From his perch on the rail he cocks his head and fixes me with a chiding glare.

"What am I to do Eugenious?" He twitches his neck to contemplate my situation from another angle. "Do I tell him so he leaves me alone?"

Uninterested in this option, the bird scratches under his wing, ruffling his wintery plumage.

"Should I keep it secret to spite him?" He stares out over the foggy expanse, conveying his indifference.

"Perhaps I just end it all and leap off the balcony!" I sob in self pity. Eugeneous squawks at a sharp rap on the antechamber portal, and takes flight into the abyss, as I wish to do.

Mariam admits Nerses and a troop of eunuchs enter along with Lusine, who bustles excitedly to her sister while the eunuchs announce I am to accompany them to the bath house. Emotions in turmoil, it takes every ounce of my flagging energy not to fight them all. I know what this ritual means, that I am to be plucked, stuffed and trimmed to be devoured by their master.

When we get to the mausoleum, I rebelliously barricade the door closed, having decided to resist Damian's odious attentions. Shamila, the attendant, shakes her head with a sigh, indicating the futility of my plotting. Though I know she may be right; for instance, the windows cannot be barred, the obstacle will at least slow him down and keep him from a frontal attack while I am bathing.

We finish the routine quicker than usual, as I refuse to let Shamila apply depilatory to my arms and legs this time, and she is patting my hair dry when I detect the patterned march of trained guards approaching. I shrug into my robe and tie the sash tight as the portal rattles against the beam I had laid across its hinges.

"Open the door!" His command goads my ire to brashness.

"Nay!" I shout back, "I am not a slave beholden to your whims!"

"You don't know what you are saying!" His patronizing stokes the flames of anger. Let him think I am a simpleton then, his underestimation will be his downfall. "Guards, heave ho!"

The boom of armored bodies slamming into the oaken panels rebounds off the tiled walls. The wood bar and hinges jump under the pressure of their rhythmic assault. Feeding on the warrior's blood pulsing through my body, I wait until the next ebb, then throw off the beam. Two giant guards crash into the chamber, followed by another pair staggering in, and all fall over each other.

"You could have just waited until I was finished bathing!" Regal in my haughty disdain, I parade past the heap of humanity sprawled across the marble flagstones. I stride under the gaping archway, ready for war, but a different sort of confrontation stops my heart mid-beat.

"I have waited long enough. I miss you Adila."

"Majidii," I whisper, as if anything louder will wake me from fantasy.

"I was so anxious to get to you, I couldn't think right!" The power of his presence overwhelms me, grounding my feet so I can't move. "I am sorry for the intrusion."

Glancing around at the curious faces peeping from apartment windows, I digress into false bravado to challenge him.

"How could you do this to me?" I throw my arms to encompass the harem, "imprison me here by myself!"

"Perhaps we should discuss this elsewhere?" His comely brow knits in confusion. The sun has darkened his complexion to a rich chestnut, complimenting the fullness of his coral lips.

"If you had been here a month ago, we could have talked then," I hiss petulantly, "but instead you have your guards and eunuchs bring me while you are off doing God knows what!"

"I was here," he shrugs off my verbal attack, volleying the consternation back onto me. "I watched over you and made sure that you were settled."

The memory of the faceless immortal guard floats into my awareness, thwarting my argument, deflating my bombast. Searching for blame to deflect my frightening tender feelings, I spit out a childish reply.

"You should have told me!" I wheedle, trying to keep my tone steady.

"I couldn't tell you," his composure fuels my trepidation, "and I deemed it best to give you space to adjust."

"You gave me room enough," I found my angle, "and you gave someone else the chance to move in too!"

"I left you well protected," Majidi's eyes scan the area.

"Then you are more of a fool than I thought!" Unseen audible gasps can't stop the words from bursting from me, "I am with child!"

Agape horror strikes his lovely features, emboldening me to stride past him and up to my chambers, where I slam my door and crumble into a quivering mass on the priceless Persian rug.

"He hates me now!" Goading my agony gives me a sadistic pleasure that is easier for me to bear than sorting through the layers of complex emotions. I sit in the dim receiving room and stare into the crackling fire, daring the flames to contradict my self pity. All afternoon and evening I sequestered myself with my thoughts, plotting my next steps, forgetting everything in my focus on what to do. "There is nothing for me here, not that there ever was."

"I cannot stay here," I conspire with the luminous embers, "but where would I go?"

"Gong! Gong! Gong!" The bell for Compline tolls the answer, urging me out the balcony to contemplate the ghostly monastery perched high upon the inland mountains. In the fading dusk, I can make out a thread of stones bridging the valley. I recall how I viewed the aqueduct from the tower chamber above, and how I followed its arched trail until it disappeared into the snow capped range beyond.

"That's it!" I jump into action, "I'm going to the abbey!"

It doesn't take me long to don the pantaloons, woolen tunica and boots. I find a warm cloak and roll in it a torch and flint in case I need to light the way. Not knowing how long it will take me to cross the stretch of canyon, I swallow a few bites of bread and fruit to fuel me for the climb. With one last look over my luxurious prison, I launch up to the waterway with a practiced hop and make my escape.

Moonlight dances atop the ripples to illuminate the liquid pathway, and I envision myself floating effortlessly upstream into the celestial heavens. Not even the frigid water, nor the mortal heaviness in my limbs can penetrate the dreamlike state that suspends me high above the earth. The mystical pull of the shrouded peaks steadies my balance within the stony track, grounding me in my purpose.

"You must not sleep Adila," My maman's low chant sounds peculiarly similar to the monks singing the Matins service. "Wake up child!"

"Nay Maman," the young girl in me wants to ascend this glittering path up to my heavenly father, "I do not want to wake up, tis cold and hard."

"Yes it is daughter," her faint voice is fading into a thick cloud of oblivion, "but if you fall asleep you will not awaken. You have the spirit and strength of the Gods in you, and you must continue until you bridge the gulf between us all."

Her encouraging words shock my sluggish heart and seize my stiffening muscles into action. Groaning under the weight of deadly chill dragging me into its fatal depths, I claw back to awareness, the sparkling pathway solidifying to the channel outlined in the silvery dawn. Having crawled through the night, I have but a quarter league to go to reach the slope under the monastery. Filled with renewed hope, driven with fear of discovery, I list forward and lose my footing in the greedy grasp of rushing water. For a valiant moment I teeter and grapple about, but in the end, I lose the battle to balance, and pitch headlong over the side of the aqueduct wall.

Chapter 24

Whiteness saturates every corner of my existence, whatever state of being is left of me. A floating sensation lifts me upwards to where a colossal gate emerges from the clouds. The outline of an angelic figure appearing, confirms my suspicion that my physical self is gone, and I now face my judgment at the gates of heaven. The brightness fades into the hooded specter, which spreads its robes and wraps me in snug darkness.

Excruciating pain penetrates the remains of my broken body, the smell of blood sharp in my senses. My memory fails, for I can't recall answering any questions to gain admittance into eternal paradise.

"Father God!" I cry out, "Did I not make it into heaven? Am I to swelter in Hell for my sins?"

"Nay daughter," black apparitions encircle
me, "There is work for you yet."

One of the shades comes into focus, and I perceive a low murmuring amongst the flock.

"Brother Samuel?" What is my mentor doing here in the afterlife? He reaches out and pinches my arm, and I scream with surprise at the piercing pain. "Is this purgatory?"

"Sleep child," the cape of darkness consumes me again into a pit of blissful nothingness.

The wistful caress of cool breath brushes through me, awakening my supernal senses to the luminous aura surrounding me. The jasmine scented air, the tinkling music of a lute, the cushion of cloud-like softness supporting me, all assure me that I made it. I blink my eyes open and witness the beauty of heaven, the creamy marble columns, the nebulous white curtains, and the frescoed dome above all fulfill my fantasy of what paradise would be like.

A silent cherub approaches and smiles in childlike joy. She runs away and I want to turn my head to watch where she goes, but I cannot move. Remembering that my physical body is dead, I relax into the plush cradle of God's dominion.

"Wake up Adila," the deep male voice confuses my idea of Valhalla. I regain consciousness, but this time there's a dull ache where my body should be. "Lusine came to get me, she is here too."

"Brother Samuel?" My whisper is raspy, "if I am in heaven, why do I feel pain?"

"Praise Allah!" He cries, adding to my disorientation that my brother in Christ would use a muslim name for God, "you are awake!"

"Brigida?" A female form with long flowing hair steps forth, "Am I not dead?"

"Its me, Mariam," I feel her take my hand, "and you are not dead thanks to God!"

Thanks to God, I close my eyes against the tainted beauty of the airy chamber. I try to give thanks to my savior, but I cannot conjure gratitude for my return to reality. Instead I ask for grace to carry out this purpose that continues to uphold me, endurance to perform the tasks that I have left undone, and clarity to see what it is that God wants me to do.

"Adila," the gentle bass stirs my dormant heart. "Can you move at all?"

A latent ache in my chest impels me to turn my head away from the direction of his voice. But the sound of his weeping fuels the hurt, until I feel my heart nigh breaking. There is only one masculine voice that has ever moved my emotions, but I have lost his love to his brother's depraved lust. Contrary to these addled thoughts, telling me that he hates me now that I laid with another, Majidi takes my limp hand and I feel his lips press against my palm.

"I am so sorry Adila," he sobs, "I did this to you! I was selfish to think that you would be okay here, and that I could protect you. Whatever you think of me now, I vow that I will see you hale and happy again."

Touched my his oath, I close my fingers around his and open my eyes to take in his compelling visage. Tears swimming in his eyes enhance his beauty, a magnifying glass into his true soul. The purity of his intentions and desires to do what is right, spills forth in the wetness on his chiseled cheekbones. Steeling against the pain spreading from my movements, I reach out and brush the tears from his lovely face. I smile reassuringly up at Mariam, a strange sense of belonging easing my discomfort.

"I am still upset with you Majidi," I snap in a temper a few days later when I cannot move an inch from the various splints and bandages encasing my body. "I forgive you, because I know it was my choice to cross the aqueduct, but you knew how I cherish my freedom and yet you took it away!"

"I know Adila," he props me up onto some cushions and plops down beside me to break our fast together. "I never forgot how important your independence is, and I admire that about you. I heard that the monks discovered your true identity, and thought it would help your plight to bring you here."

"Why would you think that holding me in bondage with the rest of your harem would benefit me?" I sputter between the bites that he shoves in my mouth. "I thought you knew how I ache at the thought of sharing you with other women."

"As I have told you, it was selfish of me." He stops feeding and lets his head fall back onto the bolster. His studious gaze punctures my angry wall of defense, "I wanted to have you with me, and I took the opportunity when it was presented."

"And you invaded the Armenian city per the Bishop's treaty?" Carefully gauging his reaction to my query for signs of regret, I press him for undue obligation on my behalf.

"I would have gone eventually," he shrugs, "besides, it took my mind off missing you."

"Oh posh!" My ire dissipates like the mist under his sunny smile, "you speak nonsense. Look at me! I'm a mess! I can tell my face is distorted with bruising and scratches."

Shaking my encased arm to punctuate my undesirability, sends the corners of his mouth plunging downwards. He shakes his head and adjusts my arm back onto my lap and tugs at the blanket in effort to comfort my broken body. With my good hand, I stay his ministrations until he meets my probing eyes.

"I thought you hated me Majidi," his molten orbs hold my questioning without dropping, "and that running away was my only option."

"Nay Adila," he shushes, "I was not angry with you, but I am disgusted in myself that I failed to protect you from Damian."

"Perhaps we can let bygones be bygones, now that there is no child anymore?" I had known without having to be told that the seed growing in me was gone. Majidi threads his fingers in mine and kisses them fervently. The adoration in his mien turns amorous, and he bends forward, but pulls back at a subtle movement from across the chamber. Lusine approaches with a carefully blank expression and removes the remains of our meal. "Did I hear you say that Lusine was responsible for saving me?"

"She certainly was!" Majidi beamed at her shy grin. "She came to me and kept trying to pull me to the balcony. I thought she was addled until she spoke, 'Adila, bird!' and I saw this great falcon in mortal combat with some vultures."

"Eugenious!" I gasp, fearing the worst for my feathery friend. "He fought off the buzzards? Is he okay?"

"What a fierce choice of champions! Yes he is recovering in the care of the monks who took you in and set your limbs."

"Bless you Lusine, for risking yourself for me," she curtseys demurely and departs, "and thank God for the monks for treating me. I envisioned that I was gone to heaven and they were angels!"

"Well they did a splendid job patching you up until we could bring you here and have my surgeon repair your ribs." He indicates the bandage covering my torso. "And they're very proficient with their herbs to deaden the pain!"

"Speaking of discomfort," I stifle a yawn, "I am tired, I couldn't sleep last night."

"Rest then, my dear," his lips linger on my brow, "I have work to do right there at my desk, so I will be close by if you need anything."

Dozing off to the music of water splashing in a fountain nearby, I flit in and out of respite, absorbing the peaceful setting. Rather than dwell on the itching inside the stiff wrapping around my leg, I contemplate Majidi's back as he sits poring over a stack of scrolls. A supple linen tunic cossets the taut muscles of his wide shoulders and narrow waist. Sighing in wonder at how casually he wears his comeliness, I focus outward to where the room opens into a vast terrace.

The purplish blur of mountain peaks over the forested valley is closer here in the master's chambers, the air pungent with coniferous spice. Deep contentment mantles the room as dusk settles upon the city. The ruby sunset bleeds into amber torchlight when the servants glide across the marbled expanse to light scones. Impassive guards coalesce in darkened doorways, securing this idyll of heaven here on earth. I fade into sweet repose, claiming the immunity of grace upon me.

Emerging as if part of a dream, the toll for vigil service traverses the gorge to stroke my awareness. A subtle movement beside the bed rouses me further to contemplate the figure kneeling on a rug facing the sound of the bell. Rather than bow towards the east, as I have seen other muslims do when called to prayer, Majidi kneels back on his heels and stares out the open balcony as if hypnotized by the rhythmic chanting drifting on the breeze.

Palpable confusion emanates from his posture, trapped between prayer and prostrate by an unseen ideological battle. Vigil service yields to the stillness of the night, and Majidi briskly goes through the motions of islamic devotion and rolls up his carpet. He reaches under the bed and I hear him slide something out, then withdraw to another room. In the nocturnal hush, I hear the splash of his ministrations and the slap of bare feet upon his return.

Like a thief in the night, the sight of his naked form steals the breath from my body. The glow from the torches illuminates his chestnut shoulders and sculpted haunch. How could I have forgotten the magnetic impact of his magnificence on my good sense? My dormant frame suddenly awakens, secret parts I had thought dead, now tingle in excitement as I watch his muscles glide under silken skin. I squirm against the restraining splints, trying to relieve the electricity snapping through me.

Unaware of the devastating effect of his unadorned perfection, he beds down on the pallet that he had pulled out, soft snores soon signifying his slumber. Meanwhile I toil against my restraints, the heat in my loins rising to ire that I can't move my impaired torso and legs.

"Be patient, child," I freeze from wriggling, honing my ears to where the command originated. The sound of Majidi's breath emanates evenly from the floor beside me, so it couldn't have been him. My pulse increases, I glance at the unmoving guards in the porticoes. Unable to detect anything with my carnal senses, I train my spiritual ear and am rewarded to hear God's directive, "You must build your strength slowly."

"Lord, what would you have me to do?" I stretch my arms out in supplication, curiously noting how when I relax into prayer I no longer have pain.

"Nothing, Adila," I watch the puff of his breath sway the wispy bed curtains above, "for once in your life, you do nothing but accept the aid that I provide."

Long after God's presence leaves the drapes to inhabit the lullaby of nocturnal creatures, I meditate on his instructions. Two things I am terrible at, being idle, and accepting help. A shiver rattles through me, either in anticipation of another challenge, or from the chilly wind invading the chamber. All of my writhing merely resulted in pushing the warm covers to the end of the bed and out of my reach.

"Do nothing," I repeat, studying the curtains hanging from the bed frame overhead. "Accept aide." Another gust unwraps a swathe of fabric to dangle directly in front of me, I nearly laugh aloud, "Thank you my Lord, I will!"

Deliberately, I hold onto the length and pull myself to sit up until I can grasp the edge of the cover. Smugly satisfied in my small achievement, and greatly gratified to follow God's advice, I swaddle myself in silk up to my chin and nestle into sleep's blithe embrace.

Chapter 25

"One month," the words roll off the Arab's tongue with a flourish that fell on my ears like a prison sentence. "Do Nothing for the next month."

"But Doctor Al-Zahra," I plead to the surgeon, "You just said that my wounds are healing quickly!"

"Tis not the superficial lacerations that need time," he fixes me with a stern look, "the bones inside need several weeks to knit properly. They must be kept immobile to grow back straight, thus the splints stay on."

"You have much knowledge on treating medical maladies, Adila," Majidi interjects, sitting by my side on the bed, "but Doctor Al-Zahra has been with me on the battlefield, and has treated these types of catastrophic injuries. I trust that he knows what he is doing."

"Thank you Your Eminence, but I am not beyond learning new techniques and remedies." The tidy man straightens his tunica and rummages through his sack until he proffers a corked bottle.

"Resin?" I read the label quizzically.

"Last year my master took a tumble in the woods while traveling in Russia. Some wise healer used this pine sap as an astringent, and to glue his wound together. It worked so well that I didn't believe how severe the damage was until I tried it on some of my patients." He winks conspiringly, "Now I use it all of the time!"

"You see," Majidi lifts up his chiton to expose his lean ribs and rippling abdomen. It takes me a moment to gather that he is trying to show me the faint mark on his side, "there is barely anything left of the gash!"

He drops a casual kiss on my mouth and escorts the surgeon out to the veranda. I pursue the hum of their conversation until their voices are drowned in the tumble of water splashing in a fountain. Using the dangling bed curtain, I hoist myself up and swivel my legs so that I can

261

sit upright on the side of the mattress and survey the governor's grand chambers.

Gazing beyond the vast private rooms, of which I've scrutinized every tile, column and statue, I surmise that the state rooms lie through an arched portal in the far corner of the expanse. The edge of a heavily gilded and ornate chair leads me to believe that the Strategos conducts his business of Chaldia from the adjacent hall.

That which seduces my soul, however, is the vista from the wide open balcony in front of me.

From the mosaicked dome to the marbled floor, drape lavish brocade curtains, drawn agape to frame the breathtaking view. The panorama encompasses the entire city and sea as far as the eye can see. The urge to walk out onto the broad terrace comes upon me so strong, that were it not for Majidi's return I would have tried to stand.

"What are you about, Adila?" He stands akimbo to block the intoxicating aspect.

"I'm tired of laying in this bed, I want to go out there!" I complain, pointing like a spoiled child. Correcting my tone so as not to sound ungrateful that I have displaced the Strategos from his luxurious bed, I finish, "but the doctor says I can't do anything."

"I will make a pact with you," his cooperative intelligence commands my interest, "if you will moderate your movements according to Dr. Al-Zahra's orders, I will ensure that you go anywhere you want!"

"How can I get around without walking?"

"Firstly, you will ask me for help," I hear God's words in his speech, and nod in compliance. "Secondly, I'm certain my engineer can fashion a device on wheels for you to move about until your bones are healed enough to bear your weight."

"Oh, but I don't want to be a burden on you and your..." he holds up a hand to halt my tirade.

"Most importantly, you will not fret over what you cannot do, but focus on the activities that you can do." He pauses to let the wisdom of a positive mindset penetrate my cloud of self pity. "I have lived through several severe injuries myself, and personally helped many more of my men overcome our infirmities this way. If you listen to your body and alter the way you may typically move about, you will find that you are capable of much more than you realize."

Mulling over the terms of his agreement, I begin to understand how it will work. Dr. Al-Zahra specifically said I had to keep the bones immobile, but that doesn't mean that I can't move the uninjured parts. With renewed hope, I stretch out my bruised but unbroken arm to clasp his hand.

"Its a deal!" I promise, knowing that it will be easy to comply with the physical challenge, but the asking for help may be more difficult.

"Done!" He nearly shouts in exuberance. "Lets get you a chair and break our fast out there on the terrace!"

A pair of weeks of pass by, during which I follow instructions to do nothing, and yet the days are full of doing something. As per my lifelong routine, the monastery bell calls me to the small balcony overlooking the valley in morning worship, while Majidi kneels in prayer to honor God in his way. We break our fast, then proceed to the terrace to exercise in whatever fashion we're able.

While I content myself with marching in my chair and stretching my limbs, I vicariously thrill in watching Majidi's arduous training. He is always mindful of my progress, and constantly probes my activity, testing my physical capabilities. Through continual instruction, he taxes my mental capacity to learn Armenian swordsmanship as he trains. Eventually I begin to combine the two, and practice the movements with deliberate precision.

By noontime, when the sun usually works its way through the early winter fog that swirls inland from the sea, we clean up and clad for more occupational pursuits. On the quieter days, when Majidi sits at his desk and pores through scrolls and tomes, I pluck at the lute and compose new songs that unify the chants from the abbey and strains from the minaret.

The sublime serenity of these times is equalled in excitement on the days when Majidi holds court in the adjoining chamber. Once the dignitaries, viziers and citizens are assembled, I roll my wheeled chair just outside the ajar portal and eavesdrop on the proceedings. Although the machinations of state business twists my thoughts into knots, the way in which the Strategos handles it all so expertly, yet sensitively, garners my utmost admiration.

Especially on these evenings, after he finishes tying up all foreign and domestic loose ends, we spend a few quiet hours discussing the events and issues over dinner. Some nights we play chess, music or just simply sit under the stars in companionable silence.

"You are healing quickly Adila," he observes my fluid movement as I adjust the heavy robe to cover my feet.

"Thanks to you for helping me," I delight in his approval and realize that part of my recovery is because I want to impress him. "And to God for mercy and strength."

"Yes, Allahu akbar," he murmurs, gazing distractedly to where my tunica slips down my shoulder. "Allahu akbar."

"I feel badly for taking over your bed," a shiver tingles through me at his ogling. "You should not have to sleep on the floor."

"Its nothing, I do not want to jostle you unawares," he grins bawdily at the double meaning, then more seriously, "and I worry that I might harm you. Besides, I'm accustomed to sleeping on my pallet while traveling."

"If that is the case, I am much better now to return to my own apartments."

"No!" His sharp retort surprises us both. "My apologies, that came out stronger than I intended. It is just that I feel responsible to take care of you, and I can protect you best here in my chambers."

"Well I am not comfortable putting the Strategos out of his bed," I pout slightly disappointed that he doesn't say that he enjoys my company, as I had become accustomed to his.

"Please stay Adila," he requests rather than commands, "I want you with me, not just to ease my conscience, but because I love having you around. The bed is enormous, so I will keep to one side easily enough."

Sighing inwardly in relief, I nod in acquiescence and rub my forearms as a foreboding chill shivers through me. The fissure of anxiety, a portent of growing too attached to Majidi, may be also God's displeasure over the extent of seeking another's attention. Attributing my actions to be due to the cold air, Majidi suggests that we retire and calls for Mariam to assist my toilet, while I wheel my chair in to the bedroom.

Once Mariam and Lusine help me to undress and relieve myself, they supervise the process of lifting, pushing and shifting myself into bed. Though the exercise is tedious, I strictly adhere to Majidi's instructions to do for myself what I can to regain my independence. The girls drape the curtains around the bed frame and depart, allowing him to emerge meagerly clad in the brief loincloth that he wore on our first encounter.

With the glowing embers from the brazier casting an amber hue on the sweep of his legs and swell of his chest, he slips under the covers and settles stiffly across the plush expanse of mattress. If it wasn't for his comically exaggerated concern, I would be utterly lost in the artistry of his profile etched against the dim backdrop of orange.

"Do you think that scrap will do any good?" I jest, pointing to the obvious protrusion where the loincloth fails to tame his erection.

"I just don't want to frighten you," his ponderous exhale belies his discomfort, "normally I sleep in the nude!"

"I know," the vision of him bedding down naked on his pallet flashes before me, "but we are too far along in knowing each other to be uncomfortable! Come," I pat the space beside me, "I could use your warmth to chase away the bite."

He slides over next to me, and I squirm to mold my curves to his side, using the crook of his armpit to pillow my head. Tenderly he wraps his arm around me and kisses my temple, bidding me good night. Breathing deeply in contentment, I coast on the rhythmic roll of his pulse into oblivion.

The celestial pathway stretches out before me, beckoning me to break out of my restraining splints and walk along the sparkling surface. In my dream I am whole, and I see myself dancing across the sky in pursuit of the moon. Not even Majidi's leveled snores can penetrate the mystical vision, as the heavenly bodies align to form steps up through a shimmering curtain of flurries.

The luminescent moon gracefully bows to the golden splendor of the sun as I cross the threshold of awareness. The ethereal aura that lit my path, retreats deep inside of me, filling my soul with uncontainable joy. Unable to perceive the details of my dream, I am left with a heart overflowing with love. I labor through the days ahead, toiling to complete the simplest of functions. Yet I am comforted that I can find strength if I retreat into this core of light, that one day it will return to illuminate my destiny.

"Dr. Al-Zahra is here, Adila!" Majidi is already up and dressed.

"He is early!" I dismay in keeping the busy surgeon waiting for me. These past two weeks having Majidi next to me in the bed, I have been sleeping so soundly that it is an effort to wake up.

"Yes he is," he ties back the curtain, letting the suns rays penetrate the cozy cocoon, "I know you've gotten good at doing things yourself this past month, but let me help you this once to go a little faster." Gratefully, I wrap my arms around his neck and allow him to carry me to the bath chamber. He deposits me on the touleta and discreetly withdraws to retrieve my clothes while I pass water down the opening and sponge off. I yawn sleepily as he scoops me up again, and plant a drowsy kiss on his neck. He chuckles, passing me a linen cloth to wipe my face before pulling a padded chamois and woolen tunica over my light chemise.

Our hustle is rewarded when Dr. Al-Zahra tells Majidi to set me back on the bed so that he can remove the splints. After methodically cutting away the layers of bindings, he carefully peels away the strips to free my legs. Though they look skinny and pale, I have never been so pleased to expose my legs, and I revel in the sensation of the cool air prickling my flesh. The doctor probes around the healed scars and declares the bones completely fused.

"You will be able to walk with the aid of crutches," he holds up a restraining hand as I greedily grab at the crutches. "Slowly! You must build up your balance and strength slowly. If you rush about you risk falling and reinjuring yourself. Master Majidi, see that she paces her activities so that she doesn't strain the bone structure."

"You know my methods Dr. Al-Zahra," he takes the crutches and helps me ease to my feet. He steadies me as I wobble and sway like a colt, reminding me what it feels like to stand. "Plant your feet wide Adila, bend your knees and feel the solid ground under you."

"She is not one of your soldiers, Sire," the surgeon interjects, "a mere woman does not have the mental nor physical training, and should not be pressed into remembering how to move her limbs."

"Adila, stand at attention!" The Strategos barks, bristling for me. I grip the handles and straighten my frame, "Now, March!"

Inspired by his determination to show the doctor what I, a lowly woman, can do, I tighten my stomach and lift my knees from my abdomen. After a month of doing little other than marching in my chair, I expertly execute the exercise for the enlightenment of Al-Zahra.

"Dr. Al-Zahra, this mere woman has twice the intelligence and strength as most warriors I have led into battle." His confidence in me expands in my chest, smothering my anger.

"Thank you for correcting me Eminence," the humility in his bow rings hollow, "I see what you are saying now, she is built like a man."

How can one be so brilliant, and yet so ignorant? To have such a distorted view of the prism of feminine appeal is baffling. A vision of Keket comes to mind, the innate harmony of her powerful frame, so much like mine. For a ponderous moment I search the doctor's arrogant mien for the answer, until the tendrils of God's fingertips beckon to look outward to him instead. Impudently dismissing the renown surgeon, I strike out with the crutches in stoic dignity to the terrace. Once there, in the aerie of God's wonders, a gale, rich with salty tang, scours away my angst and replaces it with awe in the splendor of his creation below.

"The seraglio looks so colorful from up here," I address Majidi when he joins me quietly by my side, head sinking into his drooping shoulders. His sidelong glance gauges my mood, "the pleasant fountains in the plaza, the merry afternoon bustle.

"One could even be seduced to think it a joyful place. Yet things are not as they appear on the outside, are they."

"Ah, so you are saying that for everything wondrous, there is a dark side?" He picks up my train of thought, and straightens to take in the kaleidoscope, "just like the good doctor? His medical knowledge is second to none, but he is an imbecile compared to a certain young woman who's fortitude I very much admire."

His genuine esteem lifts the corners of my lips to smile brightly at him and rest my head on a brawny shoulder. Wrapping a supportive arm around my waist, he kisses my forehead and tilts his head atop mine. The rising sun is already cutting through the frosty marine clouds, promising a benevolent wintery day.

"Lets go down there today!" His enthusiasm catches me off guard, and the demon in me whispers that he wants to see his concubines. "Its been a month since you have gone anywhere but these apartments, and the water in the pools will be excellent for teaching you to walk again."

Chiding my negative spirit, I nod in vigorous agreement, and accept the chaise that he orders to transport me down the labyrinth of corridors and stairs. When we reach the central piazza, I'm taken aback to the point of tears at the warm tidings from the women. I send the chair bearers away and stand in their midst, proving witness to yet another victory over infirmary, albeit by my own hand this time. As I crutch my way across to the bathhouse, I murmur my thanks to those who I now call my friends.

Closing the door on the trailing calls to wish me well, Majidi bars the portal against any further intrusion. Awkwardness seems to have rooted him to the marbled mosaic on the floor of the entryway, and he lets out a pent up breath and fusses with a short coil of hair. I grin at his adolescent manner, his discomfort around the women crystalizing in his ruddy complexion.

"Well...Captain," I ferret the proper term to address him as a soldier, hoping a dose of humor will ease him, "you have brought me here, now what?"

"Eminence."

"I beg your pardon?" Apparently wit is not the correct approach.

"Captain refers to Tarik, I go by your 'Eminence'." I stare at him incredulously until his hubris fades.

"You weren't so eminent when I found you falling from a tree in your skivvies!" I mumble sarcastically, then soften my banter when I realize his bravado is to cover up the disquiet that unmans him when confronted by his feminine horde. I stump to a settee and sit down, patting the space beside me, "I suppose if we're going in the pool, you'll have to help me remove the bandage around my ribs."

I busy myself struggling with the bulky clothing while he approaches the bench hesitantly and motions me to stand. Layers of fabric peel over my head until I shiver in my short linen chemise. Whether from cold or modesty, I cross my arms over my puckered breasts, giving him pause in his toil. He turns his attention to reducing his own attire, stripping down to the loincloth, so that we're both in undergarments.

"If you will hold up the hem, I can unwind the wrapping." The strain in his voice belies inner tension. Quelling my own trembling, I mimic his false businesslike tone and raise my slip to expose my bandaged torso. As he leans close to untangle the loose end, the atmosphere thickens so I can hardly breath. Again and again his arms encircle my waist to reach around for the growing bundle of swathe. Finally, the tail end glides off my hips, but his hands remain caressing my ribs.

"You are so beautiful," the reverence in his confession sets my head spinning. Drunk with passion, I sway into him and he sweeps me up against him and brings his lips crashing down on mine. Fierce desire reignites between us, untamed, undimmed and unforgiving. He clutches my buttock and presses my hips into his granite member, rubbing urgently against me. Suddenly he tears his mouth from mine and groans to the domed ceiling, leaving me staring in confusion at the tendons popping out of his neck. When he abruptly ceases his movements, in an incredibly erotic moment, I can feel his sex pulsing in release.

"Its been a while," he avoids my admiring gaze, sheepishly calculating the wet spot on the front of the loincloth. "And I forgot the effect that your body has on me."

"Hmmm, indeed!" I tease gently, "but I've gone to mush!"

"Tis more than physical Adila," he responds seriously, then fingers the scars on my ribs. "At least the doctor did well to reduce the damage to your lovely skin!"

Self consciously, I drop my chemise over my marred body, motivated to get back the muscle I have lost. Majidi carries me into the warm water and instructs me to hold onto the edge and start walking around. Each simple step buoys my confidence and I lose myself in the joy of moving my legs again. I walk until the passion for Majidi subsides and the heat from the water takes its place in my joints.

Every day we repeat this exercise, progressing from walking around the perimeter to striding without holding the edge, then swimming.

Hour after patient hour, he takes me by the hand and encourages me so that by the next week I am able to walk on my own without assistance.

Being back in the harem makes me realize how easy it has been to exist in a bubble within the tapestried walls of Majidi's chambers. Constrained by immobility and coddled by luxury, the complexities of the outside world had faded. While the social atmosphere in the fountain plaza calls me to join the ladies in their chattering, it has the opposite effect on Majidi. His discomfort manifests in him drilling me as if I'm one of his soldiers, which in turn pushes me to excel in regaining my strength.

The inevitable sadness further invades our fragile oasis when I witness Majidi's indifference for his concubines. As I see their individual qualities, Hayfa's prolific mothering, Indira's petite strength, Shamila's massaging hands, Keket's elegant brawn, he skirts around them without so much as a turn of his head. When we return to his apartments, he is quick to deposit me in the bedroom and seek his vizier and counsel.

Where he used to discuss his dealings of the day with me, he gravitates to his male companions to shout and guffaw with them instead.

In the refuge of night time, we finally regain the harmonious energy that draws us to curl up under the covers. For now, these remnants of our eden are enough. The feel of his hands on me and his body pressed to mine, stave off the impending reality of our futile situation.

"I miss my sister," I sigh in response to Majidi barking at me to run faster through the water. He pauses in his own exercise, balancing himself horizontal, stiff as a tree trunk on his elbows and toes, and considers me from under a furrowed brow. It has been a particularly trying morning for the both of us. Starting with his vizier chastising him about the amount of time he spends with me, then a clandestine visit from Damian, complaining about the duplicity of them both being seen in the seraglio every day.

Our trip to the pool already tenuous, the strict hand of routine pushed us down the stairs through the harem apartments. The cacophony of music and cavorting around the central plaza further threatened to pull me off course to join the singing in celebration of the rare sunny day.

The toxic mix of my longing for simple pleasures, and his angst over his obligations was bound to manifest in some way. So in typical fashion, I put away my need for softer pursuits to perform for Majidi, while he exhausted his discomfort in training, impelling me to increase my pace beyond the usual incremental progress.

"Perhaps we should end it." The doom in his statement plucks a chord of fear within me. Panting from the arduous swim, I slump to the side of the pool and drop my head in my arms so that he can't read the dread in my face at the prospect of losing our friendship again. "I've pressed you too far today."

"Tis not the exercise Majidi," I counter, "I am thankful for your training, but I fear this time has become too burdensome for you to continue. Whenever my father would take out his agitation with his sharp demands, Brigida was always there to soften its sting."

"I am sorry Adila, I just want to help you recover your strength. It is my fault that this happened, I have to make it right again."

"As I have told you, it was my decision to cross the aqueduct," my gaze bores into his in effort to get my point across, "my injuries are not your responsibility."

"If I hadn't left you with Damian prowling about, you would be whole, hale and happy." He gives me a hand stepping out of the pool and passes me a towel.

"Only God can make me truly happy Majidi, but you might help by letting me visit Liang Na?" I hazard to advocate for myself, timid that my need for female company might offend him. He is silent for so long, contemplating the mosaic of marble tiles laid in the floor, that I lose my courage and withdraw my request. "Tis but a frivolous thought, I can amuse myself in training just as well. I do enjoy the pools and…"

"Yes," he stops my false tongue before it spews outright lies, "you may see the princess, but you must be able to walk there under your own strength. I will not go with you, as you can see I can hardly bring myself to pass through the seraglio, but I will ensure your safety."

Cheered by the prospect of seeing my friend, I throw my arms around Majidi's neck and plant a hearty kiss on his cheek. From one moment to the next, a playful kiss sparks a fissure of ardor, as our lips find each other and his hands clutch at my back. Mewling as he slants his mouth across mine, I open to him, body, mind and soul. Somehow Majidi steers me to a bench and lowers me gently until my back makes contact with the marble. He kneels between my thighs and rips at the chord tying his trousers, while base memories of the last time I lay on this very seat seep through the cold stone to chill my passion for Damian's brother.

Mercifully, God holds the knot fast, and Majidi inhales a sobering breath and descends back to reality with me. He surveys the semi-private room and slumps down onto the bench.

"Not here," he shakes his head. To which I add a tacit, "Not now."

Physically and emotionally drained, I straddle the bench and wrap my arms around him once again, resting my forehead on his shoulder. He sighs and leans into me, words unnecessary to convey our mutual frustrated affections.

"Sing to me Adila," he requests, then purrs in satisfaction when I find the tune that Mariam taught me from their grandmother. Soothed and bonded by song, we help each other to gather our things and depart, leaving my crutches behind.

"How was your visit with the princess?" Majidi glances up from the scrolls on his desk to take in my disheveled state, "And why is your color high?"

"I am breathing heavily," I gasp, "because your guard was walking so fast I nearly had to run to keep up with him!"

"Probably get back for putting him to shame on your previous forays to the tower!" He chuckles at the strained snort from the sentinel as he resumes his watch in the bedroom door frame.

"I already apologized for that, and for the menial task of escorting me to Liang Na's apartment." At the mention of his third wife, Majidi sifts through the parchment leafs in front of him, in search of a distraction. "As for my afternoon with the princess, twas not what I thought it would be."

"What happened?" He leans back and folds his arms across his chest, indulging me with a quizzical brow.

"Nothing happened," I shrug out of my woolen cloak and slouch into the chair across from him, "that's the problem! We used to talk and sing, or sit in the sun and listen to her ladies play their instruments. This time she made no effort to understand what I was saying or explain what she wanted to convey. The strangest part, was there was no music, which was what first connected us years ago."

"Do you think she may be jealous?"

"Not jealous," I ponder, "but perhaps angry at me. The only sentiment she kept repeating, was to tell me that she has ten and five years now."

"The age that we are to consummate the union." He muses ruefully, then sighs and wanders through a gap in the drapes.

"She sees me as standing in the way of her honor." I mutter, following him onto the broad veranda. The grumbling sea echoes our mood, its choppy whitecaps tossing ships in the harbor in a staccato dance. "The waters are rough today."

"Aye, this time of year gives rise to fierce storms at sea and in the mountains." He points to a lone trireme bobbing placidly protected in a cove to the east. "Tis why I keep Tarik anchored in the inlet...that's it!"

"What?" I start at his sudden declaration.

"I must take troops to check the mountain passes, but I have fretted over leaving you here." He takes hold of my hands and pins me with an earnest gaze, "Would you stay with Tarik out there on his ship for a fortnight? Mariam and Lusine can go with you."

The idea of venturing outside of the citadel walls lifts my spirit and I nod vigorously in agreement. He swings me around in a crushing embrace, squeezing a giggle from my beleaguered lungs. His exuberant relief speaks to the inner conflict he's been battling between his responsibility to his empire, and his desire to see me healthy. When he finally sets me on my own feet, I silently vow to greet him on his return with renewed vigor.

Chapter 26

Spring ensues in fits and starts, with rain to replenish the land, vying with the sun to nourish life. It is Lent season once again, and I am grateful to celebrate it with the devout Admiral Tarik. The spartan diet and naval accommodations suit my mood and drive my aspirations to restore every aspect of my being to what it was a year ago. Rocked in the cradle of the Constantineous, I contemplate the drastic change in my circumstances since last Easter.

Time on board ticks away, as steady as the current lapping at the hull. Much like his commander, Tarik captains his ship with routine and precision, occupying his sailors with chores and drills. He indulges me with laborious tasks on deck to keep me active, but draws the line when I request to join swordplay with the seamen. So I contentedly pass the time toiling at odd jobs, doing exercises to strengthen my frame, and mimicking their combat maneuvers in the privacy of my cabin.

While the belly of the days are dedicated to physical endeavors, the crown of each morning begins with mandatory religious service with the crew. Tarik insists that everyone huddle together in the damp chill on deck for a few moments of devotion. In divine choreography, chants from the monks at Prote Ora sweep down the valley from the monastery, to intermingle with the solitary muezzin keening from the minaret. The uncanny duet seeps into my psyche like the leaden fog condensing through my cloak.

These quiet moments refuel my spiritual glow from the inside, just as the suns rays brighten the color in my pale face. On clear evenings, Tarik brings out his pfeife and plays, aiding my restoration. One of the other mates strums his lyra, the steward blows the dankiyo pipes, and the cook belts out his joyful bass. In the span of a week I learn the tunes and steps to the jigs, so that I join in the singing and dancing with gusto. The only stain on these merry days, is that Majidi is not here to enjoy them with me.

Unused to the confines of the ship, in the second week on board I start to gaze in yearning to the harbor abuzz with people bustling about their business. After a particularly stormy night that steals my energy and appetite, Tarik suggests that I accompany the group of sailors going ashore for supplies. The thrill of venturing unhindered to the markets snaps me out of malaise, which not even the choppy boat ride to the pier can spoil.

Armed with a list of produce from Cook, and flanked by my companions Mariam and Lusine, I nearly skip over the oaken docks and cobblestones on my way to the warren of shops and stalls on the edge of town. I'm so excited to be free of walls trapping me inside, that I soon become lost in the labyrinth of structures that funnel me deeper into the city. Far from being alarmed, however, I know to get back I simply follow gravity downhill, so I continue my quest to find the best spice stand that sells rare saffron.

After a while, I have the suspicion that I am being followed. The girls must notice that I've been glancing over my shoulder, and they linger close, Lusine clutching a handful of my skirt. We tarry at a display of fragrant soaps, when my instincts prove true.

"It is heartening to see you up and about again. Now we can see about making a new child for the one you lost." Damian's stench overwhelms the bouquet of the shop's wares, just as he overpowers and pushes me inside. His henchmen close in behind, sealing us off from the stunned merchant and wide eyed family. Instead of heeding the bruising grip on my arms, I feel a determined tugging on my skirt, Lusine is hanging on even while being dragged through the guards legs.

"Run!" I hiss to her while grappling against Damian's seizure. "Get the Admiral!"

Coldly calculating that it will take at least a half hour for help to arrive, I relax into a dangerous game of taunting and warding off, until my attacker's patience wears thin. Damian's intent grows from spite to malice, thus my lively resistance intensifies to an all out contest of denial.

Fatigue sets in sooner than expected, but panic pushes me to continue holding him off.

Growling in frustration, Damian barks at his guards to bend me over and pin me down on a table. My newly knit ribs groan under the strain of his weight pressing me into the planks, but I refuse to give in to the burgeoning sense of shame of being raped again. I twist and thrash my legs about, managing to land a kick to his groin.

"Hold her still you idiots!" Damian grits out, breathing heavily. "If I have to take you unconscious, I will!"

With that he yanks my hair back and smashes the side of my face onto the table. My head swims as he twines his fingers through my tresses in a deadly mockery of a caress, before he slams my temple to meet the oak.

"Enough!" The odious bulk eases, "Look at the commotion you have created. Don't you have enough to amuse you back at the citadel?"

"Tarik," Damian oozes contempt, "the valet boy. You can't tell me what to do."

"No, but I can tell Everyone what you do!" He firmly gathers my unsteady frame and guides me through the man-made bulwark.

"That threat is losing its power," the ominous rumble trails us outside, "the more time Majidi spends with his whore, the less he spends on other matters!"

As soon as the swelling in my eye abates to where I can see properly, Tarik allows me to train with his unit of fighting sailors. He saw for himself how I must be able to defend myself, and directs his soldiers not to spare me in drilling against me. Much akin to the Armenian warriors who honed my agility with the scimitar, Tarik's men test my arm quickness. Whereas Nicolo was a challenge of strength, sparring these men presses my endurance, harkening back to my childhood days when I needed to run on forever.

The tight quarters of the captain's cabin aid in my progression to close combat. On deck, I swing the broadsword with the men-at-arms, but inside Tarik trains me in the art of the petite dirk and rapier. Witnessing my need for protection, and believing in my own capability to do so, he relentlessly presses me to react quicker and more aggressively until we're both exhausted. By the next full moon, I am no longer responding, but attacking.

"You are ready Adila," the winded captain grips his knees, "you will return to the citadel soon, but I have no more fears for your safety."

"Thank you Admiral," I gasp, equally disheveled from sparring for the past hour, "I can never repay you enough for this gift."

"Your blessed company is pleasure enough…"

"Pleasure for what?!" My strained heart leaps at the booming voice that swallows the door reverberating against the wall. He takes in our proximity and heavy breathing, "Tarik? My faithful friend and trusted captain! What about her company?"

We ogle Majidi in disbelief, mouths agog at his gross miscalculation. His grace and power stalk into the space like a panther pacing in its cage.

"And you my lov…" The song of my rapier cuts him short, whistling to poise with deadly intent at his throat.

"Don't you dare say that word, or any other that you'll regret." I cannot bear to hear him trivialize the feelings we have shared. Glaring past my outstretched arm, I note dark smudges under red-rimmed eyes and a patchy, unkept beard. Recognizing the aspect of an overtired man, I heave a sigh and flip the weapon in my hand, offering the hilt to Tarik. "Here is your knife back, Captain. My thanks again for your help and hospitality."

"Keep it," he casts a meaningful glance at Majidi, "you will need it more than I realized!"

With a smile and a curtsy, I stow the dirk in my bundle of belongings, throw on my cloak and face the fuming Strategos.

"I await your…Pleasure," I tilt my head in a mocking bow, "Your Eminence."

Trailed by the muffled snickers of Mariam and Lusine, I sashay out to the deck and assume a posture of exaggerated humility. Slightly regretting my sarcasm, I wait patiently while Majidi and Tarik growl at each other for a spell, and quietly fall into step behind him to disembark the Constantineous. The captain of the guard pulls the oars to row us ashore, looking as tired as his master.

Without fanfare, Majidi mounts his horse, hoists me up behind him, and loosens the reins, giving the lathered animal his head to carry us up the winding road to the citadel. Several times, he sways precariously in the saddle, and as we approach the arch of the lofty gate, I all but hold him from falling off the horse and over the steep embankment. Once inside the gaping entrance, the vizier and valet take over, dragging their master toward his chambers. I contemplate my warm cloak, my bundle of belongings, and the open portal with no one watching.

"Adila?" Majidi shrugs off the manservants, extending a gauntleted hand to me. Trapped by his ebony gaze, I am lost in the tumultuous sea of affection, and hypnotically accept his proffered truce. His emaciated frame sags against me as we conduct him through the maze of corridors and drop him unceremoniously into his bed. The valet unstraps his leather armor and hauls off his tunic, his pungent aroma repelling me to the closet to disrobe. When I emerge, his deep snores already resonate throughout the room, and I nestle into the luxurious sheets beside him.

Chapter 27

The gentle plash of water lapping the edge of the pool soothes me to the core, and I succumb to its molten embrace. After a month of washing from cold saltwater buckets, the heated bath is decadent. Leaving Majidi to his slumber, I had slipped past his equally exhausted guard and made a dash for the seraglio. Its typical morning calm was punctuated only by the spray of the fountain, and the bathhouse attendant plucking her lute while awaiting the afternoon rush.

"I was enjoying your playing, Shamila," I practice Armenian with the servant, "if you can please help me wash my hair, I will do the rest so you can go back to your lute."

"As you wish Mistress," I hear the tinkle of jars as she rummages in the toiletry cabinet, "which scent would please you today?"

"The rose attar will do, thank you." I reply by rote, too complacent to give it much thought. With a deep breath, I sink under the surface and scrub at my scalp. When I emerge, I perceive the ripples from Shamila swimming beside me, and I tilt my head back so she can reach all of my hair. Her strong hands massage the soap throughout my mane, releasing an intense jasmine fragrance. The sublime perfume hushes any complaints over her mistake, and I duck under the water again to rinse for a second washing.

"My Armenian tongue is not great," perhaps I misspoke my preference to her, "I meant to tell you to bring the rose, did I use the wrong word?"

"You don't like the jasmine?" I shriek and splash around at the male bass. Soap burns in my eyes and I sputter and slap away his helping hands. Terror at my vulnerability, and trauma from my past experiences, collide to confuse my thoughts.

"Tis I, Majidi!"

"Nay!" The demon in me gasps, "I cannot see!"

"I'm so sorry, Adila," the caress of my name stays my flailing. Still shaking, I dive down and rub the rest of the sting from my eyes and the fright from my heart. Resurfacing, I take in the woebegone visage before me, pity for his disheveled state slowing my pulse.

"The jasmine is beautiful." I offer to soften my next request, "I'm not much fun with surprise visits however, so I would prefer you to announce yourself in the future."

"Of course," his expression falls further, "I have been so tired, I wasn't thinking."

"That's why I left you to sleep, you look so fatigued!"

"I must really be hideous," he laments, "but I was worried you weren't there when I awoke, and I rushed to find you before I had a chance to clean myself."

"Can we start this over?" I murmur and reach to take him by the forearms. I place a conciliatory kiss on his gaunt cheek and pull at his beard playfully. "Thank you for washing my hair, now I will do yours."

Returning the favor of shampooing is more than I bargained for, as I have to dig through the matted layers to scour his pate. Several latherings later, I restore the sheen to his raven curls and apply the bar of jasmine to his facial hair.

"Tarik told me that you liked the jasmine." I tilt my head, perplexed, "tis from the stand in the market. I wanted to get you something to show that I'm not always the cad who greeted you on his boat."

"I surmised it was the weariness talking nonsense," I grin, touched by his gesture. "Thank you for the gift, it is lovely, as are you."

"We rode hard to get home quickly," he explains how they usually return from expeditions with less urgency. Though suffering from dysentery and exhaustion, he urged his men through the mountains to hurry home. As I listen to his rigorous journey with one ear, I marvel at the change in him, that he would press his unit to rush back. Filled with warmth, and not necessarily from the heated water, I tenderly comb oil through his curls, winding the obsidian coils around my fingers. His eyelids begin to droop, so we hurriedly finish washing, emerge to peel off our wet undergarments, and wrap ourselves in clean linens.

Just as we're exiting the bathhouse, we nearly bump into a dark, bald figure shrouded in white linen, who bows and cowers back from Majidi. When we step into the noon sunshine reflecting brightly around the courtyard, I blanch in recognition of the scabbed head.

"Keket?" Majidi's tone echoes my consternation. "What have you done with your braids?"

"You should know!" A petite beauty steps protectively in front, the venom in her accusation tickles my nape.

"Shhh!" Keket tries to settle her lover, "Hush Indira!"

"We had to shave her hair off because you ripped out so much!" Her impassioned argument reverberates through the silent plaza. Astonished stares are all the response the master receives from his harem when he looks around for an explanation. While the handful of concubines are frozen in fear around the fountain, a large residence nearby sprays a brood of raucous youths of various ages. The smallest toddler races forth in a burst of giggles and runs headlong into Majidi's legs. He chuckles, reacting quickly to scoop up the teetering child. A collective gasp sucks the air out of the courtyard.

"Children, have care!" Haiyfa rushes forward to pluck her son from his arms, mumbling apologies. "Do not pester father!"

Horror twists Majidi's doting smile into an apoplectic grimace. Foreseeing that nothing good will come of the situation, I push him up the alley between the buildings and usher him back to his suite.

"My brother tests my oath not to commit fratricide," the Strategos storms across the bedchamber, "this cannot continue!"

"You have the power to change everything," I hazard a verbal nudge, deflating his anger.

"I had always hoped that I could save him from our father's debauched rearing." He ceases pacing and flops onto the desk chair, the intensity of his regard pinning my attention, "but he's gone too far, and I do not know how to reel him in. What should I do Adila? How can I fix this?"

Huddled on the spacious mattress, shrouded within draw curtains, we birth a plan so dangerous that it can only be whispered in the cloak of night. In a stolen brace of hours, we put our heads close together and weave the details of a plan with the strands of our hushed words. Our bold plight will either ensure total freedom, or absolute annihilation.

After visiting all afternoon with Liang Na, I had left the princess with my blade and her promise to use it to protect herself come what may. Then, obscured by the growing shadows, I crept over the rampart pathway and down the spiral staircase to the ground level suite. Without risking to announce myself, I snuck past the sleeping eunuch Alexander, and suffered an acute moment of embarrassment upon finding Indira abed with Keket.

"I cannot say exactly when it will be," I murmur to the outline of her bald head, having intruded their haven, "but you will know by my signal when it is time to act. In the meantime, prepare the others to either fight or flee."

"How can we trust the other women to act when it is time?" Keket airs her concern, "I will show them how to disable the eunuchs, but they are not fighters like you and I."

"We have no choice," Indira opines, "we cannot go on with this abuse. There are others, like me, who are willing to learn in order to end the horrors."

"Just be wise with who you tell, and don't say anything about Damian not being the real Strategos," I reply, "Mariam and Lusine are both in, and I have told the Princess Liang Na to barricade her tower and let no one enter but me."

"Are you daft??" Keket hisses, "Lusine is his child!"

"She hates him all the same," I can barely make out Indira's words. "He has ignored her as he does all of his children. And Mariam has done a commendable job of bringing her up to see the truth of what he is."

"'Tis true," I nod, then realize that they cannot see me either, "Lusine has helped me get around him on several occasions. I must go back now, but do I have your oath that I will take care of the master and his guards, and you will deal with the eunuchs?"

"I swear to do my best," the African warrior exhales gravely. The three of us clasp hands in the center of the bed, sealing our fate.

The wistful toll of Vigil spirals down the tower to divert me from my return to Majidi, whisking me to the balcony perch off my old bedchamber. There, enveloped in ethereal tendrils of misty chimes, I drop to my knees and beseech God for guidance and courage. Since last night, when Majidi granted his solemn approval for me to plant the seeds of insurrection, I have prayed constantly for my Lord to obstruct my plans if mutiny is not the answer.

Thus far, my way has been cleared of all impediments. Eunuchs retired for the night, guards absent from their posts, servants asleep on their pallets. There was nothing to stop me from sliding easily into Liang Na's apartment, except the princess' cool demeanor upon seeing me. After begging my friend to take Tarik's rapier to defend herself, it was clear sailing down the eddy of stairs to enlist the more warring instincts of my erstwhile foe Keket.

Upon returning to the governor's suite, Majidi is still awake in spite of his fatigue. With a resolute nod, he affirms my report that our strategy is set in motion. His willingness to give up everything, not just for me, but to do what is right, grips my heart and squeezes the words up through my throat.

"I love you Majidi," I hush him before he reacts in reply, "I feel God's presence in you, and it draws me to you in body and spirit. You don't have to say anything, because I believe that we are destined to be together."

The powerful emotion rouses a yearning for him that I had contained since our affair at the abbey. Distance, jealousy, abuse and hurt have taken turns to tamp down this desire to be with him fully. But now, at his weakest, I am attracted to him the most.

"Will you have me?" My petition is squelched under his lips, a hungry growl rumbling through his chest as he crushes me to him. I strain against him, reveling in his urgency prodding my abdomen. He snatches my tunica over my head, and I catch my breath as he latches onto my sensitive breasts. He strokes my body until I am sobbing from the flames roaring in my belly. I drag him to the bed by his trouser string, untying it along the way so that when the backs of my thighs reach the mattress, I have him boldly nude under my appreciative hands.

Guiding him with the forceful grace of my Valkrye ancestors, I swing him around and onto his back. Stalking him on hands and knees, I straddle him like a conqueror, caressing the pale fissure marking the mahogany skin stretched taut over protruding ribs. He, in turn, lovingly fingers the knotted tissue of my healing wounds, as I sink down upon him. The external world fades into oblivion overpowered by the frantic rhythm of our lovemaking. Fused by our scarred past and present passion, we shatter all barriers between us in shuddering ecstasy.

My steepled hands cleave the water, imitating how Majidi sliced through me last night. Bubbles of laughter escape into the pool, as I reminisce over my wanton mastery over the Strategos. Sickness and fatigue were no match for our need for each other, and we made love twice more in the night. Finally depleted of all bodily function, he didn't stir when I arose with the sun and sped across the chilled marble to the touletta. Even when I emerged more composed, his heavy breathing continued to rattle through the chamber. Not wanting to interrupt his much needed rest, I decided a wash was in order and sought the seraglio bath house.

Stroking my arms in a wide arc, I swim upwards to break the surface of the cool bath. Much refreshed, I brush the wetness from my eyes, blinking away the remaining droplets. Against the alabaster tiles, a sooty form sharpens.

"Do you know how I came to the harem?" The handsome Jewess startles me, as does her abrupt inquiry. Heavy features enhance her appeal, as does the iridescent midnight sari hugging her curvaceous figure. Set deep over proud cheekbones, opal studs blaze with the import of her query.

"Nay Rachel," I had never met her, but I recall Mariam telling me her name. "We have not yet spoken to one another."

"Hah!" She scoffs, tossing her luxurious chestnut mane, "that doesn't mean that you haven't heard gossip. We all have a past Adila, a story of a previous life and how we arrived here."

"I would very much like to hear yours." Since the inception of my religious education, I have been curious about Judaic laws governing sexual practices around a woman's moon cycle. Sensing her desire to confide in me, I cross my arms on the edge of the pool and give my full attention to her tale.

"The previous Emperor, John Tzimisces, sent me to the Strategos."

The rasp in her voice caresses the murdered ruler's name. "He treasured me differently than the others, and respected my monthly religious practices. When John started to fear for his life, he gifted me to his loyal commander to protect me. He trusted that the governor would cherish me as he did."

"But he hasn't," I finish, hurting for her slain love who enslaved her to a cruel master.

"He mocks my beliefs," she shakes her head woefully and slumps down onto the very bench upon which I degraded myself with the same villain. "I suspect that he even seeks me out when I am in menstrual abstention because it gives him pleasure to insult me."

"Perhaps tis a blessing that you are one of a few here without children?" I venture, immediately regretting my insensitive comment that causes her to hide her face in her hands, shoulders shaking.

"God forgive me!" She wails, "I damaged myself trying to rid my womb of his seed once, and I cannot conceive!"

The weight of her confession presses on my chest like the pressure of the water swirling around me. Keening sobs career off the mosaics, pleading for succor from the unappeased guilt of losing a child, of which I am well familiar. Relinquishing my bath, I wrap myself in a towel so that I can gather her quaking frame to me and let her sob her sorrow into my shoulder. Once spent, I grasp her hands and crane my neck to capture her lipid gaze.

"Now I will tell you My history." Briefly I recant my religious upbringing and salvation, hoping to connect spiritually with her transgressions. "I understand the burden of tampering with an unborn life, but you see Rachel, God forgives us of our sins so that we will turn back to him."

"How can God ever forgive me for killing my baby?"

"God already has! Perhaps it is time for you to forgive yourself."

"For so long I have told myself that God uses the master's sexual mistreatment to punish me," she pulls back slightly to face me fully with the gravity of her fear, "if I am forgiven, I will have no excuse endure his attentions henceforth."

"Then don't." The forbidden words hang like juicy drops in the humid atmosphere. Dampened by the swish of water lapping the tiles, I purr an appeal to her agony, offering my precarious solution. By the midday call to prayer, I solidify Rachel's participation in my plot to rebel.

This latest recruit adds to my confidence in the success of my strategy, and I decide to check back with Liang Na and ensure her safety. Pressed by urgency, I bound up the stairs two at a time and race across the parapet to the princess' tower. For once there are so many servants coming and going along the pathway, that no one seems to notice my rush in all the activity. Finding the tower portal to the apartments agape, I start to worry.

"What is going on?" I catch one of her ladies as she flits around the reception room, snatching up the cushions. "Why are you packing?"

"We are to move," exertion and dread snatch my breath, causing my head to spin as I sprint up to the roof terrace in search of my friend. In cruel irony, I find not the dainty princess, but the gloating pretender, Damian.

Whirling back to the door, a clot of guards blocks the only opening to escape the patio. Within seconds I am beset by grasping gauntlets and ducking swinging arms. I manage to pluck a scimitar from one, its lethal arc hissing a semicircle bulwark to hold them at bay.

"Enough!" Damian's roar thunders across the terrace to stop the guards from advancing further and forcing me to retreat into the pool behind me. "She will come to me now."

His smug tone arrests me more than his shouting. Hypnotized by the sun's rays winking off the twirling blade in his fingertips, my mind cannot process the painted marionette dwarfed alongside his rangy frame. He stops spinning the weapon, and awareness punches me in the gut. The dagger I gave to my friend to protect herself from this fiend, incriminates me in plotting against him.

"Liang Na," my whimper carries a quiver of confusion, even as my eyes meet the belligerent betrayal in hers. Pain pierces my shoulder, as real as if she is using my own rapier to stab me in the back. Anticipating his victory over my sagging body and broken spirit, he waves the princess away and motions the guards to take my inert arms.

"Bring the other prisoner," a scuffling in the stairway saves me from utter dejection. Where Liang Na's perfidy sapped my energy, the sight of Majidi, bound and beaten, ignites my vigor.

"Twill give me great pleasure to have the Strategos execute you for treason tomorrow in the harem!" Damian crows gleefully, "But not before he witnesses me having you one last time!"

"Naaayyyy!" Screeching protest erupts from the heavens as I lunge against the guards. In a grand flurry of snowy feathers and flapping wings, Eugenious swoops into the fray, vicious talons clawing at the guards. Swatting at the falcon, while fighting to maintain their hold on me, they lose their footing and the three of us plunge over the edge of the pool. Their heavy armor anchors them to the bottom of the reservoir, as I flail to stay afloat.

In the chaos of the moment, time slows to etch the myriad of events in my brain. Either to rescue their drowning comrades, or to recapture my floundering figure, more of the guards plunge into the frigid pool. The force of their plash repels me against the far wall, where I clutch at the balustrade. For a heart's beat, I lock gazes with Majidi in divine farewell. Then the reverberating waves catapult me up and over the slippery restraining rail into oblivion.

Yet again, God has other plans for my life. The ancient bricks, slimy with algae, provide a slick surface to slide down the sloped curtain wall and skip like a stone along the valley river. In a half faint, I imagine the branch that scoops me up to surf the rapids, is the hand of my Savior keeping me afloat. Swollen from the rainy season, the river gushes urgently along the bottom the gorge.

Through the haze of mist and vertigo, I see light penetrating the abyss ahead, as the cascade bears me to the harbor. With one last vital gulp of air, I'm spewed into the eddy where the river collides with the sea. Somersaulting in the churning water, I lose all sense of orientation and succumb to the vortex.

Chapter 28

Waves of stars undulate in a rolling course before me, a cosmic illusion of my watery resting place. I dream that I shoot along the stellar current, propelled by a supernatural force into the heavens. Not even a visceral nausea can urge me to forego the peaceful vision.

The rocking and bobbing grows vigorous, until finally I am tossed from a cushiony cloud of comfort onto wooden planks that jar me to life. The rolling passage that shimmered in the sky, now sails from one crest of waves to the next in rapid propulsion. I lay on the seesawing floor, wishing for the smooth journey of my dream, but realizing that God has purpose in this radiance in my soul.

The familiar scent of lye scrubbed boards clears my head, I recognize the captain's cabin on the Constantineous. Gratitude swells within me like the bloating tide, both lifting me up to exhilarating heights. While I continue to praise God for saving me again, the ship shutters beneath my cheek, plowing down into another trough, then groaning under the strain of full sail.

Bowels twisting in protest of the violent motion, I lurch to my feet and sway to the portal. Staggering against the seaspray slapping my face, I barely make it to the rail ere I vomit over the side of the vessel. Steadying hands grip my shoulders as I retch out the meager contents of my stomach. Spent from heaving, and humiliated by my disgusting display, I slump back against the hull, my dizzy head resting on my knees.

"Don't be ashamed, Adila," Tarik shouts over the gale, "we all get sick when the sea is rough like this!"

"Why are we sailing then?" I grin in wry relief at my friend.

"Lets go inside and I'll explain." He pulls me to my feet, calling for his first mate to take the helm for a moment, and for the steward to bring some bland and water.

While I relish the bland fare to settle my stomach, he explains the urgency of our flight. Shortly after the lookout had spotted me floating in the bay and hauled me on board, Lusine and Mariam rowed themselves to the ship with the outrageous news of Damian's treachery.

"I have been prepared for this moment for a while," he resolves, "and thus the Constantineous has been equipped to sail to Constantinople with all the speed she can muster."

"What if he kills Majidi?" I sob, grasping the need to solicit aide from the empire, "Then this race to Miklagard will be for naught!"

"I do not believe Damian will kill him any time soon." The captain's tone grows morbid, "He will want him to suffer first."

"What will he do to him?" I whimper not wanting to know the answer.

"Tis not what his brother will do to him," he ponders, "but what Damian will do to his people. That evil man knows Majidi's weakness for those under his care."

"I'm afraid I have needlessly endangered my friends in the harem," guilt engulfs me like the surrounding waves, "my intent was to free them from bondage."

"It would surprise you the drastic measures the women will take to survive in the harem." His reasoning conjures the image of his own daughter and the scars marring Mariam's face, "They knew the risks involved, but from the intelligence I have gathered, Damian has no knowledge of your plans involving the concubines."

"Do the girls know that for sure?" I assumed Mariam and Lusine to be his source.

"I have to return to the helm," he shakes his head, denying their knowledge, "but come to the galley with my officers later when the winds calm, and you will know all."

The gathering around the table proves enlightening on many accounts. The handful of men represent Majidi's most trusted servants. Among them I recognize the guard stationed outside of Liang Na's tower, who found me on the parapet and locked me back in my apartments; and the sentry in charge of the Strategos' bedchamber. The attendant who piques my interest the most is Alexander, Keket's eunuch.

289

The pieces fall into place as I listen to the accounts of events from the past few days. According to the eunuch, Damian has been growing more violent and bold of late to possess not just the concubines, but the governorship. When the princess's attendant told him about the blade I had given Liang Na, he saw his opportunity to act. His henchmen seized Majidi in his sick, sleep-deprived state, killing the Strategos' travel-weary captain of the guards. As the pair of Majidi's personal sentries galloped down the winding road to the harbor to alert Tarik, Mariam and Lusine were racing through the underground tunnel with the account of my demise.

Speed and stealth are our weapons, as no one would have noticed the Constantineous rowing out to sea at night and setting full sail to the Bosporous. With the spring storms urging us forward, Tarik estimates our arrival in Constantinople the day after tomorrow, assuming the ship withstands the smashing waves.

Due to the strict confidentiality of Damian's existence, and the taboo nature of his role, an official counterattack is impossible. We therefore, must rely on our contacts and relationships to stage a covert ambush. The first of whom will be my former host, the Abbot Nicolas. Tarik explains that the Monastery port on the Marmara, is better situated for our clandestine mission, causing my stomach to surge again with anxiety.

Each of us at the table plays a vital role in the theatre that is to be set on land and sea across the expanse of the Byzantine Empire. With his high ranking naval background, Tarik will commandeer ships from the emperor Basil's fleet, to turn around and sail back to Trebizond. Following close behind, will be a small army of elite soldiers, chosen by Majidi's guards for their ability to ride fast and fight fiercely. This unit will gain admittance to the citadel under the guise of a diplomatic envoy. Which is where I enact my part in this drama.

It is well-known that my sister grew close to Liang Na as her attendant prior to her betrothal to the Strategos. I am to return with Brigida, at the head of the land march, to visit her friend the Princess. Once inside the stronghold, our band will overtake Damian's guards and open the gates for the seamen to aid us in securing the castle. It all sounds so straight forward, until I lay eyes on the cloaked figures awaiting us at the pier.

"I admit, life has been rather mundane without you," Brother Samuel laments, reclining next to me under the star studded sky when we stop for the night. The fortnight it has taken to recruit, equip and mobilize our party of a brace of people, has felt agonizingly slow.

"You do have a way of attracting intrigue," Brigida agrees from the protective circle of Nicolo's arms. He snorts in agreement, passing his cup to share. The glow of friendly company warms me more than the fire around which we gather.

"Seems to me that you were all itching for some excitement when I asked for your help," I had made certain that my family was aware of the risks they faced, "not even Constance over there hesitated to come!"

"I hear that they're building a monastery outside of Trebizond I should like to visit." The bespeckled monk confesses. "Though the breakneck pace is a bit more than I envisioned!"

"Time is of the essence," Nicolo's military sense agrees with our haste, "if we are to catch the pretender by surprise."

"And there's no telling what Damian will do to Majidi in the meantime," his name catches in my throat. I had hurriedly explained my feelings for the Strategos to the Abbot and Brother Samuel when they greeted us on the pier, and Brigida was already aware of my love. Perhaps my absence had softened their hearts, for Father Nicolas not only blessed our cause, he granted leave for Brother Samuel and Constantine to accompany us.

Aided by a benevolent spring breeze sweeping down the mountains, we make swift progress along the road skirting the same southern coastline of the Euxine Sea that I had rode previously. After a week we reach Chaldia, but this time we toil up the Pontus mountains to access Trebizond via the tangle of inland roads. The lure of verdant gorges and crystalline lakes on our approach, strikes my heart with desire to dwell in this eden under better circumstances.

Obscured once again by the shadows of my drawn cowl, I walk unrecognized under the vaulted arches of the citadel gatehouse. A quiver slithers down my spine as the iron gate clangs behind me, resealing me into this opulent prison I had so recently escaped. The modest party we had left Constantinople with a week ago, has dwindled to Brother Samuel, Constance, Alexander the Eunuch and myself disguised as monks, and Brigida, and her serving girl. Damian's haughty Vizier had met us along the serpentine road, insisting that Nicolo and his men at arms remain outside of the walls of the stronghold.

So, with a meaningful kiss from his wife and a flash of my hidden steel, we assure the hulking viking that we will manage until reuniting with them in the next few days. Then, our unremarkable group trails the vizier, as he dispatches us to another eunuch, who guides us along the familiar route to the seraglio.

Conveniently, us 'monks' are deposited in the same tower guardroom connecting my old apartments to the ramparts that I had discovered in my search for the princess' quarters. While the others inspect the pallets laid on the oaken floorboards for us to sleep on, I focus on Brigida's heeled boots on the flagstones as they retreat down the corridor. A sharp knock indicates her destination, my former accommodations, now the royal chambers housing Liang Na.

The steadying gong announcing Typica emanates from across the valley, bringing us to the ledge overlooking the road below Automatically, we kneel along the stone sill facing the monastery, chanting and prostrating in prayer. Absorbed in the composed rhythm, I subliminally detect a shuffle on the stair. It takes all of my spiritual calm not to bolt when I hear the derisive tone of Zindor mocking our ritual to his companion.

"They stink of Greek Orthodoxy," the Archieunuch sneers in Armenian.

"We'll leave them to their groveling," Damian's hiss crawls my skin, "I hear that Adila's sister is the real beauty. I am intrigued to see her for myself!"

Steeling against the red haze burgeoning in my brain, I count their footsteps in the direction of the princess' chambers. Without knocking, Zindor bangs the door open and announces the pretend governor. Not wasting another moment, I fly into action. Under three pairs of astonished orbs, I rummage through the guards' cupboard, finding a suitable uniform and short rapier. I frantically step into the armor of an immortal, exchanging my monks robes for military garb.

"I must make sure my sister is safe!" I jerk on the mask. "I won't do anything to betray our mission, I promise I will return by vespers."

With well practiced mastery, I wade into the aqueduct, clinging to the curve of the tower until I reach the secluded balcony whereon I spent many quiet hours with my Lord. In the elongated shadows of dusk, I silently and slowly curl my body down to the flagstones, then melt into the molding encasing the door.

Damian's self-aggrandizing conversation drifts from the antechamber, I can tell that he's puffing himself up for the women. Brigida's skillful banter gives me slight ease, she is handling the situation with subtle tact for the time being. Ere long, the men take their leave, and Liang Na shows her guest around the rooms. They communicate in simple greek phrases as the party shifts to the bed chamber.

"My rooms are not as grand as my last suite," the princess bemoans, "they needed the security of the tower to house an important prisoner. Here is the bath room, though it is not big enough to hold my wardrobe."

"What is this?" Brigida sweeps the heavy brocade curtain aside to reveal the alcove. "Oh!" I sweep off my mask and put a finger to my lips, "How frightening!"

"Yes it is," the princess continues her tour, "I never go out there."

"Is this where I am to sleep?" Brigida inquires rather loudly, winking back at me and drawing the drapes.

Her muffled affirmation assures me that Brigida will be close by, and have company with the other ladies. As stealthily as I came, I retreat back up to my humble quarters and don the habit and cowl over the padded uniform. The same eunuch brings us a tray of simple fare, and entrusts us not to stray into the harem. While we eat, I inform my friends of Brigida's whereabouts and that we will have to act quickly now that Damian has taken interest in her.

A furtive tread on the stair hushes our murmurings, I fondle the sword concealed under my robe and pull my cowl lower over my face. The flicker from a taper illuminates Keket's sharp features and sculpted shoulders rounding the spiraling wall.

Nearly dropping her light in surprise, she starts when she espies the four of us crouched on our pallets.

"I came to get water," she apologetically raises her bucket, indicating to the aqueduct. Instinctively, her eunuch leaps to her aid, taking the vessel from her. "Alexander! You made it back!"

"Please don't mind us child," Constance recovers, more accustomed to dealing with other women than the other monk. Leaving Brother Samuel struck dumb by her powerful presence, I stand and sweep back my hood.

"Tis good to see you Keket," her sable complexion turns ashen, and I hasten to reassure her that I am not a ghost. I am explaining how I was saved by the buoyant arm of God, when she engulfs me in a stifling hug.

"When we heard of your fall, our hopes plunged with you." The emotion in her words moves me. "Something has been ominous in the harem Adila, I do not know what, but tis unsettling. Since they moved the princess from the tower, the parapet has been more heavily guarded than when she was there."

"Let us put an end to the fear and tyranny," I point out the others, "these are my friends, here to aid us in our plight for freedom. There are soldiers beyond the gates, but we need all of your help to secure the harem until they get inside."

We strategize into the night, until the bell for compline reminds us that we must rest if we are to carry out our plan. Though we seek our beds, sleep eludes me as I lay sweltering under my layers of garb, and the weight of my thoughts. After a few hours, I finally drift off, only to wake at the march of boots as the guards change post on the rampart path. Putting the pieces together, I surmise that Majidi must still be alive and imprisoned in the tower.

"Wake up!" The urgency in his voice shakes me to alertness, "Adila, I am forever having to wake you!"

"What is it, Brother Samuel?" I sit up, rubbing the vestiges of sleep from my eyes.

"They are taking your sister to the harem bathhouse." The information portends doom.

"He is preparing her." Constance cleans her spectacles and concludes. "We must put our plan in motion today!"

When we break our fast, for what could be our last together, we consume every morsel brought to us so as to have sustenance for the long day ahead. The ponderous tome of Trite Hora echoes our solemn mood, as we kneel in supplication to God.

Facing east, the mid morning sun encouraging juicy drops of sweat to trail down my spine, I pray that our Lord will give us strength and keep us safe in our victory.

The serving eunuch returns to remove our tray, and Brother Samuel explains that we desire to pray in the holy monastery of St. Eugeneous. He agrees to get us through the guarded entryway to the citadel, but we will have to find our way to the road outside on our own, as he has duties elsewhere. Backs rigid with resolve, we follow the servant down the corridor to the guarded barrier between the citadel and the harem.

The eunuch instructs the guards to unbar the doors and let us pass. Then he indicates the direction through the citadel grounds, and departs to his tasks. With one last nod acknowledging our point of no return, we discreetly part ways. Brother Samuel and Constantine are swallowed by the stream of pedestrian traffic through the vast courtyard. Keket's eunuch turns back to alert his mistress to assemble her feminine force for action at high noon. Which leaves me to permeate the inky corners of the guard's post to one side of the doors to scout the scene in advance.

Ascending the steep stairs to the top of the narrow tower, I have an ideal view of the upper citadel on one side and the seraglio on the other. From my vantage point, I must patiently await events to unfold as the sun steadily progresses to its zenith. I see Keket and Indira casually strolling to the fountain plaza, where they are joined by the other concubines in our allegiance. They play music and frolic as usual, appearing nonchalant as their numbers swell to a dozen.

Meanwhile, the two monks have reached the press of people at the outer gate. From there, I envision Brother Samuel finding a place to tarry, while Constance hastens to Nicolo at his camp outside the wall. God willing, Samuel will ensure the gate stays open for Nicole's men, while Constance will go on to alert Captain Tarik to attack through the underground harbor tunnel. The plot is afoot.

At the hour of Christ's crucifixion, Hekte Ora bells resonate across the valley to blend with the muezzin's cry from the nearby minaret.

Usually a period of respite from the high heat of the sun, today the combined faiths' calls to prayer portends the opposite. For our motley army, they are our signal that it is time to act. As if witnessing a drama play out under my tower, I hold my breath in suspense for the first signs of struggle in the harem plaza.

To wait patiently has always been a fierce foe, no more so than the present attacks on my idleness. Knowing however, that the women are capable of subduing their former captors, I leave them to handle the eunuchs on their own. My task is to bar the main entry, so the bulk of Damian's army can't march completely unhindered into the harem, then admit Nicolo's men when they arrive.

Ere long, a lone figure in lipid robes stumbles up the grand staircase and pounds on the oaken doors, crying for the gatekeepers to let him out. The time is nigh that I will have to take out the two guards, but the idea of having to kill Nerses as well, is distasteful, for I know he is a troubled soul. While distracted with the heavy iron crossbar, I descend from the lookout tower and dispatch the guards with such calculated quickness that I'm certain they didn't even know I was there.

Through the crack in the double door, Nerses stares agog at the two lifeless forms blocking his escape. Dragging the opening wider, I meet the eunuch's stunned eyes over the point of my dagger. Ere I can squeeze through, he bolts in the direction of my old chambers, relieving me of the odious task of slaying him too.

Straining under the weight of the solid metal bar, I manage to slide it through the locks on the inside of the harem doors, sealing us in and Damian's men out. Then, like a coiled spring released, I dash through the corridor and bound up the spiral staircase to the guard's platform where we slept. Stretching out over the ledge and aqueduct, I check the scene below on the road to the citadel entryway.

A line of dark smudges creeps along the curtain wall like a parade of ants. Nicolo's men vanish into the yawning arch, and I listen for the shouts of guards or weapons. My ears hone in on running boots, but they sound closer than they should if coming from a league below at ground level.

The strategos' private passage! My mind berates my omission. I had forgotten the secret back way connecting Majidi's chambers one level above, from where guards are now streaming down the tower stairs.

Chilling calm bathes my heated thoughts with the cold reality of what I must do. If the seraglio is overrun with troops, the plot will fail, I must plug the leak with my steel and God's strength.

The mask of the Immortal in place, the mortality of my body diminishes until I feel nothing but God's spirit coursing through my veins. Taking position against the inner wall of the staircase, I crouch in readiness to thrust upwards under the chest plate of my next victim. The soldiers descend, one by one, witlessly stomping directly into my blade with supernatural ease. As their inert bulk piles up, the onslaught trickles to a pause, giving me a break during which I strip their armor and stack their bodies to block the stairs.

A thundering boom splinters the air, the harem gate is under full attack. In between the explosions, the slap of slippers patter up the tower stairs. I retreat to the guard's niche and lift my mask to drink from the aqueduct. Refreshed, I greet the legion of warrior women with a broad smile.

Giddy over our early success, I embrace Keket and the others, joyful to see them hale and hearty. While scavenging the arms of the fallen soldiers, we brief each other on our progress and strategize our next move. The road below is quiet, so we surmise that Nicolo has penetrated the citadel, in which case we need only hold this tower until the Tarik's men flank Damian's soldiers and pick them off from behind.

A feminine scream knifes through the corridor, flaying our spirits. For a hair raising moment, Keket and I stare at one another, listening to my name ring distinctly above the sudden cacophony of shrieks. Instinctively responding to Brigida's distress, I scoop up a scimitar along with my rapier and dash to my former quarters.

Our trepidation is confirmed upon careening into the receiving room. Several guards hold the princess' ladies and my sister, while Damian holds a dirk to Liang Na's throat.

"Unbar the doors!" He spats, pressing the blade into her delicate flesh. One, two, three armored soldiers stand ready, plus another holding Brigida. If we can somehow get Liang Na from the clutches of the devil, the ten of us women and Alexander, whom I spot lurking in the archway to the bedroom, may have a chance to overcome them, as the sound of splintering oak cracks through the hallway behind us.

"Are your men so weak they can't keep us women subdued and do it themselves?" Brigida wields her sharp wit with cavalier skill. As his dull mind mulls her pointed insult, a small movement from the princess arrests my attention. From the folds of her skirt, she flashes a glimpse of the rapier I had given her. My eyes widen to meet her onyx orbs, swimming in regret.

"I am sorry," she speaks in her native tongue, her rosebud lips in a lopsided grin.

"No!" I shout, putting up a hand to stave off her suicidal intentions. Bravely stomping her spiked heel on Damian's foot, she manages to shove him away and pivot to stab clumsily at his midsection. Crimson with outrage, he plucks the knife from her and raises his arm, curses spewing from his deranged lips. Mercifully, I shut my eyes rather than witness the murder of my friend.

When I open them again, I am strangely calm amid the wails from her attendants and chiding from the guards that she was a valuable pawn. For an instant I exchange a tear streaked look with Brigida, then use the chaos of the moment to lunge at her captor.

Favor is not on my side this time, a pair of swords cross to bar my path. As I grapple and parry with two of the guards, the song of Keket's blade clashing with another penetrates my concentration. They siphon me from my group, forcing me to flee to the bedchamber, then slam the door, trapping me inside. Damian commands his men to bring their new captive, and I shout through the door for Keket to stay with Brigida.

With their exit, the din from the antechamber subsides into the distant pummeling at the seraglio doors until they finally splinter in surrender. Back inside the suite, the bedroom door cracks open to reveal the macabre, tear-streaked mask of Liang Na's first lady in waiting beckoning me to come out. The women have bound her neck with a silk scarf, creating the illusion that the life blood flowing from her body is merely the watery red fabric puddling about her shoulders. In respect of her royal position, and in reverence to our friendship, I carry her to the chaise and lay her as if in peaceful repose.

Kneeling beside her, I try to focus my prayers on her deliverance to paradise, but the stampede of boots past the apartments urges me to continue my mission to rescue Majidi. Only the true Strategos can cease the fighting before more have to perish.

Were it not for the deadly circumstances, the irony of being locked in my old chambers again would be comical. Especially given that I know how to escape along the aqueduct by rote.

With a last kiss on her cool forehead, I leave my friend to her ladies to keep vigil and step out onto the balcony overlooking the valley. The familiar smell of earth and mist comforts my spirit, as the cold water in the channel revitalizes my body.

Navigating the winding waterway in the growing shade of the late afternoon, I hazard to survey the situation below.

There seems to be a concentration of fighting around the harem entryway and grand stairs, which gives me hope that Nicolo's army has engaged the citadel guards in battle. Skirmishing along the ramparts has broken out between the tower sentries and a mix of concubines and seamen. I drop down onto the parapet and sprint the rest of the pathway up to the tower as I have so many times before.

Pausing to catch my breath, I send up a quick thanks to God for getting me thus far. Then I test the portal latch and find it alarmingly unlocked, so I slowly press the door open and slide into the murky unknown. The once bright and airy vestibule is now heavily shuttered and curtained, necessitating extra caution as I proceed. Furniture cloaked in sheets hunch like beasts in the darkness, the exaggerated sound of my pulse echoes against the walls of my mind.

The memory of umbrageous adversaries in the night from the monastery of Kiev years ago, piques my subconscious. Honing all of my senses to pick up the presence of that which I cannot behold, I advance across the room towards the stairs at the far side. Permeating the pungent turpentine saturating the oaken floorboards and ornate trimmings, a distinct sweetness suggests silken fabric covering a rotten core.

Zindor's Perfume! I start at the recollection, causing the blow to the head that was meant to incapacitate me, merely to graze my cheek and knock me down. Experience quiets my instinct to bounce up and fight, amplifying the tap of flint and the sizzle of a lamp being lit.

"Did you get her?" The Archeunuch snaps at an accomplice. "Where is she?"

299

"Over here, sire," I lay inert as Nerses slippered foot pushes me onto my back. Though my old servant is no match for me physically, his master's evil proximity prickles the hair on my neck.

"Hold the lamp," light flickers outside of my eyelids, the cloying cologne intensifies. I force myself to relax as his talons clutch my jaw. "Hah! I laid open one cheek and you did the other!" He scoffs, reaching for my wrist to tie it with a cord. I spring into action, grabbing at his arm instead, but he reacts too quickly.

Jumping back, he flings his arm into Nerses, who bobbles the kerosene lamp, strewing oil and flames into the air. Sparks shower over the three of us, though the embers fizzle and die on my sodden garb. I watch in awe however, as the glowing particles find fuel in the eunuchs' perfumed robes, igniting into multicolored flames. While Nerses pats at Zindor's clothing, his own gown catches fire, causing them both to run about in panic. The sweet odor of burning fragrance turns to the stench of singed hair and flesh. Screams fill the chamber, until the pop and hiss of the consuming fire increases to douse their agony.

Turning from the gruesome scene, I contemplate the blaze scattered about the room, and bound over the flammable floorboards and furniture to the interior stairway. The portal at the top is locked with a key that is missing, and there's not enough space on the landing to gather myself to ram it with my padded shoulder. I sail back down to the first floor and dodge the conflagration to retrieve my discarded sword.

The curved blade is ill suited to chopping wood, but after a few minutes of desperate hacking I chew away the door panel to weaken the mechanism. Breath is bursting from my chest and sweat streaming down my brow while I pry the hardware lose and batter my way past the barrier.

Smoke is already billowing up the stairs behind me, and I blink away salty perspiration to assess the second level. The empty receiving room is dark but for a swathe of white fabric pooling on a bench under the boarded up aerial window. As my eyes adjust to the soot further clouding the dim space, I imagine the clink of a chain and the white material taking the shape of a human form.

"Adila?" A hoarse croak emanates from the dormer. "Your ghost returns to haunt me?"

"Majidi!" I span the room in one leap, sobbing into his feeble embrace, "God saved me to deliver you!" I describe my miraculous slide down the wall to the sea, as I urgently test the shackle around his ankle.

"I have no strength to properly greet you." He plucks his ragged remnants of the tunic I last saw him wearing. "They refused to give me food, light, exercise...not even a change of clothes!"

"Your vigor will return," I caress his sallow, bearded cheek, "but for the moment, we must get you out of here."

"A forthright ago I contemplated escape," he shakes his head, "but I do not know if I have the energy to do it anymore."

"I came back for you Majidi," I capture his chin to lift his gaze, "because you must live to see the birth of our child."

"Do not jest with me, I told you I am incapable of siring offspring!" Disbelief fuels his vigor.

"Nay my love," I sit down close beside him so he can see the veracity of my words reflected in my face, "Zindor has been drugging your wives so they remain barren." His dubious snort compels me to continue, "And last year, I became pregnant with your seed from our time in the monastery, but I lost the baby after taking a beating. I am sorry that I never told you, twas spiteful of me."

"What are you saying?" His sunken gaze bores into me.

"I carry your child now Majidi," it was Constance again who noticed my nausea and diagnosed my tender breasts, "from the last time we were together. I want to raise this life with you by my side."

"No more regrets," this time he reaches out to me, clasping my nape to press our foreheads together. "Let's get this chain off."

He suggests using my rapier to pick the lock on the manacle, which is no minor feat with my hands shaking from exhaustion and no light to see what I am doing. While the door lock challenged my sword arm, the shackle tries my patience and dexterity with the slim dirk. To keep frustration at bay, I apprise Majidi on the state of his realm and our coordinated coup. After what seems an eternity, I pop the pin out and the iron clangs to the floor. Crying out in relieved victory, we kiss fervently until the heat rising form the floorboards surpasses our passion, urging us to ascend to the terrace at the top of the tower.

The stunning vista welcomes us to linger in her lush beauty. A siren, enthralling us in her alluring presence that all is well, though the world is burning down around us. Majidi kneels at the edge of the pool and splashes water over his head and shoulders, cupping his hands to drink in desperate thirst. Possessed by a different need, to ease my dread of becoming overly hot, I follow his lead, then sit back on my heels to contemplate our escape.

The inferno licks greedily at the door frame from whence we just came, and I turn to tell Majidi that we have but a few minutes until the wooded trusses supporting the roof tiles will collapse. In deep thought, he continues to stare into the pool, as if the answer lies in its swirling currents.

"We can go through there." He points to the bottom of the cistern. I glance at him sharply, wondering if hunger and isolation have robbed his sanity. "Every day they brought me here to bathe, but instead of tending to my bodily functions, I would sit here and pray for guidance. You taught me that."

The divine clarity in his calm demeanor brings bubbles of joy hiccuping in my throat. Elated to share this spiritual breakthrough, in spite of our circumstances, I squeeze his hand, beaming with faith in him.

"God revealed the machinations of the cloaca, and how the trap down there regulates the water flow to the lower citadel." He points to the opening, which appears wide enough to accommodate his shoulders. The groaning and splintering sounds increase to interrupt Majidi's engineering lesson, "so basically, the pipe will carry us to the aqueduct."

"It may be our only option," the doorway is completely engulfed, the hot pavers tremble beneath my knees. "God be with us."

"Feet first, deep inhale, cover your face," he instructs, "I'll go, then you."

"See you on the other side!" Refusing the finality of goodbye words, we cling briefly together, separating before the ever present magnetism between us fuses us for eternity. Inhaling deeply, Majidi pinches his nose with his fingers and jumps.

Wriggling out of my padded uniform, I pray aloud as I watch him disappear into the underwater tunnel. With a final plea to the heavens, I suck in a deep breath and plunge in his wake. The suction into the tube is more forceful than I anticipated, and I fight to keep my arms close to my body and cover my face. Much like my slippery ride down the citadel wall, I glide swiftly through the pipe as it slithers downhill through the bowels of the tower.

Sunlight bursts upon me, celebrating my triumphant breakout as I skip across the surface of the aqueduct, until the current abates to a gentle tug. I drift along the channel, absently admiring the purple and magenta streaks in the evening sky, praising my savior for getting me through yet another trial of faith and crisis. God answers in a spectacular explosion of orange and yellow sparks and loud boom from the tower interior collapsing.

"We made it!" The victorious cheer echoes my sentiments, bringing me back to the present with gladness that Majidi was right. The water pressure had propelled us to where the aqueduct intersects the ramparts, but the clamor of battle tames our enthusiasm. The Strategos wobbles to his feet and spreads his arms out, unaware of his weakened condition.

"Cease fighting!" His rasping order is swept away by the din of fighting as soon as it leaves his lips. A few heads turn to glance up, then return to the melee. Confused by their lack of response, Majidi waves his arms and hops up and down, continuing to scream until he loses his voice. Foreseeing disaster, I yank him back down into the canal.

"They don't recognize you," understanding settles his mien, "we have to get you to your throne! This way to my old bedroom."

Neither of us hesitates at the reverse of command, as I lead him through the channel and he follows trustingly. His labored breathing slows our pace, allowing the chill of the water to pucker our skin under the thin layer of clothing. Darkness conceals our progress, while complicating our plight to find the balcony underneath.

The cautious journey, stiff muscles and disorientation start to eat at my nerves, it seems we are crawling forever and should have reached the apartment already. Just as I contemplate doubling back, a plume of white sweeps by and flutters to rest a few meters below.

"Eugenious!" I laugh affectionately at my guardian angel. He squawks and dances impatiently on the balustrade, waiting for Majidi and I to drop to the safety of the balcony. Rewarding his vanity with compliments, I describe to the exhausted man how the great falcon has saved me, allowing the strategos time to recover. I scavenge a loaf of bread from the bedside tray and share it among us, fueling us for the final push to the governor's state rooms.

The antechamber is bright with lamplight, where I warn Majidi that his wife is laid out and her attendants are watching over the body of their princess. His voice is raw as he sobs a prayer over her, promising to avenge her death. Numb to the pain of losing my friend, I train my mind on the task of how to get out, expecting to have to deal with yet another obstacle.

The latch clicks easily, the door unlocked, releasing a flood of gratitude to inflate my resolve. The corridor is empty but for a few armored corpses, and the muffled clash of swords emanating from the ramparts on one side, and the harem gates on the other. Selecting a battle ax and a rapier, I take only weapons, no armor. It is Majidi's turn to take charge, and we speed to the secret passageway to his chambers.

Blocking the entry to the royal bedroom is one of Damian's guards, crouched and ready. Leaping in front of Majidi, I draw my rapier and engage the imposing Armenien. Remembering the left handed soldier to be a formidable foe from previous entanglements, I switch the dagger to my left hand so I can swing the ax with all of the strength of my dominant arm. He seizes the shift to slice down at me, grazing my abdomen before I can retreat.

The burn of pain triggers buried memories of beatings and abuse, releasing the red cloud of fury from monastic bondage. Brain addled in crimson haze, a howl rends my throat, and I parry and hack at the guard. The ferocity of my attack drives him across the threshold, where I face him with the brunt of violent recollection. Behind his helmet mask, his visage morphs from the ruddy complexion of my father, to the mean sneers of childish tormentors, to Damian's smooth veneer.

Contempt of these men fires my belly, and with a savage bellow I swing the axe upward, lopping off his arm in one brutal motion. Swiftly putting him an end to his torment, I spin around and chop off his head. Sobered by disgust, I toss down the gored axe, finally noticing the score of eyes trained in my direction.

Shock in its many forms manifest in the stares of those scattered about the rooms. Lurking in the dim portal, I first pick out Majidi's flinty pools of grim admiration. Sagging against the door molding, Keket clutches her arm and sags in relief. Circling to my right, disbelief raises Tarik's brow, and he crosses himself in holy apprehension. Several of his seamen, drop their skirmishing with Damian's personal guards, register astonishment in their gaping mouths.

Illuminated by the full moon glaring off the terrazzo marble, I read sorrow in Brigida's comely countenance. Blurry reflections of the azure sea beyond, her eyes swim with pity, for she alone knows from where this hatred comes from, and what it does to me. Tears stream down her chin, and drip silently on the knife poised at her neck.

Expressionless in the midst of horror, Damian's maniacal countenance caresses my sisters pate, disinterested in my disturbing display. Squinting into the shadows behind me, his orbs glaze over and a pronounced tic bulges at the side of his jaw.

"Everyone lay down your weapons," the composed order from the true Strategos contradicts his brother's bombast. Majidi steps into the halo of luminescence, watching the men lower their swords. "Tis over Damian, drop your dagger and let her go."

"He's an imposter!" Madness twists his smooth features into a lopsided mask of a lunatic. "She is coming with me, I will be back to reclaim my realm! If you try to stop me, I will kill her."

Not wanting Majidi to rile him further, I put out my hands, as if to freeze the tableau with the power of my will. Damian hoots at my unintended aid, and shuffles backward to the same stairs that I had trod numerous times to rehabilitate my body after his debauchery broke it. My nostrils flare as I cast about for a way to prevent him from doing the same to my sister.

"He won't get away," Majidi whispers, I whimper at my impotence, as the fiend edges to the perimeter of torchlight, Brigida in tow. Out of the darkness, a streak of white flashes up the grand staircase, the moon's icy rays glinting off cold steel.

Damian stumbles, his hold loosening, his dagger slipping away from her throat, and my sister sways precariously on the top step.

In a singular motion, a blonde giant scoops her up in one arm, and withdraws his bloodied dirk from Damian's back. As Satan's mortal form topples into oblivion, Nicolo cradles Brigida against his broad chest and buries his face in her shoulder. Harkening back to the day on the roadside, when the Viking pledged his protection over us, a jumble of emotions clogs my throat. Humility, over the power of fate. Respect, for the work of our team. Relief, from the presence of evil. Love, and its enduring strength to conquer all.

Chapter 29

Celestial sparks cluster to form cobbled steps, which I climb into the enchanted mist. In my dream, I am not alone, for my fingers are intertwined with those whom I bring along in my journey to ethereal perfection. Emulating Eugenious, I fling my arms wide as if soaring aloft, only instead of feathers, my family and friends hold me up. Molting this plumage, I scatter them like a collection of rare gems across the velvety heavens. Satisfied that they pirouette their own pathway to individual destinies, a deep peace permeates my vision.

This sense of freedom, rooted in the assurance that God will care for all of my loved ones, remains as I stand on the balcony watching the sun gild the seraglio. A year ago I stood in this same spot, lamenting the duplicitous beauty of the harem. Today however, the vibrant industry buzzing throughout the lower citadel, is a true representation of life among the women still living there.

In the forthnight since the concubine revolt, the Strategos of Chaldia courageously reconstructed his harem. By official decree, he permanently destroyed the doors of the institution of sexual slavery, and freed the women from bondage. By my counsel, he helped those who desired to return to their families, and a few chose to follow Mother Constance to found a new abbey. Many however, accepted his offer to remain in the women's quarters and serve the community.

The Eunuchs who survived the purge at the hands of their former mistresses, were extended similar options. Brother Samuel gleaned three young castrati for the choir at St. Eugeneous across the valley, where he has been residing temporarily, and most of the others stayed in service under Keket's eunuch, Alexander.

Which leads to the biggest change. Since the captain of the guard was killed by Damian's men when they imprisoned the Strategos, Majidi promoted Keket to oversee his personal security as his new captain. It was a moving moment when the citadel sentries all bent a knee to her, and pledged to protect the governor according to her command. She and Indira will live in her original apartments with a comfortable salary for the remainder of their lives.

"How goes the progress with the hospital?" Majidi's lanky arms encircle me from behind. He still hasn't regained his former weight from before his sickness and captivity. "Has Mother Constance discharged any patients recovered from battle injuries?"

"Yes, Zoe and Shamila seem to have bonded in their healing, similar to how they allied in their efforts to rebel." The two sirens had lured a guard into a silken trap of saris, thinking he was going to have a rare treat of the master's forbidden fruits.

Instead, they enticed him into the fountain pool and held him under the water while he thrashed about in panic. Shaking my head at the bold use of weapons at their disposal, I was supremely relieved when Constance told me they would live after sustaining significant injuries in the struggle. "Mother Constance has identified them as potential candidates to take charge of the hospital, while she organizes the nunnery."

"There is much to do Adila," Majidi circles to my side and gestures around the citadel, "and I hope to have your counsel in doing so. Once our baby is born, will you accept the position of Vice Vizier, to work with Comneus on domestic affairs?"

"I would prefer that you have me as a confidant," his frequent mention of Our Child never ceases to bring a modest flush to my cheeks, "no need for titles between us, Your Eminence."

"Very well," he chides my giggle, "if you won't be my Vizier, perhaps you will be my wife." The cacophony in the background blurs, and I suck in my breath as he kneels and takes my hand.

"I love you, Adila, and I want you with me always." His unfathomable soul lays open in appeal, probing mine to answer. "Brother Samuel says that he can annul the other two marriages because they were not in the Christian faith and there were no offspring. I will convert if you want."

"No!" I cry, remembering the Bishop's mission that I convert the

Strategos. He stands up, startled by my vehement response. "I mean...I know you love me Majidi, so there is no need for such formalities."

"I understand your hesitation to wed," his crestfallen visage prompts me to clarify, but he grasps my hands and continues, "but I beg you to think of our child. Our daughter especially, must have the protection of my name."

"I love you, Majidi, and I will marry you," his smile radiates the joy of heavenly beams, "but only if you do not convert. Our differences are what magnify our attraction to each other and our understanding of the world."

He stands and snuggles me under his arm, resting his head atop mine. In that moment, I reflect on Liang Na's symbol of Yin and Yang, black and white flowing together harmoniously. With the eastern sun shining across our embrace, I imagine us to appear similarly dark and light, complimenting each other to create something extraordinary.

"Sing to us Adila," he requests, rubbing my abdomen.

There was once a spirited child, who dreamed of dancing across the night sky streaked with the aura of the Norse Gods. The lighted pathway sustained the youth through many seasons of toil and hardship.

Journeying far from home, the waif grew into a girl tiptoeing through the darkness of her uncertain future. Her path was illuminated with experience, education and knowledge of God to give her faith in her purpose.

Traversing the years, the young woman navigated the soaring heights and plunging valleys of romance. Her way was guided by her relationship with God above all else to illuminate her divine will.

Through the dark days of sin, captivity and torment the woman orbits the celestial sphere in search of escape from evil. Enlightened by forging new relationships, she survives to discover a greater fate in sharing herself with others.

After her fall from grace, the wife and mother to be embraces her salvation, releasing those she had held imprisoned in her mind to their own unique fate in God's vast universe. The light that she once hoarded deep inside erupts into brilliant rays, forever dissolving the walls that kept it inside.

Printed in the United States
by Baker & Taylor Publisher Services

Printed in the United States
by Baker & Taylor Publisher Services